Kim Lawrence lives on [...] her university lecturer h[...] arrived as strays and ne[...] one or both of her boomerang sons. When she's not writing she loves to be outdoors gardening, or walking on one of the beaches for which the island is famous—along with being the place where Prince William and Catherine made their first home!

Bella Mason has been a bookworm from an early age. She has been regaling people with stories from the time she discovered she could hold the dinner table hostage with her reimagined fairy tales. After earning a degree in journalism she rekindled her love of writing, and now writes full-time. When she isn't imagining dashing heroes and strong heroines she can be found exploring Melbourne, with her nose in a book, or lusting after fast cars.

KEEPING THE ENEMY CLOSE…

KIM LAWRENCE

BELLA MASON

MILLS & BOON

First published in Great Britain 2025
by Mills & Boon, an imprint of HarperCollins*Publishers* Ltd,
1 London Bridge Street, London, SE1 9GF

www.harpercollins.co.uk

HarperCollins*Publishers*, Macken House, 39/40 Mayor Street Upper, Dublin 1, D01 C9W8, Ireland

ISBN: 978-0-263-34493-6

12/25

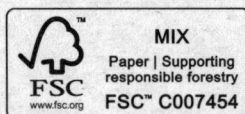

MIX
Paper | Supporting
responsible forestry
FSC™ C007454

This book contains FSC™ certified paper
and other controlled sources to ensure responsible forest management.

For more information visit www.harpercollins.co.uk/green.

Printed and Bound in the UK using 100% Renewable Electricity
at CPI Group (UK) Ltd, Croydon, CR0 4YY

RECLAIMED ON ROMANO'S TERMS

KIM LAWRENCE

MILLS & BOON

For Stella.

PROLOGUE

THE LIGHTS THAT had been on earlier when they left the house were still blazing as the car turned into the long tree-lined driveway of the Manor. In the driver's seat Amy's father was silent, as he had been the entire journey back from the hospital.

It wasn't a relaxed, comfortable silence; it was a tense, nerve-stretching absence of sound. The only times he had even acknowledged her presence was when he'd delivered a series of poisonous icy glares when she had dared risk a surreptitious glance at the numerous missed messages on her phone screen.

Amy's fingers remained curled around the phone but after a swift sideways glance at her father's profile—even his double chin looked furious—she didn't pull it out. A spasm of self-contempt tugged the corners of her lips downward.

Not so brave now, sneered the voice in her head.

Earlier, it had been a different story.

She had stood defiant in the face of her parents' reaction, even though normally her mother would act as the voice of moderation whenever she incurred her father's displeasure, but not this time.

Her parents had been united in their horror.

Amy shook her head as though the action would physically block the scene that continued to play out in her head in a loop.

It didn't.

'How far has this gone?' her father thundered inside her head as the replay loop reached the cliffhanger moment.

'How far has it gone…?' she'd repeated. 'No further than I wanted it to.'

Her mother whimpered and gasped, *'My baby!'*

The memory of that response twisted the knife of guilt a few painful inches deeper in Amy's chest.

'Mum, this isn't a Victorian melodrama and I'm not a child. I'm nineteen next week.'

Lost in her own miserable thoughts, she didn't notice the engine had been switched off until her father opened the car door, still ignoring her. Amy caught his sleeve and he swung around, his eyes sliding from her face to her hand grasping the tweed of his jacket.

When she let go, he smoothed the fabric as though she had contaminated it with her touch.

'Mum will be all right, won't she, Dad?'

Despite the doctors' confident assertions, Amy still found it difficult to believe, even after her prayers had been answered and her mother had regained consciousness.

Amy would have promised anything at that moment, and she had.

She flinched now as her father's response was a slammed door.

The security lights came on as he marched towards the front door they must have left wide open in their hurry to leave in the slipstream of the ambulance's blue flashing lights.

Biting her already raw full lower lip, Amy extricated herself from the passenger seat and stood in the shadows of the semi lit forecourt. The night air hit her, cooling her skin but not the swirling mass of tormented emotions twisting in her head.

Out of habit, she glanced up at the clock tower above the arch that led to the stable block, her eyes widening when she saw it was one-thirty. Had it *really* only been six hours earlier when she had stood, bag packed, telling her parents of her intention to leave? She knew her over-confident declaration had been defensively aggressive to compensate for the fact her knees were shaking and her stomach churning in apprehension.

Having spent her life wrapped in cotton wool that had come to feel like a strait jacket she was breaking free of, taking a massive step into the unknown and facing parental disapproval, it was small wonder her knees had been shaking.

Six hours—which meant that Leo had been waiting for her for five hours by now. She had allowed herself a comfortable hour to get to their prearranged meeting spot. She had been terrified of being late and somehow missing him.

Was he still waiting?

What had he thought when she didn't show?

Amy's cold fingers tightened around the phone in her pocket. She wished she could regain some of her earlier bravery, that utter certainty of several hours ago that had buoyed her.

That certainty had dissolved as she'd witnessed her mother's body jerk like a broken doll in response to the shock from the paddles the paramedics had administered. The horror she'd felt had killed all her confidence stone dead, even before her father had snarled, '*You did this!*'

Amy was no longer made brave by the naive conviction that love would make everything all right. The conviction that had made her stand quietly throughout a storm of accusations and threats, culminating in her father's parting shot.

'Walk through that door and that's it—I have no daughter.'

The ultimatum had shaken her but she'd held her ground. 'You won't accept that I'm with Leo, but I love him and I know we're meant to be together. I have no choice.'

She knew differently now; there *was* a choice and it was one she had made when her mother had regained consciousness and pulled off her oxygen mask long enough to plead.

'Don't do this, Amy, don't go with him—promise me, promise me.'

'I promise, Mum.'

Amy walked towards the open door, but her father had already disappeared from view. The elegant chandelier illuminated the graceful curving staircase that Amy had been halfway down when her mother's anguished cry had made Amy turn in time to see her clutch her chest and collapse.

She had a vague recollection of running back up the stairs and falling on her knees by her mother's prone form.

Her father had been there too, his face as red as her mother's had been pale. 'Are you happy now that you've nearly killed her?'

Amy blinked back tears as the scene continued to relentlessly play out in her head. She stared at the phone in her hand, remembering how she'd had to yell to make herself heard above her father's abusive flow of bitter accusations as she gave the requested details to the emergency services.

'Is she breathing?' she'd been asked.

'I don't know!' Amy had wailed, frustration and gut-clenching fear making it hard to respond to the calm instructions of the person on the other end of the line.

'Yes, I think her airway is clear…but her lips are blue. Chest compressions? I… Right…'

When the paramedic had appeared, she had literally sobbed her relief, the floodgates opening and tears falling in a river down her cheeks as she fell back onto her heels and manoeuvred herself out of their way.

The journey behind the ambulance remained a surreal blur. The arrival in the casualty unit was equally dreamlike, but certain details stood out, like seeing the heart emoji on her phone screen when they had been asked to switch off mobiles as they walked through what felt like a sinister forest of bleeping machines to the cubicle where her mum lay, surrounded by a scary number of medical staff.

As she reached the first of the flight of steps that led to the front door, Amy heard footsteps from inside the house and braced her shoulders, fighting an urge to delay the moment when she would be alone with her father.

She was working up her courage when a rustle made her turn her head in time to see a tall, lean figure separate itself from the purple-shadowed glossy undergrowth.

'Leo!' Shock and longing were intertwined in her gasp as she identified the figure standing there. 'I… I… *You* can't be here.' She looked nervously over her shoulder. The situation was awful enough without Leo, who didn't have a clue what it was like to be on the receiving end of her father's temper.

He took a step forward, the light illuminating his features. It highlighted the sharp cheekbones, the symmetrical planes and hollows, his perfect features dissected by a narrow blade of a nose, the sculpted sultry curve of his incredible mouth.

The shadows did nothing to dilute his masculine aura, the tingling charge of danger he gave off. The danger had initially attracted her, but it was his passion and sensitivity that had kept her with him, that had turned her lust to love.

The high-octane masculinity hit her now like a shock-wave, grabbing hard at the muscles low in her belly, the longing so strong she could barely breathe. The sense of loss that followed felt like a hard, dark weight lodged behind her breastbone.

'Where have you been, Amy?' He moved closer and the light hit his face, leaving half in darkness, half in light. The emotions in his dark eyes reached out to grab her. He wasn't angry, just frustrated and confused, his dark brows drawn into a questioning line above his hawkish nose as he stared at her. 'I waited for you...'

She knew it was crazy but it was a fact; she could *feel* his voice. Deep velvet with a fascinating back note of gravel, it vibrated through every cell in her body.

'What have they done to you?'

She stood there on the balls of her feet, poised to run into the arms he held open in invitation. An invitation she longed to accept, to walk into his arms to feel the hardness of his lean body, smell the warm male scent of his skin. The longing rose up in her and she wanted nothing more than to lay her head against his chest and hear his heartbeat and feel his strong arms close protectively around her.

She wanted the rest of the world to go away and there to be nothing but her and Leo.

When Leo was with her she felt braver and stronger; it always felt as if he'd peeled away a layer and exposed the real her. With him, she was more *herself* than she had ever been before she'd met him. The same way his lovemaking seemed to somehow drive her deeper into herself, making her self-aware at a cellular level in a way she could not define.

'Is sex always like this?' she had asked him after that first time, because she'd had nothing to compare it to.

'Not for me it isn't,' he'd replied, looking as stunned as she had felt.

Her eyes on his face like a sleepwalker, she took a half step towards him, remembering as she did so how she'd felt the first time she'd set eyes on him. Her nervous system had gone into meltdown, her brain short-circuited. She had never experienced anything so *visceral* in her life before.

He had terrified her, not because there was anything threatening in his behaviour; despite his physicality, the opposite was true. The way his big hands with their long, tapering brown fingers had moved down the nervous colt's flanks was incredibly gentle.

She had been too stunned in the moment by the whirl-wind of sensation inside her to register how the skittish animal responded to the soft words the most beautiful man she had ever imagined was murmuring into its ear. Sensing her presence, he had turned his head, brushing his hands along the torn denim that covered his muscular thighs.

Amy had shivered as fire crackled along her nerve-endings when his dark eyes connected with her stare. She could see the flare of awareness flash in his, and then he'd smiled and she was lost.

'I am so sorry, Leo,' she pushed out, feeling the heat of tears that pressed against her eyelids. The deep ache of loss in her belly.

From nowhere, the rain came. Under the shelter of the porticoed porch she stayed dry, but in seconds Leo was drenched—not that he reacted to it, or the water that ran down his face, glossing his golden skin—skin she loved to touch.

In her peripheral vision she was aware of her father appearing in the doorway behind her. She half turned and saw that he was holding a phone in his hand, wielding it like a weapon, not looking at her but at Leo.

'I've already called the police to tell them we have an intruder. I'm filming this, so keep your distance!' he added, even though Leo hadn't moved. But without moving at all he suddenly seemed taller and even more imposing.

Leo stared her father down before his glance shifted to Amy, lingering on her face for a long moment. There was no doubt in his face, just encouragement. The fact he believed in her and had total confidence that she would take the hand he stretched towards her made not doing so the most painful thing she'd ever experienced in her life.

Amy saw the brief look of confusion flicker across his chiselled features before he switched his scrutiny to her father.

'I didn't come here to argue with you. I just came here for Amy.'

Amy stared again at the hand extended to her, the internal conflict that was raging inside her finding release in a series of white-faced, agonised gasps. 'You don't understand, Leo.'

For three seconds their eyes held, then he broke the contact as his hand fell down. 'I think maybe I do. You want this.' His hand lifted again but this time his sweeping gesture encompassed the illuminated manor house. 'You like your designer life, you love it…the tennis clubs, the skiing holidays. You were never going to walk away from it all, were you?' His shoulders lifted in a shrug as one dark brow elevated. 'I get it,' he ground out, his gorgeous voice now sounding like broken glass.

'No, it's not like that at all! I just can't…'

'Amy.'

Her father's voice stopped her in her tracks.

'I am so sorry, Leo, but—'

His head reared back as he made a cutting gesture with his hand. 'I don't need buts. Goodbye, Amy. It's certainly been an…experience.'

He turned and walked away, taking something of Amy with him.

CHAPTER ONE

Nine years later

LEO ROMANO, WHO WAS walking and talking as he spoke into his phone, paused by the glass wall that afforded thrilling views across the City landscape. But he ignored the view as he ended the call with a crisp, *'Ciao.'*

He slid the phone into a pocket of the tailored dark jeans he wore and applied the towel hanging loosely around his neck to his wet hair before discarding it in a crumpled heap. It landed wetly on one of the designer leather chairs arranged to enjoy the view as he shook his head, leaving speckles of moisture on the dark blue of the silk shirt that he had not yet buttoned. It hung open, revealing a slice of his golden, densely muscled torso. His broad chest had a light dusting of dark body hair, his flat belly was ridged with muscle. The dull gold buckle of his unfastened belt was a shade lighter than his skin.

Fastening his shirt one-handed, he paused by the open laptop set on a table. The screen was frozen on a shot of a slim figure. In the background, the building she was leaving was totally blocked out by hordes of press wielding sound booms, microphones and cameras. There was no sound on the clip but it had to be bedlam, yet she appeared calm, if very pale, with her eyes fixed on a point up ahead, her tilted chin displaying the graceful curve of her neck.

The rich caramel-coloured hair—hair he had once tangled his fingers in—was drawn back from her face in a thick glossy braid that was pinned around her oval face. The puritanical hairstyle left nothing to hide behind, but there was nothing to hide.

Amy Sinclair was beautiful, more so now than she had been nine years ago.

The delicate bone structure of her face and melting softness of her wide-spaced, darkly-lashed brown eyes were perfectly balanced by feathery dark brows and the lush curve of her mouth—a mouth that had launched a thousand fantasies. Many of those fantasies, he thought grimly, belonged to him.

Leo looked away, resenting the degree of effort it took to break the connection, unable to deny the scalding rush of frustrated heat that had settled in his groin. It was humiliating for a man who prided himself on his total objectivity, the ability to take the emotion out of decision-making or, for that matter, from life in general. Amy's rejection had made him the man he was today, so he had that much to thank her for.

Taking a couple of deep breaths, lips compressed, hands clenched tight with his long brown fingers bone-white from the pressure, he forced himself to turn back. It would have been simpler to pretend he felt nothing, but after nine years the act was wearing thin.

The moment had come to break the cycle of denial, face his weakness and conquer it.

Some might say not before time, he thought, his nostrils flaring as he huffed out a snort of impatient self-contempt.

For nine years he had told himself that the Sinclair family were history, consigned to some dusty corner of his mind.

He had moved on.

It was a self-delusion that had been exposed the moment

the George Sinclair scandal had spawned a wealth of banner headlines: Wealthy Financier Caught with Hand in the Till.

It would have been reasonable, given their shared history, to indulge in a few moments of what-goes-around-comes-around satisfaction, raise a glass to karma then get on with his life.

Instead, he had become totally...*obsessed* with the story. Even admitting to this weakness in the privacy of his own head, just *thinking* the word made him clench his teeth, but what else could you call his encyclopaedic knowledge of every tabloid headline, every online podcast covering Sinclair's trial and eventual incarceration? He'd also hoarded every scrap of information, including every photo, old or new, of Sinclair's daughter, whose *loyalty* and *quiet dignity* had apparently won her a fan base.

There were a lot of photos and he had looked at every single one of them.

Leo had read it all and filed away the opinions of both the crazy people and the serious commentators. Those who loved Amy Sinclair for being a dutiful, loving daughter were countered by an equal number of conspiracy theorists who had concluded she was the criminal mastermind behind the crime and she'd got off scot-free, while the real crazies framed a possibility that she came from Mars.

He had read it all, watched it all—and all because nine years ago Amy Sinclair had rejected him.

Something he had recovered from completely.

Having the lie revealed for what it was meant he was not well-disposed towards the author of his humiliation or, more especially, himself.

It wasn't as if he was the only person in the world to be rejected by his first love, and it wasn't as if rejection had been a new experience for him. Sure, his mother hadn't exactly *rejected* him, but she had died, which as a child had felt pretty much like the same thing.

Then came the foster homes, where a couple of unpleasant experiences had left their mark, but most carers had been well-intentioned, or even kind, but by that point in his life Leo had been wary of *kind*. Even the better people he'd come across had found the aloof kid he'd been too self-contained. A child who didn't smile or cry was hard to warm to.

School hadn't supplied the sort of stimulation his quick mind had craved. His last report had basically read: *a bit of a loner, but good with animal*s. When he'd met Amy Sinclair, he'd been working at stables that ran a sanctuary sideline for old and abused horses. She had been one of the rich kid volunteers, the sort he'd normally steered clear of.

Amy was the first person in his life who had believed in him. Except, of course, she hadn't. She'd simply strung him along as they had created a future together in their heads, but when push came to shove, the novelty value of slumming it had inevitably worn off. And when faced with the prospect of actually leaving her spoilt, fairy tale princess lifestyle for a life with a *no-hope loser* as her father had so charmingly phrased it, she had revealed her true self.

Leo didn't look back on the immediate post-Amy era of his life with any pride, those weeks and months when he had wallowed in self-pity, often found in the bottom of a glass. But he had eventually come out the other side and moved on, telling himself, and really believing it, that he had shrugged off the past and learnt from it. He had viewed, and still did, the gullibility of his old self with a mixture of embarrassment, scorn and disbelief.

And there were even positives to the experience, which he had acknowledged; he had definitely learnt some very important lessons.

He'd never thought of a woman as *his* again, and never would. The term *soulmate* had been expunged from his vocabulary. Somewhere between the bottom of a beer glass and deciding to fight back, Leo had discovered that being a lone wolf and thinking outside the box did not make you a loser.

Actually, those traits could be positive ones when it came to making money, as his early success in crypto had shown. The self-belief that success had given him had helped him deal in a pragmatic way with the next bolt from the blue when it came.

He had family in the form of an Italian billionaire grandfather, who appeared to think that Leo would view this news like a lottery winner and run after the dangling carrot he'd extended. Whereas, actually, Leo's first inclination had been to tell this stranger, who had turfed out his only daughter because she had fallen in love with a man he didn't approve of, to take a hike. Leo had no interest in being the chosen one, and he was more than capable of making his own success; he didn't need to inherit it.

'You think I care about the Romano name, or how old and *noble* this family is, or how much money you have? *You* came looking for *me* because there isn't anyone else, but maybe you should have thought of that before you threw my mother out. I'm not about to kiss your ring or anywhere else, old man, because you need me more than I need you!'

A faint, ironic smile tugged at Leo's lips at the memory of that first encounter, which had been, to put it politely, *stormy.* Over the years, there had been several storms while he worked alongside his grandfather, and even now that the old man was no longer taking an active part in the day-to-day working of the Romano estate, there were still occasions when they butted heads.

Men who threw their daughters to the wolves did not fill Leo with admiration, but over the years an understanding of sorts had developed between the two men.

His heavy-lidded glance strayed one last time to the screen.

He wasn't filled with admiration for weak, compliant daughters who supported their guilty fathers, either.

His half-smile had vanished, and his eyes were cold as he closed the laptop with a decisive snap. He had allowed ghosts from the past to take up space in his head. Now, he needed to free up that space and reclaim his life, which, as lives went, was a pretty good one.

Nine years ago, he had not been in a position to take revenge on the family responsible for humiliating him.

Flexing his broad shoulders, he reached for the leather jacket he had discarded earlier. He was the one calling the shots now.

As he slid into the driving seat of his car, he glanced at the time on the slim platinum-banded watch on his wrist. It was a thirty-minute drive to where the fast-food truck where Amy produced culinary miracles, according to the reviews he'd read, was parked up.

She had gone from being the head chef at a fashionable Michelin-starred restaurant in the capital owned by her father to running a fast-food truck. Her fall in social and professional standing had been as meteoric as his journey in the opposite direction had been.

According to his research, she would still be there. Apparently, she always put in a long day and her only help was a kid on a government employment scheme and a well-known chef who had fallen off the wagon and on hard times.

Amy *should* have fallen apart without *Daddy* to tell her

what to do, *Daddy* to buy her a restaurant as a plaything, *Daddy* who, for all he knew, still had to approve her boyfriends.

Yes, Leo had confidently waited for her to fall apart.

But she hadn't.

It was common knowledge that she had received multiple offers from tabloids to tell her story, casting herself in a favourable light. But it turned out she had not taken up even one of the book offers that would have established her as a professional victim, with her story eventually serialised profitably in one of the red-tops.

Leo assumed she had money stashed away and was biding her time to push the price up, a risky strategy. But there hadn't been a bidding war, no sob story; instead, she'd resurfaced as the part owner of Gourmet Gypsy, a glorified greasy spoon food truck—not anyone's idea of an easy route.

Despite being a social pariah, she obviously still had a few friends in the industry, because some low-key publicity for her down-market venture had emerged. A couple of food critics had written good things, and she was making a living of sorts.

She was called resilient; she was called imaginative and hard-working.

It took a tough person to do what Amy had, but Leo knew she was *not* tough. Reading praise, however faint, of her was like hearing a nail scratching a chalkboard.

Then when her father had been released from incarceration early and the information filtered through to Leo about the sudden increase in Sinclair's cash-flow, he finally understood what was going on. Amy always had followed Daddy's orders and this was all part of her father's long-term plan. Her business was just a front for him to help out his new friends with a bit of money laundering.

Could she really be part of this latest con, or was she just a dim, unwitting pawn? It was time to find out.

Half an hour later, Leo had parked up.

His position, giving him a view of the SilverStream with *Gourmet Gypsy* written along its sides, was pretty much perfect. The interior was still illuminated and he could make out a figure moving around inside.

Then the lights went out, the door opened, and he watched as a small figure, slim beneath an unattractive padded coat that reached to mid-thigh, pulled down the shutters and locked up.

She seemed unaware of a group of three or four youths in hoodies sharing a bottle they passed between them, their lurching progress suggesting they were not just high on booze.

Like many parts of London, extreme deprivation sat cheek by jowl with wealth and privilege. The Gourmet Gypsy van sat squarely on the dividing line between the boarded-up windows and the chic, expensive shops, in a sort of no-man's-land.

Leo got out of the car and, as he did so, the irony hit him. He had come to punish her and instead he might actually end up saving her.

CHAPTER TWO

AMY WAS DOG-TIRED, although she almost welcomed the exhaustion as it stopped her worrying. She worried a lot, but lately, since she had agreed to her father's suggestion that she put her name to his new venture, she worried even more.

She was, of course, glad that he had regained some focus and proud that he wanted to rebuild his life and repay the investors who had lost out because of what he called his *bad decisions*. He'd complained that there were unfair obstacles stopping someone like him rebuilding their life, making a success of himself.

It had been a relief to see the fire in his eyes when he had come up with a way to overcome those obstacles. Since he had been released early from prison, he had accused her of watching him like a hawk and, although she denied it, she was.

Amy would never forget that terrible night after he had been given bail before the trial, when she'd found him lying on the sofa surrounded by empty pill bottles. She hadn't been watching him then—she'd been so angry with him she'd spent as little time in his company as possible, and he had almost died.

'But I don't understand—what are they investing in?' There was no way her business was worth a fraction of the sort of sums she had glimpsed on the documents her father had wanted her to sign.

She had been wary, but was terrified of how he might react if she didn't show she had faith in him. Though, in all honesty, she couldn't see the business justifying the investment and the suppliers she already had were cheaper than the contracts her father was so proud of negotiating. She was already working twenty-four-seven to keep her head above water, to make a go of Gourmet Gypsy without the additional overheads, and what sort of influence would these investors want for their money?

But she'd wanted to make her father happy. He was, after all, the only family she had left after her mother had died just before he was arrested.

He had assured her that the investors would not interfere. All he needed was her signature—a lot of signatures, it seemed to Amy, and when she had wanted to read the papers she was putting her name to, her father had looked hurt and asked her if she didn't trust him.

He had served his time and paid a heavy price for his crime, he'd declared. He deserved a second chance, and if his own daughter wouldn't give him one, who would?

Amy fished out her phone from her pocket and glanced at the clock, estimating what time she'd arrive home. Despite her father being pretty sniffy about the flat, she couldn't really afford it. But she'd needed a second bedroom for him when he was released, and she liked it. The top floor afforded views of trees and while the brick, purpose-built block wasn't pretty, it was quiet Also, it was only five minutes from the Tube, so all she had was a ten-minute walk the other end.

She hadn't put the phone back in her deep pocket before it was snatched out of her hand. Amy jolted back to the moment with a thud by the adrenaline dump into her bloodstream, and she took in the boys, faces invisible, that she had been oblivious to. Boys now circling her...laughing, jeering. She let out a sharp cry of protest and ignored the voice in her head that suggested she should run.

She couldn't afford a new phone and her whole life was on it.

'It's a really old phone—you don't need it, I do.' She tried to inject calm reason into her voice but could barely hear her words, let alone the intonation, above the thud of her own heartbeat vibrating in her eardrums.

'Need it!' mocked the one holding her phone. '*Posh*, isn't she...?' He turned with a flood of expletives and a titter and found his companions were not where they'd just been. He couldn't think why they had run and the phone he had just been tauntingly holding up had been snatched back. 'Bitch!' he snarled and grabbed her.

Amy had sometimes imagined how she would react in a situation of this sort, never actually thinking it would happen. Because it didn't, did it? Things like this happened to someone else. She had always decided that a brains rather than brawn response would be the best plan, given she was only five foot three. Her first option was to run, and she was actually quite fast, but if that wasn't an option she would try talking her way out of the situation.

Resorting to violence had never been one of the options.

It turned out that reality differed from theory big time! Blind instinct along with panic kicked in and she began to struggle wildly as she wriggled, feeling a small moment of satisfaction as she stepped down hard on something she thought—she hoped—was a foot.

The grunt and curse suggested it was. But then the arm around her neck tightened and ice-cold brain-numbing fear conquered every other emotion.

She felt darkness lower across her vision and nerveless fingers dropped the phone—but then, quite suddenly, she could breathe again. As her brain sparked into life she was aware, in her peripheral vision, of someone who was very tall. Like a puppet whose strings had been severed she fell to her knees and stayed there, breathing hard. Aware too that things were happening off-camera while she fought the urge to vomit.

She eventually got to her feet and, with her eyes still squished closed, addressed her hoarse question to a point over her shoulder. 'Have they gone?'

'They have gone.' A few harsh words followed in a language she could identify but didn't know.

The voice she could identify in any language.

Amy didn't need to look. She knew that voice at a cellular level, as well as the person it belonged to.

She had no clue in the world how he was here, but he was.

Had she gone mad?

Or sustained a knock on the head?

Both seemed a lot more likely than Leo being here in this place, now. Her heart hammering against her ribcage, she lifted her braced hands off her thighs, her palms slick with sweat. She straightened up slowly and, with one hand anchoring her messed hair that had come adrift during the short, frantic tussle, she opened her eyes.

He'd found a wall to lean his shoulders against, looking nonchalant and unbelievably sleek and exclusive. He didn't even have a single hair out of place.

'Leo?' A whisper was all she could manage as she stared in shaky disbelief at the tall figure, cataloguing every detail of his patrician features, every shift of expression on his face. It was still all angles and intriguing hollows, with strong classic features creating a miracle of symmetry. Looking at him acted like a trip switch that turned her brain off as she experienced a weird collision of past and present.

Seeing him that last time, the hurt and disillusion in his face before he'd walked away, had always stuck with her. There was no hurt now; his dark eyes were shuttered, stance relaxed, though there was a telltale tension in his flexing jawline that some might miss. But she knew that face so well, or at least a younger version of it, that she didn't miss anything. Not the tiny scar by the side of his mouth—she remembered tracing it with her finger—nor the waves of sinful male magnetism that poured off him.

A debilitating weakness slid through her and she wrapped her arms around herself as if that would keep the tight ball of her suppressed emotions in place. She was shivering despite the tendrils of heat that were breaking out across her skin, leaving a fiery trail.

Leo was there—impossible but a fact, the same but different. Nine years had built muscle, hardened the lines of his extraordinary, fascinating face, with its broad forehead, sharp commanding nose, a mouth that was all sin…and eyes that felt as though they were reaching into your soul.

She recognised, as her brain kicked into life, that it was better to acknowledge this was nothing more than sexual attraction. Admittedly on an atomic scale, but it was all just hormones and chemical reactions.

Nothing more.

Of all the things she could have said—should have said—she heard herself gasp accusingly, 'You speak Italian!'

His lips quirked and her traitorous stomach flipped. 'It seemed only polite to learn my mother's tongue.'

'Of course—congratulations. It must be nice to have family.'

'That must have hurt.'

She shook her head, struggling to make sense of the tangle of emotions flooding her thoughts. Shaking her head, she said, 'I don't understand what you mean by that…'

'It could have been your family too—that must have hurt.'

An angry retort trembled on her tongue, but then she remembered her father's reaction to the news. 'I was happy for you, whether you believe it or not.'

'Most people would say you do sincerity very well.'

'Did you hurt them, those youths?' She needed a moment's reprieve from thinking about the past and Leo's clear scorn for her.

'We had a civilised conversation and they left. There's no need to thank me.'

His devil-may-care wide white grin did not extend to his eyes, framed by the dark, dense, curling lashes.

'I won't. I had it under control.' She saw something that could have been surprise flicker in the inky blackness of his eyes and lifted her chin a little higher.

'Yes, I saw that.'

She ignored the sarcastic jibe. 'Well, I don't know why you are here, but I don't believe in coincidences, so…?'

'Then you have changed, because you used to believe in the Easter bunny,' he ground out, his hard expression countering the pretend amazement in his voice.

'It's been nine years. Of course I've changed, Leo.' She had not let herself say or even think his name in that time. Excluding her dreams; she'd had to cut herself some slack where her subconscious was involved.

She would have known him, his voice, in pitch darkness, but he had changed too, she realised as she took in the minute details, looking up at him through her lashes and noting the power in his broader leather-covered shoulders.

The fact he looked slick, polished and expensive, attired head-to-toe in designer labels, did nothing to lessen the sheer force of him that had captivated her the first time she'd seen him all those years ago. Now there was an additional layer, an overall hardness to everything about him. Not just the planes of his superbly, *austerely* beautiful face, but in his stance. He carried himself with an arrogance that had not been there nine years ago. He exuded the absolute confidence of a male in the prime of his life who knew he was right at the top of the food chain.

The illicit shudders that shamefully ripped through her body as she stared up at him were no less primal than they had been that very first time she'd set eyes on Leo. She acknowledged the fact with a stab of self-disgust, but took comfort from the fact she was no longer running recklessly towards the excitement he represented. Despite the shameful heat between her legs, *she* had changed.

She knew about consequences.

Giving him up had been the hardest, most painful thing she'd ever had to do. Watching him walk away from her, thinking that she had betrayed him, had added an extra layer to that pain.

And now she had no idea what was in his head. His blank expression left her totally off-balance and in the dark. He had become an unknown entity.

He had always been, and still was, beautiful—the most beautiful thing she had ever seen—but the lanky, coltish quality he'd possessed at twenty had hardened.

Exciting.

The word popped into her head unbidden and she lowered her lashes in a silky screen while she fought for composure, or something that passed for it.

His presence was more disturbing than the young thugs he had seen off, but in a very different way.

Leo watched as she straightened her spine and lifted her

head, cloaked in a coolness that didn't fool him. It amused him to think she imagined he couldn't see it for what it was—barely even skin-deep.

Amy was reacting to him the way she always had. Nine years was a long time, but it hadn't taught her how to conceal the fact that she was lusting after him.

'You should have given them your phone!'

For a split second his cloaked expression fell away and she could see his anger, hot enough to make her take an involuntary step backwards.

He clamped his lips tightly, as if to hold back further remonstrations, but his gaze continued to move over her face, studying each feature with disturbing intensity, travelling from her neck to her chin and lingering on her mouth before finally settling on her eyes.

She didn't react; indeed, she barely registered his words. The impact, the impossibility of him being there, the stream of questions tumbling through her head, made it a struggle to maintain a façade of anything even approaching calm.

Her tongue flickered across her dry lips, drawing his eyes and an inarticulate sound from his throat.

The noise jolted her free of her trance as her gaze shifted from his face to the phone he'd picked up, which he was now holding out to her.

'You were willing to fight for it, so take it.'

She ignored the sarcastic reminder and reached out, a deep shudder running though her body as their fingers grazed for a split second. Her eyes darted everywhere but at the face of the man she had once loved as she closed her fingers over the phone and brought it up tight against her chest.

Loved and left.

It had taken her months after that fateful night to stop

reimagining the scene, replacing the facts with alternative outcomes, but none of the other scenarios had a particularly happy conclusion either.

Some people were just not meant to be together.

She tipped her head awkwardly in acknowledgement. Her eyes lifted as she shook her head and forced her lips into a smile. Not a great smile and it hurt, but she was definitely smiling, which was better than the alternative—which was gibbering incoherence.

'My whole life is on this phone...' Her attempt at a laugh didn't work out brilliantly and his only response was a scowl.

'Your life!' He expelled the words through gritted teeth. 'Walking alone at this time of night in an area like this doesn't suggest too much concern for your life!'

'This area is perfectly—' She stopped and took a deep breath, recognising that arguing with him wasn't going to de-escalate a situation that needed some serious de-escalation. 'Look, I'm grateful, but I could have handled it. I was handling it.'

'Oh, is that a fact?'

This fresh display of blatant sarcasm brought a faint flush to her pale cheeks.

'Yes!' she retorted, pausing and trying to stick a hairpin back into her once neat braid, which immediately tumbled back down. So much for dignity.

How dare he comment on where she ran her business, where she lived her life? Him, with his new family, his new life—he knew nothing of hers any more.

She flung the unravelling braid over her shoulder and cleared her throat. 'Sorry. Obviously, I am grateful, but I just...' She swallowed convulsively as emotion rose in her throat, thickening her words and, worse, bringing the sting of tears to her eyes. 'I just want to go home now.'

Aware that her voice had risen to a shrill plaintive wail, she took a deep breath, calming in theory but less so in reality. She cleared her throat again. 'This is just all a bit *weird*. You, here? Looking like this…' Her voice stalled. She fought the urge to say something daft like *Do you work out?* and said nothing at all.

'You have no security?'

The taut condemnation in his voice wrenched an ironic laugh from her. His comment showed just how far removed this man was from the Leo she had known.

'Sure. It's their day off.' She studied his face; he *used* to have a sense of humour. 'Seriously, this is normally a quiet time of night, and I've taken self-defence classes.' She hadn't, but she didn't want him to know his criticism had got to her.

'You did?' He raised his eyebrows in challenge. She could tell he'd seen straight through her falsehood.

Sometimes it was irritating that she couldn't follow through with a perfectly good lie.

'No, but I intend to when I have the time, and I've read a lot of self-help books.'

'What, to whack little shits across the head with?'

She laughed and she didn't know why, because laughter in this situation was not a sane reaction, but for a second he had sounded so like the Leo she had once known that a wistful sigh left her lips. Before reality came flooding back in and she realised that he was no more like the old Leo than she was the old Amy. They never could be. It was time to say goodbye, once and for all.

CHAPTER THREE

'LOOK, THANKS FOR your help but—'

'Get in.'

'What?' Until the long, sleek designer car they were standing beside bleeped, she had no idea they had been walking while they talked. He had basically been herding her like a sheep as they spoke and she hadn't even noticed.

'I was always told not to get into cars with strangers,' she said, trying to inject some levity, admittedly strained, into the situation.

'I'm not a stranger, Amy.'

Her head tilted to look him full in the face.

Yes, he was.

It was as if he had been stripped back to a shell and re-built as a harder, scarier version of the Leo she had known and loved.

'The Tube—you can walk me to the Tube. That's it.' It was a meeting him midway offer that he appeared not to recognise.

'It's either home or the police station,' he said in a voice that left no room for negotiation. She was starting to suspect it was the norm for this Leo.

'Police?'

'To report the attack and theft.'

'I still have my phone and they won't class it as a mugging, so what would be the point?'

'You sound like an expert.'

She shook her head. 'I'm just stating the obvious.'

'In what world is that obvious?'

'My world, Leo.' But no longer his.

He said something in Italian and looked at her oddly.

'We can stand here arguing all day or you can get in.'

'Night,' she corrected, adding, 'not day.'

He looked bewildered and utterly vexed by her pedantic insertion. She took a deep breath and weighed her limited options.

'All right,' she said, sliding into the leather seat and sinking into the padded luxury that swallowed her up.

It probably made her shallow, but she missed that part of having money—the comfort, the space, the security and the *smell* of luxury. She inhaled, and Leo's scent hit her. Warm, clean, male. With an elusive hint of an undeniably expensive fragrance.

The engine was silent so when the car moved off she gave a little gasp of shock. 'Don't you want to know where I live?'

He flashed her a look before pulling out into the traffic. 'I know where you live, Amy.'

That could have sounded sinister... Actually, there was no *could* about it, it *was* sinister.

'Now,' he said, flashing her a smile that didn't reach his eyes, 'isn't this more comfortable than the Tube?'

She could lie and tell him that no, she would feel more comfortable packed in like a sardine with her face in someone's armpit. It wouldn't even be a total lie. Being in a confined space with this version of Leo was proving to be just as stressful. On a much deeper, chemical level.

Luckily, he didn't feel the need to make conversation because she was not capable of it. She sat there with a dazed look on her face as he drove, trying to build up some resistance to the aura of maleness he exuded. Trying not to tax her sex-whacked brain as she struggled to work out how he'd just happened to be passing by.

Obviously, he hadn't just happened to be passing by. This had all been planned. But what, exactly, was he planning now?

By the time he drew up outside her apartment block, she virtually threw herself out of the car.

He followed her. 'I'll see you in.'

If this had been an argument she could have won, she'd have fought it. But she knew resistance would be futile. She wouldn't win, not against *this* Leo.

To regain any amount of control she could, she avoided the lift in favour of the stairs. Being alone in a small space with him wasn't wise right now. She wasn't about to make that mistake twice.

He wasn't subtle when he strode straight past her into the living room of the flat before she'd barely opened the door. Her nostrils flared in annoyance. He was invading her space but she was in control, she reminded herself. She clung with bloodless fingers to the illusion.

'So, you live here alone?'

Her lips quirked into an ironic smile as she directed a look at her uninvited guest, who was taking in every detail of her home. Maybe he was thinking of when she had smuggled him into the Manor when her parents were absent, no doubt enjoying the fact that she was no longer living in the lap of luxury.

'I think maybe you know I don't, Leo.' He knew where she lived so it wasn't such a massive jump to assume he knew that her father lived here too.

He shrugged. 'Is your father around?'

'He's away for the weekend.' She caught her full lower

lip between her teeth and tried to disguise her worry about the situation beneath a shrug and a smile.

Her dad had been cagey when she had challenged him about where he was going, and who with, adding another hurt, *'Don't you trust me?'* to end the discussion. Because actually, no, she didn't trust him, but there was no question of her voicing the fact. Her father was vulnerable; he had already tried to take his life once, and she hadn't been there for him.

He needed support, not a guilt trip, she reminded herself. He'd done his time.

'Why are you here, Leo? Nothing about this is accidental, is it?' she charged.

'You think I arranged for you to be attacked?'

'Of course not! But you weren't just passing either, were you?'

'True.' He performed a ninety-degree turn. 'This is a nice place.'

Her eyes narrowed and she couldn't bear it any longer. 'Stop it! Why not say what you mean? How the mighty have fallen! Enjoy the moment, that's fine! I guess I owe you that.' She extended her arms wide in invitation. 'If you must know, even this place is more than I can really afford, but Dad...' She bit her lip and shook her head, wondering why she had volunteered this much information.

'Wouldn't enjoy slumming it?'

Her eyes slid from his intuitive dark stare. Her father had made his opinion of the flat very clear, and it hadn't been positive!

'When will he be back?'

Amy continued to shrug off the inappropriately thick coat to reveal a pale blue denim shirt tied at the waist. Her jeans were a shade darker and clung to her thighs and when she bent down to unzip the ankle boots she was wearing the fabric pulled distractingly tight across her firm, rounded bottom. Her waist-length glossy hair, which was working its way loose of the braid, fell over one shoulder as she straightened up and kicked off the soft ankle boots she wore.

Leo was still struggling to take control of the testosterone-charged heat in his groin when she lifted her head.

'Monday,' she said, giving the knot at her waist an extra sharp tug. 'Like I already explained to you, he's away for the weekend, staying with friends.' Her hands landed on her hips as her chin lifted to a defensive angle, drawing his attention to the narrowness of her waist and the curve of her hips. Her supple, streamlined figure, the smooth curves of her body and her natural elegance had always made him think of a sleek cat. With claws, he added silently, thinking not just of the marks she had left on his shoulders on occasion, but the way she hadn't hesitated before cutting him out of her life. It was a good reminder of what he was here to do.

'Is this an interrogation?' she asked with a frown.

Leo looked at her and laughed again.

At eighteen, Amy hadn't had a clue about the sort of power her beauty gave her, let alone how use it to her own advantage. The fact that she still didn't amazed him.

'Have I said something funny?' she demanded, the hoarse note of belligerence in her voice shaking loose a memory— a memory of that throaty little whimper, low in her throat, she would let out when he kissed her, promptly negating any control he'd ever had around her.

'You're very touchy, *cara*.' He shifted his stance slightly to ease the ache in his groin.

A man might ask himself at this point just who was being

punished here, he thought, permitting himself a flicker of an ironic self-mocking smile.

'I'm not.'

It might be a piece of poetic justice, his plan to rub her little nose in their flipped fortunes by bringing her into his world, allowing her to see what she had missed out on, but he hadn't factored in the fact that she wouldn't be the only one made to feel uncomfortable with the arrangement. She was still the most incredibly sensual woman he had ever met.

Amy, reacting to the tension buzzing in the air like static, closed her eyes, bringing her lashes down to act like a glossy but inadequate protective shield, casting a shadow across her high smooth cheeks. It was then that he noted the purple smudges under her soft brown eyes.

'Do you ever sleep?'

She shrank under his critical stare, clearly suddenly aware of what a wreck she looked. So different from the flawlessly glossy women he was used to escorting.

'Thank you for your concern, but being self-employed means I need to put in the hours, and I like being my own boss.'

The look she gave him suggested that wasn't entirely true. But he didn't care to explore it further. He was more interested in furthering his cause.

'Do you like your father's new friends?'

It took Amy a moment to retrieve the thread he had picked back up. Where was he going with this? Why did he want to know?

'*New* friends—?'

'Well, I doubt if many of his old golf club buddies hung around, and you said he was away with friends.'

'After he was…arrested…' she silently mocked herself for the small tell-tale hesitation '…we were toxic, but who needs friends like that, anyway?' she countered with a shrug, thinking miserably that her father needed them, he desperately needed them, his old life, the club memberships and committees.

Leo just shrugged and, not for the first time, Amy wondered how he had become so invulnerable. Hard as steel.

'But not you—you stood by him,' he stated.

Amy's glance slid from his. She remembered, all too well, wishing that she could walk away. 'He's my father. I know he's not perfect.' And she also knew how vulnerable he was.

Leo's harsh, mocking laugh brought an angry flush to her cheeks. Partly because of the guilt she felt at not having been there, not in a way that counted, when her father *had* needed her. She'd been too angry with him to guess the level of his desperation.

Leo responded with an infuriating languid half smile as he walked over to the mantelpiece above the electric fire and peered at the photos that lined it.

'So you haven't always been afraid of horses,' he said, picking up one of a curly-haired child sitting on top of a chunky pony, holding a rosette. 'You used to be a lot fairer.'

Her hand went automatically to her hair, despising that she cared what she looked like in this moment.

'No, that's not me, and I'm not afraid of horses.' She loved horses but the bargain had been that she was allowed to help out at the stables, but she must never get on a horse.

Having lost one daughter in a riding accident, the ban had not been that surprising. Amy had understood why her parents were overprotective, but that didn't make it any easier to accept the restrictions. Restrictions that had made her the odd one out growing up, because it hadn't just been the horse-riding her parents had deemed dangerous; there were so many other things she'd never got to do either, no sleepovers, no camping trips. The list of things she had not been allowed to do had seemed endless.

She hadn't told Leo about Alice back then, about why she'd felt she had to be the perfect daughter. Good enough for both herself and the child they'd lost.

But, of course, she never had been. Had Alice been perfect? Would it have been different if her sister had grown up, become a rebellious teen first? But Alice hadn't. She'd never flunked a maths test, never had a teenage strop or an unsuitable boyfriend.

Long before she'd met Leo, Amy had stopped competing with the perfect ghost of her sibling, and stopped trying to make her parents proud, recognising it wasn't possible.

Leo, of course, was an excellent horseman. One of the first times she'd seen him he'd been on horseback, and she'd been riveted. Watching the tall stranger, as he'd been then, on the frisky half-schooled mare.

Her stomach flipped and quivered as she recalled the shocking impact, the visceral reaction she had experienced. Sexual attraction that she had been too inexperienced to hide.

She snatched the picture from his hand and replaced it on the mantelpiece. 'It's not me—it's my sister, Alice,' she said, straightening the photo frame.

'You have a sister?' The furrow between his brows deepened. 'Older, I'm assuming?'

'She would have been.'

An alert expression slid into his eyes. 'She died.'

It was a statement, and one she didn't respond to.

'You miss her?'

'I never knew her.' Reacting to what might have been pity

in his voice—pity she didn't want or need—she responded more sharply than she'd intended. Softening it, she added, 'It happened ten years before I was born. My parents were no longer young when I was born; for the first six months she was pregnant with me, Mum thought she was experiencing the menopause.'

'You never mentioned you had a sister.'

Amy felt a wave a guilt, remembering how good it had felt to be with someone who didn't bring her dead sister into the conversation at every opportunity, who didn't compare her with the ghost.

'I'm sure there were things you didn't tell me.' There were a lot of things she hadn't told him, and then suddenly there had been nothing to tell him.

No baby.

Nine years later and the thought of her miscarriage still came with the same pain. She ignored the tight feeling in her chest and the dull ache.

Revisiting the past wouldn't help anyone. Least of all her.

'You weren't just passing, Leo, so what's this all about?'

'So how old was your sister when she died?'

She sighed out her frustration when he ignored her question.

'She was ten.'

She glanced at another photo of a curly blonde cherubic smiling baby. 'They thought I might get fairer as I got older, but I never did. I got darker, except for—' She touched the blonde streak that sprang from her forehead that no one ever believed was natural.

'So where are you?' he asked, scanning the gallery line-up of photos, seeing the same child at various ages, but none of a dark-haired child.

'Oh, no one prints out their online photos these days.'

Especially if you never quite lived up to expectation, she thought, dodging his eyes, determined not to allow him to spotlight her insecurities. He was no longer twenty, no longer in love with her. He didn't get to know about her insecurities.

Suddenly, she felt every month of her twenty-eight years, and it was hard to think that she'd ever been so happy, living in the moment and never thinking ahead.

It wouldn't have worked.

It *couldn't* have worked.

Unbidden, the memory of Leo standing outside her family home, his hand reaching out to her, drifted into her head. For a split second she was back on that emotional ledge, wanting to take his hand and knowing it was impossible.

The look on Leo's lean face…the expression in his dark eyes under his long messy fringe had been so intense and real as he'd willed her to take the hand he held outstretched to her…was spotlit in her memory, every detail frozen in time.

She shook her head and she saw the realisation of what she'd been seeing in her mind's eye slide into his gaze in the shift of muscle as his jaw clenched.

She took a deep breath and dragged herself back to the present. 'Look, we have established you were not just passing. That's not to say I'm not grateful you got me out of that situation, but really…'

'You realise the more you tell me how grateful you are, the less grateful you sound?' he observed, sounding amused.

'Why, Leo? If you are here to see how the mighty have fallen, well, that's fair enough. I suppose I deserve that, but not Dad. He's an old man trying hard to rebuild his life. So if you're just here to tell me how great your life is going, that's fine. You're about to be married… You've won the lottery… Whatever it is, good luck for the future, and goodbye.'

Not that he needed luck, from what she had read.

She held open the door, anxious for this farce to be over.

'Actually, I'm here to offer you a job.'

CHAPTER FOUR

THE SILENCE STRETCHED.

'Me, work for you?' She stared at him, her eyebrows hitting her hairline. 'Have you been drinking?'

'No, but if you're offering…?'

Her lips tightened. 'I'm not,' she retorted unsmilingly. 'Unless it's escaped your notice, I already have a job.'

'I imagine it must be tough coming down in the world—a hard landing.'

She lifted her chin. 'I'm not complaining.'

'Your margins must be very tight.'

She stayed silent, likely sensing something was coming. The *something* made her visibly tense in anticipation.

'What I'm suggesting is temporary.' Long enough to enjoy the satisfaction of seeing her in *his* world, out of her depth. Because, despite the fact that she had lost everything, she had retained the innate attitude of a winner. Where the hell did her strength come from?

He pushed away the stab of admiration that came with the thought, focusing instead on the inexplicable way she had defended her father. When she wanted to fight for something, she did so like a tigress.

Yet she hadn't fought for him.

Amy shook her head and gave him a stubborn blank look.

'I need a chef for an upcoming event.'

'Is that meant to be a joke?' She pointed to her face. 'I am not laughing. There are a lot of chefs out there, Leo.'

'It's a tough gig and I understand if you don't feel up to the challenge.'

'It isn't a matter of feeling up to anything. Nothing in the world would make me work for a man who…'

'Was your social inferior?'

The colour flew to her cheeks. 'I wasn't going to say that.'

'It's true, though.'

'You never forgave me, did you?'

'I almost forgot you existed,' he lied without hesitation.

She flinched, but after a split second and a convulsive swallow she lifted her chin.

There was a reason why Leo had risen to the heights he had, a reason why the business world revered him. His ruthlessness was unrivalled, so it was infuriating that he felt the need to remind himself that *nothing* about Amy was authentic, not the bitten lip or the unshed tears.

'And then your father's case hit the headlines, and you stayed a daddy's girl to the end. It reminded me that we have unfinished business, Amy.' He paused, his contemptuous dark eyes narrowed, trained on her face for a long moment before he asked, 'Are you, Amy?'

The lethally soft question made her shiver. 'Am I what?'

'A daddy's girl. What would you do for your father? How far does your devotion and blind loyalty go?'

'What do you mean?' she asked, even though she was pretty sure she didn't want to know.

'We have established that working for me is not something that sets your soul alight with joy. The question is, would you work for me in order to save your father from another stint in jail? For a second offence, he might not have the option of an open prison.'

The possibility that he wasn't bluffing sent an icy chill through Amy. In her mind, she could see the scattered pills on the floor amidst empty bottles and her father's body on the floor, unmoving. She knew with total certainty that if faced with that shame again, he wouldn't get as far as prison.

'He's not going back to prison.' Amy could hear the note of panic in her voice. 'He's turning his life around.'

Leo refused to recognise the stab of guilt that speared him when he saw the fear in her eyes—that, at least, was authentic. 'Those new friends your father made behind bars, they have friends on the outside who have large quantities of cash made illegally, which they need to launder through a legitimate business.' He arched a speculative ebony brow. 'Have your accounts been looking more healthy of late?'

She looked at him, loathing shining in her eyes, hating how what he was saying made sense. 'How do you know any of this?'

'It's easy to *know* things when you know where to look. Your father is not a master criminal, although in his arrogance and greed I'm quite sure he thinks he is.' His voice dropped to a foreboding purr as he tilted his head and scanned her face with a clinical detachment that made her feel like a bug under a microscope. 'Are you in on the scam, Amy?'

She stepped forward and lifted her arm in the same moment. The action was pure reflex and she barely registered what she was about to do until fingers like steel wrapped around her wrist.

Her eyes widened in shocked horror, which was supplanted when instead of releasing her hand he dragged her towards him. He bent his head and she literally stopped breathing, her eyes drifting closed as his head lowered.

The warmth of his breath on her palm sent a shiver through her body and then she was free. Apart from the tangled emotions churning inside her as she rubbed her palm hard against her thigh.

She made herself meet his gaze. His taunting smile made it obvious he knew she had thought he was going to kiss her.

The only question was, did he also know she had wanted him to?

'What do you want, Leo?' she asked, making her voice cold, even though it did nothing to lower her internal temperature.

'I've already told you I need a chef… I think a six-week contract will suffice.'

Six weeks of working for him and he would have the satisfaction of seeing her fail. Amy would be begging to leave; she had developed unexpected steel, but in a war of attrition there was only one winner.

'My business…?'

'I will pay for a temp to fill in for you. I am assuming that your alcoholic helper will be able to cope without you.'

Anger blazed in her soft eyes as she drew herself up to her full height. 'How do you—' she began and stopped. It was pointless to ask why Leo's position gave him a reach that she couldn't even begin to imagine. 'Ben hasn't had a drink in ten years and he is my business partner, equal partners. He put money in, and his knowledge has made all the difference.'

'An older man to lean on,' he mused, pressing a finger to his chin. 'Am I seeing a pattern here…?'

'My father is trying hard—'

'To do what, exactly? Set himself up as the go-to man for drug dealers with some cash to launder?'

The blood drained from her face, the colour change so dramatic that any doubts that she had any involvement in George's extracurricular activities vanished.

'Drugs?' she stuttered out. 'He wouldn't!' Hearing the question in her own voice, she rounded on him furiously. 'I suppose you don't believe in second chances.'

'I believe they're wasted on most people.'

'God, when did you get so cynical?' she flared.

'I think you can take some credit for that, *cara*.'

He managed to make the endearment sound like a mocking insult. 'Stop calling me that!' she hissed in frustration.

'I'll take that as a yes, shall I?' He smiled and turned towards the door, pausing as he swung back. 'Oh, and as my employee I think a bit of courtesy might be in order for our working relationship.'

She lowered herself into a mocking curtsey.

'I'll have the contract sent over for you to sign.'

'What, in blood?' she snarled.

He laughed and she remembered a time when his smile had not been an exercise in cynicism. Remembering all the times he had teased her and made her laugh, she was seized by a quite crazy sense of loss.

She had lost Leo years ago.

'We leave on Friday.'

She shook her head, her brow pleated in a perplexed frown. 'Friday? Where to?'

'For Tuscany.'

'Tuscany in Italy?'

He arched a brow and regarded her as if she'd just made a totally facile comment.

'That's too soon. I will have things to—'

He brushed aside her objections. 'You don't have to do anything except just be ready. You do have an up-to-date passport?' he asked, already moving through the door.

She nodded and he was gone.

CHAPTER FIVE

FRIDAY CAME AND as Amy sat waiting with her bag packed she began to wonder again if this had all been an elaborate hoax. It had the hallmarks of an elaborate 'gotcha' for someone who had too much time on his hands. He wasn't going to show; she was just going to sit here all day.

She had signed the contract, not in blood but in black ink. Not that it had made the act any easier. Before she had signed the next six weeks of her life away, she had confronted her father, hoping, *willing* him to deny everything, tell her this was some terrible mistake.

It wasn't a mistake, it was the truth, and almost as shocking as his eventual admission after a lot of waffle was his utter lack of remorse, the way he had taken no responsibility at all for his actions.

Reminding herself that he was vulnerable, she had held tight to her anger and the seething sense of betrayal while taking in his reaction to being challenged. His mood shifting from initial shock and denial to indignation, to the inevitable tearful hurt.

She had stood by him throughout his trial and sentence, she'd been there when he got out, and he'd not only lied to her, he'd used her. Things were at the point where the only option was to call him out on his manipulative behaviour or physically remove herself from the scene before she said something that she would regret.

She had walked away knowing that a lot of what her father did was an act, but the fragility was real. If something she said, even a true something, pushed her father to another suicide attempt she would never be able to live with the guilt.

Was the promise she had extracted from her father worth anything? She wanted to believe that he would end his association with his shady friends. *She could only hope.*

Every night since she had signed away her immediate future she had barely slept and, when she did, she woke up in a cold sweat. That was bad enough, but the hot sweats when she woke aching, yelling Leo's name, were infinitely worse. When even her father, not the most observant of men, asked her if she was ill, she knew that the sleepless nights were showing.

Or maybe it was living with the knowledge that she was still attracted to Leo, a man who now hated her enough to blackmail her. It was a terrible, wicked thing to do, and she wanted to hate him for it. And she did, but at the same time she kind of thought she deserved it; she had not set out to make him hate her, but she could see why he did. She had broken his heart.

Small wonder that she tried to focus on the basics and let the deeper meaning sort itself out. Basics being thinking about Tuscany, an exciting test of her skills, and she did love a challenge.

The challenge, she suspected, was not going to be culinary but emotional. It was one thing to empathise with Leo's take on the situation; it was quite another to allow him to grind her down and make her doubt her own ability, which she suspected was his game plan.

Amy was sure that the next weeks would be much simpler to navigate if she could return that hate, but instead she was fatally attracted to him.

It was eleven-thirty when her doorbell finally rang. Her father had gone for coffee with an old friend who he had reconnected with, and his mood had been ebullient when they had parted. So she hadn't needed to invent a reason for him not to be there.

Luckily, he had accepted the basic facts she had supplied—she'd accepted a short and well-paid contract, having been recommended by a former colleague. He hadn't pressed for the details, and Amy had not filled him in.

She had wondered what his reaction would be if he knew that Leo would be her boss. Would he be furious and go into meltdown at the suggestion? Or—and actually this was the worse option—would he see an opportunity for her to pick up where they'd left off? The fact that Leo Romano was now mega-rich no doubt made him a lot more acceptable to George Sinclair.

Either way, she didn't want to know.

A middle-aged man, suited and booted, stood there.

'Miss Sinclair.' His smile was polite and friendly. 'I'm here to take you to the airport.' He saw her looking past him. 'Mr. Romano is already in Italy and he will meet us at the airport. These your bags?'

'Yes—oh, no, I can manage.'

He ignored her and picked them up. 'You travel light.'

The man carrying her bags walked ahead to a gleaming limo taking up several parking spaces.

Amy paused at the door being held open, butterflies rioting in her stomach.

What are you doing, Amy?

The driver spoke, and the sound jolted her, cutting through her paralysing apprehension.

She blinked, having no idea what he'd said, but she managed a half smile and nodded, taking a steadying breath before she slid inside the luxurious interior. The door was closed silently behind her, but to Amy it sounded like the clanging of a metal prison door.

She reminded herself that she wasn't a prisoner, she was here of her own volition. She didn't need an escape plan—six weeks, that was all. Six weeks was nothing.

To distract herself she began silent calculations of how many days, hours, minutes were involved in six weeks and barely noticed the route they took through London.

'We are here.'

The information relayed through the intercom made her start. She focused on slowing her galloping heart rate while the driver parked up, and waited while he went around to open the passenger door.

'When is the flight?' she asked, pleased that she sounded calm and in control.

The driver looked at her oddly. 'Take-off is in about ten minutes.'

Amy couldn't understand how he appeared so calm. The last time she had flown, she had arrived three hours ahead of time and still nearly missed her flight. Then the penny dropped.

'This is a private airport,' she realised, taking in her surroundings.

'That's right.'

'And that's a private plane?' The question was redundant as the jet on the runway had *Romano* in gold written along its wings.

* * *

If she'd been less nervous and apprehensive about what awaited her, she would have enjoyed the flight with her every whim being catered for. Not that she had many whims, other than a deep desire for no turbulence.

That wish was granted.

Amy, still on the receiving end of VIP treatment when they landed, wondered if the smiles would stop if they knew she was just the cook. She didn't test the theory but her entourage deserted her completely anyhow when a tall dynamic figure appeared.

Leo did not appear inclined to encourage the official groupies and after a brief exchange he made his way to her side.

'Good flight?'

It was such a normal thing to say in an abnormal situation that she almost laughed, though it seemed doubtful if she could have forced anything past the emotional occlusion in her throat.

She gave a tiny tip of her head, which seemed adequate.

'Do you want a transfer or will you walk?'

'You live close by?'

'To the helipad.' He looked at her sharply as she blanched. 'Is that an issue?'

'No, not at all,' she lied stoically. If he wanted to see her fall apart he would have to do better than a chopper ride.

They had been airborne for ten minutes before he spoke. 'You do know your eyes are closed?'

'Well, it didn't happen accidentally.'

'You don't like helicopters?'

'They are delightful on the ground.'

She opened one eye and saw that he was laughing and looking far too human and ridiculously attractive.

'Sadistic bastard,' she muttered, perhaps a little louder than she had intended.

She kept her eyes closed until she sensed the sharp descent. Her curiosity finally overcoming her fear, her eyes blinked open. Her stomach flip was nothing to do with the distance from the ground but the dark eyes that were watching her. How long their gaze stayed connected she had no idea, but she blinked first, just before her internal temperature had reached a critical point.

'Oh, my God!' She blinked at the sheer scale of the building that dominated the landscape. The view from the air was even more impressive than the one she had seen online. 'It's a real castle.'

'What did you expect, a flatpack? Actually, it's more of a fortified manor, but the ramparts are still intact and the towers.'

'So beautiful it makes me wish I could paint.'

'It has been painted by many artists.'

She expected him to mock her for her sharp cry and her white knuckles on landing, but he displayed unexpected tact and pretended not to notice. Or then again, she mocked herself, maybe he wasn't as obsessed with her body language as she was with his.

'Our carriage awaits.'

The carriage turned out to be a Jeep, and her bags had already been thrown into the back when she climbed in beside them. Leo got in the front with the driver. The two men kept up a conversation in Italian as they drove into a courtyard.

She climbed out dragging a bag with her.

'Leave it; someone will bring them.'

He opened a door and Amy preceded him into the short corridor, lined with various stores and a cool room.

'Kitchen,' he said, pointing to the door ahead. Despite the

closed door, the sounds of a noisy argument in full swing reached them.

Leo felt a stab of annoyance at the tickle of guilt he felt. He could have allowed her to settle in first after the flight, but the fact was he didn't *want* her to settle in.

It was irrational to feel guilt. This was the perfect situation to reveal the real Amy who hid under this new persona, the one that would run away when the going got tough. He just hadn't expected it to be *this* tough so soon.

Knuckles resting on the door, he pushed it in a couple of inches and was greeted by a particularly crude epithet and winced. Pained frown still in place, he glanced down, only to discover Amy was not looking shocked, more amused by his reaction if the twitching lips were any indication.

'Relax, Leo, I've heard worse. This is a kitchen, after all, although I must admit that is a new one on me. So inventive! I should have asked—who do I report to?'

'Me.'

She slung him a look. 'I mean, who is the head chef?'

'You are. I thought that was understood.'

The way he was watching her reminded her of a cat playing with its prey. Refusing to give him the satisfaction of seeing her fall apart, which was presumably the plan, she lifted her chin.

'Oh, I understand totally.'

Displaying a combination of self-possession and determination, she gave the high ponytail she wore in bouncy defiance a determined swish and lifted her chin before stepping into the room. Leo followed her. He had sat through many boardroom battles, but this was different, much more earthy. The blood on the walls in this argument might be tomato-based but it was all a lot more *real*.

Despite the fact that a full-scale war appeared to have

broken out in the kitchen, Amy immediately felt some of the tension leave her shoulders. This was her world, and she took in at a glance a very well-equipped kitchen that any restaurant would have been proud of, though no kitchen she had ever worked in had ancient beams sitting cheek by jowl with the latest in culinary high-tech.

It was actually a relief to have something to distract her from the things that Leo's presence did to her. The prickle caused by the man who had guided her was still there, just under her skin, but her stomach had stopped its athletic flips and it was a relief to be able to split her focus and concentrate on something other than his dominating presence and, of course, her reaction to it.

Taking advantage of the fact that no one seemed to have noticed she was there, she allowed herself a few moments of invisibility to absorb the scene of general noisy chaos and diagnosed too many bosses, too many egos and an excess of testosterone. The ratio of male to female accounted for that, though she knew from personal experience that any woman here could give as good as they got.

First one person and then another noticed their visitors, until only the two main swaggering protagonists continued to eyeball each other, the noise now just the insults they were still hurling.

Amy put some extra distance between her and Leo, the action both professional and personal. She didn't want to be seen as part of the management, acknowledging that while not out of sight or out of mind, it helped her brain function to distance herself from all that undiluted masculinity.

'Don't look at him,' she said, thinking, *Excellent advice, Amy, take it yourself,* before inserting herself into the centre of the drama and adding in a soft, cool voice that nevertheless carried, 'I'm in charge.'

A ripple of shock moved through the room like a wave, leaving shocked silence in its wake. A silence broken by the sound of liquid boiling over from a pan, sending plumes of steamy acrid smoke into the air.

Amy strode over to the stove and switched off the gas, directing a frowning stare into the contents of the pan while muttering. She slid a sly sideways glance in Leo's direction. '*He* wouldn't know a remoulade from a roulade.'

Someone laughed, which Amy, ever the optimist, took as a good sign.

'Right.' She swung back with a smile that gave no hint of the fact that her heart was hammering against her ribs, or the fact that the tall figure she had just mocked had his obsidian stare fixed like a laser on her.

She didn't wilt. Instead, she channelled the adrenaline.

'I'm Amy and…well, we can do the introductions later,' she continued briskly, waving a hand around the room before walking across to a board where a menu was pinned and took it down. 'So—' her eyes flashed from the paper to the tall lanky man who had been at the centre of the disagreement '—dinner, for how many?'

'Thirty,' a voice supplied.

'And the issue you were arguing over is…?'

'I ordered lobster and this…'

'I ordered what you said, and you said crab—'

Because the two men looked ready to face off again, Amy spoke over them.

'Always annoying when there's an order mix-up,' she agreed with a *been there, done that* sigh. 'I worked with an Italian guy who used to say *granchio* when he made a mistake—it means crab, doesn't it?'

There were several nods of agreement and several grins in recognition of the irony.

Someone threw out a remark in Italian.

'Sorry, guys, my Italian is purely culinary based. English and French are my limit. I love that challenge, don't you, to use the ingredients at hand? I remember when I couldn't make the chilli crab salsa to top a pea risotto that I had planned. Of course, the crabs arrived too late, which is typical.' She paused to allow the mutter of rueful agreement. 'But the coconut crab rice the next day proved a massive hit, and it actually became our signature dish.

'As the newbie and as we're on the clock, how about I'm the runner tonight? Any spare whites?' Amy asked, teasing her ponytail into a knot and producing extra pins to secure it there.

'Not that would fit you, Chef.'

Someone shook out a black apron. 'Will this do for tonight?'

'Perfect!'

Leo watched as the diminutive figure wrapped the apron strings three times around her narrow waist and smiled sunnily at her audience before she picked up the hot handle of the burnt copper saucepan using a cloth.

'How about I put this pan in to soak and make another batch of...' she arched a brow and picked up a bottle off the counter '... Marsala sauce?' Amy said, picking up another bottle that lay beside a work station, glancing at the label with an approving nod before applying herself to a pile of shallots.

She was well aware that her knife skills were being marked out of ten by her audience. But as she was quietly confident that she was a twelve and a half out of ten, she was not bothered by the scrutiny.

After everyone had begun to drift away to quietly take up their own tasks, Leo watched her for a few more moments in silence. The other staff gave him some wary glances that managed to convey he was in the way. Amy, completely immersed in her task, appeared to have tuned him out completely.

His chagrin at the situation held a thread of self-mockery. He had orchestrated this and it had not produced the result he had anticipated. Far from finding herself thrown into a situation she couldn't cope with, Amy hadn't seemed even slightly stressed.

Cope? The woman had *conquered* without even raising her voice. She had turned his imagined scenario on its head. Instead of falling apart, she had calmly taken charge and seemed on the brink of winning over her very critical audience. An audience that had already managed to make three, that he knew of, very experienced chefs hang up their chef's hats and walk.

Avoiding someone who was wildly whipping something in a massive metal bowl, he moved to where Amy stood, receiving several slightly nervous but distracted head nods on the way.

'Don't you want to see your room, unpack?'

Amy threw him a quick, incredulous glance over her shoulder. 'Now?' Her astonishment at the suggestion shone in her soft brown eyes. 'I'm working, but fine, later…someone here can show me the way, I'm sure.'

Leo's jaw clenched, shock and outrage flashing cold in his eyes, then his sense of the ridiculous reasserted itself as he tried to remember the last time he had been dismissed.

When was the last time he had laughed at himself?

'Fine.'

Without looking at him, she waved a fluttering hand of dismissal.

His exercise in humiliation was not going to plan, but

Leo was a long way from admitting defeat. Amy was in her element now, but there was a big difference between a dinner and the upcoming gala event.

His phone vibrated and he glanced at the caller identity, his mouth twitching into a smile as the image of a svelte six-foot blonde with a penchant for six-inch heels formed in his head. She was ambitious, voracious and enjoyed sex without emotional *mess,* as she called it.

He continued to walk, ignoring the call and shoving the phone back into his pocket, the image swiftly fading from his mind and replaced by the small dynamic figure he had just left in the kitchen.

The kitchen was the one room in this building where people didn't bow and scrape when he appeared, but today he had been totally invisible; there was another star shining too brightly. He had to admit to being surprised and, also albeit reluctantly, impressed.

Pretty hard not to admit that Amy had handled a room full of massive egos like a pro, which, of course, she was—a fact that was only just bedding in.

It might, he conceded, not be as easy as he had antici-pated to make her want to run for cover. This Amy was not averse to a bit of manipulation herself… The acknowl-edgment made him smile. Though the smile faded as his thoughts made the leap to the other ways she might have changed and grown…and the people—the men in particu-lar—who might have joined her on that journey.

Amy knew there could have been improvements—the chef basting the sirloin had been a bit stingy with the butter in her opinion—but the meal was apparently a success which, in this environment, seemed to amount to a win. Especially as Leo's grandfather was visiting, a figure who, reading between the lines, seemed to inspire awe rather than affection.

Amy was not someone who thought a kitchen worked better on fear, insults and a lot of curses thrown into the mix. As with any organisation, the message at the top filtered down. It did not make her feelings warm towards Leo, who was boss here.

A boss, she had been mournfully told, who didn't much care what he ate. He even came into the kitchen and made himself toast and things that he called sandwiches. She was amused by the complaints but hid it. It was always frustrating to cook for someone who thought of food as fuel and not a sensory experience.

Luckily, it seemed that he did entertain quite a lot when he was in residence. Amy wondered what this army of artists did when he wasn't, but she didn't want to stir up trouble so she kept her thoughts to herself.

It was fifteen minutes since the last of the staff had left at her suggestion. Her initial assessment was that they were a good bunch with a couple of personality clashes but nothing major.

Amy didn't mind the clean-up post service; she found it kind of relaxing. Sleeping straight after a tough service when her adrenaline was still high was hard, though a dinner party of thirty, no matter how indifferent to food artistry the host was, was not what she would class as tough.

She was cleaning the seals on the last fridge, an area too often missed, when she heard the door swing open.

'I'll be with you now,' she tossed out, assuming it was someone assigned to showing her to her room.

'Why are you cleaning? There are staff—'

Her stomach fluttering, she spun around so fast she almost lost her balance. She did lose a couple of hairgrips that fell with a gentle clatter onto the floor, and she immediately dropped to her knees and chased them, sticking them haphazardly back into her hair as she straightened up.

'What are you doing here?' She addressed the accusing question to the sinfully beautiful man dressed in a dinner jacket, his tie hanging loose, his broad shoulders propped against the wall as he stood there watching her.

His entire attitude seemed languid but his eyes were very alert and, now that she looked into them, she read annoyance and something else that she hastily skipped over in the ink-dark depths.

'More like, what are you doing here?' He noted the faint purple smudges beneath her eyes again and felt his aggravation rise. It was as if she was trying to make him feel guilty, but she wouldn't succeed, he decided, nursing his resentment. 'I brought you here for a tour of the kitchens, not to—'

Nostrils flared, she sucked in a deep breath. 'You brought me here to watch me become overwhelmed, maybe cry a few tears. Or were you expecting me to seek a strong masculine shoulder to weep on?'

Her eyes went of their own volition to the area under discussion just as his broad, muscle-packed shoulders left the wall and his physical presence became even more dominating.

'Sorry to disappoint,' she sneered. 'But you'll have to do better than that. I have worked in kitchens a hell of a lot tougher than this one.'

'I thought you were self-taught?'

The mockery in his voice was something she had heard before. 'I had no formal training, yes. My training was all hands-on. I learnt on the job and worked my way up.'

'I'm surprised Daddy allowed you to get your hands dirty.'

She laughed. 'Oh, he was about as contemptuous about me doing *menial* work as you.'

Outrage at being compared with George Sinclair flashed in his dark eyes. 'I have never termed any job as menial.'

His outraged stance was not exactly screaming equality and another time she might have laughed in his face, but she settled for saying, 'You don't need to, Leo, you have perfected the sneer.'

She might have been imagining it, but she thought her mocking admiration drew a low growl from him.

'*Dio!*' he cursed, seething through gritted teeth. As much as he would have liked to react to the provocative glitter in her golden-brown eyes, he refused. 'So there is something you care enough about to disobey your father.' Annoyed that she had pushed him into a retort that had revealed an open wound he would not own even to himself, he closed his eyes.

They stayed closed long enough to miss her flinch and the blood draining from her face.

'I was only nineteen, Leo.' *But I'm not now.* This was what he wanted—to get under her skin. Why let him see that he had succeeded?

'I am sorry if I hurt you back then.'

The sincerity shining in her face only fed his anger. Did she really think saying sorry made a difference now? Her attitude only hardened his resolve to see this thing through.

'It's ancient history.' He produced a dismissive shrug, comfortable with the lie that came easily. 'But I don't want to see you weep.' In his head, there was a line between retribution and bullying, and making a woman cry crossed that line—*any* woman, he emphasised for his own benefit.

Amy's response to the admission which seemed dragged out of him was a cynical little smile. 'But it would be a bonus?'

His tense jaw tightened another painful notch, her reaction making the guilt he had been fighting off throughout the evening with each successive course delivered to the appreciative diners even more irrational.

Her ability to play on his emotions was a weakness he had to acknowledge in order to guard against it.

'I'm sure you've found enough sympathy and a few protective shoulders to cry on over the years.'

She arched a brow. 'For the record, I do not gently crumble and cry out for strong masculine shoulders or even weak ones.' She narrowed her eyes to show her self-reliance, which was real.

If it hadn't been, she wouldn't be here today, it was that simple. She pushed away all the painful memories she had built a protective mental wall around—watching her mother fighting for her life, losing first Leo and then the baby Amy hadn't even known she'd conceived, her mother's death and then shortly afterwards her father's shameful conviction.

She lifted her chin and thought, *You're tough, Amy, so act like it.* 'If I did need a shoulder, it wouldn't be yours,' she declared and immediately wished the rather childish addition unsaid. It did rather shake her off her firm footing on the high ground.

She took a deep breath and, channeling a calm she was a million miles from feeling, continued. 'I am fulfilling my part of this deal and if it isn't as painful for me as you obviously hoped, that's tough! I am good at what I do.' She planted the spray she was still holding on the work surface and suddenly sagged, gripping the copper surface for support, her voice losing a little of the angry venom as she finished with a waspish, 'Sorry if that makes you unhappy, but it's a fact.' She swallowed. 'It's been a long day.' Then wished she hadn't added that because it sounded as if she was fishing for the sympathy vote.

'Have you actually eaten anything while you've been producing miraculous food?' he demanded, sounding less sympathetic and more annoyed.

Amy had decided the best way to deal with him was to maintain a snooty silence but her professional pride kicked in. '*Miraculous?*'

'Well, even my grandfather didn't complain. I think he actually said it was *quite nice,* and that in itself translates as miraculous.'

'Did you like it?' *Oh, God, I sound so needy.*

'Yes, I did. Sit down before you fall down, Amy.'

'I...'

A sound of hissing exasperation left his lips. Before she had any idea of his intention, he spanned her waist with his big hands and with a casual display of strength lifted her up onto the counter surface of the kitchen island, which should not have impressed her or made the heat unfurl in her belly.

It did both and she despised her weakness.

He was rifling through the contents of one of the fridges. 'There's nothing to eat,' he complained.

Despite herself, Amy laughed. 'I thought you liked the food.'

'It's not for me, it's for you—but I'm a big guy; I need quantity, not pretty.' She might be the exception, he admitted as his eyes travelled over her delicate features. She was a classic example of small but perfectly formed and just looking at her made him hungry. 'What's this?' he asked, turning his attention back to the fridge as he pulled off a cover and sniffed the contents of a large bowl.

'Oh, there were some chicken livers left over and I couldn't waste them, so I made a bit of paté.'

'A bit?' He eyed the massive bowl as he planted it on the work surface. 'Bread?' He walked to the huge terracotta crock and lifted the lid, pulling out a loaf.

'Yum, that treacle bread is just divine. Jamie has a gift, seriously, she does.'

'Who is Jamie?'

'The only female in the kitchen?' she said, her sarcasm losing its force as the level of surreal in this scenario finally hit her.

'Other than you.'

'Yes, I suppose so, but I don't count. I'm just your token blackmail victim.'

He turned his head as she swung her legs and yawned. He turned away quickly, but not before the image had set free a protective surge of emotion that he told himself was nine years out of date. He had wanted to protect her back then and she had thrown it back in his face.

Now, the person she needed protecting from was him.

'Who told you that you don't count?'

Amy couldn't have put a time stamp on the moment she'd realised that she would never really count. Nobody had said it outright, but it had been obvious from what they hadn't said that she would never live up to her parents' memories of the child they had lost.

The harder she'd tried, it seemed the more she'd failed, and when their disappointment had started to feel like knife thrusts she had decided to stop trying—it was just too bloody painful.

It had been about that time when Leo had entered her life and, for the first time in her life, she had not felt second best.

'Have I said something amusing?'

A look of confusion crossed her face as she dragged herself back to the present. 'What do you mean?'

'You laughed.' If you could call the strangled sound that had left her lips a laugh.

'Tickle,' she said, touching her throat, not quite meeting his eyes as she produced a very unrealistic cough behind her hand.

'The butter, it's just in there,' she said as he turned to the fridge door. 'That's right, second shelf,' she said, indicating the prettily decorated butter pats lined up. 'The one on the right is black garlic and that one is beef, both gorgeous.'

She was happy thinking about food. Food had always been a way to express herself—the tastes, the textures, the combination of spices, the routines—it had been her salvation because it all made perfect sense to her.

She blinked and fought the strong urge to close her eyes as she watched him methodically select the items he wanted and place them on a scrubbed wooden board, which he dumped on the freshly scrubbed copper surface beside her.

'What are you doing, Leo?' she protested wearily as she fought off the impulse to close her eyes. 'I've just cleaned this.'

'I am feeding you because you are clearly too stupid to feed yourself.'

'I'm not hungry.' But actually, she realised, she was ravenous.

She blinked and opened her eyes wide at the sound of him slicing into the loaf. She pinched herself to stay awake, or maybe she actually wasn't awake and this was all some bizarre nightmare as she watched him putting a generous slice on a plate and push it towards her. 'Eat.'

Dry bread was his version of food? It was funny, but her depleted energy levels didn't even allow for a smile, let alone a mocking laugh. 'You...?'

'I have eaten plenty.'

'Why are you being nice?' He had glanced at her but was busy dolloping some butter on the bread, along with a generous helping of the paté. 'You didn't bring me here to be nice.'

She took a bite, and felt her energy levels surge.

'So why do you think I brought you here?' He stepped back and watched her devour the food the way she had once devoured him.

'To rub my nose in it by showing me the life that could have been mine.' She wiped the crumbs from around her mouth. 'A bit obvious, but probably part of it is also about… control? You have it and I don't.' If this was what they called *speaking truth to power* she couldn't understand why it wasn't more popular. It felt great, also scarily addictive.

'Or maybe you wanted to see me overcome with lust?' Her eyes dropped, her scornful laugh sounding forced as she added quickly, 'Anyway, this—' her over-the-top gesture encompassed their surroundings '—is all a bit of an overkill. You didn't have to bring me here to prove you are some sort of irresistible sex god; you could have done that in London.'

One corner of his mouth lifted in a wicked smile and he watched the horrified panic spread across her face as she realised what she'd just said.

'Now she tells me,' he drawled, enjoying every moment of her discomfiture, not that she was telling him anything he didn't already know.

Amy might have changed but she still couldn't hide her physical response to him; he knew for a fact if he laid his hand against her breast he would be able to feel her heart trying to pound its way to freedom.

'I was just thinking of all those wasted air miles,' she bluffed. 'For the record, it doesn't matter what the location is, *nothing* is going to happen between us.'

'Was that declaration for your benefit or mine?'

Her nostrils flared as she glared. 'Your problem is—' She stopped the flow of words to give her brain time to catch up with her tongue by the simple expedient of biting down hard.

'Don't stop now; this is fascinating.'

A fresh wave of angry colour flooded her face. 'You know exactly what I meant,' she countered crossly.

'I think I do, yes.'

'Not that,' she snarled, longing to wipe the self-satisfied smirk off his face. 'Your problem is you've had too many casual hook-ups telling you how perfect you are because they know they'll never have to look at you with crumbs around your mouth.' Even as she spoke, her eyes zeroed in on the perfectly carved outline of his mouth, which was a mistake.

She cleared her throat. 'Seriously, although I'd love to pander to your ego with some more foot-in-mouth moments, it's been a long day and I've had enough,' she added, sliding the plate away.

'You've barely eaten anything, except me with your eyes.'

His silky taunt brought home the fact she was still staring at his mouth. 'Probably why I have indigestion.'

Her spiky riposte drew a laugh from his throat and an appreciative gleam to his eyes.

'Eat!' He slid the plate back to her.

'I'm sure that wasn't in the contract,' she grumbled, loading another slice of bread with butter and paté and taking a bite of a tomato before addressing the bread. 'I can feel my arteries clogging.'

Curious, Leo sampled the paté from a knife, belatedly aware that she was staring at his mouth again.

Amy lowered her eyes, admitting in a grudging mumble, 'I was hungry. I did need food, but it's hard when you're cooking to actually eat properly, especially when you finish late at night.'

He watched her lick some butter off her lips and angled his head, lowering his eyelids to hide the predatory gleam he couldn't prevent. Then he wondered why he was even bothering to hide anything when there was nothing covert about the electricity in the air or the hunger clawing at his gut.

He laid the knife down. 'It's good.'

She tipped her head in acknowledgment of the compliment and looked at him through her lashes. 'I went a bit heavy on the brandy.'

'Ever the critic.'

'I'm not into false modesty.'

'So you usually fall into bed after service.' *Alone?* he wondered, his eyes sliding of their own volition to the third—yes, he had been counting—button that had popped open at the neck of her blouse.

'That would be nice,' she admitted, directing her gaze away from the satiny gleam of the dark olive skin of his throat and at the rack of copper pans hanging on the stone wall instead. 'But it's hard to switch off after a busy service. Not that tonight was particularly busy. I've never worked in a kitchen so *over*staffed before.'

'So you like to keep busy?'

His words brought her eyes back to his face and, captured by his ink-black gaze, Amy couldn't have looked away if her life depended on it.

Why try? asked the unhelpful voice in her head. *He is extremely good to look at.*

She gave a twisted smile. 'When I'm not laundering money or entertaining my shady business partners, of course.'

He huffed out an impatient sigh. 'Don't be so damned

prickly. But now we're on the subject, you do know that he was using you, that the bastard would have let you take the fall for him.'

Tears stung her eyelids as she nodded.

'Then why? Why the hell would you let him get away with it? Why let yourself be used that way?'

The muscles of Leo's face were clenched, pulled taut against his perfect bones. His sensual lips were compressed flat, almost bloodless as his nostrils flared, making her think of a jungle cat about to rip its prey apart.

'Can't you see he preys on your weakness?'

'I'm not weak. Caring about someone isn't weakness.' Her empty plate scraped along the gleaming copper surface as she pushed it away before pressing her hands, sweaty palms down, to lever herself off the surface and jump to the floor.

CHAPTER SIX

HER ATTITUDE INFURIATED him beyond reason. 'Care? Your father used you, screwed you over, and you are still putting your life on hold for him.' He pointed out the basic facts in what was intended to be an expressionless monotone but the anger he struggled to contain seeped like acid into his voice. 'You think that is a badge of courage? *Dio...!* It is stupid! And what sort of message does that send out? Here's my other cheek!' he snarled, turning his head to one side and poking a finger at his own lean cheek.

Amy was seized with a compulsion to reach out and lay her hand against his brown cheek, feel the stubble under her fingertips. She was unable to take her eyes off his face, all the passion in him drawing her like a moth to a flame.

'What are you staring at?'

'You are so Italian here.'

'It's not about geography; I am half Italian everywhere.'

'Well, you have certainly embraced the Latin thing.'

'Do not change the subject, Amy.'

'I'm not, I'm… Well, maybe just a little bit,' she conceded. 'My father—' she sighed out, dodging his accusing stare. 'He is my father; you must understand that, for all his faults. Your own grandfather—'

'Rejected my mother.' He enunciated each word slowly, the heat that had been in his voice becoming an icy coldness as he related his past. 'I barely remember, but she came from here. Imagine what it must have been like to go from this to the life she had. Her own father sent her into a life of penury and back-breaking misery. She was a single mother with nothing and…' He paused, the muscles in his throat working as he swallowed, visibly gaining control of his emotions as he finished in a voice now devoid of all emotion. 'Forgiveness does not come as easily to me as it appears to for you.'

'You have forgiven your grandfather, though.'

'I have *accepted* who he is; it is not quite the same thing.'

'After Mum died and then Dad was arrested and bailed…' she said slowly.

Some of the heat died from his face. 'Your mother always seemed like a nice person.'

She nodded, tears crowding her eyes. 'She was, but I think when Alice died… Losing a baby, a child, like that, it has to change you.' Hand on her throat, her chest lifted in a shuddering sigh. 'I always wish I had told her—'

He watched as she stopped, a stricken self-conscious expression, quickly banished, flashing across her face.

'Told her what?'

'Dad was devastated by her death and then… I was furious with him after the arrest, you know, especially after the police rolled up at Mum's funeral. We had massive rows and for the first time in years, I went to the stables. I even got on a horse.' She vented a hard little laugh at the memory. 'Just to punish him.'

'Did you enjoy it?'

The question made her smile wryly. 'I do love horses, but it turns out I'm not too good with heights.'

Her attempt to laugh at herself brought an ache to his throat. Leo was fully aware of the irony of his reaction. He had brought her here to punish her and he had fallen into the trap of wanting to protect her, but it was an impulse he had no intention of surrendering to. 'It is hardly surprising you were so angry with him.'

'I know, but…one night I came home. He'd been bailed awaiting sentencing the next day, but I still went out and left him. When I walked in there were empty pill bottles everywhere, and he was unconscious…'

The shock of her stark description nailed him to the spot. 'Your father attempted to take his own life?'

She nodded. 'It was lucky I came home when I did.'

Leo compressed his lips. Expressing his suspicions was not going to make anyone feel better, but he had to wonder, knowing the man as he did, if Sinclair had not very carefully timed his suicide attempt. Whatever the truth was, Amy being her father's protector now made much more sense.

'I don't know why I told you that.' Amy's smooth brow pleated as her eyes lifted to his face. It was stupid, considering he had appointed himself as her enemy, but she felt a sense of relief in finally having shared it.

Her legs felt shaky and she just hoped they would hold her up. During the to-and-fro of their conversation, a heat and a heavy raw awareness had been building until she could almost see and feel the blue crackle in the air, and not just in her legs.

'You've not eaten enough to keep a sparrow alive.' His voice was a sexy, dark silk rumble as he pre-empted her intention to move away by coming to stand in front of her, effectively pinning her with her back to the counter.

'I've had enough. I was breaking more health and safety rules than you can dream of by sitting on the work surface,' she said, her voice sounding a little high-pitched.

'I never dream of health and safety rules. Do you want to know what I dream about, Amy?'

Playing for time, she tucked stray strands of toffee-coloured hair behind her ears. The delay didn't help as when she opened her mouth a squeak came out. Not that Amy heard it past the mindless clamour in her blood—a driving desire to touch him becoming so loud it drowned out everything else. A bomb could have exploded and she wouldn't have heard it.

Her head lifted, her eyes half-closed, she could see the dark shadow of him through the delicate membrane.

'Your mouth.'

She blinked her eyes open to see that Leo was staring at the mouth he'd just mentioned.

'I dream about your laugh too...full-throated and the sexiest sound in the world.'

She gave a laugh now but it was nervous and breathless, more a sigh than a laugh.

'I dream—'

Unable to stand further revelations, she cut across him. 'Not of revenge?'

Her words hit him like a bucket of ice water.

The sexual tension moved below critical point as he acknowledged the charge with a careless shrug.

'Another day, maybe? Right now, I want...' He leaned in and touched her cheek with his thumb, running down the soft curve until it came to rest at the side of her mouth before moving to the curved seal of her lips. 'I would like to explore every moist, warm crevice.'

Amy's lips parted on a gasp as his mouth replaced his thumb. The kiss was feather-soft.

Her world seemed to otherwise stop as their eyes met and

he kissed her for real, hard and hungry, driving her head back against the support of his hand.

The heat was instantaneous, as was her loss of control, and Amy was on a high as liquid warmth spilled between her legs.

It was that familiar, often dreamt of growling sound that vibrated in her throat that made him pull back. It was either that or obey every raw instinct that was urging him to sink into her, take her right here on the damned kitchen floor.

She deserved better than that.

For a man out for revenge, Leo, you're showing way too much consideration, mocked the voice in his head.

'That felt like revenge.'

He looked stunned by her response.

'It was a kiss.' His shrug dismissed it as nothing.

It was calculated, it was Leo exploiting her weakness, her desire for him, and when she compared it to the kisses they had once shared, kisses filled with lust, love, laughter and tenderness, she wanted to weep for what she had lost.

She brushed the back of her hand across her trembling lips as though to wipe away the touch and saw his eyes flare hot with some sort of emotion she didn't have the energy or inclination to translate.

Blinking, she stalked over to the row of sinks and picked up a cloth.

'What are you doing now?'

'I'm cleaning up the mess you've made.' The real *mess,* the tangle of conflicting emotions in her head, was not so easily dealt with, not with a wet cloth anyhow.

Maybe a bit of self-control required here, Amy.

The cloth was plucked from her hand and flung into a sink.

'Are you *trying* to be a martyr? You've been up since dawn and you've seen nothing but the kitchen—'

She gave an indignant gasp. The cheek of the man! 'And

whose fault is that? You brought me in by the servants' entrance.'

His grimace was not guilt exactly, but something that came as close as she had ever seen or was likely to on his face, and a moment later it was gone.

'No one expected you to go straight to work.'

She fixed him with a narrow-eyed glare. 'What did you expect, Leo?'

Good question. 'Not what happened. Come on, I'll show you to your room.'

She curled her lips into a sarcastic smile. 'A cosy cellar somewhere, I can't wait.'

'I think we can at least manage hot and cold running water.' He caught her gaze moving to the work surface and the plate and his lips tightened. 'Leave it; someone else will attend to it.'

'My, you really have grown into the arrogant billionaire lifestyle, haven't you, Leo? I *am* the someone else that does the attending,' she muttered, but her heart wasn't in it. Weariness was washing over her as the day's events finally caught up with her.

His eyes had narrowed but as he studied her face he simply shrugged. 'I'll give you the grand tour tomorrow, but we'll use the shortcut tonight.'

She hadn't noticed the stone spiral staircase in the lobby when they had arrived.

She was too tired to argue, too strung out on the emotions he'd dragged out of her, from the depths of her past.

By the time she had followed him to the top she had stopped counting the floors they had passed and was breathing hard.

'This is the direct route from the service section to the east tower wing.'

Amy pictured the castle as she had arrived, the square twin towers that had loomed over the iconic edifice. 'So we're in the tower now?'

'Yes, both towers, along with the defensive wall, were here before the rest came along in the mid-fourteenth century. They are no longer separate but part of the house itself.'

'Your family have lived here all that time?'

'We came along in the fifteenth century.'

'Almost newbies then.'

He might have smiled at her quip but he was too far ahead to tell and she was almost skipping to keep up.

'The castle transformed over the years into a fortified mansion rather than a castle; there is one floor above us.'

'How many floors are there?'

'Seven. This floor links with the wing above the library.'

She blinked, finding it impossible to visualise the layout. 'It looked pretty much like a castle to me. Do the other staff have accommodation here?' she said, lowering her voice as they walked down a wide, shallow flight of stairs and entered a hallway. They passed by several doors. A few of the deep windows to her right were open and she could hear the sound of the sea, her nose twitching as she inhaled the salty tang in the warm breeze that was underlaid with the mingled scents of cypress and thyme.

'There are converted outbuildings, stable blocks,' he explained, not slowing his stride. 'But most live in the village, a few commute from town.'

Her weariness outweighed her curiosity so she resisted the temptation to ask for more details, but decided that she would find out about the village as it would mean less interaction with Leo. Because after that scene in the kitchen, which she had barely escaped with her mind intact, it was clear that even a distant glimpse of him was not going to be good for her equilibrium. Though she was clinging to the very realistic hope that he wouldn't be here often.

Wanting to plaster herself against him while simultaneously wanting to push him away was making her head ache. Just looking at him made the rest of her ache. His antagonism hurt, but the small snatches of conversation that came close to the easy intimacy they had once shared were even more painful reminders of what she'd lost.

She half tripped, steadied herself and bit her lip, determined not to ask him to slow down even though she was virtually skipping now to keep up with his long stride. A more considerate man might have made allowances for the disparity in their leg lengths, she decided, nursing her resentment.

'Here we are.'

He had stopped outside a double door, the only door in this section of the hallway that she could see. With any luck, this meant she would be less likely to bump into any guests; she already knew that twenty were staying the night after the dinner.

'Thanks.' She stood, waiting for him to move. 'I just hope I will be able to find my way to the kitchen in the morning.' She kept the doubt out of her voice to keep things light.

'You won't be needed in the kitchen in the morning.' He watched her stick her little rounded chin out and sighed. The image he carried of a soft helpless creature who needed someone to make her decisions for her was fast vanishing.

Who was he kidding? It had already gone, and he was feeling quite nostalgic for it. Despising her had made it easier to keep any lingering sexual attraction that remained from their youthful fling at bay.

Obviously, Leo no longer mistook the high voltage sparks that flew between them for love. The wild hunger they both still felt might be nothing more than chemistry, but it was still an obstacle—certainly to a good night's sleep. But it went both ways, and he had no qualms about using it against her—using it to his own advantage.

'I will be needed.'

His jaw clenched and her expression suggested she took pleasure from contradicting him.

'It's *breakfast!* I am sure the rest of the army down there can cope without your guidance.'

'Do I tell you how to do…whatever it is you do? The morning isn't just breakfast, it's deliveries and menus and prep,' she enumerated, mocking his ignorance.

Though it turned out he wasn't as clueless as she had imagined when he said, 'Deliveries aren't really an issue as almost everything is produced in-house, so to speak. You can literally walk around the kitchen gardens and select your fresh produce. Our herds are all organic free range, and even most of the wine is produced here, or it will be. You asked what I do, and the winery is my pet project at the moment.'

She looked impressed, which gave him a feeling of smug satisfaction.

'And *your* morning will involve meeting my grandfather,' he added, pausing to watch her eyes widen in predictable shock, probably dismay too.

If she knew his grandfather it would definitely be dismay. He could have made an excuse when the old man had announced he wanted to meet this new chef and possibly steal her from Leo, on whom good food was wasted, but Leo had decided that the demand fitted well into his plan to make Amy's life uncomfortable.

So far, he'd not had the success he had anticipated in that regard; he'd been overconfident. Amy had responded to every challenge and the kiss that should have unsettled her hadn't done so either!

'But...'

He cut across her wavering protest. 'A courtesy, just to say hello. He was really impressed with the food tonight.'

'Does he not live here?'

'No, he stepped aside from the day-to-day running a few years ago. He currently lives in Florence, so now I'm the one paying your wages.'

'How much?'

A raw laugh was wrenched from his throat. 'You didn't read that page?'

'I didn't see much point. This is blackmail, not a job, so I didn't think I could really negotiate my salary.'

His head reared back, an expression of hauteur spreading across his lean face.

'You're *offended?*' she cried incredulously. 'Sorry, but it's the truth! If you must know, I hadn't thought about it; you're paying the salary of my replacement at the food truck, so I assumed...'

'What, that you could just sit back, whip up an omelette and wait for this to be over? You will earn your pay.'

Outraged at the suggestion that she wouldn't, her golden-brown eyes sparked. 'I am *not* work-shy.'

'I had noticed that.'

His dry response mollified her slightly. 'So when is this *audience* with your grandfather?' As much as she disliked the idea, she couldn't see any way around it.

His expressive lips quirked at her choice of words. 'We should be able to do the tour first.'

'*We?*' she said warily.

'I will give you the tour, then introduce you to my grandfather.'

'I could wander around on my own—'

'And get lost.'

'I happen to have an excellent sense of direction,' she lied. 'But fine, I'll do the tour. Go for it, show me all the things I missed out on, rub my nose in it…'

'What the hell are you talking about?'

She raised one well-defined brow. 'Oh, come off it, Leo. I may be dim enough to let Dad dupe me, but I'm not that dim. This is obviously part of your payback; you want to show me the life that could have been mine, had I stayed with you. The thing is, even if I had gone with you, we likely wouldn't be together now. Have you seen the statistics on young marriage?'

'I don't recall ever proposing.'

Swallowing the urge to weep because he'd probably like it if she did, she shrugged. 'True, we weren't that foolish, but you know what I mean.'

As he finally stepped aside, Amy virtually threw herself into the room but, before she could close the door on him, he brushed past her and went inside. She took a deep breath and turned slowly to face him.

'I don't need a guided tour of my room—' She stopped mid-sentence, her stunned gaze moving around the room, even though her initial thought was that it was a mistake.

This was not a bedroom, but a sitting room. A further internal door was open and she could make out an elegant antique pale wooden half tester bed hung with pretty drapes.

This room had a feminine vibe too, the furniture a blend of antique and high-end modern. The pale linen upholstery on the comfortable-looking sofas was brightened by an eclectic selection of cushions. Similarly, the rugs on the polished wooden floor provided vivid splashes of colour, as did the antique rugs, probably too precious to walk on, glowing against the stone walls. She tracked the gorgeous scent that filled the room to the antique bowl set in the carved open fireplace that held lavender and roses.

She hadn't been expecting…this.

'This is beautiful,' she said, wandering across the polished boards of the floor to the open doorway of the bedroom, her expression one of genuine pleasure.

'Right, so you were thinking more a dusty attic and slave labour; that explains your decision to spend half the night outside the door picking a fight with me.'

'I was not picking a fight. I was *winning* a fight.' She paused. Actually, they had been talking; she had not expected that being here would involve so much talking. 'And, besides, you were…'

'I was?' he prompted.

'It doesn't matter.' She had no intention of explaining that because entering the room involved physical contact with him, it had not been an option. They were not touching and the heat rising from the pit of her belly was already shamefully distracting.

He was watching her with an uncomfortably alert expression in his midnight inky stare. When he spoke it was slowly, a discernible edginess in his deep velvet voice.

'We could always just do it instead of skating around it; just cut to the chase and get it over with.' He took a step towards her and Amy, engulfed by a wave of sheer panic, mirrored the action, two steps to his one, which took her into the bedroom.

'Get what over with?' Her attempt at bewilderment drew an impatient shake of his head and an eye roll.

'Don't pretend you don't know what I'm talking about, Amy. Neither of us are starry-eyed kids any more, calling sex *love*.'

She stood there, her insides molten, her mind floating somewhere outside her body.

He watched as she bit down on her full upper lip, the soft cushiony pinkness taunting him. Her hurried shallow breaths and dilated pupils sending messages that were louder than words.

He could almost hear his control snapping. He moved and at the last second from somewhere he dug out the strength to control the desire that was pounding at him.

'You've got to stop looking at me like that if you don't want this to happen, Amy.'

Amy couldn't have broken free of his hypnotic stare if her life had depended on it. Moreover, she didn't want to.

'It is true, I do want sex…with you.' His inner tension added a sexy rasp to his voice. 'Are you trying to tell me you don't want it too?'

She met his hypnotic gaze and said nothing. The only sound in the room was the distant ticking of a clock and the audible breathy rasp of her forced respirations.

'I… You…' She shook her head, *needing* to touch him so much it was a physical pain.

He could see her shaking and had to forcibly stop himself from reaching for her. Knowing a woman wanted you was an aphrodisiac; knowing *this* woman in particular wanted him was an incredible rush.

'I need to hear you say it. If you want me, *cara*, come and get me!' Sweat dampened his skin as he threw out the challenge whilst ruthlessly checking the painful need rising up in him.

Nine years ago, she had sent him away, so it was important, *essential,* to him that this time she be the one begging him to stay.

She counted the steps as she maintained contact with

the molten heat of his stare, only stopping when there was barely an inch of air separating them. The heat coming off his body made it feel like a furnace.

'I want you.'

The heat burst white-hot around them as their lips connected.

He groaned as she slid her tongue sinuously between his lips and, framing her face between his hands, he plunged deeper into the warm, moist recesses of her mouth.

Her breasts flattened against his rock-hard chest as she strained against him, drawing herself up on tiptoe to link her fingers behind his head.

Desire burned away everything in her head but Leo. They stumbled backwards, lips still connected, to the bed and fell down together onto it.

Leo rolled onto his side, bringing her with him, before he stood up, drawing a cry of loss and protest from Amy until she saw he was fighting his way out of his shirt.

She pulled herself up onto her knees to watch him, taking gloating pleasure from eyeing his lean tanned torso, from the perfect musculature of his broad chest down to the ridges corrugating his flat belly.

His burning eyes left hers to deal with his belt buckle. 'You carry on looking at me like that and things might be over before they've even begun,' he purred, the molten heat in his stare stoking the fire inside her.

'You're shaking,' she pushed out, consumed by an ever-escalating sense of urgency. 'Let me,' she demanded fiercely.

The blood burning in his veins, Leo sank his fingers into her hair as, head bent, she worked on the buckle before she moved to the zip. Swiftly, he caught her hands, holding them wide.

Unable to resist her sultry smile, he bent down, kissing

her while he opened her shirt by the simple expedient of pulling hard, sending a shower of buttons across the room as he peeled the fabric off her shoulders. She fell back on her bottom and had wriggled her jeans over her slim hips in a matter of moments.

The man who women generally considered a slick, polished lover fumbled to strip off his own trousers, but this was no sex by numbers; it was raw and elemental, no rules, just anger and need. He had never wanted a woman this much in his life.

Amy gasped as his mouth trailed heat and moisture over her bare shoulder and neck as he joined her on the bed. Head flung back, she linked her arms around his waist as he freed her breasts from her bra and turned his attention to the quivering peaks, cupping, stroking, kneading as she arched her back to give him full access.

Pausing for a moment, he removed his boxer shorts, allowing his erection to fall straight into her waiting greedy hands, and they closed over the shaft, drawing a deep feral groan from the depths of his chest.

He returned to pay homage to her breasts once more, his tongue flicking a taut nipple. As need pounded through him, Leo fought for some sort of control when all he wanted to do was plunge straight into her softness.

'You're beautiful,' he rasped as he removed the tiny panties she wore and propped himself up on one elbow to stare down at her now totally nude body.

She took his hand and guided it to the apex of her legs and the soft fuzz there. Her eyes drifted closed as he began to stroke her.

Her body was ready for him before he even touched her, so wet and hot as his fingers slid over the intimate folds.

Throbbing with need, he kissed his way up her body before sliding between her open legs. Her back arched as he rotated his hips before sliding incrementally deeper inside her, and she closed around him, tight as a glove.

As they moved together seamlessly, Leo felt the loneliness he never acknowledged melt away in the heat of their union, the softness of her body, the total surrender she offered him.

As the firestorm of sensation built inside her, Amy not only forgot how to breathe, she forgot where she ended and Leo began. It was a total immersion in a perfect, decadent storm of ecstasy that only ended when it finally exploded and annihilated them both.

Lying there, breathing hard, stunned by the intensity of the moment, she felt him kiss her eyelids and couldn't help a nip of fear. She was affected too much by what had just happened.

Confused by the flurry of movement from Leo, Amy opened her eyes and watched him, at first bewildered and then understanding, as she realised there would be no intimate aftermath.

'You're going?' she said, keeping her voice carefully neutral as she pulled the sheet up over her cooling body.

Retrieving his shirt from where it had fallen, his eyes brushed her face and, ignoring the hand squeezing his heart, he nodded. He had to keep moving because he hadn't wanted to leave the bed at all; he had wanted to stay there and hold her.

That should not happen when you scratched a carnal itch, he thought, and it was a relief to recognise the loneliness he usually wore like armour settle firmly back into place. As he dressed, he welcomed the return of the hollow ache inside that was a permanent part of him.

'Get some sleep, Amy. I'll see you in the morning,' he

called over his shoulder before he left the room, closing the door behind him.

She heard the door slam but didn't see his exit because she had turned over and was pummelling the pillows with her fists as mortification rolled over her in waves.

She really hated him for doing that to her.

She wasn't too keen on herself either right now, for being such a total pushover.

Outside in the hallway, Leo leaned his shoulders against the wall and thrust his long fingers into his hair. Tilting his head back, he gently banged it against the wall, the sinews in his neck standing out like cords under his olive skin.

He stood there for several moments until his erratic breathing slowed and became regular again. He was in danger of complicating things, and he refused to do that. They shared a natural chemistry, that was all. Yes, it was hot, but it would inevitably cool, and so the sane thing to do would be to enjoy it while it lasted. Some heavy-duty sexual release would be both curative and pleasurable. It would wipe the slate and his head clean of the lingering chaos Amy had left behind.

It should have been a cut and dried deal. Logically, it would have been, had she not changed. He'd been deeply invested in her being the same sweet, pliable and ultimately weak Amy he'd known her to be.

He'd needed her to be *that* Amy.

His teeth gritted in a frustrated grimace. Instead, she was *this* Amy.

The one who had stepped outside the box he had put her in and then crushed it under her small heel.

The one who stood up to him, who was not anxious in the slightest to please.

And the hell of it was, he found this new Amy even more attractive.

He shook his head, the groove between his brows deepening as he relived the staggering moment that peace had broken out when she'd stepped into a kitchen of warring egos, without even raising her voice.

She had managed them and they didn't even know they were being managed. Was there a fear that she would manage him too, if he let her?

CHAPTER SEVEN

THE LAST TIME Amy had glanced at the clock it had been four a.m. As she reached for her phone and glanced blearily at the screen, she saw it was now half-past seven. She lifted a hand to shade her eyes from the light that was shining through the window as she hadn't drawn the blinds last night.

Carefully, she pushed off the covers and tentatively swung her legs over the edge of the bed. Her head was pounding like a metronome. The events of yesterday, especially the last part, flickered through her head in slow motion. The way her body had become so quickly attuned to his again, the realisation that she had wanted him so badly, frightened her.

Even though she still wanted him.

She opened one eye. Had she packed her migraine medication? She already knew the answer was no, but screaming would have hurt and escalated the issue, so instead she walked across to the window and searched for the mechanism that closed the blinds.

The relief when the sun was blotted out drew a deep sigh from her. Locating her handbag, she found the strip of generic painkillers which would be a lot better than nothing, especially if they kicked in before the migraine developed claws and took hold.

She lay back down on the bed and waited for the meds to kick in; she knew how this worked. Half an hour later, she tested the water by sitting up. The fact that she could, without feeling dizzy or wanting to throw up, suggested the painkillers had done their job, which was a massive relief. Whatever else Leo had in store for her today, meeting his grandfather, who did not sound warm and cuddly, would require her to be on her A game.

A fuzziness persisted but she was able to open a selection of doors revealing generous storage without wincing when they closed. She finally located the door that led to the bathroom, which turned out to be enormous, bigger than her entire flat in London. So big she could have lived in it. Even in her downbeat mood she paused to lust a little over the incredible copper bath.

This was her fantasy and Leo's real life.

They had no future together. He had everything he wanted at his fingertips…*including her.* And when he didn't, when the spark fizzled out, she thought of all those years of crushing loneliness she had fought her way free of. What had she been thinking, opening the door to it happening all over again?

That it had been a mistake hardly covered it, and yet she knew that if she could live last night again, she'd do exactly the same thing.

Eyes closed, she walked into the shower. The water wasn't cold but it did drown out the condemnatory voice in her head.

She spent an age standing under the steamy jets of the walk-in shower with the space-age controls, being pounded from all sides. It was hedonistic. How long was it since she had lingered like this in a shower? A smile curved her lips as she enjoyed the self-indulgent luxury of it. She enjoyed the luxury too of wrapping herself in one of the stack of fluffy bath sheets, until she realised she didn't have a clue what time it was.

Amy was stunned; she *always* knew what time it was. Her life revolved around being at work on time and working systematically through the long list of tasks she needed to complete. That was how she made it through each day. She could never let up because if she did her life would immediately spin out of control.

And her real fear, the one she didn't acknowledge, was that *she* would also spin out of control.

She shook her head and immediately regretted the action. Too many people had expected—still expected—too much from her for that to happen. Even when she'd lost Leo, she hadn't allowed herself the opportunity to break down, to let go. She'd hassled the hurt away.

In search of her phone, she squatted down and went through the pockets of the clothes she had just dropped in a messy pile on the floor when she had stripped off last night.

It had fallen out of a pocket and it was low on charge but intact. When she saw the time, she gave a worried frown.

What if Leo appeared?

And how was she going to play the morning after the night before?

Or maybe after last night he wouldn't want to see her, she speculated, worrying when she recognised the thought was not as cheering as it might be—*should* be.

She took one of the robes that were hanging on a rack, then wrapped a towel turban-wise around her dripping hair. Tying the belt on the robe, she hurried through into the adjoining room as she worked out her coping strategy for dealing with him. For starters, she was going to turn it into a drama.

There was no sign of her suitcase.

After a lot of searching, she discovered her case and her clothes behind the last door she opened. Her clothes were all neatly hung up and folded.

Half an hour later, fully dressed and her hair almost dry, the damp braid hanging down between her shoulder blades, she had returned to the bathroom to retrieve her clothes when there was a knock that appeared to be coming from the direction of the outer door. She froze, listening, then heard a female voice call something she could not make out and a moment later she heard the door quietly close again.

Some of the tension left her shoulders; at least it wasn't Leo. Ignoring the anticlimactic feeling this realisation brought with it, she checked herself out in the mirror. She was now as pink as she had just been pale. Scowling at the reflected face of the person who stared back at her, she thrust her clothes into a linen hamper and, taking a deep breath, opened the door.

The bedroom was empty, and so was the pretty sunlit sitting room. She blinked in the sunlight and squinted, shading her eyes with a hand. The person who had entered before had opened a window and delivered the tray responsible for the gorgeous aroma of coffee.

In deference to her fragile head, she half-lowered the blinds and eagerly followed the scent to the table where the tray and coffee pot sat.

Did staff get coffee delivered to their rooms?

Did they have rooms like this?

Or only the ones who slept with the boss?

The attention, while very nice, made it hard to gauge her position on the upstairs-downstairs gradient. It was going to be hard to establish a working relationship with the other kitchen staff if they thought she was getting preferential treatment.

Or sleeping with the boss.

Was this about Leo not losing an opportunity to drive home what he now had, and she didn't? The best response to him trying to make her feel uncomfortable was to enjoy the perks, she decided. So she poured herself a cup and sipped contentedly as she took the time to examine her surroundings in a little more detail.

The first thing that caught her eye was a small button on the floor by the open bedroom door. Remembering how it had got there sent a hungry hormonal rush through her body.

She had decided to put down her behaviour last night to a combination of serious exhaustion and the fact that her sexual appetite had been virtually in hibernation for the past nine years.

It had taken Leo to reawaken it.

The thought sent a bolt of sheer panic through her as, with perfect timing, the door opened, not preceded by a knock, polite or otherwise.

Leo stood framed there for a moment, the image of his tall figure managing to imprint itself on her retinas.

His nostrils flared as his glance was drawn to the tray. 'Is there a spare cup?'

She delivered a sweet smile before looking at him and, when she did, it stayed pasted there. She cleared her throat.

'There is. Anyone would think someone knew you were coming when they ordered it.' She had decided that if he mentioned last night she would just shrug and be cool, maybe even slightly amused that he was making a big deal out of nothing.

He hadn't mentioned last night yet; he hadn't done anything except send her pulse into orbit.

In her defence, he would do that to anyone, rocking up without warning in track bottoms and a damned running vest that clung damply to his golden skin which, gleaming against the black fabric, oozed pheromones from every perfect pore.

She fiddled with her hair as she tried and failed to look anywhere but at him.

'Sorry, I ran for longer than I intended.'

She pressed her fingers to her temple, but she had no intention of telling him about her migraine, revealing any weakness.

'Sorry as well about...' His gesture took in his running outfit.

She licked her dry lips and swallowed, privately thinking that his smile was less apology and more taunt.

'I didn't want to keep you hanging around before we started the tour.' With a frown, he walked across to the first window and raised the blind, before performing the same action on the other two.

She was stubbornly unwilling to ask him to lower them again. The discomfort was preferable to admitting a vulnerability to Leo. She adjusted her seat with her back to the windows and watched in silence as he poured his coffee.

He took a long swallow that caused the muscles in his throat to ripple before he folded himself casually into one of the armchairs. It wasn't really built for someone of his stature but he was incapable of doing anything that wasn't elegant and coordinated.

She practised a cool reply in her head but was fatally distracted. His body hummed with energy but underneath she could sense the tension vibrating off him.

Well, she reasoned waspishly, it only seemed right that the life of a billionaire should have some degree of stress. Maybe those articles she had read that claimed he slept the moment his head hit the pillow and woke up refreshed six hours later were part of the fictional narrative that surrounded him.

The women weren't fictional though.

She experienced a moment of stomach-clenching nausea that she refused point-blank to acknowledge as jealousy.

'I didn't think it was a firm—'

'Date?'

'*Arrangement,*' she inserted, her smile insincere but the accompanying scowl very authentic as she ignored the mocking note in his voice. 'Another day will do just as well and if you're busy it might be quite fun to explore on my own.' Actually, a pair of dark glasses and some fresh air might, with the help of the painkillers, see off the incipient migraine.

'It was firm, and I'm not in any hurry.' He turned towards her as the light shifted and fell on her face, bleaching her skin of colour and emphasising the size and brilliance of her soft brown eyes. He frowned.

'Did you sleep OK?'

'Like a baby,' she lied cheerfully. 'Did you have a good run, or workout, or—' She swallowed as her eyes remained unwilling to stop following the progress of a bead of sweat that slid down his chest.

'There is a gym and a pool inside and out, so feel free to make use of them.' He had made full use of them both before his run. He had exhausted his body though not his mind, which had only eventually cleared as he had pounded the forest trail.

He was overthinking everything. There was no problem to work through; he was not a hormonal teenager, and neither was he one of those men who waxed lyrical about emotional connections.

Last night had been sex, pretty mind-blowing, excellent sex, to be sure, but just sex.

'I don't expect I'll have time,' she said, resurrecting a little defiance.

'Do you have an issue with what I'm wearing?' he drawled, setting his drained cup back on the tray.

Her lips pursed tight as she glared at him and thought, *Thanks for drawing attention to the fact I can't take my eyes off you.*

'I was just thinking that you're not looking very executive today.'

No, just sexily gorgeous.

And he knew it.

Swallowing, she forcibly removed her eyes from the second bead of sweat that was tracing a slower path down the glistening skin of his throat.

Behind his half-closed, heavy lids she could see the gleam in his inky eyes and she tensed, preparing for another jibe. Only she was left stunned when instead he said, 'You look beautiful this morning. We never did get to spend a night together, did we?'

Despite her innocence, or for that matter his own, she had not been overendowed with inhibitions. In fact, Leo thought, she had usually taken a wicked delight in shocking him.

He'd had more skilful lovers since her, but not one of them had ever come close to living up to the youthful, carnal initiation they had shared.

Until last night, he had sometimes wondered if he was guilty of embroidering their fireworks in bed with nostalgia.

Now he knew he hadn't.

He watched her through his lashes, the angle of her jaw, her shell-like earlobe… *Dio*, what the hell was happening to him? He was getting aroused by a woman's jaw!

Everything she did was just so… He took a final gulp from the nearly empty cup and got to his feet, moving rest-

lessly around the room. His research into her life would have
revealed any long-term relationships, but he considered it
impossible that a woman with her innate sensuality would
have lived the life of a nun.

Still, the knowledge that she was OK with casual hook-
ups did not totally erase the unease he felt about last night,
but he shelved the idea of the faceless men who had passed
through her life, not finding it a subject he wanted to dwell
on. At the same time, he was well aware that, considering
his own lifestyle, his disapproval of hers was incredibly
hypocritical.

'Last night…'

'A mistake, I know.'

'Inevitable is what I was thinking.'

'Oh!' She folded her hands primly in her lap and lowered her gaze.

'I was… I mean I…don't always act with so little…fi-
nesse.'

She looked up and was astonished to see embarrassment
flit across his face.

'You were perfect!'

Her blush amused him.

'So were you.'

'This could get complicated, Leo.'

'What are you agonising about? We're not in a relationship, so why should there be any complications?'

Not for him, maybe, because he didn't even like her,
whereas she… 'I don't like the assumption that you consider me being here as your sex on tap. That really isn't in
my contract, not even the small print.'

He looked astonished by her outburst before he laughed.
'Don't stress,' he said, studying her face. 'Let's play it by
ear, shall we? For the record, I'm quite happy to be your sex

on tap for the duration. You going to eat this?' he asked, lifting the cover on a croissant and putting it in his mouth before she replied.

'I don't eat breakfast.' It was a lie, but he didn't need to know that.

'You're eating me up instead.' Underneath the sly, mocking accusation there was a tell-tale layer of tension that communicated itself directly to her tingling nerve-endings. The prickling sensation spread like a hot rash under her skin.

The automatic denial died on her lips when she realised she was staring at his mouth. She yanked her gaze upwards, connecting with his eyes, but the expression in the dark glimmering depths provided no safe space from the debilitating awareness that permeated her body.

'With your eyes,' he elaborated, presumably just in case she hadn't got the drift.

'You do think a lot of yourself, but actually I was thinking you might have showered before you invited yourself in,' she said with a fastidious little sniff as she shoved her hand in her handbag and pulled out a pair of oversized sunglasses and slid them on her nose.

Her eyes hidden, her chin took the heavy lifting when it came to challenging him to comment.

His response demolished any illusion that she was in control of this situation.

'You have changed. You used not to have any issue with my sweat. Quite the opposite, in fact.'

Her nostrils flared as she remembered the taste and smell of his damp skin.

She cleared her throat and blinked away the tactile images crowding into her head as Leo levered himself out of the chair with stomach-flipping, casual grace and rubbed his hands together.

'So, shall we get this thing over with?'

'What over with?'

'The tour. What did you think I meant, *cara*?'

'Will you stop calling me that?' she snapped out irritably, hating the way his tongue curled around the endearment, dragging each syllable out.

'Why? I am Italian. It's natural for me to say it.'

She turned her head, trying to avoid the smell of the coffee in her nostrils, a fragrance she normally loved but the migraine messed with all her senses.

'Did you never realise that you had family here? Did your mother never speak of…? Sorry, I didn't mean to—' She hesitated, not sure she should ask, not sure she had the right.

'Poke your delightful little nose in?' He shrugged, his eyes detaching from her face.

Amy's shoulders sagged. She was relieved both to escape his scrutiny and not be called out for her curiosity.

'My mother…no, never.'

Amy had the feeling that his words were not really addressed to her. He was barely acknowledging her presence; it was almost as if he had forgotten she was there.

He was still speaking.

'At least until she got ill. At the very end, she was on strong medication and she did speak of this place, though I didn't know that then as she kept sliding into Italian.'

'It seems odd she didn't speak Italian to you growing up.'

His flickering regard landed back on her face. 'What is this, twenty questions?'

She expected him to end the conversation and was surprised when, after a pause, he disclosed some more.

'I think my mother was trying to erase her background. I did know a few words, actually, and some phrases she said sometimes. When she called out for her *papà*, I assumed he was dead. I carried on thinking that for a long time.'

'It's so sad, but it must have been marvellous to know you weren't alone,' she said softly.

He imagined her eyes behind the dark sunglasses glowing with an empathy that struck him as ironic in the circumstances.

'I had thought once before I wasn't alone, but it turned out I was mistaken.' He brought his white teeth together, his shark-like smile more like a grimace as he watched her pale and virtually ooze guilt. 'Don't look so worried, Amy. What doesn't kill you and all that. So, are you ready?'

'I just need my...' She flung the words over her shoulder as she quickly disappeared into the bathroom. She needed a minute. She had reached the point of no return on the tears that refused to be blinked away behind the misted tinted glass.

What was she crying about, anyway?

He was never going to forgive her, she knew that. For a long time she had struggled to forgive herself, but she knew that if she had to make the choice again, she still would. That didn't make it the right decision but, right or wrong, she had to live with it.

And she had been living with it, in a water-under-the-bridge, moving on kind of way, but now, being here, seeing Leo, and remembering who he had once been...

He had moved on and so had she. Their lives were briefly connecting again, that was all.

On that tear-drying, pragmatic thought she snatched a tissue, blew her nose and wiped the mist from her glasses with her sleeve and went to locate her trainers from where she must have kicked them off last night. If Leo wanted to give her a tour, he could give her a tour. Anything that got them out of this room was a bonus.

* * *

Leo had watched Amy leave the room, admiring the view. He was still struggling to keep his libido in check when she returned, still pale in the face and huffing out breaths as she balanced on the foot that was shoved in an unlaced trainer, while with her knee brought up almost to her chin she tried to put the other on.

'There's no fire. Sit down before you do yourself an injury,' he barked out roughly.

She obeyed, quite literally dropping to the floor and straight into a cross-legged position, where she proceeded to push her bare foot into the trainer before leaping to her feet again.

Had she always been like that? Always on the go, rushing around? There were certainly things that had changed. Her face was a little thinner, the youthful softness of her features had become more refined, her rounded cheeks more pronounced, her stubborn chin a little sharper.

But her figure seemed exactly the same as he remembered it.

An image from the many stored in his head surfaced unbidden through the wall he had erected to hold back what he had mentally filed as juvenile fantasies.

Except this fantasy had been real.

Amy, the rosy tips of her breasts showing through her silky hair as she bent over him, her hands either side of his head, her hair brushing his chest.

He fought free of the images that belonged to a time in his life when he had actually wanted ties, a time when he had not understood the advantages of no obligation, uncomplicated, honest sex.

Being transfixed by the rise and fall of her breasts beneath the loose cotton covering was an expression of nothing more complicated than a physical need, no more meaning-ful than slaking a thirst.

Sure, think of her as a glass of beer, Leo, mocked his in-ternal voice. *That's really going to work!*

Oblivious to the fact that Leo was fighting against mem-ories, Amy was focused on coaxing her features into a neu-tral expression that didn't hint at the painful friction caused by her breasts pushing against the fabric of her white shirt while she trawled frantically for a response, because the truth was not an option.

'Let's get this over with. I have work to do.' Work was her salvation during tough times, all times really. When she was thinking of spice combinations, tastes and textures she could shut out the background noise—or at least turn down the volume.

He opened the door into the corridor she vaguely recalled from last night, and she really wished all her memories of last night were as vague.

She stepped past him, walking into the corridor in day-light giving the brief illusion that she was stepping into the sea and sky. When the illusion faded, she realised that there was solid ground under her feet and the sea was sev-eral hundred metres beyond the ten-foot-high windows. She lifted a hand to offer another level of protection from the bright sunlight.

'You're not a fan of delegation then?' he wondered, join-ing her.

Light spots dancing across her vision, she turned away from the vista that another time she would have enjoyed. Her retinas made Leo a dark, threatening shadow against the light.

'I don't ask anyone to do anything I can't. I've never been what anyone would term an *executive* chef. I'm hands-on, even when I was working at the restaurant,' she explained, throwing a glance at her small hands with the neatly trimmed pearly nails. 'We might not have kept the Michelin star, even if we hadn't closed. There's a lot of pressure to maintain it, and for me it was never about attracting an elitist custom base. I just wanted to serve good food that only the elite could afford.'

Leo followed the direction of her gaze. Other than last night, he hadn't seen those elegant fingers chopping and dicing, but he had plenty of first-hand experience of them stroking and touching his flesh, featherlight and skilful. His body hardened, helpless to resist the ache of hunger in his belly.

His teeth clenched as he told himself he wasn't helpless; he was fully in control of himself.

'Very egalitarian of you.'

She ignored his mockery. 'In my experience, throwing around orders isn't the quickest way to gain respect.' She felt her shoulders relax. They were not retracing their footsteps from the previous night and the windows framing the views had been replaced by stone sconces containing bas-relief figures carved in the niches. They looked intricate but not friendly.

'Do you need respect?'

'Well, it's handy, especially when there's a kitchen full of professionals way more experienced than I am.' She had realised that when she'd recognised the names and a quick internet trawl on her phone had confirmed her suspicions; the level of experience in the Romano kitchen was staggering.

'They are being asked to perform at a level way below their pay grade, so it has to be frustrating. It explains the atmosphere last night when we walked in, and it wasn't just me being foisted on them.'

'Are chefs meant to be so self-deprecating? I thought arrogance came with the job.'

Her eyes widened a second before her lips began to twitch and she choked back a laugh. So ironic, considering the man who'd just said that oozed arrogance from every perfect pore!

'Share the joke?'

She opened her eyes behind the smoky glass, this time not trying to stifle her laughter. 'Oh, I doubt you'd get it if I did. I'm just impressed that *self-deprecating* is in your vocabulary. And, for the record, I'm not underselling myself. I'm good at what I do, but—'

'But nothing,' he interrupted, recovering from the novelty shock of being mocked. 'The reason those highly qualified people are working under you is because they accepted a lot of money to do so—I only employ the best of the best.'

His comment had confirmed what Amy had suspected. 'Too many leaders, too many egos. But none big enough to compete with yours, of course.' She paused, seeing they had reached a gallery. The hallway continued on to the right, almost to infinity, it seemed, and they stood directly at the head of a staircase.

Curving and graceful, it led down to a massive space. On a raised dais at one end, a grand piano took pride of place, and the marble floor had a pearlescent quality warmed by the ancient vibrant frescoes on the walls.

Amy blinked, the breath catching in her throat as she imagined what the room would look like when the chandeliers suspended from the coffered ceiling high above were lit, illuminating the intricately carved supporting pillars and bas-relief sculptures.

'The ballroom.'

She shot a self-conscious sideways look at his dark profile and closed her mouth with an audible snap. Though, in her defence, if ever a space deserved openmouthed admiration this was it. Then, unable to resist the impulse, she ran her hand across the smooth inlaid wood of the curving bannister, enjoying the tactile sensation.

'What's the scent?' Finally, something that wasn't making her feel nauseous.

'Cedarwood.'

'I can imagine people making quite an entrance down this staircase,' she said, tilting her head back to look at the frescoes above and immediately regretting it when a sharp pain stabbed through her temple.

'It's only used occasionally these days. The gala will be the first time this year.'

'When is the gala?'

'About six weeks away.'

'And that's why I'm here.' She cocked her head in challenge. 'Isn't it?'

He cut across her. 'For the record, I like to keep a degree of separation between work and pleasure.'

While he spoke he had taken a step towards her, but in every other way he felt further away.

Humiliation swelled like a balloon inside her, but she didn't let it explode. 'That works for me.'

'I think you'll enjoy it.'

'Is this work we're talking about now?'

'I wouldn't have said it if we were not talking work, but unless you're a very good actress I know you enjoyed last night.'

She longed to throw his damned arrogance back in his beautiful smug face but he was right—she really wasn't that good an actress.

'The takeover we are celebrating was last month, but

we felt it would be good to have a joint celebration for my grandfather's birthday also.'

'He'll be there too?' she blurted.

'Save your horror until after you have met him.'

'It's not horror, it's a genuine concern. I'm meant to be in charge of this thing, so a little more information would be useful.'

'I'll forward you the guest list. I think you'll know quite a few names on it, old friends and the like; it's a small world. I'm sure you'll enjoy catching up.'

But you're secretly hoping I won't, she thought, keeping her face blank. 'I won't be catching up with anyone; I'll be working.'

'Actually, the staff here will be supplemented by some outside caterers. Obviously, our kitchen—well, your kitchen,' he corrected with a slight smile, 'will be overseeing the menu. I would imagine it's not too late to make adjustments to your predecessor's arrangements if you want to put your own stamp on it, but your role will strictly be as executive chef, and as such you'll be expected to appear front of house.'

So that had been his plan all along: throw her in with a lot of people from her old life and introduce her as the hired help. 'How very not daunting at all,' she said drily.

His short, hard laugh echoed off the rafters. 'I think it would take a lot to daunt you.'

'Is that a compliment?'

Not an intentional one. On one level he knew that if he were objective he'd have been impressed by her resilience and her determination.

He wasn't objective.

'An observation,' he returned smoothly.

'Well, I won't be there. As I said, I'm very hands-on. I like to be in the kitchen at all times.'

'Hands-on…that's good to know,' he drawled smoothly and watched her blush like a virgin, which he knew she wasn't. He felt a stab of self-contempt. He had drawn the line in the sand, professional one side and personal the other, secure in the knowledge that all it took to blur that line was the scuff of a shoe.

'Besides, I don't have a thing to wear to that kind of occasion,' she rebutted, aware that her pounding head was not up to a full-scale battle on the subject—not now, anyway.

'I think we can fix that. I've always liked you in red.'

Amy clenched her teeth and resisted the temptation to rise to the bait. 'I don't want to be fixed or dressed.'

What about undressed? The thought formed in her head before she could stop it. In desperation, she changed the subject. 'Where does that hallway go?'

'There is access to the ramparts further along.' He gestured ahead. 'The view from the walk along them is worth seeing. But—' he glanced down at the sports watch on his wrist '—we'll need to cut the tour short as my grandfather is a creature of habit and routine, and since the pneumonia he usually rests before lunch.'

'I'm sorry, I didn't know he'd been ill.'

'He is not frail, but it takes a little longer to recover at his age.'

'I understand.'

'This way.'

She walked down the steps, wistfully imagining all the women in delicate heels and ballgowns who had gone before her. She frowned at herself and felt a surge of annoyance. She refused to feel envious of those Romano women, picked no doubt for their breeding and fortunes.

Once she had been a pale version of one of those women, expected to make a suitable alliance.

She felt sorry for them now.

She wasn't Leo's besotted lover.

She wasn't her parents' disappointment of a daughter.

She wasn't the rich girl who had been bought a restaurant.

She was just Amy, taking it one day at a time, and despite the worry over bills, the terror that her father would land himself back in prison, and the daily torment of being exposed to a man who made her remember she was actually a woman, she was happy to take responsibility for her own life.

Her hand slid down the smooth bannister. She had not belonged in the society that her parents had wanted her to inhabit, and this world that Leo navigated was so beyond that in every sense of the word. At least she had never been forced to be confronted by that reality at a time in her life when she would have struggled to cope.

If they had still been together when Leo had learnt of his Romano inheritance, an unlikely situation, given the limited shelf life of youthful passion, all it would have done was hasten the inevitable end.

Wealth changed people, and Leo would have left her behind.

But she was the one who had left him behind, and a man like Leo was always the one to walk away. What was going on between them now had a lot to do with bruised male ego. Nothing more. And that she could handle.

Her feet landed on the marble and she took a step back before Leo joined her.

'What is your grandfather like?'

Leo paused. 'He's like a man who threw his daughter away because, unlike you, she followed her heart.'

'Or her hormones?' she suggested, hiding layers of hurt under aggression, which came easy right now because the relief from generic painkillers had worn off and the telltale signs of an encroaching full-blown migraine were getting harder to ignore. 'And where did following her heart get her?'

'The situation is not comparable. My mother was pregnant and he drove her away. She was bringing up a child alone in a foreign country with no support.'

His empathy for his mother did him credit. Would he have been as empathetic if he had discovered she had unknowingly been carrying his child when they'd parted? It was a question she had asked herself many times over the years. Her instinct had made her want to run towards Leo, but maybe she was lucky she hadn't found him.

What if he had been horrified at being stuck with a baby at his age? She felt the familiar ache as an image of a little boy with dark hair and Leo's eyes drifted into her head. Would he one day have children of his own?

'He gave her an ultimatum: dump the boyfriend or...'

'So they ran away together?' *Like we planned to do.* The thought made the empty space in her chest expand as, behind the tinted glasses she brought her lashes down in a silky shield so he wouldn't guess the comparison she was making, though he probably knew anyway.

But he'd never known about the baby. Never would, as what was the point in telling him now?

'No, he went back to his wife.'

She winced but closed her mouth over a sympathetic response. His expression suggested it would not have been well received.

'So your grandfather always knew he had a grandchild? When did he start looking for you?'

'No, he didn't know about me.' The admission sounded cold.

'So he didn't know your mother was pregnant?'

He flashed her a look. 'He sent her away because she wouldn't fall into line.'

In the same situation, she had stayed. She and Leo's mother were two sides of the same coin.

'I don't know your grandfather and I'm not defending him but...' She shook her head and winced as the vice tightened around her chest. What could she say without revealing too much? 'Sorry, it's not my business. You obviously have a relationship, so that's good. It's not easy to let the past go, but you clearly understand one another.'

She almost added that you could always let the past go, but then she realised that Leo was not a *let it go* sort of man.

He never forgave and never forgot.

CHAPTER EIGHT

'WHAT'S WRONG?'

'Nothing.'

'Then why are you hiding behind those sunglasses?'

'I'm not hiding, I have a headache.'

His brows lifted. 'Take an aspirin.'

'Empathy is one of your most endearing qualities,' she muttered, her sarcasm wasted on his broad back as she followed him along the echoing corridor, refusing to be distracted by the mad light show she was seeing the world through. Her brain foggy, she barely registered the network of rooms. She made a couple of grunting sounds when a response seemed to be indicated as she walked through open double doors.

Amy stayed where she was as Leo walked towards a figure sitting in a carved chair beside a window. Of course it was a window! Oh, God what was it with this place? Had no one told the architects that ancient castles were meant to be dark and gloomy?

Aware there was some uncharted swaying going on, Amy caught hold of the carved back of a chair to steady herself and waited, by this point not caring about what impression she made, like it mattered anyhow. She focused on what really mattered, which was not throwing up.

She caught snippets of the two men's conversation, not

that it made much difference. They were speaking in Italian, which was perfectly natural and not part of some grand scheme to make her feel even more isolated, but the result was the same. On the bright side, if there was one, the room was not built on such cavernous proportions as many she had seen, though cosy would have been pushing it.

As she stared across at the figure sitting on the throne-like chair—not that he needed accessories to look regal—through a haze of shimmering lights, the delicate Italian greyhound dancing at his feet suddenly peeled away and trotted towards her.

'Good girl,' Amy whispered to the creature. She trailed her fingers for the dog to lick. 'I want to stroke you, I really do, but—' But if she bent down now the consequences might not be pretty, she finished in her head.

She was genuinely curious about the man that she had built in her head to be a fearful monster. She had anticipated he would be a big man but, unlike his grandson, he was smaller than average, almost slight, his dark hair heavily threaded with silver, his well-trimmed beard all silver. The only similarity she could detect was the hawklike nose.

His eyes appeared to be far lighter than Leo's and were set beneath grey-flecked, bushy brows. They swivelled her way and caught her staring.

He clicked his fingers and the dog at her feet ran, tail wagging, to his side…or was that click meant for her? Amy wondered.

'Chef!'

She flinched and half-closed her eyes. Whilst he was a relatively small man, his voice was not small at all, and the volume increased the pain in her skull. She tilted her head in cautious acknowledgement of the imperious summons and felt the room spin.

'The meal last night was quite acceptable. I go home tomorrow and, before I do, I wanted to thank you. My grandson is being quite mysterious about where he found you.' He flashed a look at Leo, who simply raised an eyebrow in response.

Watching them face off, Amy struggled to work out what they reminded her of—before it came to her.

'Like two silverbacks,' she murmured, not really aware she had voiced her observation out loud until both men turned their heads to stare at her.

Whether they minded being compared to two gorillas minus the chest-beating was not a priority, because Amy's priority was finding a bathroom.

'Actually, could you point me in the direction of—' Her hand clamped to her mouth, she looked around desperately.

Leo appeared to take in the situation at a glance. 'This way.'

Hovering outside the bathroom door, Leo's face twisted into a grimace of sympathy and concern as he listened to the sounds coming from inside. He had never seen anyone look as pale as Amy had looked as he had half-carried her to the nearest bathroom.

The sounds seemed to have subsided and when he cautiously opened the door this time all he heard was running water. No voice yelling, *'Go away!'* like the two previous times he had attempted to invade the space. Not that it would have mattered; he had already decided that enough was enough and he wasn't going away.

He stepped inside the room, alarm shooting through him as he saw the small figure sitting cross-legged on the floor. He switched off the tap that was still gushing water before he squatted down beside her. She was grey now rather than white. He felt a pang inside his chest that hurt, even though he had long ago conquered the tender protectiveness she evoked in him.

She had done him a favour, actually. He could now enjoy sex with no emotional connection. Because it was not the sex that was dangerous, it was the emotions. That had been a life-changing discovery and he had Amy to thank for it.

'Are you all right?'

Morning sickness. Out of nowhere, the thought took root in his head.

She couldn't be pregnant.

Why shouldn't she be?

The idea that Amy was carrying another man's baby was not one he could contemplate. It was a rejection that had nothing to do with logic and everything to do with the irrational emotions he had banished from his life.

The same way Amy had banished him. Now she was back—and he had brought her back. He had slept with her and the more contact they had, the less his reasons for bringing her here made sense. He was meant to be congratulating himself on having escaped a weak, spineless creature, sure she would reveal her true self when the props were removed.

Well, that's working out well for you, isn't it? Leo mocked himself.

What Amy lacked in inches she more than made up for in guts and sheer determination, not to mention sheer bloody-mindedness.

When she gave no indication that she had heard him, he repeated his question. 'Are you all right?'

Amy batted away his hand. For an intelligent man, he asked some very stupid questions. 'No.'

'Can you open your eyes?'

'I could but I don't want to,' she mumbled through

clenched teeth. 'Will you just leave me alone with my splitting head and let me die in peace?'

He snorted. 'You're not going to die.'

She considered the response inhuman.

'This is a headache?' He couldn't keep the doubt out of his voice.

'No, it's not a bloody headache, it's a migraine. It's a headache like a tornado is a gentle breeze.'

Listening to her response, at how Amy managed to pack an incredible amount of aggression and loathing into a whisper, Leo felt something painful break loose in his chest. She was so fragile and yet so tough.

'I'll take you to your room. Can you walk? Oh, I know you can, but you don't have to.'

'My balance goes.'

'Not a problem.' He bent down to scoop her up.

'You can't carry me,' she whimpered as her head, which she couldn't hold up, found the support of his shoulder, and she discovered another scent that did not make her feel queasy—Leo.

'Actually, I can.'

And he did, although the journey was all a bit of a blur to Amy as they negotiated a myriad of corridors and passageways.

Lying on her bed in a blissfully dark room, she made objections when someone who she didn't want to identify but knew was Leo unlaced her trainers.

She grunted and rolled into a foetal ball of misery.

'The doctor will be here presently.'

'I don't need a doctor. I just need you to go away.'

'You are a very bad patient.'

The unexpected tenderness in his voice made her eyes

seep weak tears that ran silently and unchecked down her cheeks before blotting into the pillow.

'Ah, here he is now. I will leave you.'

She wanted to yell *Don't go*...but, ashamed of her weakness, she managed to stop herself. She was not so incapacitated that she had lost sight of the fact that safety was the last thing that Leo represented. Not to her, anyway.

The doctor was gentle and kind, he didn't drag out the consultation and the only questions he asked were pertinent.

He told her he would arrange a prescription for her normal medication should this happen again.

The jab he gave her, he explained, would deal with her nausea, vomiting and pain.

'You just need some quiet and to sleep.'

She didn't really expect to sleep, but when the door closed and she was alone, able to lower her defences virtually immediately, she did fall into a deep sleep.

When she woke, her initial disorientation morphed into relief as she registered that the hammer inside her skull was now just faint background noise.

At the first little groan she emitted, Leo rose from his seat by the window and laid down his laptop. By the time he reached the bed, Amy was levering herself awkwardly into a sitting position.

'Don't—let me,' he said, masking his concern under a layer of brusque irritation. He recognised that his irritation was ridiculous, given that the entire object of this exercise had been—what? Revenge? To make her feel vulnerable and uncomfortable? But he'd never been aiming for torture, which was what her pain level had apparently been.

Of course, she could have simply admitted the problem, explain that she was unwell, but it seemed to him that this Amy admitted nothing, certainly not to him anyway. She had looked so damned vulnerable and fragile as she'd slept, her dark lashes spread like butterflies' wings on her scarily pale cheeks.

He had countered any feelings of irrational guilt on his part by focusing on the blindingly obvious. Which was that Amy was the author of this situation, simply by not owning up to a weakness and also not bringing essential medication with her.

Did it not occur to her that he had better things to do than keep a bedside vigil?

Nobody asked you to, the annoying voice in his head argued. *You could have delegated.*

'Like I have a choice,' Amy muttered, leaning against the conveniently placed pillow behind her back. Then gritted out a grudging, 'Thank you, but I'm not an invalid.'

He tilted his dark head in mocking acknowledgment. 'You're most welcome.' He scanned her face, the sarcastic glint in his heavy-lidded eyes fading as he took in her pallor and the violet smudges beneath her eyes, hating that he had no control over the surge of protectiveness, an emotional response he thought he'd left behind nine years ago.

This was the woman who had ripped out his heart and stomped all over it. What the hell was he doing or, more importantly, feeling?

'So, how are you feeling?' The ice clinked in the jug as he poured her a glass of water and passed it to her.

She looked at it without reacting.

'Employment law frowns on employees not being hydrated.'

She huffed out a sigh and took the glass because her mouth and throat were dry.

He watched as, holding it in two hands, she glugged the liquid greedily.

'Slowly, you don't want to throw up again.'

The reminder made her pull the glass from her lips and set it down on the bedside table. 'I'm not going to—' In the act of flinging off the throw that had been laid across her legs, her eyes widened with horror as a pained version of the morning's events flashed through her head. *Oh, God, talk about first impressions!*

'Your grandfather—'

'He is grateful you didn't throw up on his shoes.'

'I'm glad you think this is a joke. He didn't really say that, did he?'

'No. The two of you should get on; his sense of humour is a little underdeveloped too. Don't worry, he took it in his stride and has decided to blame me for the entire incident. And as I couldn't make myself available to dance attendance on him, he has left early. He never stays long, though. It was hard for him to relinquish the reins in the first instance.'

'Was he really all right about it?'

Leo sighed. 'Actually, he suggested I sack you.'

This professional insult roused her from her lethargy. 'I'm a better chef than you deserve!'

'He's decided you're pregnant.'

She was unprepared for that and had no defence against the bleakness that washed over her in a wave.

'I'm not. And as it's unlikely I'll ever see your grandfather again, I'd be grateful if you'd tell him that. Also, employment law means you couldn't sack me even if I was.'

'You will see him at the gala.'

'I'm not going to allow you to wheel me out like a prize example of how the mighty have fallen.'

He bit back a retort, aware that he had an unfair advantage here. He wasn't as weak as a kitten—a kitten with claws, he thought, making that all-important clarification.

'He's a bit of a foodie and he loves talking about food. He says, at his age, food is better than sex. Apparently, this is something I have to look forward to, but for the moment food is simply fuel.'

'What about sex?' The words tripped off her tongue before she could stop them.

'Sex is one of the joys of life.' He could imagine a man finding sex with Amy to be one of life's necessities, like oxygen. A man who was not him, of course, as he was a man who was never going to care enough to be hurt again.

Only Leo could turn a conversation about food into one about sex and make it sound so impersonal.

'You're obsessed,' she accused.

'Maybe we both are, and you introduced the subject.' Head tilted to one side, he stood back and surveyed her burning face. 'Now you're looking a much better colour; you have some warmth in your cheeks.'

She flung him a killer glare. 'Why,' she added, swinging her legs over the side of the bed, 'are you even in here?'

He was watching her progress with a critical frown. 'I'm delivering the medication, as per your doctor's instructions.' He nodded to the parcel on her bedside table. 'He tells me that, taken early enough, these usually stop the progress of a migraine.'

'Mostly.'

'You, I understand, did not bring your own medication.'

She slung him an irritated look, not appreciating the preachy tone he had adopted, as if she were some recalcitrant six-year-old. She toyed with the idea of just flicking him the finger and crawling back under the covers. It was a non-starter as options went but thinking about it tugged the corners of her mouth upwards into an almost smile.

'I had to leave the house in rather a rush.' She bit down

on her lower lip. Damn him, she even *sounded* like a six-year-old now!

Their child would have been eight now.

It was several years too late for a big reveal, which she was glad of, as the idea of telling Leo filled her with icy horror.

She had tried once, though… When she had discovered she was pregnant, the first thing she had done was to ring him. But her call, and the many that had followed, had been blocked.

So she had packed a bag and decided to follow him. Tell him he was going to be a father.

It was a measure of her panic and desperation that she had ever imagined that was a sane idea. Not after the way he had left. She hadn't really thought the plan through; actually, she hadn't had a plan at all. She had been running to him on pure instinct, more homing pigeon than sane person.

Except, of course, Leo had never been her home, although having him here, looking out for her, she couldn't help but imagine what her life would have been like if he had.

Life hadn't disillusioned her enough to make her lose the belief that a person could be your home—the right person. She just no longer believed she would find the right person for her.

As time had gone on, it had grown increasingly unlikely. Besides, her work had never allowed for a lot of dating and the men who asked her out usually wanted to use her to advance their careers, when she had been in a position to do so.

But she had tried to do the right thing, despite how hard it was. She'd left a note for her parents, telling them not to worry and she'd be in touch. She had been on a train going to London when the cramps had kicked in.

She had made it back home again before her parents had

found the note. Other than the hospital staff and the cleaner who had found the discarded hospital identity bracelet in her bedroom and silently handed it to her, and hugged her, she had told nobody.

'Are you all right?'

Amy pulled her head up cautiously but still managed to loosen another hank of silky pillow-tousled hair. 'Fine,' she said giving up with a sigh of frustration on refastening her braid. Instead, she began to remove some of the remaining hairpins, lining them up on the bedside table before sliding her fingers into the already unravelling braid to loosen it.

'If you want me to admit it's my fault that I almost threw up on your grandfather's shoes, then fine—mea culpa,' she said, continuing to work on her hair, which had been damp when she had fastened it and now fell in a mass of Pre-Raphaelite ripples down her back.

Sensing he was watching her, she looked up, and there was something compulsive in his stare that sent her stomach muscles into a nosedive.

'Why don't you wear it loose any more?'

'I work in a kitchen, so it's a matter of health and safety. I actually cut it a few years ago, but it was more work keeping it—' She stopped, thinking, *Oh, yes, Amy, because your hair down the years is a really fascinating subject.*

'You have beautiful hair.' The stark delivery, combined with the mesmerising heat in his stare, added another layer to the rapidly thickening atmosphere.

'I remember you sitting astride me and your hair brushing my chest—' He halted, his smoky stare managing to be fierce but also soft and seductive.

Amy stopped breathing. She was shaking, except she wasn't. The tremor was not superficial; it was deep inside her.

Remember?

She remembered crying herself to sleep for days and weeks and months. And she remembered feeling utterly bereft, never sharing her secret, her grief, with anyone, because there was no one to share it with.

She had wanted Leo so much. Him being here now, looking out for her, brought home just how badly she had needed him back then too.

'I try not to relive the past, Leo.' Because it hurt too damned much. 'That's why none of *this* is a very good idea.'

'I'm not trying to relive the past. I'm trying to exorcise it and the ghosts and enjoy the present.'

She stared, fascinated by the magnificent symmetry of his face as it tightened, pulling the gold-toned skin across his perfect bones, before his expression changed and he produced a charisma-loaded smile, his eyes gleaming through his ludicrously long eyelashes.

'In fact, I think we should enjoy it together.'

CHAPTER NINE

AMY STARED STRAIGHT AHEAD. She barely came up to his shoulder, so his chest was straight ahead. A trick of the light, the fineness of the shirt fabric or her wilful imagination, but she could see the suggestion of a sprinkling of dark hair. It sparked tactile images of her fingers stroking the hair-roughened satiny skin, tracing the ridges of muscle on his flat belly, before…

This was crazy! She was not a particularly sexual person—and certainly not someone who allowed dark fantasies to take over. It had only ever happened with Leo. It didn't take any effort on his part; all he had to do was breathe to bypass all her defences.

It had always been Leo.

'In bed, you mean. You're not interested in me anywhere else.'

'I was thinking more of a walk in the fresh air, but…'

She flushed. 'I should be in work.'

'No one is expecting you today.'

His hand slid down her back, the featherlight contact sending electric flutters of sensation along her spine before his fingers came to rest lightly on her waist.

She told herself he'd pushed in closer but it was a lie; she had done the pushing and all the denial in the world wasn't going to change the fact. He held up his arm to reveal the slim, silver-banded watch he wore on his wrist, displaying a light sprinkling of fine dark hair as he flicked the cuff to display a sinewy forearm.

'It's five thirty-four.'

He dropped his arm, shifted his stance and the brain-debilitating contact was broken. It took a few deep breaths for her to fight clear of the sexual thrall that had immobilised her.

Amy cleared her throat and met his eyes, her defiance slipping several notches when she read the total understanding gleaming there. She knew that he knew *exactly* what he was doing to her, and she wanted to crawl away and hide.

'You shred my control too, you know that.'

He voiced the devastating truth almost casually, but there was nothing casual about the muscle clenching and un-clenching in his lean cheek, visible through the shadow of stubble that hadn't been there earlier.

Amy breathed through the heart-thudding, shocking moment and, before she had formulated any sort of response, he moved towards the door in a dizzying change of direction in his body language and his voice.

'Even I don't jump on women who have just got out of their sick bed.' Which didn't mean he wasn't tempted. 'How about I let you freshen up and have something light to eat sent up? Then we will explore the grounds. It might put some colour in your cheeks.'

Amy knew she had plenty of colour; her cheeks were still burning in fiery reaction.

'There's no need for you to do all that.'

'But I don't trust you—' He paused, his glance landing for a few tense moments on her mouth.

'Trust me to do what?'

'To not return to the kitchen and get in everyone's way. They're already aware of the situation.'

'You mean they know you're blackmailing me?'

'No, that we're having sex.'

She went white then saw the unholy amusement in his eyes and cursed. 'Was that meant to be a joke?'

'Would it be so bad if they did know?'

She regarded him incredulously. 'Too right it would! And it was sex in the singular!'

'The day is still young, but I actually meant that they know you're unwell.'

'Being unwell cuts no ice in a kitchen, believe you me.'

'Yes, I'm sure you are very tough, and well able to drag yourself to work with a broken leg or share your flu with your colleagues. But being unwell *does* cut ice in this kitchen when I make it clear to everyone that you are to rest and recuperate.'

'That sounds like an abuse of power.'

He breathed out a sigh and folded his arms across his chest as he looked down at her. 'That's an interesting take on an employer who looks after the welfare of his workforce.'

Amy decided that this was the point when it made sense to stop digging the hole she was sinking into while she could still climb out. She bit her lip and pointed out, 'I have rested.'

She still couldn't get over the fact that she had slept so much of the day away.

'I think it will take more than a couple of hours to re-dress the fact that you appear to have been functioning on the edge of exhaustion for weeks, possibly months…'

'So you brought me here for a holiday?'

He reacted to her sarcasm with a frown as he raked a hand through his dark hair. 'At this point I don't know why the hell I brought you here!'

She was still blinking when the door closed behind him with a forceful click.

CHAPTER TEN

WHEN AMY CAME out of the bathroom in a fresh change of clothes she could see through the opening into the sitting room that the tea tray and sandwiches that had been delivered earlier by a fresh-faced maid had been removed.

She felt a lot better, though she was reluctant to acknowledge her relief that she wasn't due in the kitchen.

She sat down in front of the mirror and opened her make-up bag, but after a reflective moment closed it, having extracted some lip gloss. She didn't want to make it look like she was trying too hard—or, for that matter, trying at all.

She never wanted to be like her mother, desperate to please a man. Getting up at the crack of dawn so her husband wasn't offended by her face without make-up, and splashing cash on the latest craze to eliminate any signs of ageing.

It didn't take her long to braid her hair into one thick plait, which she threw over her shoulder. About to get up, she paused and unzipped the make-up bag again, deciding that a smudge of neutral eyeshadow and a flick of a mascara wand couldn't really be considered *trying hard*.

At the tap on the door she took a moment to compose herself, which wasn't so easy when her heart was drumming so hard she could feel it in her throat.

Amy had reached the door, where a steadying breath and

being ninety-nine percent sure of who would be on the other side didn't prevent her experiencing the shockwave impact of seeing Leo standing there.

Brain numb, her senses so acute it hurt, she stayed glued to the spot.

'You look…' His eyes flickered down her slim figure, taking in the narrowness of her waist in the full-skirted cotton. The butter-yellow of the sleeveless bodice made the golden-brown of her eyes pop. 'Better.'

'Better than bedraggled is not a high bar, but I'll take it,' she said pertly, flinging back the braid that landed in the middle of her back.

'I like the fifties vibe of your dress.'

'Thanks,' she said lightly, closing the door behind her as she stepped out into the wide corridor. 'How?' she wondered, looking at the view through the window. 'You have the sea view this side and through the bedroom window.' She turned to glance at the door to her suite, which faced in the opposite direction. 'Did I somehow miss the bridge? We're not on an island, are we?'

'No, a peninsula, so we look out on the Tyrrhenian Sea from all sides.'

'It's an incredible place.'

'A long way from my bedsit above the garage with the view of the petrol pumps.'

Amy turned away; she didn't want to think about the stolen moments they had shared in that poky bedsit. Peeling wallpaper and threadbare carpet notwithstanding, they were the only times in her life when she had experienced true happiness. 'I could do with some fresh air.'

Leo didn't comment on the hint of desperation in her overly bright response. 'This way.'

He led her in the direction Amy recalled as being the

route from the kitchens, but before they reached the stone staircase he led her into a lift.

'If you want to go out, this is your quickest route.' Unlike her, he appeared oblivious to the skin-peeling tension in the enclosed space. Tension that made her virtually throw herself out when the doors swished open.

Directly opposite, a solid metal-banded oak door was open and she stepped out into the early evening sunshine and paused to take in her surroundings.

She was standing in a courtyard. The space was filled with the trickle of water and the hum of bees that hovered above the lavender which spilled from the raised beds and the wild thyme that grew in the cracks in the stone-gravelled footpaths. There were a couple of wrought iron benches and tables set beside a fountain. The stone walls of the castle were on three sides, leaving the south-facing fourth side open to a vista that was breathtaking. It must make this a sun trap most of the day, she thought.

The area directly ahead sloped, the green manicured lawn giving way to immaculate terrace gardens where flowers spilled from several beds onto what appeared to be a grove of olives. Through the foliage she caught glimpses of what she took to be a white sandy beach beyond. The blue of the sea itself was almost indistinguishable from the blue sky.

'This is so beautiful.' She didn't bother disguising her uncomplicated admiration for the beauty of the place. Despite herself, she felt excited at the prospect of exploration.

'This way.'

Her feet crunched on the gravel as he led her out of the courtyard and onto the grassy expanse of the lawn. She turned around and looked back at the castle, her full skirt skimming her calves as she twirled.

Despite the reason for her being here, and the man whose

presence by her side meant that she couldn't totally relax, she laughed, unable to regret experiencing this place.

She just regretted the reason she was here.

He wasn't sure what he'd expected her reaction to be, but her laughter and her almost childlike pleasure in her surroundings was not it.

He fought off a smile—her uncomplicated delight was contagious. 'You like it?'

She flashed him a look, her face a mirror of her amused astonishment. 'That's a joke, right? It's beautiful, Leo, and I'm happy for you that you have such a beautiful home.'

His own expression blanked as he searched her face, but he saw nothing but genuine sincerity.

Underneath his composed expression, his jaw was practically hitting his chest. What sort of woman got treated the way he had treated her and then pronounced herself *happy* for him?

'It must be like living in a fairytale.'

'I do not believe in fairytales or happily ever after endings.'

And that was how to kill the moment! Was she in part responsible for his inbuilt cynicism? The possibility drained away the last of her optimism and left her feeling flat as she walked on.

Seeing the happiness fade from her face sent a slug of irrational guilt through Leo. 'This way,' he said when she had wandered off aimlessly towards the right.

Amy was standing above the highest level of the numerous terraces when Leo, standing below her, turned and held out his hand. She regarded it suspiciously for a moment before laying her own lightly on his. Leo turned his hand and interlaced his fingers within hers and took the first step.

'It's a bit of a drop for—'

'The vertically challenged?'

'I wasn't going to say that.'

'You were thinking it,' she snapped back, recalling his racing stable of tall leggy blondes. 'Though,' she added with a conciliatory smile, 'I'm glad I didn't wear heels. This,' she went on as she followed the narrow path that connected the layers of lush greenery and brilliant blooms, 'is mountain goat country.'

'Do you want to sit down for a while?' he asked as they reached a gazebo. A couple of stone cherubs on the wall behind them gushed bubbling water into the trough below the stone seat, and behind it irises grew in profusion in the mossy ground. It was a cool and calm spot.

'No, I'm fine, thanks.' She caught sight of the name engraved in the stone seat. '*Luisa Romano,*' she read. 'Your mother?'

He nodded though his body language had already indicated her guess had been correct.

'It's very beautiful.'

'Simple. I'm no designer, but I like to work with my hands.' He held up his hands, his long fingers splayed for a moment.

Amy remembered how skilled those hands were and felt her insides dissolve. So she rushed into speech. 'I didn't know you could do self-deprecating.'

His laugh lowered the tension by several degrees.

'This,' he said, running his fingers across the stone surface, 'was one of our bonding moments.'

Her brow puckered at the cynicism in his voice. 'You and your grandfather?' she asked cautiously.

'We try, but the history makes it hard.'

The flicker of pained anguish in his eyes was there and gone, maybe even imagined on her part, but Amy's tender heart clenched in her chest.

He turned his head and saw the empathy shining in her eyes. This woman wore her feelings so close to the surface she might as well wear a sign saying, *I'm a soft touch—take advantage of me.*

Which, of course, he was.

His jaw tightened as he experienced a fresh stab of guilt.

'Maybe I could actually do with a rest,' she murmured, sliding onto the bench. It was a simple repurposed slab of stone, worn smooth with age. While the area was now out of the sun, it retained the warmth of earlier in the day and she could feel the heat through the cotton of her skirt.

After a moment Leo joined her. He sat beside her but apart.

'Sounds like you've both put some effort in,' she observed softly.

'There isn't an ocean between us, but I still wouldn't like to swim it.' He stopped dead. She was wandering around in his head and the hell of it was that he had invited her into it—actually, he was giving her the guided tour.

What on earth was he doing?

'Are you a good swimmer?' She swivelled sideways to look at him, thinking he was definitely more handsome than any man had the right to be. He was certainly built for swimming and she could easily imagine him, streamlined and sleek, cutting through the water.

Leo turned his head and captured her gaze. 'Better since I moved here. The sea, the pool, are perfect opportunities to improve technique and stamina. My technique has, I like to think, improved greatly over the years.'

She intercepted the challenging carnal gleam in his eyes and the message wasn't exactly subtle. Subtle or not, she was helpless to resist, a sexual flush travelling over her skin until the rosy tide had suffused every tingling inch of her body.

Amy shook her head, willing her panicked heartbeat to

slow as she pushed her hands into the deep pockets of her skirt to disguise the fact they were trembling.

'That is a very obvious deflection,' she managed coolly as she got to her feet and brushed down her skirt.

He arched a brow. 'From where I'm standing—'

And he was standing now, the difference in their heights immediately putting her at a disadvantage.

'It looks like it was a pretty good deflection. You going to blame that on the temperature?' he wondered, looking directly at her breasts under the yellow top.

She didn't need to look to know her treacherous body was betraying her, but at least not all of her giveaways were as prominent as her tight nipples.

'Has it occurred to you, Amy, that you're not exactly the best person to be handing out family advice?'

She flinched as his hit landed, her eyes widening in protest at the suggestion. 'I am not handing out advice. I was trying to figure out why you are such a bastard.'

'Oh, I'm a self-made man,' he drawled through bared teeth. 'Of course, I have had a little bit of help along the way.'

Her lips clamped tight. He never lost an opportunity to turn the knife, did he? But part of her didn't blame him.

She shrugged, her eyes straying once more to the engraved name on the bench before she stepped out of the shaded area and into the warm evening sun. 'You'd probably be happier if you let go of the past.' She tossed the words over her shoulder and walked ahead of him, making her way down the rows of terraces, all the time aware of his footsteps behind her, though he made no attempt to join her.

He had spoilt her pleasure in the beauty of her surroundings.

She had reached the flat ground that led onto the copse of olives when he caught up with her.

'That path leads to the beach, or do you want to go back?'

Amy was torn. She could have said something stinging, along the lines of her voluntarily spending more time in his company was about as likely as…well, something that was very unlikely.

On the other hand, she had really wanted to see the sea up close ever since her first glimpse of it. Now she could smell it and the draw was impossible to resist.

She wasn't aware she had sighed until she glanced up and saw the sardonic amusement painted on his dark fallen-angel features as he watched her struggle.

It was very hard to shake the conviction that he could read her like a book. It wasn't a two-way situation; he remained frustratingly enigmatic.

Trawling through her recollections, Amy realised he always had been, really. He had given out very little information in the past, and she hadn't pushed him for anything back then because the mysteriousness of him had fed her romantic fantasies.

'I'll be masterful and take charge, shall I? Beach.' He gestured to the path off to the left.

After a short pause she followed, walking behind him between the straight lines of the trees. It was cool and quiet except for her frantic heartbeat as she surveyed the movements of the tall figure up ahead.

She had been determined to maintain a cool silence but, as they walked on, the idea felt childish. Also, the need to fill the silence grew impossible to resist.

'Do you produce your own olive oil?'

'We do, but this area is no longer commercial. We have productive groves to the south on the mountain slopes. This part is actually a little neglected, hence why the wild perennial flowers underfoot have taken hold.'

'They are pretty.'

'It's tough to control them without using herbicides, which bring their own issues; it's ultimately about sustainability and, of course, the health of the land.'

A frown appeared between her brows as she flung her plait back, waving her hand to deter the insects buzzing around her face. 'I didn't realise that you took such a personal interest in the estate. I thought you were just about—'

He paused and turned back, looking at her with his usual mocking grin. 'Making money?' His smile faded. 'Did you use some insect repellant?'

'I didn't think I'd need it.'

'Well, you will.'

'I think they like me,' she admitted, swatting her arm.

'Come on.'

The pace he set for the next few yards felt more like a jog for Amy but when they emerged onto the beach all thought of complaining faded.

The wide curved stretch of white, sugary sand was empty, and the sun reflecting off the turquoise-streaked sea was dazzling.

He watched as her wide smile emerged, her pleasure and excitement unfeigned.

'This is simply incredible.'

'Take off your shoes; the sand gets everywhere.'

She saw that Leo had already kicked off his shoes. He stood there in his cut-offs and a tee-shirt that exposed his impressive biceps, looking very much at home and a million miles away from the images of him which were distributed for PR purposes. And even further from the man usually seen on red carpets with his arm around beautiful blondes.

The sea looked so tempting that she sighed as she walked

across the hot sand to the water's edge. 'I should have brought my swimsuit,' she mourned.

'You don't need a swimsuit; there's nobody here.'

She could not allow the provocation to pass or, for that matter, for the pleasure of the moment to be ruined.

'You're here.'

'I can fade into the background.' He touched the tee-shirt stretched over his broad chest. 'See, camouflage.'

She threw back her head and laughed. The idea of Leo fading into any background, anywhere, in any circumstances was one of the funniest things she had ever heard.

He watched as she wiped tears from her cheeks, her laughter morphing before his eyes into broken sobs that lifted her chest.

'Amy…?'

Her eyes went from his outstretched hand to his face, which was creased with a wary, quizzical expression that indicated she must look like lunatic. She pressed a hand to her mouth in an attempt to physically suppress any further outbursts and took some gulping breaths, mortified by the unrestrained spillage of suppressed emotions.

'It could be worse; I could be crying.'

He felt a surge of empathy shake free inside him and sidestepped it, not ready to accept his own feelings—the feelings she shook loose in him.

'Are you waiting for me to do empathy?'

She swallowed a bubble of laughter. 'Don't, or you'll set me off again. It's the migraine; it can leave me feeling a bit…'

Insane.

In lust.

In deep, deep trouble.

'Let's get you back to the house.'

'Castle,' she was unable to stop herself correcting. 'And I can get myself back.'

'Give me strength.' He would certainly need it, he decided as he watched her tramp with a gentle sway of her hips up the sand, the full skirt of her yellow dress whipping around her legs in the sea breeze.

He had brought her here thinking of revenge, never dreaming that what he was really doing was locking himself in a room with a live, primed sexual grenade.

Another school of thought, jeered the voice in his head, *is that you knew exactly what you were doing, Leo.*

She'd hurt him once; only a fool would invite her to take a second shot. And he wasn't a fool.

'I wasn't offering to carry you, *cara*.' And he wasn't offering her another shot at his heart either. 'Once in one day is enough; you are more solid than you look.'

Determined not to give him the satisfaction of responding, she twisted her lips and stalked off.

There was no cosy conversation during the return walk; there wasn't even any confrontational conversation. The couple of glances she risked throwing in Leo's direction suggested that his thoughts were elsewhere.

'Will you be able to find your way back to your suite?' he asked when they reached the big oak door.

'Of course,' she replied with a calm confidence she was far from feeling. 'Thank you for the guided tour.'

'We hardly scraped the surface, but I'll arrange for someone to give you the full tour soon.'

Someone, not him. She got the message and obviously she was glad.

'We thought you'd prefer to have your dinner in your room.'

She assumed the *we* was him, but she said nothing. She

didn't even point out that someone could have enquired about her preference, which required great restraint on her part.

He made to move away and stopped. 'Oh, the garden lighting on the beach paths is temporarily out of service for some repairs. So if you do decide during the week to take any night air, stick to the gardens around the castle. The kitchen garden is that way and the tennis courts and swimming pools are just a little further on.'

She tipped her head in acknowledgement and walked in through the double doors without looking back.

She was waiting when her dinner was served.

The maid looked startled to be greeted by Amy, who took the tray and joined her in the hallway. 'I think I'd prefer to eat with company in the kitchen.'

Her appearance was greeted with surprise and more sympathy than Amy had anticipated, as she assured them that she wasn't here to work.

'I was going a bit mad just talking to myself.'

There were fewer staff than the previous day, which made sense. Apparently, they were only serving two—plus the staff—who, from what she saw, ate very well.

As she sat on a stool eating the really delicious monkfish kebabs with a crunchy side salad and subtle tikka sauce, watching the interplay between the staff, several of them came across to talk for a moment or two.

Conversation was about food, with a bit of juicy gossip thrown in for good measure, and Amy found herself relaxing for the first time since she'd arrived.

Occasionally, she glanced towards the door, wondering what Leo's reaction would be if he discovered she had ignored his edict to stay in her room. Well, maybe not an *edict,* but he had been extremely high-handed. If he had appeared, she would have told him so, not that she was looking for a fight—or him.

She would have liked to linger in the kitchen, but it felt wrong to be there and not work and she was feeling extremely tired again, which was often the way if she allowed a migraine to develop.

When she went to carry her tray over to the dishwashers it was firmly taken off her.

Amy didn't protest; she was actually quite touched by the kindness.

Would she have been so touched if Leo had been the one offering the kindness? The inconvenient question stayed in her head as she made her way back to her own suite.

It wasn't *what* he said; it was the *way* he said it.

The next time she saw him she would tell him so, she decided tiredly before she lay down in bed. She was asleep before her head hit the pillow.

She didn't actually see Leo all the next day; he did not put in a disruptive appearance in the kitchen or highjack her along the long hallways. There was no request for her presence, which meant her day was harassment-free and rather productive.

The evening meal left the pass looking like a work of art and she knew it tasted as good as it looked. There was, after all, no harm being a perfectionist.

She ate supper with the rest of the staff and they discussed their own individual versions of French meringue, as retro floating islands were making a comeback on menus.

The idea of the sea drew her, and the draw had nothing whatever to do with a childish impulse to ignore Leo's instructions. The summer days were long and she would be back at the castle before darkness fell.

She thought she might have met someone as she trod the same path she had yesterday, but it was both deserted and silent, except for when the noise of a helicopter above made her look up and watch until it vanished behind the forested area to the east, presumably to land in the same place she had when they'd arrived.

Would there be more guests to feed tomorrow? Courtesy of the kitchen gossip, she had learnt that Leo's female companions never visited the castle. He appeared to keep his life strictly compartmentalised.

Amy took a few moments when she reached the beach to drink in the view. Leo had said he swam here but, not being the strongest swimmer in the world, she had taken the precaution of checking the tides and asking about any dangerous currents.

It took her a few moments to pull off the wraparound skirt and her white cotton top and arrange them neatly on top of the canvas bag containing her towel and the book she had brought.

The sand was warm underfoot as she ran down to the sea.

She was happy to paddle for a little while, meandering up and down the beach in the warm, crystal-clear water before she walked out until she was deep enough to swim. Her slow breaststroke was never going to break any records and she was careful to keep parallel to the beach and not go out of her depth, until she grew tired and flipped over onto her back to float lazily, seeing the sun through the delicate skin of her eyelids. With just the hiss of the waves breaking on the shore and the odd bird screeching overhead, she felt her cares and tensions slip away.

She eventually opened her eyes and wondered if too much relaxing was bad for you. She had floated further out than she'd intended and was, without a doubt, out of her depth. But it wasn't *too* far.

She didn't allow herself to panic, though it was nipping at her heels as she determinedly set off for the shore. It seemed to take an incredibly long time to reach the shallows and stand on her feet, water streaming down her body, her heart hammering with a combination of the physical effort and relief as she waded to the shore.

She spread out her towel and collapsed onto it, lying there with her ribcage lifting in tune with her rapid exhalations, which gradually slowed as the relaxing heat seeped into her limbs. Her adrenaline levels lowered as she closed her eyes.

It wasn't cold, but it was the perceptible change in temperature that woke her. She sat up and looked around, initially confused before she realised that she had fallen asleep. There was no sun; instead, the beach was lit by moonlight and the sea was now silver-streaked and dark, and was lapping only a few feet away from her.

She ransacked her bag to find her phone and gasped when she saw the time. It was close on midnight. Scrambling to her feet and swearing under her breath, she struggled into her top and then fastened her skirt over her bikini, which was now bone-dry. Even her rope of hair, which usually took an age to dry, was barely damp.

Retaining her phone before pushing everything else into her bag, she slung it over her shoulder and headed for the trees. Without the moonlight and the light of her phone it would have been pitch-black. Even with these light sources, the olive grove felt very different than in daylight, the trees' skeletal outlines in the dark seeming sinister and unwelcoming. Heart pounding, she began to run, every snap of a twig and animal call raising her heart rate.

It was a relief to emerge, but she didn't pause. Jogging

across the flat ground, she didn't stop until she reached the lowest terrace.

Her nervousness now seemed foolish with the soothing aroma of night-scented stocks and roses filling the air. She wasn't in a wilderness; she was a few hundred metres from a building with dozens of people in it. Though it might have been better to have remembered that she wasn't afraid of the dark five minutes ago.

By the time she reached the third level, the illuminated castle came into view and the last of the tension bunching her shoulders loosened. She even took the time out to linger a little to admire the spotlit iconic building.

CHAPTER ELEVEN

'I CAN'T DECIDE if you're stupid or stubborn!'

Amy screamed and spun around, fists raised, to face the owner of the voice, who seemed to materialise out of the undergrowth, a dark, sinister shadow looming over her.

Then the darkness was broken by a powerful beam of light that made her blink, and the dark figure took form and shape.

Feeling stupid, she hit out with a querulous, 'What are you doing? You gave me the fright of my life!'

'What am *I* doing?' he barked.

'Get that thing out of my eyes!'

Not just out of her eyes but out of the way full stop, and the darkness descended again. Other senses compensated when you couldn't see. And her well-developed sense of smell was busy compensating. Amy tried and failed not to breathe in the clean male scent Leo exuded.

The dark was dangerous, but the danger that lurked in the shadows wasn't ghouls or ghosts. People did things in the dark that they wouldn't do in daylight; it freed up inhibitions, not that she'd ever had any of those where Leo was concerned.

'Can we skip the part where you work yourself up into a foot-stamping temper tantrum, because it isn't going to alter the fact you are in the wrong. I explained that this area was off-limits at night until the electricity supply is—'

She made a scornful noise in her throat. 'There is no light issue; the place is lit up like a Christmas tree.' She was making a pointy-fingered gesture to the brightly lit castle when the lights went out, along with the moon.

'You were saying?' drawled the dark shadow.

'Someone switched off the lights.'

She could hear the hissing sound of exasperation escape his lips. 'It is automated, our contribution to the elimination of light pollution.'

'But you are almost self-sustaining; the hydro and—'

'My, you have been busy educating yourself. Light pollution isn't just about energy; it's about the adverse effects on the natural environment—animals, birds, insects.'

'Oh, well, I wasn't in the dark. I have my phone.'

He gave a disgusted snort. 'You call that a torch?' He waved a high beam light in her face again, and it was an assault on her retinas.

'Stop that!' she squealed, covering her face and turning away. 'Now look what you've made me do,' she added as the contents of her bag spilled out. She dropped down to her knees.

Leo retrieved the paperback that had fallen under some foliage, glanced at the title by torchlight and dropped it into the open bag. 'So you like happy ever afters,' he observed, sounding amused. 'And it's a clever trick, reading in the dark.'

'It wasn't dark when I left the castle,' she retorted. 'I fell asleep in the daytime and when I woke up it was night.' She shrugged and reached out for something to retain her balance as she rose to her feet and realised it was the stone seat of the gazebo erected in his mother's memory. Her eyes flew to his face. 'Oh, you were...' She traced the engraved name with a finger and felt her throat thicken with emotion. 'I disturbed you, I'm sorry,' she said softly.

'Disturbed me?'

His tone sounded strange, and his face, just a blur in the dark, gave no added information.

'Come on, I'll see you back up to your room.'

'Oh, no, I'm fine. I'll…'

'For once in your life, don't argue!'

'All right, all right, there's no need to bellow.'

Above her head he swore, and after a pause she followed the uneven path ahead, which was lit by his powerful torch.

'We were not all Boy Scouts,' she grumbled.

He laughed. 'I wasn't a Boy Scout either. I have never been a team player. Though the local gang took quite a lot of convincing of that fact.'

'Gang?'

'Young men are pack animals, and I wasn't raised in a leafy suburb.'

The matter-of-fact description of his childhood chilled Amy's blood. She had zero idea of what his life had been like in the years before they'd met, and he had rarely mentioned anything beyond the basics. She knew he had lived in several foster homes and had left school with little or no qualifications, which had seemed strange to her at the time, because it was very obvious he was super smart.

They had reached the lawned area.

'I can manage the rest and I'm sorry, I really didn't intend to be out in the dark.'

'I'm going your way.'

'Weren't you going to swim?'

'I might use the pool later, and the next time you feel the need for a midnight skinny-dip you might think of using it yourself.'

Accustomed to the dark now, she could make out the outline of his classical features and it didn't take much imagination to envisage the mocking gleam in his dark eyes as he taunted her.

'I wasn't skinny-dipping; I have a swimsuit on and—' She hesitated.

'What?'

'People might see me in the pool.'

'And that is an issue, why, exactly?'

She hesitated and then admitted, 'Well, there have been a couple of comments, nothing nasty or anything, but staff aren't normally housed where I am and they…we don't have access to the pool and tennis courts or the leisure facilities. I don't want anyone to jump to the wrong conclusions,' she finished, glad the darkness concealed her burning cheeks.

'*The wrong conclusions?*'

Her jaw clamped in response to this display of feigned ignorance. 'You know exactly what I mean.' His torch had been trained into the distance but, as he spoke, he brought it up on her face again like a spotlight. 'And it was only once.'

'Oh, is that why you're so cranky? I've never been anyone's dirty little secret before. Oh, well, a bit of creeping around can be quite stimulating, so I've been told. Or are you talking about a discovery fantasy?'

She batted wildly at his hand, panicked by the insidious tug of desire she felt at his taunts. She heard the sound of the torch hitting something hard a second before they were enclosed in a velvet blackness, as the moon had been swallowed up by a cloud.

The smothering darkness created a dangerous illusion of intimacy and she could feel it like a spider spinning its silken cords around her.

'I don't have anything to keep secret. I know I'm not here long, but it's hard to work as a team if… I just don't want any awkward questions, that's all.'

'Stay still.'

She froze and felt a hand land on her shoulder. 'You were about to step into a pond.'

'How do you know?' she asked, puzzled. She couldn't even see the outline of the castle. She could still feel its presence, though not as intensely as she was aware of Leo's. All her senses were attuned to him.

'I have excellent night vision.'

'Of course you do.'

He laughed at her dry tone. 'That's it,' he added when, encouraged by his guiding hand, she took a step towards him. 'Do you want to have one?'

'Want to have what?'

'Do you want a secret?'

Her throat was dry, her heart beating fast. 'Is that code for something?'

'You know what I'm saying, but I'll spell it out for you so there is no misunderstanding. Fantasies are not enough. Once is not enough, not nearly enough. I stayed away yesterday because of your migraine but I am asking you now. Amy, do you want to have sex with me?'

'Yes.' She was a mess of screaming hormones, but he didn't have to make beautifully indecent propositions to do that to her. He just had to exist.

He took a deep breath and let it out slowly. His calm was illusionary and it was in danger of shattering at any moment. He was in the grip of a lust that showed no sign of diminishing and the only logical cure was to satiate it.

'You have no idea how glad I am that you said that. We need to finish what we started nearly ten years ago. It doesn't need to be complicated; it's actually very simple.'

She couldn't see his eyes but she was hypnotised—hypnotised by his deep voice, which was like smoke that seemed to wrap around her and vibrate deep inside her like a pulse. The pulse was everywhere, but especially focused between her legs.

'It's not that simple,' she whispered, her protest feeble as she thought, *It's dangerous because I'm falling in love with you again. It's possible I never stopped loving you.*

He leaned in then and she pressed into his hardness as his hands swept down her spine before settling on her bottom, drawing her in even closer.

A sibilant sigh left her lips. 'But you make me ache, Leo.'

'I think we can do something about that ache, don't you?' he rasped against her mouth, and as his tongue flicked along the outline his thumbs were on the corners of her jaw, positioning her lips perfectly for him to plunder.

'I…' The rest of her words were lost inside his mouth as his tongue plunged between her parted lips.

Resistance didn't even cross her mind as she kissed him back with a raw, almost feral desperation, her fingers sliding under his tee-shirt to feel his smooth skin. Revelling in the strength of his hard body and the ridges of muscle that contracted under her touch, she experienced a slug of power as she both heard and felt his groan.

'Is this real?' she wondered, not even realising she had voiced her thoughts out loud until he took her hand and curved it over the rock-hard, pulsing outline in his shorts.

'Does that feel real to you, *cara*?'

'Very, very real…' she mumbled thickly, tightening her grip until he groaned out a protest.

They were stumbling but she didn't know where to until she registered a light… Maybe she was dying and this was the end of a tunnel?

She wasn't dying; it was the swimming pool, with its underwater lighting creating a stunning rippling illuminated effect that was reminiscent of the northern lights.

'I'm never going to make it to a bed,' he bit out.

'Don't apologise,' she mumbled.

Still kissing and half carrying her, he dragged the cushions off one of the recliners on the terrace and threw them on the floor before sinking onto them with her clutched in his arms.

Kneeling face to face, he ripped off his tee-shirt, pulling it over his head in one fluid motion.

She barely registered that the sound that emerged, part gloating greed, part awe, part longing, came from her own lips. Hands resting on his bare shoulders, she kissed her way down his bronzed torso, pulling up only when she reached the waistband of his shorts. Holding his gaze, she slid her hands lower, biting her lip, her eyes fierce with satisfaction when he groaned again.

He jerked her back, his big hands framing her flushed face. 'This isn't going to be *just* sex, *cara*, it's going to be mind-blowing, head-banging sex,' he growled out.

After the *just sex* part, she felt unshed tears press at the back of her eyes. She wanted more than that, but if she told him what she wanted, what she felt about him, it would be a deal-breaker. It was kind of ironic, really. That she had once turned away the man who would now run for the hills at the mention of love or commitment.

She lifted her chin and bit the lobe of his ear and whispered, 'Prove it!'

With bewildering speed, she was flat on her back, the improvised bed of cushions protecting her from the hard surface of the ground.

She felt his body on top of her, but more she felt the staggering power that poured off him, the hunger, the sheer *maleness* that excited her more than she would have thought possible.

He left her alone for a brief moment and peeled off his shorts. The scent of jasmine that spilled from the nearby containers would always, in Amy's head, be associated in future with the sight of him standing there naked and fully aroused, a perfect image of primal male virility.

He was her fantasy in the flesh, made real just for her.

Kneeling, he pulled off her skirt and top and peeled the bikini away from her skin. A moment later she was naked and then he joined her and she was no longer an observer; she was fully involved in this primal mating.

He abruptly interrupted their mutual touching and kissing. 'Protection?' he slurred.

She bit his neck and thought, *Kill me now.*

'You're right, you never were a Boy Scout.'

'I can still make it good for you.'

'I want you inside me!' She nipped his lower lip, drawing a pinprick of blood in her frustration.

'Hang on, let me check...' He rolled over and reached for his shirt and pulled out the wallet he had shoved into his pocket along with his phone.

He emerged triumphant with a silver foil packet.

She smiled and snatched it off him. 'Let me.'

She took her time moving down his body, using his knee as a useful aid to her rising frustration.

His body was slick with salt by the time she took him into her hand. The sinews in his neck distended with the strain he was under as he lifted his head. 'Just do it! I...'

Tipped onto her back, she looked at him, challenge glowing in her eyes as, feet flat on the ground, her knees open in carnal challenge, she waited to be claimed.

It was not a long wait.

A second later, sheathed in her tight slickness, every muscle in his body pumped and primed, he began to move.

Each thrust drove her deeper into herself, and she was aware of him at a cellular level. Each thrust was more pleasure and more torture, the pressure building and building before exploding in a stunning shower of stars.

She floated back to her body slowly, the image of their entwined bodies imprinted behind her closed eyes.

He rolled off her with a grin. 'Witchy woman,' he said, touching the white-blonde streak in the dark of her hair.

'That was…'

'Sex does not have to be complicated.'

'No, it doesn't,' she agreed sadly. *Love* was complicated.

'Shall we take this to a bed? Or do you fancy a swim in the pool?'

'Another time, maybe.'

They ended up in her bed, the transfer taking a little longer because she made him go back and gather their clothes from the poolside, even though they were both more than adequately swathed in towels.

The second time in a bed was gentler, less rushed, more tender, but not any less intense.

Sex for Leo did not usually involve any kind of aftermath; he was an expert at silent dressing in the dark.

So as he lay there in the dark, making sleepy conversation with Amy about modern vinery techniques, which somehow led on to discussing his relationship with his grandfather, he didn't immediately register what was happening.

He was breaking all the rules that he had established over the years for a very good reason—to keep sex a million miles away from an emotional connection.

She sensed his withdrawal and immediately misunderstood the reason for it.

'It's fine, I understand. It's hard; family is so complicated... I wish I had more of a relationship with my mum before she became so ill.'

About to roll away, there was something in her voice that made him lie still. He threw an arm over his head and listened to her soft voice talking in the dark.

'The doctors said I wasn't responsible for the first heart attack. That it was a genetic defect she had been born with.'

He turned on his side to look at her face. 'Why would you feel responsible for her heart attack?'

'I'm not... I wasn't...'

'Amy?'

His tone of voice was uncompromising, and she sighed. It was probably past time to tell him.

'She had her first heart attack when I told them I was leaving to be with you. Dad told me I'd nearly killed her.'

'So this was when you sent me away?' he asked, rigid with tension.

'We had just got back from the hospital. Mum made me promise I would stay. I loved you so much, Leo, but she'd nearly died.'

Hand over his eyes, Leo fell back onto the bed.

He had based everything he'd done over the last nine years on the belief that she had rejected him, that she hadn't truly loved him... But the truth was so much more nuanced than that. Ultimately, his revenge had been to punish her for something that had always been out of her control.

He lay there, stunned, feeling as if a hand had just thrust into his chest and it was squeezing what used to be his heart.

'Why didn't you tell me?' he rasped, seeing her standing there in the doorway that day, the tears gathering in her eyes.

'I… There was no point. It wouldn't have changed anything. And look, it didn't turn out so badly. If I had gone with you, then most likely by now we'd hate one another. Instead, we are having sex, beautiful, fantastic sex.'

'Sex,' he repeated in an odd voice.

'Don't worry, I know you don't want anything else. I know it's just sex and it won't last, but even you have to admit it is totally beautiful.'

She was saying exactly what he wanted to hear, so why did he feel…aggrieved to hear her describing what his perfect relationship would be?

The long pause before he responded made her fear that she had said something wrong, that he had realised the truth—that she still loved him. She had never stopped loving him, but voicing that love would be the end of this and even though they might have no future together, she was going to extract every last scrap of pleasure from the present.

'Yes, totally beautiful.' His voice was husky.

She gave a sigh of relief. It felt as though a barrier between them had fallen, and she felt physically lighter now that she had told him, though of course she hadn't told him all of her secrets.

Her final one was still too painful to share.

CHAPTER TWELVE

Amy woke and turned her head on the pillow, her warm fuzzy feeling dying when she saw the empty space beside her. Leo had been away for two days but was returning today in time for the gala.

As she lay there stretching she saw the scarlet dress hanging behind the door in its transparent cover emblazoned with the designer's name. Her outfit for the gala.

Leo had produced it like a magician before he'd left, expecting her to be pleased. She knew her reaction had disappointed him—she loved it, she really did, and she felt sexy and powerful in it. It wasn't even the fact that she had reservations about being present at the gala. It was more that it was an echo of all the times her father had demanded final approval on her mother's outfit for an event.

Her phone rang and she reached for it, grimacing when she saw the caller's identity.

She would ring Ben back. It had only been the previous week when he had rung, asking her if she would consider selling her share in Gourmet Gypsy. The temp, who had worked out really well and had increased their profits, was keen to buy in.

She was torn as the food truck was very much her baby, though it had only ever been intended to be a temporary stopgap, leading to better things. The better things had not involved staying in a Tuscan castle and becoming the mistress in everything but title to the most gorgeous man in the world.

Leo had already suggested she stay on after the gala, that their arrangement could become open-ended, but she hadn't given him an answer yet. She adored him, she loved him with every cell in her body, but the longer she was here, the harder the inevitable heartbreak would be when it came. And when the man who you loved felt the need to slide the words *just sex* into the conversation every single time you made love, hanging onto any kind of hope was pointless.

She pushed away the decision yet again and instead fingered the red silk of her dress as she walked to the bathroom. Leo would be back later, and for now that was enough.

It was afternoon when the kitchen door opened; it was a quiet moment and she was alone. Amy looked up, emotions she struggled to dampen flaring and dying as the man delivering micro salad from the home farm walked in carrying their order in a cool box.

She was pathetic, she told herself. Even if Leo hadn't been absent for the past two days, she wouldn't have seen anything of him because she was too busy to see him.

Soon she wouldn't see him at all. Even if she took up his offer, there was no promise of permanence, no commitment, but deep down she still had hope and she knew that she wouldn't leave until she lost every scrap of that hope.

She pushed away the thought, which was more than a thought—a reality—but there was no point crying over something that hadn't happened yet. She'd be damned if she was going to waste what time she had with him worrying about the future.

He had texted her when he had arrived back, checking

she'd be able to make their meeting. Their so-called *meetings* were often on the beach, sometimes by the pool, when he teased her for having a sentimental attachment to the second place they had made love. *Little did he know!* But mostly these meetings were late at night or early in the morning, before he left her room in cover of darkness.

Several of the staff emerged from the staffroom, where they had been taking a break.

'Have you seen this list, Amy… Chef? We might as well serve this woman fresh air!'

Amy eyed the tablet Jamie was scrolling through. 'Someone with a lot of allergies?' she asked, wondering at the younger woman's annoyed tone. It wasn't as if they weren't all accustomed to accommodating guests' dietary requirements aside of the usual vegetarian and vegan alternatives.

Sensing the unspoken query in Amy's voice, the young chef pushed the tablet along the counter towards her. 'Allergies,' she said as Amy began to read, 'I can do. Food intolerances I can do. Vegan options, well, I'm a vegan. The calorie count that we cannot exceed on each course is also fair enough. But have you seen the dictate on the food groups we're not allowed to combine on a plate? These are not just dietary requirements; it's a straitjacket for any chef! Creativity will go out the—'

While Amy sympathised with the other woman, she adopted a soothing tone. 'Yeah, it doesn't leave much leeway but—'

'But you'd better get used to it, Jamie,' the chef who had been standing at the nearest work station interrupted. 'Because that lady is going to be our new boss.'

'With luck, she won't be spending too much time here,' the younger woman said, displaying crossed fingers before returning to the tablet. 'Do you think they'll be making the announcement tonight?' she wondered gloomily. 'I suppose we could do—'

Her suggestions were a static buzz in Amy's head.

'Our new boss?' she said, aiming for casual and producing strangled.

'You haven't heard?' someone on the other side of the kitchen said in a surprised tone.

'It seems he's serious this time. Apparently, they've been secretly engaged for months. Her name's Sophia.'

'No ring yet, though,' Jamie intervened, typing up notes with a frown. 'And that paper—or rather, scandal sheet—is the rag that wrote that article on the Queen, the old Queen, still being alive. That squid recipe of yours, Amy, do you use…?'

Amy automatically listed the ingredients. 'So Leo is engaged?'

Someone else laughed. 'Do you have *any* footprint on social media?'

'I follow some people.'

'All food-related, right…but there's a whole other world out there.'

'Of bile, gossip and innuendo. Leave her alone.'

Amy didn't have a clue how she got through the rest of the morning. On autopilot, she delegated the task of coordinating the staff who had been brought in for the gala, then waited for the couple of hours that were pencilled in for her time off—supposedly for her *meeting* with Leo.

Her knife skills had raised a few eyebrows as she'd sliced and diced as though her life depended on it. She didn't have a clue who this woman was, but she already hated her. But not as much as she hated Leo and herself, and not necessarily in that order.

He had not promised her anything, but she had *hoped*—she had really hoped—that this had meant more than just sex for him. And all the while he had been planning to make a life with another woman.

She walked through the olive groves that bordered the beach, glad of the shade. When the stony ground gave way to sand, she removed her sandals.

She was early for their assignation, but so was Leo. He was already standing facing the sea when she reached the secluded cove. A voice in her head suggested now was the moment to pause, to get her thoughts in order, but her mortified anger was firmly in charge.

His dark hair was ruffled, his black tee-shirt was tucked into a pair of faded denim cut-offs. Barefoot, Leo was standing on the water's edge, staring out to sea, shading his eyes—perhaps to see the boat with a red sail bobbing on the horizon.

As if sensing her presence, he turned when she was still fifty feet away and watched her approach.

She paused a few feet away from him, the light breeze whipping her hair into a tangled skein across her face. Even knowing what she now knew—basically, that despite all his simple honesty he was a lying bastard—she had unpinned her hair.

She had worn it loose because he liked it that way and she felt angry with herself for wanting to please him, wanting to hear him say she was beautiful just one last time.

She didn't pause for preliminaries or even notice the smile of welcome on his face morph into an expression of caution.

'Is it true that you are engaged to this Sophia woman?'

For once she had surprised him, but she was too angry to celebrate this triumph over his damned insouciance.

She watched the shock on his face meld into anger. 'How is that relevant?'

Outraged breath hissed through her flared nostrils as she pulled herself up to her full and unimpressive five foot three. 'You can ask that?'

'I just did,' he pointed out mildly.

She scowled furiously. 'I don't sleep with married men.'

'I'm not married.'

She threw him a narrow-eyed challenge and gritted out, 'But you're engaged?'

Now the question was out, there was no going back, no pretending, and she felt an icy fist of dread tighten in her belly. Because, beneath her aggressive façade, Amy was willing him to deny it, or laugh at the suggestion.

He didn't, and she died a little bit inside.

'Can I ask where you got this inside information?'

He had the utter, unbelievable cheek to act offended. 'Everyone knows, apparently.'

Except me.

Humiliation tasted bitter in her mouth.

'The entire kitchen is talking about it, about *her*...' The venom in her own voice shocked her, as taunting images of the gala's guest of honour, the subject of Amy's recent furtive internet searches, flashed before her eyes.

The blonde with the trashy reality television credentials was a perfect match for the Romano heir. The men her name had been linked with were all rich and famous, and none of them said a bad word about her. She had been equally discreet.

The perfect partner for Leo.

'You're jealous.'

She clenched her fists and tossed her head as she glared up at him. 'Grow up, Leo. I don't care who you marry! You can have a harem for all I care, but I do object to not being given the information to make an informed choice. You obviously don't give a damn when it comes to cheating but, call me old-fashioned,' she hissed, 'I bloody do, you bastard!'

She finished her diatribe on a breathless gasp, doubled over at the waist.

'I thought you had more sense than to listen to gossip.'

Her head came up with a jerk. 'Don't you dare patronise me, Leo!'

He stepped forward, clasping both her wrists, and pulled her upright.

'You are aware that I am supposedly being married off to at least three women a month?'

'Your modesty is one of your most charming characteristics.'

There was zero warning as he reached down and ran his hand over the brand-new silk kimono she wore over a strapless bikini. 'That's new—I like it, but I prefer you without it.'

The sound of her hand connecting with his cheek was shocking.

'Oh, God, I am so, so sorry! I shouldn't have… You just make me so mad! How the hell did you think it was appropriate to make a pass at me at this moment? I've never hit anyone in my entire life. I am mortified…'

He caught the shaking hand she had pressed to her mouth and pulled it to his lips, holding her eyes as he spread her fingers and kissed her palm. 'I'm sorry I wound you up, *cara*. I admit I was a bit of a bastard.'

Amy blinked at the unexpected climbdown, shock combining with confusion, hot tingles spreading like a web from her palm along her nerve-endings.

'I really shouldn't have done that, though.'

'Your vicious little tongue does a lot more harm than your left hook, *cara*. You barely touched me.' The levity in his words were not reflected in the tension-carved angles and planes of his face, which projected an intense, driven quality.

'I should be immune to gossip. I *am* immune.' Or he'd thought he was. 'I usually ignore it when people write lies about me, when I find human rats going through my recycling bin looking for private information. It doesn't matter to me what strangers think.'

It mattered what Amy thought of him, though.

The discovery of this vulnerability had not made him overly sympathetic to her distress and he'd deliberately goaded her until she'd snapped.

Her eyes flickered down to their single point of contact, which still hadn't been broken. He hadn't let go of her hand and there was something hypnotic about the way his thumb was tracing tiny arabesques on her palm.

When she drew her hand back and nursed it against her chest, he made no attempt to prevent her. 'I am not a stranger,' she said huskily.

'No, you're not, and I shouldn't have reacted like that. I am not engaged—not to Sophia nor to anyone else. Despite my grandfather's constant matchmaking, I remain single. Do you believe me?' His ink-dark eyes scanned her face.

The reply came without a pause. 'Yes, I do…' In her head she could hear herself saying those words standing in a church but, before her fantasy could solidify, she pushed it away. 'Believe you, that is,' she tacked on, hastily adding, 'I suppose it's only natural that your grandfather wants an heir.'

He might be holding out but one day, perhaps when his grandfather realised that Leo did not react well to being pushed, he would oblige, and produce the future Romano generation.

An image of dark-eyed children arranged by height flashed before her eyes. Children they might have had together in another life.

'I know what we are…or rather what we are not. What we share is just sex. I get that.' She should do; he'd said it often enough. *As if she was likely to forget when he recited it like a post-coital mantra.*

'But honesty is important to me and there are some lines that I am not willing to cross.' Lines, she realised, that could look very blurred just because she burned so fiercely for this man.

But if she bent her own rules and crossed those lines once, she would never stop crossing them, and she would end up a paler version of the person she was.

Someone she didn't like.

She jerked as a wave lapped over her toes with a hiss and retreated.

'Sophia is coming to the gala,' he said.

Her toes dug into the wet sand. 'I know this, and me being here is still an exercise in humiliation.' Her throat closed up as she angrily blinked away tears. 'Was she supposed to be part of it? I just didn't realise how far you would take it… I feel pretty stupid right now.'

'You feel stupid? How the hell do you think I feel?'

Unnerved by the raw anger in his voice, she took a step back.

'Do you think any of this is going the way I planned?

Nine years ago, I felt happier than I'd ever been, ever dreamt I could be, and then you walked away from me. Well, maybe it was all for the good. Before my grandfather found me, I had already discovered I had skills, a knack for making money. Initially, it was just about trying to prove myself to you and your family, then I discovered I was really good at thinking outside the box.'

'And making even more money.'

He nodded and gave a negligent shrug. 'Yes. Seeing you reminds me of what I once thought my life was. It reminds me of all my weaknesses.' His heavy lids drooped.

'You think I'm a weakness?'

Amy was half fascinated and half repelled by his admission.

'I think you are my nemesis.' He paused, his chest lifting as he sucked in a deep breath. 'You have a face and a body that would tempt a saint and I am definitely no saint.' He gave a devil-on-steroids white grin and caught her by the waist and…did he drag her towards him, or did she throw herself at him?

Amy wasn't sure. It was one of those moments when the cord that seemed to connect them was almost visible as she strained to press closer to him.

'It doesn't matter what I say, my body betrays me…' The groan that followed his laugh had a tortured sound that she physically felt. 'As does yours,' he said, his mouth moving down the column of her throat. 'I can smell it on you. You're ready for me now.'

She whimpered and his dark eyes flared before his mouth covered hers in a devouring kiss.

Their mutual frantic kissing took them several feet from the water's edge, where they collapsed to their knees onto the sand, pulling off each other's clothes, hands on hot skin as they fell onto the sand.

'Sorry, I'm squashing you.'

'No!' She placed one hand on the back of his head and held him where he was. 'I like it.'

'This is…' he started to say.

Just sex.

'What's wrong?' he asked sharply.

She shook her head, an intent expression settling on her face as she traced the sharp angles of his face with the forefinger of her free hand. Then she arched her back to increase the delicious friction of their bodies.

His eyes were black as he turned his head, taking her palm and kissing it before catching her probing finger and drawing it into his mouth and sucking. His hands moved up and down her body before he lowered his head and kissed her, sliding his tongue between her parted lips.

This was no practised technique; it was all fire and raw need, and Amy felt as though she was burning up from the inside.

'Open your legs for me,' he urged throatily.

A hungry sound, half growl, half moan of longing, left her lips as he thrust into her willing heat. Her breath left her in one long sibilant hiss as her body stretched to accommodate him and hold him tight, her head flung back in sheer pleasure.

She could feel him plunging deep inside her, hot and hard, every cell aware of him. She moved as one with him, swiftly climbing to the peak with him and then leaping off the top with such a tumultuous freefall of sensation that she didn't know where he began and she ended.

They lay sprawled on the sand, both breathing hard.

'Don't move,' she begged when he began to roll off her.

He lifted his head and kissed her flushed cheek. 'I have to—there are drinks before the party with a select few guests and my grandfather has arrived.'

He stood up in one fluid motion. She sighed dreamily. His body was a work of art, utterly perfect in every way.

'And I suppose I should go back to work,' she said, not moving.

He was fastening the clip on the waist of his shorts when he paused.

'What is it?' she asked, sensing his unease.

He paused but didn't meet her eyes as he said, 'I'm sorry if I hurt you.'

She suddenly just wanted to hug him—not in a sexual way but to provide comfort. 'I'm really not so fragile.'

He gave a half nod and felt a rush of relief. Lust had never taken him over so totally before and the idea of hurting her was more painful than a knife blade.

'You didn't hurt me, but maybe I hurt you?' She rose from the sand and stood behind him, running her finger along the small, raised crescents on the satiny skin of his muscled back, from her fingernails clutching him in sheer ecstasy. 'I don't think I broke the skin, though.'

'My little cat.' He turned and caught her in his arms and kissed her, hard and hungry.

'You're the one purring,' she retorted, wading through the sand to where her bikini top had landed. 'Where are my...? Thanks,' she said as he handed her the bottom half of her bikini.

He watched her slide the bottoms over her slim, shapely thighs while he struggled with what to say. He never usually shared, he never explained, but it was a concession of sorts. 'Just to warn you, Sophia will also be at the pre-party drinks.'

Amy felt a pressure in her chest as she adjusted the string ties of her bikini bottoms.

The long beat of silence lengthened.

'Listen, Amy, I...'

'Is this some sort of test?' She rounded on him.

'No, of course not.'

'Then why did you tell me that?' And spoil a perfect moment.

'*Dio*, but I can't win with you, can I? You wanted me to *share*.'

'You call that sharing?' She hooted. 'Rubbing in the fact that you'll be upstairs with *Sophia* while I'm cooking her dinner in the kitchen.' She managed a shrug. 'Well, the joke's on you. The kitchen is actually where I prefer to be.'

'Yes, I know you are queen there. As for Sophia, our paths may have crossed, but we have never been lovers. I'm not her type.'

Her eyes widened fractionally. 'So she is—'

'In love with someone else who... Well, it's not my story to tell, but I can tell you that she wants to make this some-one—'

'Jealous?'

He shook his head. 'More like make them realise that she will not wait around for them forever. This is only an assumption on my part, you understand. I'm not getting in-volved. I just agreed to say nothing, and it gets my grand-father off my back for a few days.'

Not getting involved... So, nothing new there, she thought, pushing down her resentment.

'You're not going to tell me any more than that, are you?'

'No,' he agreed with an enigmatic smile.

'Did anyone ever tell you that you have a terrible atti-tude?' Amy broke off, gasping as a wave washed over her feet, swirling around her calves until it retreated with a soft hiss. A second wave peaked as it approached.

Leo caught her hand and pulled her back onto the dry sand. The impetus brought their bodies onto a collision course.

The air left Amy's body with a soft oomph as she stepped back. She went to take another step back but his hands came to rest on her bottom, and the impulse to pull free vanished in a puff of smoke.

She tilted her head back and looked into his face. He brushed the hair from her cheek and hooked a finger under her chin, bringing her face up to his. The featherlight touch made her think of his hands on her body, his fingers inside her body, and the things he did with his tongue.

She cursed her imagination, and her breathing had slowed to almost nothing as his nose grazed hers. His breath was warm on her cheek as his mouth moved soft as a whisper over her lips.

'While it lasts, we are exclusive.'

She blanked the *while it lasts* and focused on the *exclusive* part as she nodded in agreement.

'You don't leave me much energy for anyone else, anyway,' he murmured against her mouth before his tongue sank hungrily into the sweet welcoming depths.

She kissed him back, her hands winding into the dark hair at the nape of his neck. 'It's been a bad morning, and everyone is a bit tense about tonight, especially with the entire gala hysteria.'

'You love a challenge,' he said with a heartless lack of sympathy as he lifted her into his arms so she could wind her legs around his waist and began to deliver a series of slow open-mouthed kisses down her throat. 'I'm looking forward to seeing you in that dress. Next year you'll be...'

His words cleared the sensual fog that suffused her and she became achingly aware of the carnal pressure of his erection against her core and the fact she was grinding against it to increase that delicious pressure.

Hands on his chest, she shimmed down until she was standing in front of him, her chest heaving.

'Next year? I won't be here next year. I was only meant to be here for six weeks.'

The truth was she had been drifting, avoiding the good offer from Ben's friend, partly because she didn't want to think ahead. She wanted to enjoy every moment.

'Who knows where any of us will be next year, so live in the moment.' His voice had a hardness to it, but not as hard as his stare, which was skewering her. 'Don't act like I'm holding you here against your will.'

He didn't need to, and he knew it. She wore the dresses he wanted her to, she went to parties she didn't want to go to...and suddenly her resentment rose.

'I couldn't walk out before the gala, that wouldn't be fair.'

'That is so bloody kind of you.'

Her jaw tightened at his sarcasm.

'We're having fun. Why are you so afraid to admit it?' he asked.

'I know it's just convenient for you, having me around when you're here.'

A raw laugh erupted from his chest as, hands in his hair, he turned back to the sea before, moments later, swinging back to face her. 'Convenient! You are many things, Amy, but *convenient* is not one of them.'

'You're never going to forgive me for the past, are you?'

A hissing sound of exasperation left his lips. 'Let it go, Amy. I appreciate that the situation with your mother was horrendous and you felt obliged to stay, but you could have contacted me, explained.'

She could tell by the way it exploded out of him that this had been eating away at him.

'I did try to contact you.'

'Just leave it, Amy.'

'You don't believe me! I did ring you, but you'd already blocked me and then it was number unknown. I even tried to follow you on social media, I was so desperate. But then…'

'Fine, you tried, I believe you, but just let it lie now, Amy.'

His attitude, as if he was doing her a massive favour, snapped something inside her.

'I got on a train, even though I didn't know where I was going, just because I needed to tell you something important.'

'What,' he mocked, 'that love conquers all?'

'No, that I was pregnant.'

In the aftershock of her explosive reveal there was a pulsating silence that seemed to go on for ever.

'You were pregnant and you didn't tell me?'

She couldn't take her eyes off the pulse throbbing in his cheek.

'I just told you I tried to call you.'

'My baby?' He turned to look at her, his dark eyes bleak and filled with nothing resembling love or even liking. 'Where is he now?'

'I had a miscarriage.'

'And you could have told me that how many times over the past weeks?'

'What would have been the point? It's history.'

'Is it? Or is it your version of history? How do I know there was ever a baby? How do I know you didn't get rid of him or have him adopted? I could have a child out there…'

She listened to his increasingly irrational flow of accusations, growing colder and colder inside.

'If any of that is what you truly think me capable of, I think you should start advertising for a new chef and do not expect me to work my notice. Also, this Cinderella doesn't wear ballgowns and I hate red!' she shrieked.

CHAPTER THIRTEEN

THE THING AMY had always feared had happened. She'd always been secretly afraid that if he had known about the baby he would have rejected her and now, nine years later, that was exactly what he had done! There were no tears, though, not even when her hot emotions cooled to cold misery as she jogged back to the castle, not looking back. She slowed to a more sedate pace as she went past the musicians who were setting up in the marquee and the lighting technicians who were putting the last touches to the laser display that was timed for midnight, and went straight to her room.

She would leave tomorrow, she decided, looking at her dry-eyed reflection in the mirror, but she couldn't leave them in the lurch tonight. Ben could have the business; she wanted a total change.

The annoying stitch in her side took a long time to go away and by the time it had subsided there wasn't really time for a shower. But she made time before dressing for work, glancing at the dress still hanging up. She shook her head and straightened her shoulders before she donned her kitchen whites.

She walked into the kitchen and realised how much she would miss this place.

But not him—she hated him. He had made her love him all over again and she would never forgive him for what he'd said to her. Those accusations, they were… She shuddered when she thought of his words, remembering the emptiness in her life after she'd lost the baby.

Leo didn't watch her leave. He turned in the opposite direction and stood there, staring out at the sea, his thoughts churning.

He *had* blocked her calls, he remembered now, taking petty satisfaction from the action, or maybe he had just been protecting himself from the fact that he didn't think she'd try to contact him.

The idea of her being alone, like his own mother, coping with the tragedy of loss with no support, crushed something inside him. Maybe he should be asking himself why she hadn't trusted him enough to tell him about the baby when she'd finally opened up about her mother.

And when she had told him about the baby, what had he done? He'd blown any chance of them being together, of having a family together. A look of shock flickered across his face as he turned his back on the ocean. He *wanted* a family. He wanted a family with Amy. He loved her to distraction—he always had and he always would—but he'd been too much of a coward to admit it to himself, let alone to tell her. He'd been emotionally cut off and she had…she had given everything and asked nothing from him in return.

He walked back across the beach, realising that he was in danger of becoming just like his grandfather, alienating everyone he loved.

'What time are you heading off to mingle, Chef?' Jamie teased when the party was in full swing and they were enjoying a lull.

'I'm going to give it a miss.'

'No, you have to go, to represent us.'

Jamie's voice died at a nudge from someone.

'You not feeling too good, Amy?'

'Not really,' Amy admitted. 'But I'll be fine,' she said, producing a grin that didn't fool anyone.

'Why don't you head off, have an early night?'

Like a drowning man, she clutched at the suggestion even though she wasn't sure where it came from. 'I think I might. I'll just... Oh, dear!'

She could hear voices, see faces, but then she swayed and only saw black dots dancing before her eyes.

'Leo!' she cried before the blackness encompassed her.

It was a graceful faint and, luckily for her, a good catch.

'Jamie, find a doctor!' one of the other chefs ordered.

She came to and groggily tried to lift her head. 'I need to...'

'You need to lie down.'

'I am,' she said, her hands warm against the stone of the floor she was lying on. 'I should get up.' Then she felt pain and realised she couldn't.

His grandfather looked at the glass in Leo's hand and raised a brow.

'That isn't your first drink tonight.'

Leo flashed a sardonic smile at his grandfather. 'And it probably won't be my last, but don't worry, I won't disgrace the family name.'

'So where is our chef?'

'I don't think she'll be coming. In fact, I'm pretty sure I'm going to need a new chef.' He waited but there was no reply.

'What, no lecture on the reckless disregard for social structure or even the dangers of sleeping with the help?' he mocked, sliding deeper into his chair.

The old man's expression didn't change, despite the languid pose and the provocative attitude of his heir. 'So, I take it you're just going to sit there feeling sorry for yourself all night.'

Leo surged to his feet. The action and his fierce masculinity combined with the air of danger he was projecting, drawing stares.

'You're an idiot, this I already knew, but I had no idea until this moment that you were also a coward, Leo. I am ashamed.'

His eyes flashing fire, Leo towered over the older man, but he only held the pose for a split second before his shoulders drooped.

'So am I,' he said with a lopsided smile before he drained his champagne glass. Guilt had made him lash out at her—the knowledge that she had needed him and he hadn't been there for her.

It was fear that had stopped him from following her, from begging for her forgiveness. Fear that she would reject him for the last time, and he wouldn't blame her if she did.

'I can change.'

'Don't tell me—tell her.'

A suited figure appeared, sensing the atmosphere but squaring his shoulders anyway, and interrupted two generations of Romanos. 'I'm sorry, but I thought you should know that…'

A prickle of icy premonition ran down Leo's spine. 'What, man?'

'Miss Sinclair is unwell. She just collapsed.'

'Where is she?'

'She's still in the kitchen. We thought it best not to move her until a doctor had seen her.'

Leo flashed a frantic look at his grandfather, who just said, 'Go!'

He looked at the messenger as Leo vanished and said drily, 'Like I, or anyone else, could stop him.'

The kitchen had been cleared of staff, so the only people present were the young female chef and a doctor who was here as a guest, not professionally.

The icy hand of dread in his chest tightened. The guilt clawed at him like a fist as he thought of the last words he had said to her. He'd found her again after nine long years; she was his heart and his home, and now he could have lost her.

She was young; she couldn't die.

But his mother had been young and she had died.

He closed off the internal dialogue, his attempt to run to her side foiled by the doctor.

'A word first, please.'

Leo flashed a look at the pale, immobile figure on the floor. She looked so small, so fragile, so broken.

Swallowing his impatience, he allowed the doctor to take him a little to one side. 'What's happened?'

'I assume I'm speaking to you as her partner and not her employer?'

It didn't even occur to Leo to deny it and he gave a tight nod. 'Yes.'

'Well, it will be for the hospital to confirm but it appears that she could possibly be miscarrying.'

'What? She can't be… You're saying she's *pregnant? Now?*'

The doctor raised his bushy brows. 'Yes. Miss Sinclair didn't realise it either but, from our conversation, I would suggest it's still very early. It's not unusual at this stage but, given her history…'

'But that was nine years ago…and yes,' he added fiercely. 'That was mine too. Is she in danger?'

'I'll be much happier if she's in hospital.'

The blood drained from Leo's face. 'The baby?'

'I'm afraid I couldn't get a heartbeat, but that's not diagnostic; the hospital has much better equipment than my stethoscope. The air ambulance should be here directly.'

Leo usually prided himself on being the master of his emotions, but appearing supportive and not scared out of his mind was one of the hardest things he had ever done.

He took a deep breath and squatted down beside the prone figure who was covered in about ten coats. He glanced at the young girl beside Amy and nodded his thanks.

She smiled back. 'Chef, shall I…?'

'You go—and thanks, Jamie.'

After Jamie left, Leo took Amy's hand.

'You're missing your party. No, you can't shout at me,' she added when he looked ready to explode. 'I'm the walking wounded… Well, there's not much walking.'

'Are you in pain?'

'No, I'm fine.'

'You're a terrible liar,' he said, gently pushing a strand of hair from her cheek.

She didn't respond but she didn't agree either. She was a good liar—she had been lying to herself for so long that she had, until recently, actually believed the lies she'd told herself. The *I am over Leo* lie, the *I don't love Leo any more* lie.

Knowing she was carrying his baby and that it was likely she would lose it had ripped the plaster off those particular lies in the most painful way possible.

'I'm sorry about this. I know we were usually careful about protection, and that this is the last thing—'

He pressed a finger to her lips. 'Hush now and don't tell me what I want or feel.'

'Oh!' she fretted. 'You're being so kind to me. Jamie won't tell anyone about us, I asked her not to. And I think maybe I said stuff about you to the doctor too, because I panicked a bit.'

He swore the air blue and cradled her face gently between his big hands. 'You know I'm never kind and Jamie can shout it from the rooftops if she wants to, for all I care.' If he wasn't so engaged with the immediate priority he would have been doing some shouting himself.

He kissed her forehead with a tender reverence that brought tears to her eyes because she knew he was only doing it because of the baby.

He turned at the rustle of activity around the doorway. 'The ambulance is here.'

She closed her eyes. 'I hate hospitals.'

'Everyone hates hospitals.'

Her gaze was fluttering around the room in panic. 'Mum was in and out so many times, and there were so many deathbed scenes before the real one. She liked me to read to her and—'

'Don't worry, I will be with you.'

Her brown eyes focused on his face. 'Promise?'

He caught her hand and didn't let go. 'I promise.'

Amy didn't remember much about the helicopter flight to the hospital, she just remembered clinging to Leo's hand as though it were her lifeline.

It was a blur of white ceilings and test after test, but the only one that mattered to her was the ultrasound. The moment when they heard the heartbeat.

'Do you want to see the baby?' the doctor asked with a smile.

Leo's grip turned her fingers white and when she turned to look at him, tears streaming down her cheeks, his were wet too.

'Mr Romano, I can talk to your partner or—'

'Together.' He flashed a look at Amy, who nodded her approval. 'We will face this together, Doctor.'

'As you now know, the baby is well, but there are issues.'

'Is it like last time?' Amy asked, her voice shaking. 'I have to know.'

'From what you've told me, that is a possibility.'

'There was a lot of blood. Are you sure the baby is fine?'

'A little can look like a lot, Miss Sinclair.'

'Please call me Amy.'

'Well, Amy, you have what we call a placenta praevia, which means the placenta has developed low down in the uterus. Sometimes, it can completely block the cervix, but in your case there is a partial blockage. The bleeding you experienced was from a tear in a blood vessel.'

'That doesn't sound good,' Amy said in a shaky voice.

'Cases of placenta praevia can, and do, resolve themselves as the pregnancy progresses, in which case normal birth is possible. Otherwise, a C-section is advised.'

'So that's the positive stuff; what about the scary stuff?'

Leo did not often feel humble, but he did now as he watched Amy face this situation head-on, even though he could feel she was shaking with terror.

She was the strongest person he knew, he thought as possessive pride surged through his body.

'Well, premature labour is a possibility, especially at this very early stage, and a rupture of a major blood vessel is a danger for mother and baby. However,' he added quickly to forestall Leo's interruption, 'that is the worst-case scenario. Further pregnancies would need to be carefully monitored.'

'There is a risk to Amy?' Leo asked hoarsely.

'Future pregnancies could be perfectly normal,' the doctor said, with what seemed like unnatural cheer to Leo.

Leo set his jaw firmly. There would not be any more pregnancies. Amy was his family; she was all he needed. Losing her wasn't a risk worth taking. Would Amy be OK with adoption?

'Many cases resolve themselves at this stage. Most don't even require bed rest, just not activity that puts strain on the pelvis. However, in your case, as there's still a small amount of bleeding, I personally would prescribe bed rest.'

'That means I have to stay in hospital?' she faltered, the idea filling her with horror. But she lifted her chin and squared her shoulders; she would do anything to save this baby.

'Actually, when circumstances allow, we are quite happy for the situation to be managed at home, monitored, obviously…'

'Yes,' Leo said immediately, then turned to Amy, who gave a small nod of tentative relief.

'I'll leave you to discuss things in private. If you have any questions, I will be available.'

Amy waited until the door closed and they were alone. The room contained one less person but now they were alone it somehow felt smaller, or maybe Leo felt bigger. Ignoring the urge to clutch his hand, she unwrapped her fingers from his and pulled her hand away.

She sighed. 'You're being supportive, incredibly supportive, and I appreciate that, I really do.' Because of the sort of man he was, he'd put his own feelings on the back-burner.

'I know you won't believe me, but I really didn't know about the baby.'

'I do believe you,' he shot back.

'Oh…w…well, that's good,' Amy stuttered out, thrown by his swift, unequivocal response. 'I'm still in shock,' she admitted. 'I mean, I think it must have been that first time. I mean, we were in such a rush…'

'I can identify with shock.'

'Look, I can see you were in an awkward position there with the consultant, but I understand that you don't want your life disrupted to this extent. I'll be fine in hospital.'

He pressed his hands palm down on the bed and leaned in towards her, capturing her tear-filled eyes with his dark, intent stare.

'Well, I *won't* be fine with you staying in hospital. In fact, the only way you're staying here would be if I moved in with you.'

'But…'

He placed a finger to her lips and looked at her from under the sweep of his crazily long, dark eyelashes. 'You are carrying my child, Amy. I wasn't there for you last time and I will never, ever forgive myself for that, but this time I'm fully on board. I owe you an apology for the way I reacted when you told me about the first pregnancy. I didn't mean any of it, but it was still unforgivable.'

Her heart fluttered in her chest as she studied his face and saw total sincerity.

'You have forgiven me for not telling you?'

'There's nothing to forgive you for, but I'm not sure I've forgiven myself for being so judgemental.' His lips curled in a grimace of self-disgust. 'It was my guilt talking and I took it out on you. It seems that being in love does not make me any less a coward or a bastard.'

'In *love*?'

'I never stopped loving you, Amy. I understand now that when you pushed me away you were in an impossible position, all alone. And my response was to block your calls. I'm disgusted with myself.' The ring of truth in his voice made her eyes fill. 'You are brave and strong and never let me get away with a thing. I have been lying to myself about my feelings for you for the past nine years, because I couldn't own the pain, the hurt. I never stopped hurting after I lost you.'

She sniffled and he brushed a tear from her cheek. 'Please tell me that this means you're happy?'

'I am, of course I am, but this can't work,' she said sadly. 'If I lose this baby,' she said, pressing her hands protectively over her belly. 'And it could happen—'

'If it does, there will be no more babies. You will not risk yourself. I will not permit it. If I lost you, I would never recover! And I never want to relive that moment when I saw you lying on the floor.' He shuddered.

'But your grandfather wants an heir. I don't want to come between you and him.'

'He has me,' Leo declared, looking and sounding every inch the Italian autocrat. 'If that is not enough for him, he can reproduce himself! The only thing that matters to me is being enough for you, *cara*.'

Tears spilling down her face, she nodded and held out her arms. 'You are very much enough for me, Leo.' A flicker of a smile curved her lips upwards. 'In fact, there are times when you are too much for me.'

He kissed her as though she were made of precious glass, gentle but with the sort of tender emotion that made fresh tears spring to her eyes.

'None of this seems real,' she said, taking his big hands

between her smaller ones. 'This is so crazy—I'm lying in a hospital bed, terrified more than I can explain, and yet I'm also insanely happy because I love you, Leo. I don't have the words to tell you just how much.'

'We will get through this together, my love, and you never need be afraid again, or alone.'

EPILOGUE

LEO, WHO HAD been walking up and down the library with the pushchair, stopped when Amy appeared in a rustle of silk with the photographer in tow. He stopped dead, a look of awe spreading across his face.

'Leo!' She performed a graceful twirl.

'You look beautiful…' He took a deep breath and stepped back, bowing at the waist in homage to the figure in ivory silk.

'Isn't it bad luck for you to see me in the dress before the wedding? Actually, you don't look bad yourself.' That had to be the understatement of the century.

'That dress has been hanging in our bedroom for the past two weeks.'

'Good point,' she conceded, her nose wrinkling critically as she squinted at her reflection in the full-length mirror. 'You don't think it's a bit too tight still up top?' she queried, pressing her hands to her chest. 'I know it's already been let out, but the feeding is making me a bit…'

She tiptoed across to the pushchair. 'Is she asleep?'

'See for yourself.'

A big pair of golden-brown eyes looked up at her. 'You know she's bound to bawl during the service, but then I sup-pose without her we might not be getting married.'

Leo frowned. 'Are you suggesting I only proposed to

you because of our spectacularly beautiful daughter, our miracle baby?'

'Of course not!'

'Or that you said yes because of her?'

'No, I said yes because…' She gave a contented sigh and rubbed her hand lovingly across his lean cheek. 'I love you, Leo,' she said huskily. 'This…us, everything…it all seems like a lovely dream sometimes.'

Leo glanced across at the photographer, who was scrolling through the photos on his camera, oblivious to their conversation.

'And to answer your question, it is perfect *up top,* as you so quaintly phrase it, and in every other place too, as are you, *cara.*'

As Leo leant in and whispered in her ear she flushed and angled a warning glance in the direction of the photographer, who was still engrossed in what he was doing.

Leo rolled his eyes and muttered, 'He's in a world of his own.' before raising his voice. 'So how did it go? Lawrence?'

The photographer looked up with a vague expression. 'Sorry?'

'How did the shoot go? Is it in the bag now?'

'It looks great to me.'

'It looked great to you the last time too, but my wife— who I'm pretty sure is your worst nightmare client—had other ideas.'

'Oh, no, she isn't, not at all. She's just a perfectionist.'

'Ignore him, Lawrence,' Amy interrupted, throwing her husband a killer look. 'I just wanted it to be right, and it's perfect now.'

'I'll send you the proofs for a final review,' the photographer promised her.

Amy turned to face her husband as the other man left. 'Now you have my full attention.'

'You know you take multitasking to a crazy level. A wedding, a christening and a photoshoot.'

She grinned. 'Sorry, I had no idea he was going to roll up this morning. We had arranged it for next week, but he got his calendar confused.'

'Will I pass?'

'You have baby sick on your shoulder.'

'Oh, God!' he groaned, turning to try and see his shoulder. 'Will anyone notice?'

'I can smell it.'

'Well, you have cream on your behind.'

'I do not!' she said, trying to resist the temptation to look and failing. 'Oh, no! I knew I should have waited to change until *after* the shoot.'

'I can smell you as well, and you smell delicious. In fact, you make me hungry.' She fell into his arms with a sigh as he framed her face, his long, tanned fingers pushing into her hair. 'I love your witchy streak.'

'Leo, I knew it was a bad idea to have this photoshoot today. I mean, who in their right mind writes a cookery book when they're pregnant?'

He nuzzled her neck, the tiny moist bites sending sensual shudders throughout her body. Fighting the urge to relax into his embrace, which the small sane portion of her brain told her would be fatal, she pressed her hands to his shoulders, but the sinewy strength felt so good she ended up holding on, not pushing him away.

'You do.'

Amy blinked. She had forgotten the question as her finger trailed down his freshly shaven cheek.

'Admit it, you would have gone totally crazy on bed rest for all those months with no distractions.'

She laughed and returned his kiss with enthusiasm. 'It's true, I would have.'

It hadn't just been the inactivity; it had been the constant fear of losing the baby. She had been utterly dismissive when Leo had first pitched the idea that she write a cookery book but, once she had begun, it had been a sanity-saver—a marvellous distraction. She had never expected that it would be published, that had been a bonus, and she was still nervous about the outcome.

But today wasn't about the book, or the mouthwatering photos that seemed to now be in the bag, it was about the commitment they were about to make in front of, if not the world, the people that mattered in their lives, plus her father, who, despite everything he'd done, still mattered to her.

Amy was just grateful that Leo hadn't vetoed his invitation and understood she needed him there, even though the two men were never going to be friends. In fact, Leo loved her so much that he'd also helped extricate her father—and Gourmet Gypsy—from all involvement with his former 'friends' from prison. Now, George Sinclair was living a legitimate, albeit very quiet, life in forced retirement.

A cry made them both turn to the pushchair, where plump legs were kicking.

'But oh…it was worth it, wasn't it, Leo?'

Leo's eyes went to the small bundle with a mop of dark hair. 'Worth it? My God…she is just so perfect—' His fervent agreement morphed into a laugh when the perfect dark-haired bundle in the pushchair started to wail. 'That child has a real set of lungs on her.'

She saw the expression in his eyes as he looked at their daughter and felt a burning ache of love in her chest.

'She needs changing—'

'No, let me,' he said, leaning past her. 'Your dress.'

'I thought it was already ruined.'

The baby on his shoulder calmed as he patted her back. 'I was joking—you look perfect. You always look perfect.'

She laughed. 'Now I know you're lying.'

His expression grew solemn. 'You, my love, my life, are my truth.'

* * * * *

If you were captivated by
Reclaimed on Romano's Terms, *then be sure to check out these other steamy stories from Kim Lawrence!*

Her Forbidden Awakening in Greece
Awakened in Her Enemy's Palazzo
His Wedding Day Revenge
Engaged in Deception
Last-Minute Vows

Available now!

SNOWED-IN ENEMIES

BELLA MASON

MILLS & BOON

All the women who have to work harder and longer
for recognition.

All the women who have had to prove their
knowledge and passion.

All the women burdened to bear the expectations
of the world.

This one's for you.

PROLOGUE

Three years ago

THE SCREAMING REVS of V6 engines attached to cars that had more in common with a jet than anything Katherine Ward ever drove circulated around the Melbourne track. The noise, the vibration, was like a pulse in the ground. In the air. In her chest.

Katherine had made it.

All the years of study and single-minded determination had led her here: to the paddock of Alpha One. Single-seater racing was her greatest passion. A passion she shared with her father. One that she knew made him proud. And growing up, there was nothing she'd wanted more than to be an Alpha One journalist.

Now she would be doing just that.

Support cars were on track, which meant there were Alpha One drivers around who she would have to interview as the new pit lane correspondent for VelociTV. Drivers such as the world champion Lukas Jäger, who she was excited to talk to.

She could hardly control her elation. Her pounding heart. She was living her dream, and she would let nothing spoil this moment. Not even the burning anger and irritation that still lingered from earlier. Katherine had known being a woman in a male-dominated sport would be hard, but she'd hoped that good manners would prevail.

She was sorely mistaken.

Which was why she was currently in a secluded spot in the paddock, where she could breathe and find some much needed patience to deal with her VelociTV colleagues.

Katherine was the only female on the team, and she was certain if the others had anything to say about it, she wouldn't even be there. She had been excluded from the dinners at the hotel restaurant. The night before, the others had gotten a table with enough seating for only them and considering they had an uneven number of people, it must have been a deliberate arrangement. So she had sat by herself, quietly stewing until she was joined by two other women. Both of whom were Alpha One engineers, and now, valued contacts.

But it hadn't ended there. With the internet abuzz with the sexist comments made by back-marker driver Roman Poulet, conversation had been steering towards the topic for days.

'He's right,' her producer had said as he stood by the OB van earlier today. 'This sport is no place for women. I can bet you anything that the rest of the team are having to pull the weight of those female engineers.'

'Not just the engineers,' her cameraman had added, 'it's the wannabe drivers too. They don't have the strength or mental fortitude for racing.'

'Or understanding. I refuse to believe any woman could understand this sport like we can.'

Katherine had heard enough. She'd known they could see her examining the equipment that she would have to carry around as she did the day before. She hadn't been trying to hide her presence. She'd walked away then.

It had been clear they didn't want her around and being so new, there hadn't been much she could say to defend herself or any other woman in the sport. Which was why she was trying her very best to calm herself and thicken her skin. It didn't matter what they thought, she knew this sport inside out and she wasn't going anywhere.

She was just about to leave her place of refuge when her every cell went on high alert. She turned to find Lukas Jäger strolling through the paddock, chatting with Roman Poulet. The man who'd said women belonged in the home. That a woman could never physically compete with him. A man that raced for a back-marker team because he was too slow to earn a seat higher up on the grid.

All the Zen she'd attempted to achieve melted into disappointment as she watched Lukas smiling at whatever Roman was saying to him. Roman was a problem the sport was scrambling to fix and yet here was Lukas making no effort to keep his distance. He hadn't made a statement condemning Roman's opinions either.

Was this a secret side of the champion? Did he hold similar beliefs to Roman? The two of them seemed friendly and Katherine wondered if this was a case of 'birds of a feather.'

She stored the information away for a possible story. But right now, she needed to make her way to the press area.

Once she was miked up with her cameraman behind her, Katherine put on her brightest smile, speaking to as many drivers as she could, waiting for her moment to speak to the champion.

And then it was happening. Lukas Jäger was about to enter the pen.

Almost in slow motion, she saw him walk towards her, his manager by his side, her anticipation ramping up. *This* was what she had worked so hard for. It was only the second day of the season opener, but she had so many questions for Lukas.

She never took her eyes off him. She couldn't. He was magnetic. So she saw when he looked at her and his expression turned cold, his brows drawing in a frown. The antithesis to how broadly he had smiled with Roman. She'd wondered if they held similar beliefs and Katherine felt like she was getting her answer.

She saw him mutter something to his manager and attempt to turn away, but almost instantly her producer was there, and she held her breath hoping he was trying to convince Lukas to give her a moment. Ultimately, they all wanted great footage for VelociTV.

Her hands wrung the microphone in a hard grip. It was the only sign of her anxiety, because she had to remain calm. Professional.

And then her heart sank.

Lukas walked away.

She watched his retreating back in utter disbelief. Never in all the years that she'd spent building her career had anyone refused to speak to her.

'Come with me.'

She startled at her producer's words, spoken right beside her. Uneasiness crept in her belly. What had Lukas said? She wanted to know what was happening but didn't dare speak as she followed him to the OB van.

'Everyone out,' he instructed, leaving Katherine alone with him. Then the door slid shut.

'We took you on because your lecturer vouched for you,' her producer said. 'Asked us to give you a chance. But that means nothing if the drivers won't talk to you. You're no good to us if the *reigning champion* won't talk to you. You're done here. You're fired.'

'What?' Katherine cried out in disbelief, utterly shocked at the gross overreaction. 'You can't be serious. You can't just fire me! I've done my job. Who doesn't want to talk to me?'

'Lukas Jäger. He's competitive. He's always competitive, always going to be in the title hunt, which means we'll be speaking to him a lot. That makes you a liability. So yes, I can fire you.' He stated it as if Katherine's world imploding made no difference at all.

'Did Jäger actually tell you this?' Katherine demanded. She

didn't understand why he would refuse to speak to her. Even if he was secretly against women in the sport, he had given interviews to women before. So why was he singling her out? Regardless of his reasons, his word shouldn't be enough to get her fired...but she suspected what was really going on.

'Or is this a convenient way for you to get rid of me? Don't think I haven't noticed how I'm the only woman reporting on Alpha One for VelociTV, or the way you all speak about the handful of female correspondents here. How you think the female strategists and engineers are somehow a liability. Just be honest!'

'First of all, yes, Lukas did say that to me. Second, you're no longer employed, so I don't care what you think. If you're going to be sensitive about it, go cry on some talk show. Give me back your pass. You're out of here.'

Katherine pulled off her lanyard, tossed it at him and threw open the van door. As she walked away, she tried to leash the utter devastation coursing through her. She'd gotten to live her dream so briefly before having it ripped from her, thanks to a misogynistic ass who happened to drive a car well.

That was fine, because this wasn't the end. She would find a way to show the world exactly who Lukas Jäger was.

CHAPTER ONE

THE CLACKING OF quick-fire typing on a mechanical keyboard died with an enthusiastic punch of the enter key.

'Done,' Katherine said to herself in the stillness of her home office. The sounds of London beyond the window returned in full force after the vacuous silence of moments before. The shelves of her office—lined with books and Lego plants, the only type she didn't kill—rematerialising as she came back from the place she disappeared into whenever she wrote an article. She was exceptionally proud of this one. A feature on Lukas Jäger, former Alpha One champion, currently without a drive for next year, and the man she hated more than anyone else.

Katherine was arguably one of the most popular journalists in the paddock. But it hadn't always been that way. She'd worked hard to become a key part of the presenter team of the official broadcaster, Aero TV. A position that had also won her her very own column on the network's sporting site.

It hadn't all been smooth sailing. Lukas Jäger was the reason for that. The reason she had been fired from her first position as an on-track correspondent for VelociTV, a smaller, but well-respected motorsport news network.

She still remembered that day three years ago when he'd taken one look at her, turned around and walked away. She remembered the hope that had filled her when she saw her producer talk to him, thinking that maybe he would convince a media-shy driver to give her five minutes of his time. But that had never happened. That day her producer shattered her dream.

You're no good to us if the reigning champion won't talk to you. You're done here. You're fired.

Reporting on Alpha One had been Katherine's dream job, the sport a point of connection with her father. Something that was just for the two of them. Growing up, it was during those races that he'd noticed her, given her the attention she so craved but wouldn't ask for. Then because of an entitled chauvinist, that dream had almost died before it had even really begun. And she couldn't speak about her experience because she'd had to make sure another network or publication would hire her afterwards. One where a 'sensitive woman'— which the misogynists would undoubtedly call her—might be no more welcome than at VelociTV.

To protect her dream, she'd had to remain hireable.

Now here she was, writing a feature on the man whose name had constantly been churning in the rumour mill, whether he would secure a drive next season or if his career was over. And she hadn't held back.

Regardless of how Katherine felt about Lukas Jäger, she was a professional and, giving her article a once-over, she was satisfied with the balance of her reporting. She had presented the facts. Feeling more than a little pleased, she submitted her article, then took a look at the gold smartwatch on her wrist.

She smiled. 'I'll be early to dinner.' A dinner with her family that she had been looking forward to all week. Well, it was more her parents that she had been keen to see.

She picked up her phone to send a message to the family chat to say she was on her way when she noticed her father's message.

Dinner is postponed. Paige got into a spot of trouble. Sorry.
Love you, Kittykat.

'Of course,' Kat breathed. Her high from moments before dulled into the ever-familiar disappointment that came
attached to mentions of her sister. Her twin sister. People
often thought twins had to be close. That they would have to
be alike and have a near telepathic connection, but that had
never been the case with them. Where Katherine had succeeded, Paige had languished. When Katherine had chosen
the path of academics and responsibility, Paige had chosen to
party and move in the wrong crowd. And yet Paige was the
one doted on by Christopher, their big brother. Paige was the
fun one Nicholas—her younger brother that Katherine had
helped raise—wanted to spend time with. Her parents had
focussed most of their time on her siblings, especially Paige,
because they needed it more than her.

Katherine was used to this. It wasn't a big deal, she always
had work to do.

And as if the universe had heard her thoughts, the phone
in her hand began to ring, flashing her producer's name.

'Hi, Robert,' she greeted.

'Kat, I need you to pack.'

'Okay. Should I come by the office?' Because of course
there would be a meeting—an urgent one, by the sounds of
it. And since her dinner plans had fallen through, there was
no reason she couldn't drop everything and rush over before Robert had even uttered a summons. She glanced at her
watch. 'I can be there in twenty minutes.'

'Good. Bring everything with you. You'll be flying out
straight after.'

Well, there went dinner, but if Katherine was honest with
herself, she would much rather work than sit at a table where
she was reminded how different she was from her siblings.

How she would never relate to them like they did with each other. If she was working, it would mean that she was being responsible. Ensuring that she was successful. Being the daughter her parents never had to worry about. The one who would one day take care of them in their old age because her siblings wouldn't be able to. Take care of Paige, the free spirit—a nice way of saying 'selfish and irresponsible.' Katherine had to. Her parents would never be able to retire, never be able to relax if there wasn't a safety net for Paige. They would always be run ragged.

At least, thanks to Paige, Katherine wouldn't have to run out on dinner, leaving behind a father who was proud of his Alpha One journalist daughter and a mother who was disappointed that Katherine wouldn't settle down to a quiet life of marriage and children. Bear the grandchildren she so desperately wanted that Katherine had no interest in. They had their hands full tonight.

'What's the rush? What am I covering?' Katherine asked, her curiosity well and truly piqued at the urgency. The season was over. Teams were on winter break. News was less urgent right now. Well, apart from the fact that a couple teams hadn't confirmed their driver line-up for next season yet. It was unheard of for them to wait quite so long but she had a sneaking suspicion that Lukas was at least a part of the reason why.

'Lukas Jäger's publicity stunt.'

She let out a noise of frustration. 'Robert… Anyone but Lukas.'

'I don't care, Kat. You will be there interviewing him,' her producer said firmly. 'It's a closed track, he'll be driving, you'll be asking questions.'

The very last thing she wanted was to be stuck in a car with him for hours on end.

'Viewers love seeing you two together and we're going to leverage that.'

She knew what the viewers thought. It was in the comments of every social media post that showed them together.

Wouldn't it be amazing if Lukas and Katherine dated?

There's something between Lukas and Katherine. I guarantee it.

#lukat for life!

There absolutely was something between her and Lukas: mutual hatred.

'I have no choice, do I?'

'None.'

You're doing this for your career. You need to be a success. You're not going to end up like Mum.

'Fine,' she replied. 'Where am I going?'

'Please tell me you're joking.' Lukas Jäger stared his manager down. 'I'm not going to Lapland with Katherine Ward, Dominic. Anyone but her.'

'Tough.'

Lukas let out a growl of frustration and walked away from his friend. The man who had managed his career from the moment he graduated from karting at fourteen and was ready to step into the feeder series. Now at thirty-three, he'd known Dominic for two decades, trusted him, and yet couldn't remember a time when he'd been more annoyed with the man than he was right now.

He stepped out onto the terrace of his Carré d'Or penthouse apartment looking out at Monaco, the bite of the chilly December air on his skin a welcome distraction.

Lukas didn't want to be anywhere near Katherine. He had worked so hard, his family had sacrificed so much for him to achieve this life. To be an Alpha One world champion. And he had done it not once, but thrice. But that didn't matter to Katherine. She'd taken every opportunity to cast doubt on his talent, on his character, on his commitment. So much so that he could see how it affected the way people treated him. Affected how many offers he received from teams, because it cast doubt on his talent…his ability to race in the future. When he'd lost his seat at the team, she'd gone out of her way to promote the driver who had taken his place. It had massively impacted the way the public viewed the change.

Footsteps sounded behind him but he didn't turn to look at Dominic. Instead, he folded his fingers around the metal railing that wrapped all the way around his three-storey apartment.

'You know how I feel about her,' Lukas said, eyes fixed on the steel-coloured water.

'I do, but, Lukas, this has been a bad season…'

'You—'

'It was a bad season because you didn't win the championship. Yes, we both know the car was a big reason for that,' Dominic said, cutting him off and coming to stand beside him. 'The second half of the season did a lot of damage. You had no pace in that car to mount any kind of challenge, and I know what it took for you to drag it to the podium. But regardless of the reason, you lost your drive. You need some good PR.'

'She's the reason I need good PR, Dom.' Lukas turned to face his manager. 'The shit she's been saying about Easton Rivers is exactly why no one cares how unfair it was that I lost my seat.'

'I get that, Lukas,' Dominic said patiently. 'But the things she says are true. Easton Rivers won his junior championship, he showed pace in his tests…'

'None of that matters!' Lukas raged. 'He's Thomas Dudek's driver. Dudek created a seat in the team he runs for the driver he manages! By dumping me!'

'I know, Lukas.'

'Plus, Easton comes with money. Dudek didn't have to give

him my seat. Easton could have bought one! He could use all that sponsorship money for a back-marker team like Brock Racing who would gladly paste the name of his backers on their car. Those teams are uncompetitive, he could make a difference there and pay his dues. And what about the fact that we were promised a contract renewal? I met with Dudek, he assured me that there was no truth to Katherine's reports about Rivers taking my place. That it was all rumours.' Lukas paced like a caged animal.

'I had a similar conversation with him,' Dominic agreed.

'And we have no recourse? You know there is only one reason he waited until all the top teams' seats were filled before he announced Rivers as his driver.'

'I know, Lukas. You're right. He did it so that you wouldn't have a competitive seat. He knows that you would take another team to a driver's and possibly a constructor's title. I know it hurts that after all these years with the team he made you think he was announcing a renewal but announced Rivers instead. I *know*, Lukas. But we have to face reality. Your now former teammate, Will, is young and recently signed. They would never get rid of him. Not after one season and not with him being an academy driver. Not even with you finishing second and him eighth. And Rivers is in the other seat. Nothing will change that, so we need to look at alternatives. Negotiations will be difficult because you do have a "first driver" stipulation for any contract we pursue.'

Lukas slumped against the gold Art Deco porch post that served no other purpose than being decorative. 'Have I told you how much I love it when you're blunt?'

Dominic chuckled sympathetically. 'I know it isn't fair, but we need to work on what we can change. We can't undo anything that happened this year, but maybe we can salvage next year and get you something worthwhile and lucrative.'

Lucrative.

When Lukas had been a child racing around the local go-kart track in the foothills of the Ybbstal Alps of Austria in a kart his father built, with tyres cast off from rich parents looking to get rid of them, money had been the farthest thing from his mind. It had all been about the dream: to make it to Alpha One. Now so much of the negotiation revolved around money, but he would happily take a cut in earnings if it put him in a *competitive* seat. He didn't want to be at the back of the grid. He wanted to drive…and win.

He owed his father that much. Especially after he'd cost his father his marriage. A comfortable life. A stress-free life.

Would his father be disappointed in him after this nightmare of a year?

He couldn't know. Couldn't contact the dead. All Lukas *could* do was make every choice that would take him back to the sharp end of the grid.

'Whether you like it or not,' Dom went on, 'Katherine is loved by the fans, so you need to work with her. Leverage the public's opinion of the two of you.'

Lukas scoffed. 'You mean play into the idiotic fantasy of the two of us being a couple? Hell will freeze over first.'

Dominic sighed.

'Dom, you know how I feel about the media. The off-season allows me my space. My privacy. But more importantly, I don't want to be around the woman who championed the driver who took my seat. If you recall, it was Katherine who said that it was a "no-brainer" to replace me with Easton. She questioned whether other teams like Brock Racing would actually consider taking on me, a driver at the end of his career. Do you remember that?'

'I do, but think about how it will appear if the person who is so against you is in a car appearing to have a good time with you. Asking you questions to keep the world thinking about you.'

Lukas laughed as he ran a hand through his hair. He understood exactly what Dominic had done. 'You asked for her to do this, didn't you?'

His friend and manager simply smiled. 'You need to keep in the public eye to keep your prospects alive. If the teams that haven't yet finalised their line-up for next year don't consider you, you will be without a drive. And then your only option is retirement. All the reserve driver roles are taken. Every single one of them is younger than you. Even if we do manage to wrangle up some sort of additional driver position, are you going to be happy doing publicity stunts and sim work?'

'No,' Lukas admitted. But those weren't his only options. There was another. One he hadn't mentioned to Dominic or anyone because he didn't want to consider it at all.

A new team would be entering the sport next season. A small team that had approached Lukas to lead them. It would make him the youngest team principal in the sport's history. The car had less than no chance of winning in their first season, let alone scoring points, but it would be an opportunity to grow the organization and grow as a leader with it.

Lukas Jäger: boss of an Alpha One team. He couldn't picture it. Or rather, he didn't want to picture being in charge of the day-to-day running of a team. Overseeing the team and car's performance from an office and the pitwall. Lukas didn't want that. Didn't want to consider it even for a moment because it meant his career as a driver would undeniably be over. There would be no way back into the cockpit.

No way to repay his father for all the sacrifices.

'Fine. I'll go to Finland, but I have conditions.'

'I knew you would. Let's hear it.'

Lukas fought a smile at how well Dominic knew him. 'It's obvious we'll be forced to stay there at least overnight, so I want my accommodation away from Aero.'

'Fair enough. What else?'

'Katherine Ward only has access to me while we're shooting.' There was absolutely no way he was going to make it easier for her to gather ammunition on him to further spit her vitriol.

CHAPTER TWO

LUKAS STOOD AT the large wooden door of his luxury cabin, pulling up the zip of his thick insulated jacket, then buttoning up the fabric flap that covered the zipper. His feet were already in a pair of black snow-boots. Knowing how cold it could get out there, he made sure to prepare for it.

He placed his hand on the door-handle and inhaled deeply. This publicity stunt was the last thing in the world he wanted to do but here he was. There was no turning back now.

Lukas yanked open the door and stared at the wonderland that was Lapland. There were tall pine trees everywhere. Their barks taking on a greyish hue from the snow caught on every bump and knot. They were topped in white, like nature's very own dusting of powdered sugar. It was truly beautiful and, were it not for the events planned for that day, Lukas would quite happily have gone snowmobiling or sledding or snowshoeing and then returned to sit at the large window with the fire roaring and something warm clutched in his hands.

But that peaceful fantasy would never happen whilst he was forced to be around Katherine.

Lukas stepped out and shut the door behind him. There was a driver waiting in a dark four-wheel drive SUV. The most efficient way to trek across the snow was the most efficient way to get anywhere: in something with an engine. And at least that made Lukas smile.

'Good morning, Mr Jäger.' The driver, who'd donned a

thick black jacket with bright splashes of colour, greeted Lukas as he climbed into the front passenger seat.

He was far too cheerful. Especially when Lukas was dreading the next few hours.

Put on your media face, Dominic had begged when Lukas Zoom called him earlier.

'Morning,' Lukas grunted. Thankfully the driver caught the hint and said nothing more. Lukas needed to hold on to all of his finite patience if he was to make it through filming with Katherine.

Katherine.

The very thought of her name was like a poker in his frontal lobe. He tried to focus on why he was doing this. To save his career. To make his father's sacrifices worth something. To get back in an Alpha One car. He never felt so alive as he did when he blasted down the pit straight in his single-seater, at 350 kilometres an hour. The world a blur. A tunnel focussed on one point: turn one. When he got his braking just right and nailed that first apex—he always knew at that point if it was going to be a good lap or not. And then he would put those laps in. Time after time after time.

He never felt more alive, but he also never felt closer to his father. He could feel his father's pride then, and Lukas could forget for a moment that he was the reason his mother left.

He needed to race. It gave his life meaning, so he would do this. He would grin when he had to, and bear this invasion.

As they approached, Lukas could make out part of a track that had been carved and smoothed in the snow. The closer they got, the more he could see. A simple course that weaved through the trees and back again with a section over the frozen lake.

The SUV came to a stop near a two-door sports car. One that had no affiliation with any of the Alpha One teams on track. So, unlike all the other stunts he had done in his career where the cars had always been linked to his team. Another reminder that Lukas was a driver without a tether. That he needed the day to go well.

The car was bright red. Easily filmed. Dynamic in the monochrome environment. There were cameras fixed to the outside of it in several places, plus three that he could see on the inside. He and Katherine would be on show. Nowhere to hide. He couldn't allow a single expression to give away his reluctance to be there.

He stepped out of the vehicle and noticed the team of people like little black specks on a white canvas. Equipment everywhere even though he knew they would be invisible in the end result. Every one of these people would be ghosts, and all anyone would see would be him and Katherine.

Then would come the posts that set his teeth on edge. Lukat. He hated the portmanteau. The absurdity of the very idea.

'This way, Mr Jäger,' the man who had driven him said.

'It's Lukas,' he replied, looking at the profile of the corners of their track as they walked together. At least that would be fun.

'Lukas!' He heard his name being called as they reached a large tent from which the snow track was no longer visible. And, in what felt like a flash, he was surrounded by people. One attacked him with makeup while another affixed a mic to his clothes while a third and fourth briefed him on what he would be doing. For most people this would be too much, but he wasn't most people. He heard and understood every word being said, felt every swipe of the sponge on his face, was aware of exactly where the mic was clipped and the wire run. And still he felt the air change. Felt her very presence before he even saw her, and despite hating her for the things she'd written about him, for playing a part in him losing his seat, Lukas turned to find the burning blue eyes of Katherine Ward staring back at him. Her red hair, perfectly styled to look effortlessly elegant, hung over her right shoulder. Her skin was like porcelain. And her plump lips, the bottom a little fuller than top, pressed together in a thin line.

A prickle travelled under Lukas's skin but he kept looking. Looking at her jacket that appeared warm but Lukas knew it wasn't. A fashionable piece of apparel designed to look good in pictures and videos. He had seen tourists come to his town, the chilliest in Austria, dressed as she was, ill-equipped for the intense cold of the mountains which attracted thousands each year, only for them to run into trouble and rush back into town or worse, have emergency services rush out to them. The longer he looked at the jacket the more irritated he became, and he knew it was settling into his expression. An expression that was mirrored on hers.

'We'll give you two a moment while we get ready,' the director said. 'We'll start shooting with you both putting your helmets on. We only really have about two hours of good light to get everything done so we need to hustle.'

'Understood,' Katherine replied, but Lukas said nothing. All he did was cross his arms over his chest.

Katherine had watched Lukas keenly as she had approached. He stood maybe two inches shy of six feet. Though hidden in a thick jacket, his body was still clearly in peak physical shape. Light brown hair that was so very nearly blond crowned a head that sat on a thick, muscular neck. This man was an elite athlete. A weapon crafted to withstand the immense forces of an Alpha One race car, and the off-season hadn't dulled him at all. And when she saw him, she fought a shiver. A knot in her stomach that formed whenever he was close.

You're no good to us if the reigning champion won't talk to you. You're done here.

This man had been the reason she was fired and yet he had the audacity to look at her as if *she* was some irritation. The gall!

'Nice of you to join us,' she sniped.

'I'm perfectly on time,' he said, adjusting the cuff of his jacket. It was thick and bulky. Not in any way sexy. Not chosen for the cameras. He looked utterly comfortable in it. Warm. Yet she had to fight off shivers as the wind bit through her jacket. Had to look impeccable for the cameras.

Are you some incredible beauty? Because you're not getting on camera if you aren't.

Words from her university lecturer, the man who had given her the incredible reference that led to her job at VelociTV, who had promised to never hide the unspoken side of being a media personality. His words had made her go home and look at herself in the mirror, and make an effort to look good every moment of every day. Because it didn't matter how much she knew, no one would give her the time of day if she wasn't also a pretty face. If she didn't have a beach-ready body throughout the year.

So seeing Lukas's warm jacket turned that knot in her stomach into a ball of fire.

'And yet I could find it in me to get here a few minutes early.'

'That's your job, not mine.' His grey eyes looked almost bored. He hadn't uncrossed his arms. Had barely spoken to the people around him. Katherine had to be 'on' at all times. Keep that bubbly, media personality up around everyone she worked with. It was exhausting. But men like Lukas…they got to be grouchy and ill-tempered, and people would find an excuse for his behaviour. She hated it.

Hated him.

'And what is your job, Lukas? Certainly not racing. Not currently, at least.' She took great pleasure in the way his eyes narrowed. In the frown on his face. Her pulse galloped as he stalked towards her, knowing she had gotten under his skin. But nothing she said could even remotely make up for the fact that he had gotten her fired. That he had nearly destroyed her and her father's dream.

'You must be enjoying this immensely,' he said through his teeth in his hard accent. 'This is exactly what you wanted. It's right there in your little articles. "Lukas Jäger Is Done." Well, I'm not.' He stood right in front of her, making her look up into the grey eyes that looked so at home in the icy surroundings.

'I report the truth, Lukas. If you don't like it, maybe you need to look at yourself for a solution.'

'Kat!'

Whatever Lukas was about to say died as they both looked at one of the production assistants, who waved her over. She didn't bother excusing herself from him. She owed him no politeness. She simply walked away.

But she felt him follow behind. She fought off another shiver.

'Stupid jacket,' she mumbled.

'We're ready to go,' the production assistant informed her. Soon a transmitter that her lavalier mic plugged into was hidden in her clothes, sound checks were done and they were making their way to the track. Another production assistant was waiting for her and Lukas there, holding their helmets.

'Given how slow you've been this year, you should be able to manage the course easily enough. Though your edge seems to be pretty dead at this point, so we could end up in a snowbank.' Was antagonising the man who was about to drive her in a high-powered car on ice a wise move? Probably not, but Katherine had a need to make him as irritated as his presence made her even if she knew deep down that he wasn't slow. That he was as competitive as he had always been.

'You would love that, wouldn't you?' Lukas replied, snatching the helmet out of the hands of the innocent bystander, who was undeserving of his bad mood. 'After all, vultures are only happy when there's death.'

'How dare you?'

'You wanted me to face truths, maybe you should heed your own advice.' He rounded the car, helmet in hand. Katherine could feel the burn in her cheeks, but had to force the outrage down because there was a countdown in her ear. And just like that she plastered a smile on her face.

She noticed Lukas staring at her. Shaking his head in disgust. Whatever. She was here to do a job, and she would be the professional.

She placed the helmet on her head, but couldn't get the belt fastened. It wasn't a side release buckle clip as she had been expecting but rather a double D-ring and without a mirror she just couldn't figure it out with her gloved hands. She could bend down to have a look in the side mirror of the car but that would be a terrible angle and with so little good light, every frame had to be perfect.

And that's when she felt a hand on her shoulder. As if it burned straight through her jacket and singed her skin. She looked up to find Lukas, who grit his teeth before his lips relaxed into a small smile.

'It took me a while to get the hang of these while wearing gloves,' he said.

He was helping her. Why? 'It takes some practice,' she heard herself say.

He smirked. 'And I have plenty.' He reached past her to open the door, allowing her to catch a whiff of his cologne. It made her feel warm. Conjured images of a fireplace and a goblet of cognac.

She grinned, remembering they were on camera and every movement was being recorded. 'What a gentleman.'

'I hope you don't have a weak heart,' he teased when he climbed into the driver's side.

'Oh, don't you worry. It's perfectly steady.' That was a lie. It was pounding. Whether from anger or the shock of his one-eighty, her heart was anything but steady.

'We'll see about that.' There was a twinkle in his eye just as he started the car that roared to life. 'Ready?'

She checked her seat belts and nodded, ignoring how his presence filled the space. 'Let's do this!'

The engine screamed as he took off in the snow. The back end of the car fishtailed with the lack of traction and Lukas grinned. Katherine did too. She couldn't help it. His excitement was contagious but it wasn't just that, this right here was what she dreamed of as a child. Being in a fast car with an Alpha One driver in the most unimaginable places and she whooped in delight as they drifted around a corner, a tree flashing by in a blur. And she heard Lukas chuckle. A deep rumble that seemed to come straight from his chest.

'Okay, Lukas, you still need to answer these questions,' she said for the cameras.

'Not if you can't read them.'

He dropped a gear and floored the gas, nearly sending them into a spin that he controlled effortlessly, even though it nearly sent her papers flying. He laughed harder than she had ever heard before. But even with him trying to make her job difficult, she managed to ask all the questions she had prepared and some that she thought of in the moment, and when the car came to a stop where they had started, the director yelled 'Cut!'

'That was fantastic! You two were great!'

'Yeah,' the production assistant agreed. 'Viewers are going to *love* this, Kat.'

Once she and Lukas stepped out, whatever truce they had

found within the confines of the car was obliterated. The scowl was back on his face.

'We just need to do one more take of the ice section and then take it from there,' the director said.

'You have to be kidding,' Lukas groused. 'Why?'

'We have great footage of you and Kat in the car but had some technical difficulties with one of the exterior cameras, so we're just swapping that out and we'll be good to go. You two can get back in the car in the meantime.'

The man walked away and Katherine retrieved her helmet from the assistant, who still stood close by.

'This is ridiculous,' Lukas muttered, drumming his fingers on the roof of the car.

This man was so aggravating. 'You know this entire stunt benefits you, Lukas. You could stand to be more gracious about it.' She jammed the helmet on her head and let the assistant do up the straps this time. 'I have it so much worse. I have to be stuck in that car with you, but you don't see *me* complaining.'

'Oh please,' Lukas snapped. 'What do you have to complain about? Your face is on TV. You'll get enough content from this to fuel more of your distorted reports.'

'My reports aren't distorted. No one else has a problem with them, it's only you! And you know what?' She stepped away from the assistant and rounded on Lukas, the car between them. 'It's entirely your own fault. *You* didn't win the championship. *You* are difficult to work with. There's plenty of footage proving you could be nice if you wanted to be, but you don't.'

Which was why Katherine was proud of the article she had written. After it came out, the world would question the kind of person Lukas really was. Because if they could see him now, there was no doubt in her mind that others would question his authenticity too. 'This is who you are. A grouchy, unfriendly, snob. Those nice things you do for fans, it's a farce. You're a two-faced hypocrite and it's my job to report on the truth.'

A two-faced hypocrite?

That was what Lukas got for trying. He hated being in front of the cameras. Inviting people into his life. Allowing strangers to attempt to read him. Performing with a smile when his skin crawled at the idea of being in the media.

Lukas didn't even really have social media. He had profiles that his publicist managed. He gave them a few hours of his time to create content and he never had to document his private life for anyone.

But here he was, in his time off. Time that he usually used to decompress from life in the fast lane. When he could relax and breathe and put the hyper-competitive side of him away. When he made time for his mother, just in case, even though he knew she wouldn't call. Wouldn't ask him to visit her in Salzburg.

Right now Lukas couldn't do any of those things. His need to find a drive forced him to be in situations like these, where he had to spend time with the media he so detested.

They were always so unfair to him, but he just had to bear it. And yet Katherine had the audacity to call him a hypocrite? Say *he* was the one who wasn't gracious?

'What would you know about the truth?' he spat and got in the car before she had a chance to respond. When they called 'action' again, he poured his frustration into the car. Felt the very instant the front tyre went from contact with compacted snow to ice. When the car began to slide. Heard Katherine squeal. In delight. In panic. He didn't care. She was far away to him now, because in the moment he was a young boy in a kart his father had built with used, cast-off tyres—the only tyres they could afford—on a small icy track close to home.

And he was free. Ice, snow, a fine spray of water flew out from beneath his tyres and this was love. This was the feeling he chased. In that moment, he could have almost sworn that he saw his father standing on the side, cheering as no one else ever did. He couldn't abandon this feeling to be a team principal. Couldn't turn his back on the memories of his father. He felt Florian's presence when he drove.

Lukas could hear Katherine talk. Was certain he was answering her. If it wasn't for the fact they had to wrap up filming, he would have happily spent the rest of the day out on this frozen lake.

'That was incredible!' was the first thing Lukas heard when he got out of the car. 'This segment is going to be amazing.'

It probably would be, but would it be enough to create more of a buzz around him to get his phone ringing?

'We have a little bit of good light left so we were thinking of shooting one more segment. Get some action shots. Those would be great for promos. Maybe Kat can drive,' the director said.

That caught Lukas's attention. 'What?'

'There's a storm coming later so if we could get extra footage, it would be great.'

'I love the idea!' Katherine beamed.

Of course she did.

'Absolutely not,' Lukas said in a voice he rarely used. 'I'm not trusting her to drive this—' he patted the car '—out there. I'm not risking an injury.' He counted down the seconds to Katherine's explosion in his head. It was barely two.

'Excuse me!' Katherine very nearly shouted.

'Um…yes…well,' the field producer said, 'it would still be good to get those extra shots, so you two can head over to the tent for some touch-ups and a warm drink. We'll call for you when we're ready.' He and the director walked away, leaving Lukas and Katherine to head for the tent set beyond the tree-line, well away from where they filmed.

'You're such a misogynist!' Katherine accused as soon as they were away from the rest of the team. No one around to see them eviscerate each other. 'Just because I'm a woman you assume that I'll be a bad driver. God!' She was quite literally red in the face.

Lukas was well and truly tired of how lowly Katherine thought of him.

'It's not because you're a woman. It's because you're you. I don't trust *you*.' He wouldn't trust anyone from this crew in those conditions. Things very easily went from fun to dangerous on a track, never mind a frozen lake and snowy landscape where the trees beckoned.

Lukas sought thrills, but he was never reckless.

'I cannot be around you for one minute longer, Lukas Jäger,' Katherine huffed. She turned around and stormed off.

'Where are you going? That's not where the tent is,' Lukas called.

'Away from you!' she yelled back.

Fine. Let her go off. She wasn't his concern.

CHAPTER THREE

KATHERINE DISAPPEARED FROM VIEW.

Lukas just wanted to be done with the day. Time alone would be welcome, but Katherine having walked away left him feeling uneasy.

He felt the direction of the wind change. Knew there was a storm incoming that night. They should all be away from there by the time it happened but then he thought of that ridiculous jacket Katherine was wearing and cursed. She should be safe…but the mountains he'd grown up around should have been safe too, and he still remembered careless tourists perishing while trying to explore.

They weren't in Austria now. Nor were they in London. Storming off was a stupid thing for Katherine to do and try as he might, Lukas's conscience wouldn't let him leave without knowing she was okay.

He cursed once more for good measure and walked in the direction that Katherine had gone, then stopped. A rope, coiled loosely, sat in the snow. Someone from the production team must have dropped it there with the intention of fetching it later. Instinct from living so close to the mountains took over and he picked it up, draping it over his shoulder, then set off to look for the woman he hated more than anyone else.

'Katherine!' he called, after walking for ages and seeing no sign of her. The wind had picked up speed and glancing overhead, he saw that dark, ominous clouds had gathered. The storm was coming in much faster than they had anticipated and by the looks of it, would be worse too.

'Katherine!' he called again. Louder. He needed to find her soon because they wouldn't have much time to find shelter. Then he thought, what if she wasn't answering because it was him who was calling? He could see her being that petty. Everyone else on the shoot had called her 'Kat.' Even in the paddock hardly anyone used her full name. But Lukas did. He always did.

So as he walked a little farther, he shouted 'Kat!' as loud as he could manage.

'I'm here!' came a soft, strained response and his body simultaneously sagged in relief and went on high alert.

'I'm coming! Keep talking!'

'I'm in a crevasse. I fell.'

Lukas's body went cold. Those were the last words he wanted to hear. He ran in the direction of her voice, sliding to a stop as snow sprayed over the edge of a narrow gap like a powdery waterfall.

Lukas lay on his stomach, flattening himself on the snow and crawling slowly to the edge. Peering in, he saw Katherine on a ledge.

'Lu-Lu-Lukas?' she could barely get his name out for how badly she was shivering. Her skin was bright red. The edges of her lips where she had bitten off her lipstick were starting to turn slightly blue. He needed to get her out now.

'Are you hurt?'

'I hurt my ankle when I fell but otherwise, I'm okay.'

That was a relief to hear. 'Hang on, I'll get you out.' Lukas looked around. There were no trees where they had come. Nothing but snow in all directions. This was less than ideal. He would have to be the anchor to pull Katherine up. He couldn't afford for anything to go wrong. How ironic it was that he hadn't wanted Katherine to drive, because he didn't trust her in a car on a safe track, and yet now, if anything went wrong it could be the end of them both.

Lukas grabbed the rope, tying a figure eight knot like his father had taught him, ensuring the loop at the end was big enough to go around Katherine, and made his way back to the edge.

'Put the loop around you,' he instructed as he lowered the rope down. Once it was around her torso and her shoulders free, he gave her the next set of instructions. 'Hold on to the rope tightly. Don't try to climb it, I will pull you up. Got it?'

Katherine nodded.

'Yes or no. I need to know you understand.'

'Yes,' she said, through chattering teeth.

Once he was satisfied that she was following his instructions, he moved away from the edge lest he fall too, and pulled. One hand over the other. The rope burned his palms but he didn't care. He was singularly focussed. He pulled, and kept pulling until he saw hands and the top of a jacket hood emerge. Lukas, keeping tension with one hand, lunged with his other and grabbed ahold of Katherine's forearm, pulling her out of the crevasse and placing her safely on the snowy ground.

'Th-th-thank y-y-you,' she stuttered through chattering teeth. Lukas knew he had to get her warm immediately.

He ignored her thanks. Instead he looked her over for any signs of injury. Anything that could complicate their next mission: finding refuge from the storm. The wind was already whipping around them.

'Can you stand?' he asked as he helped her to her feet.

'I think so,' Katherine replied but struggled to keep her balance as she hobbled two steps in the snow. The wind was picking up the snow on the surface and curling it around them. They didn't have time to hobble. And with her shaking so badly, progress would be slow. Lukas had only one choice. He placed his arms around her back and under her knees, then lifted her against his chest. His body came to life as if he'd been struck with a bolt of electricity the moment he held her to him. He ignored the feeling, not willing to analyse it when there were more important things at hand.

Her body, racked by shivers, trembled in his arms and he cursed her ridiculous jacket. There was nothing he could do about it now except fight his way through the storm that was already upon them. And as hard as it was to struggle through the wind and snow that was stinging his face, it was nowhere close to as bad as it would get.

Lukas noticed Katherine's eyes starting to droop.

'Don't sleep,' he instructed.

'I'm so tired,' she slurred.

That wasn't good.

'Talk to me.' He needed to keep her awake.

'About what?' Snowflakes landed on her lashes and he had to fight the urge to brush them away. He had to keep walking. The cabins weren't far from the track. He just had to keep going and he would get them there.

'Eyes open,' he commanded, and she obeyed. Blue irises peered at him through half-closed lids. His heart rate sped up, which was ridiculous. He wasn't exerting himself enough for it to do so this frantically. 'Anything.'

'I like polar bears.'

'There are no polars bears here.'

'That's a shame.'

There were no polar bears but there were trees. Trees he recognised and as Lukas made his way through them, he saw the cabins come into view.

Cabins that were dark even though the vehicles were out front. It made sense for his cabin, there was no one there, but not the other.

Lukas climbed up the front steps to the small porch that was already covered in a layer of snow and, balancing Katherine's body against his, managed to open the door. When he stepped inside, he saw that nothing had been packed up. Items that belonged to the crew lay on several surfaces but there was no fire in the fireplace. No lights switched on.

'Hello?' Lukas called but no answer returned.

The crew were gone.

They were alone.

When they realised how close the storm was, they would have likely been airlifted out. And Lukas was annoyed. Annoyed that the production team had been operating on outdated information. Annoyed that Katherine had stormed off because no one had seen them walk away. The evacuation would likely have been chaotic. Lukas was certain both teams would have just assumed that he and Katherine were with the other. Their absence would only have been noticed once everyone was together. And now, with no one on the team having any idea where they could be, they would be deemed missing.

No one would come looking for them in a blizzard. No rescue would risk more lives for the chance of finding them.

'I hope you're happy now,' he grumbled but Katherine's response was unintelligible. Her skin getting a bluish tinge.

'Dammit!' He placed Katherine gently on one of the couches and raced to the closest room where he ripped a thick duvet from the bed and returned to her. 'I need to get you out of these clothes.' A sentence he never thought he'd say.

The snow had dampened them, making them a hazard. He removed her jacket first, flinging it across the room as if it was to blame for all that had befallen them. He took off her shoes then stripped off her socks, blouse, jeans and lastly her thermals, exposing her fair skin. Her toned body. Soft dips and peaks of her abdominals that she obviously worked hard for. Lukas had never thought he would ever be in this position: exposing Katherine like this. Once maybe, for a fleeting moment when he first saw her in the paddock and was struck by her absolute beauty. But he hadn't spoken to her. He hadn't wanted to. He hadn't wanted to be attracted to someone he would never allow in his life. Not when he was already in a vulnerable place. And now here he was, wanting to run the backs of his fingers down her face, along her body.

But he couldn't do that. He wouldn't. Not when they hated each other so much. Not when he knew she wouldn't want him to touch her at all if they weren't in this emergency. This want was a physical reaction and he was able to control his body. So he checked that her underwear was dry and when he was satisfied that it was, he wrapped her in the duvet.

He cradled her face, forcing her to look at him. 'I need you to stay awake. Can you do that for me?'

She nodded her head yes, then shook her head no.

'Try.'

He left her on the couch and went to the fireplace. Thankfully there were dry logs stacked beside it and he quickly got a roaring flame burning.

'That should do it.' He stood and stripped his own clothes, then picked up Katherine and sat with her on the rug in front of the fire with his back against the sofa. Her skin scalded his despite how cold she was. And with tense muscles, he wrapped the duvet around them both.

'You're freezing,' he said, wrapping his warm legs around her cold ones and rubbing her chest, trying his best to get warmth into her. But the contact of her skin on his made him tingle everywhere they touched. He ignored it. It was just the temperature difference that made him feel that way. Nothing more. She was the reason they were in this situation at all but when he looked down at her half-open eyes that looked like they were barely seeing anything, some of that anger melted away. He just needed her to warm up. To get her fire back.

Why do you care?

Lukas had no answer. All he knew was that he needed her to be okay. That he would only feel relief once she was bickering with him again. He didn't want to recognise how good he felt having her in his arms. This embrace, while it wracked him with worry, also calmed him. His mind had been going a million miles an hour since his contract hadn't been renewed, but right now, he didn't think about how he had been wronged. All he thought about was Katherine.

He could feel her slowly warming up, so it was probably safe to leave her long enough to make her a hot tea.

'Are you still with me?' he asked softly over her shoulder.

'Hmm' was all the reply he got.

'Can you sit here by yourself for a bit?' He tried to push off the warm rug, but Katherine's weak grip tightened around his wrist.

'No. Please don't go.'

Lukas could feel the shock on his face. Here was the woman who hated him asking him to stay. That look of vulnerability on her face, lit only by the fire in the dark cabin, was difficult to bear.

'I'm just going to get you some tea.'

'Stay with me,' she begged. 'Please.'

And against his better judgement, he sat back down, adjusting both their bodies so they were lying on the rug. Warm.

'I'm not going anywhere,' he promised, knowing how temporary a promise it was because as soon as she was back to normal, as soon as it was safe, he would very definitely go back to keeping his distance from her. This reporter who— no matter how beautiful she was—was as unscrupulous as they came.

CHAPTER FOUR

WARMTH. TOO MUCH WARMTH. Katherine could feel heat radiating on her back. A heavy weight draped over her. A weaker heat warming her face. None of this made sense.

She forced her eyes open and as her sight cleared, saw the dying embers in a fireplace she had no recollection of settling before. That was obviously the source of the warmth on her face but couldn't be responsible for the heat on her back. And as the fog lifted from her brain, she felt the softness of a cushion under her head. The hard, unyielding muscle of a well-toned arm under her neck. Another arm over her torso.

Heart racing with confusion and apprehension, Katherine followed the line of the muscular arm to a bare, sculpted chest. She shut her eyes.

'Please, God, don't let it be who I think it is,' she prayed and when she opened her eyes, was met with the sleeping face of Lukas Jäger. She swore and tried to push away, but when she threw the thick duvet off herself, she saw that she was only in her underwear and clutched the covers to her chest.

'Calm down,' a sleepy voice said. She watched him roll to his feet, clad only in a pair of tight black boxer briefs.

'Please tell me we didn't,' she whispered tightly.

'Relax. I prefer my partners a lot less comatose.'

'What the hell happened last night?' She couldn't remember coming back to the cabin. Scrunching her eyes shut, she tried to piece her memory together. She'd stormed off after their argument and hadn't noticed the crack in the snow that gave way when she stepped on the edge of it. She'd twisted her ankle.

She shoved the covers off her foot to examine the injury, noting that the joint was only slightly swollen and nowhere near as tender as it had been.

'It's not sprained or broken. The muscle tenderness should go away in a day or two,' Lukas said. He was obviously watching her but she couldn't look at him. He had pulled her from the crevasse but her memories after that were foggy. She couldn't remember how they'd gotten back.

'Why am I almost naked? Where are my clothes? Where is everyone? Why are *you* here?'

'I'm here,' Lukas said lowly, 'because I'm the only one who came to find you. Because everyone else left before the storm hit. You're almost naked, Katherine, because if I hadn't removed your clothes, you would have developed hypothermia and I really didn't want your death on my conscience.'

'You removed my clothes? You looked at me?' The thought of being in that vulnerable position with Lukas of all people was horrifying.

'I'm an Alpha One racing driver. I think I am perfectly capable of removing your clothes without looking.' His nonchalance was triggering.

'Turn around,' she snapped and tossed off the duvet to go in search of her clothes. 'So you took off my wet clothes and planted me by a fire.' The thought of having spent the entire night in Lukas's arms made lava flow through her veins.

Why would the Fates send the man she hated the most to rescue her? Why would he stay with her? He never wanted to be around her. He would never have done this out of the goodness of his heart. The man who got her fired had no heart.

She shoved her legs into her thermals and then into the jeans that were nearby. Why did you stay?' She hastily put on her blouse but now that she was no longer under the covers with Lukas or close to the embers, her skin erupted in goose bumps. She needed her jacket but it was nowhere to be found.

She heard Lukas's mirthless laughter. 'So ungrateful to the one person who kept you alive,' he spat.

Katherine caught a glimpse of the jacket on the floor, finding it balled up. Obviously having been thrown. Evidence of Lukas's anger at having helped her. 'Because why would you? You do nothing without an ulterior motive. The only reason you're even here in Lapland is because doing publicity suited you. How does helping me suit you?' She turned around to find Lukas fully dressed. His eyes flashing as they raked over her jacket.

'It doesn't suit me,' he gritted out. 'But I'm not an animal who would leave someone to die as you seem to be insinuating.' He turned towards her, grey eyes offended. Angry. An icy fire burning in them. 'You try to turn the world against me…' A step towards her. '…insult me…' Another step. The air slowly being sucked out of the room. '…could not even bother to thank me for saving your life when it's your fault we're in this mess.' One more step. Why did he loom so large? 'Your fault the world will be thinking that we're missing. *I* am the reason we made it out of that storm. So push me away.' He was in front of her now. 'Slap me across the face for undressing you and tell me to leave you.' He crowded her against the wall. Katherine wasn't breathing. An electrical storm brewed in the space between them. 'But you can't, can you? Because I'm the only one here.'

He had a point, but she couldn't give in to him. She couldn't *not* fight him. She couldn't give him the benefit of the doubt. Not ever. 'No one asked you to be here and I didn't turn the world against you. I told the truth, Easton Rivers is the future of that team. You aren't.'

Lukas shook his head. Katherine could feel the passion of

his hate burning in his gaze. 'You still can't say "Thank you for saving me, Lukas. Thank you for not letting me succumb to hypothermia and ending my miserable career that way."'

Maybe he was right about that one point, but she couldn't get her mouth to form around the words. So she said nothing.

Of course, she said nothing. Lukas expected nothing less. She couldn't show him gratitude and she couldn't be apologetic for what she had written even though she knew he was still fully capable of winning another championship.

He pushed off the wall, needing to get away from her. Needing space, but that was secondary to *their* most important need, which was surviving. So whether or not she thanked him, it made no difference to what he had to do.

'Get a fire going in the kitchen stove.' He forced himself to be calm. To push aside his anger and frustration. He had to clear head. 'I'm going to see if I can call for help.'

'You mean you haven't tried yet?' Katherine accused.

'No, and you should be glad of it because if I had, you'd be dead or comatose.' How different she was now to the woman who had begged him not to leave her. He could throw that in her face. Tell her how she'd clung to him, but what good would that do?

Lukas left her standing in the open plan living area to search the cabin for anything he could use. If he could just get word out that they were safe, he could get ahead of any crazy stories that might spread through the media. He could get word to Dominic…and his mother. Would she be worried?

He went through each room. Opened every cupboard. Searched every drawer until he found the answer to his prayers. A handheld radio. Lukas turned the device on and the screen lit up in blue. The battery still held some charge. He was about to try calling for help on it, try every frequency he could, but he couldn't do so alone in that room. Katherine had a right to hear what he found as well. She also wouldn't believe him no matter what he reported, so he took it into the kitchen and sat at the table. The chair slightly scraping the wooden floor caught Katherine's attention and she approached the table that now had the radio and Lukas's cell phone side by side. He tapped his phone screen—the status bar read 'No service.' He'd known it would, but he had to see it again anyway.

'Have you tried it yet?' There was hope in her voice.

Lukas shook his head. 'I thought you would like to be present if I managed to get through to anyone. Understand, it's a long shot.'

Katherine nodded. Lukas picked up the radio, praying it would work, and tried calling out but all he got back was static. He tried a different frequency but it was the same. And another and another.

His stomach sank and he realised how hopeful he'd been that it would work. Hope was dangerous in a situation like this. 'We just have to wait it out.'

He scrubbed a hand down his face. He had no idea how long the storm would last. It wasn't blowing as hard now as it had been the night before, but it was still impossible for anyone to be moving around in that weather, which meant he had no idea how long he would be stuck with Katherine. A woman so stubborn that she hadn't even started the fire in the stove. Certain she was just being difficult, he did it himself with gritted teeth.

'You need a better jacket and to drink something hot,' he said curtly as he closed the stove door. The flames beyond the glass licked the fresh logs, scorching the surfaces black.

'You may have assisted me last night, Lukas, and I am grateful, but *you* do not get to tell me what to do.' She crossed her arms over her chest, leaning against the kitchen table, refusing to look at the stove at all.

'What?' The nerve of this woman. He could have gone back to his own cabin. He would have been happier there but he'd stayed to make sure she was alright.

'You heard me. I'm a grown woman. I can take care of myself.'

Lukas threw the lighter that was in his hand on the table with loud clatter. 'You know what? Have at it. At least in my cabin I'll have some peace.' He stormed to the door. 'Good luck.' He didn't even bother looking back as he opened the door to howling wind and slammed it shut behind him.

CHAPTER FIVE

KATHERINE WATCHED HIM LEAVE. Heard the glass rattle from the force.

'Great!' she yelled at the closed door, relieved to see him go. Her chest rose and fell as if she had run a sprint. That was how Lukas affected her, how much he agitated her, and in his absence she could slowly calm down. But in the wake of his leaving, it had grown quiet.

'I don't need him,' she said to herself. 'I've been on my own for years.'

She could hear her every breath. Feel the chill settling on her skin once more.

'I need to get warmer.' The kitchen stove had already begun warming the cabin but it wasn't enough. She went to the large fireplace, happy to find that some of the embers were still glowing. It wouldn't take much for the fire to get going again but when she went to retrieve wood from the storage beside the fireplace, she noticed just how low she was running. Obviously Lukas had used some the night before and again to get the stove going, but that left her with very little and when she walked to the back door of the cabin and peered outside, everything was covered in a thick layer of snow. Where on earth would she find more wood? They were supposed to have left this morning. This was never meant to have been a concern for her.

'I could go outside and look for more logs,' she mumbled

to herself, but her ankle was still tender, so she could run into trouble. The last thing she needed or wanted was Lukas's help again. She'd only just got rid of him.

He left in this weather to walk to his cabin.

'That's not my problem!' she half yelled. 'He could have been pleasant but he never is.' She walked away from the door. 'It's fine. I need to keep what I have for that stove.' She glanced over at the large cast iron appliance. The red-gold flame dancing behind the glass. She had never used one of these things before. When Lukas had asked her to get the fire going she had been lost. She'd tried looking it up on her phone but with no cell service it had been impossible, but she hadn't been able to admit that to him. For now, she had a source of heat but the stove was useless to her because unless she was scrambling eggs or making ramen, she was an utterly incompetent cook. It never seemed like something she needed to waste time learning. Not when she lived in London and travelled for work all the time.

'Okay, Katherine, think. The storm is dying, so it won't be long before someone comes back. The team's equipment is still here.' That got her racing towards the bedrooms. 'So are their clothes.' She rummaged through the cupboard, finding a big thick jacket. 'Perfect!'

She threw off her jacket and pulled on one of the sweaters and then the jacket, almost immediately finding relief from the chill.

'Snacks.' That was next on the list. She hadn't brought any. There had been no need. They'd only been meant to be there for two nights. Katherine especially wouldn't have needed snacks when she was so disciplined about how she ate. But discipline didn't matter now. She rummaged through the kitchen cupboards finding a box of granola bars. Tearing one open, she devoured it right there before taking another and huddling on the couch. Knees to her chest. Her arms wrapped around herself.

Hopefully they would all come back soon.

Lukas fought his way into his cabin, brushing the snow off his clothes the moment he closed the door. With no fires going, the cabin was cold. A sacrifice made to ensure Katherine's safety. And all he'd gotten for his trouble was more accusations hurled at him. But she was alive and that was all he really needed.

Even though the woman had a way of getting under his skin.

He'd never met a more stubbornly proud person.

Well, now she could take care of herself since she so clearly wanted to. She was no longer any of his concern. He had done the right thing and now he could wait in the comfort of his own space.

He started a fire in the fireplace before doing the same in the kitchen. He was ravenous. It had been nearly a full day since he had eaten anything and even longer since he'd worked out. Working out would have to wait as much as it annoyed him. It set his day off-kilter. But it already was off-kilter, thanks to Katherine. He needed a shower and then food.

Mercifully, there was still warm water. When he stripped off his clothes and stepped under the jets, his body relaxed. His muscles had been tense; bunched for a whole day, it felt like he had let go of a weight now. And in the warm, relaxing water, his mind drifted. Images of toned, milky skin and red hair flashed behind his eyes making him groan. Streams of water ran down his arms over hands that clenched as he remembered Katherine's softness. It was cruel that his body would react so readily to her when he hated her so much. But there was no arguing with how attractive he found her when the evidence of that was hard and throbbing.

He shut off the taps with an irritated growl. After changing into clean, warm clothes, he made his way back into the kitchen and pulled ingredients from the cupboards and fridge to make the same breakfast he started every day with. He enjoyed cooking. It reminded him of his father and it was easier to remain in the peak physical condition needed for racing if he prepared his food himself.

Lukas meticulously added the ingredients to a saucepan, stirring it on the heat until it was thick and rich, then poured the hot porridge with berries and honey into a bowl adding a few more berries on top. He placed a spoon into the bowl but he couldn't lift it to his lips. Katherine hadn't even tried to make a drink before he left. Did she have anything at all to eat? Why did he care? Why should her well-being affect whether or not he could dive into his steaming hot breakfast?

He let out a long string of expletives. Why couldn't he get her out of his head? And why on earth did the air crackle whenever they were together? He felt it every time. Had felt it the moment he looked at her in the press pen three years ago. Time had turned to sludge that day. In his mind, he could still see her as she'd looked then in the VelociTV kit. A headset clamped over her ears, but her red hair still fluttering in the breeze. Clear blue eyes sparkling as the light caught them. A microphone in her slender hand, gold ring shining on her finger. And a smile on her lips that had stopped him in his tracks.

He'd known instantly he couldn't talk to her, he couldn't have allowed himself an attraction to a member of the media. Not when his relationship to the woman he loved and should have married had come to such a hurtful end right before.

You need to figure this thing out with the media because they are never going away, but I am.

The last thing he'd wanted was another relationship to hide and protect from them. So he hadn't allowed himself to get into Katherine's orbit. What would that spark have turned into? A charge so intense, like they'd harnessed the very lightning. Whether he was attracted to her or hated her.

Lukas had read about crackling hate between people and always dismissed it as fantastical but maybe there was truth in it. Maybe what he had initially felt was her undiluted hatred towards him. Why else would she attack him so consistently? He hadn't even said a word to her.

Right there was a perfect reason why he shouldn't care about Katherine.

Cursing loudly, he pushed his bowl away and grabbed his jacket, doing it up firmly before stepping back out into the storm.

'This is ridiculous,' he muttered, risking his life as he stomped through the wind and snow towards her cabin. A cabin she should have been sharing. It was ridiculous that he was taking any risk for this woman who would see his dream, all that he and his father had worked for, crash and burn. She would never understand what that was like.

When he reached her door, he was well and truly in a black mood.

He tried the handle and found that it was unlocked. 'Seriously? She's alone and she couldn't even lock this.'

Again, why do you care?

He ignored the voice.

He entered into the large living space and Katherine's head snapped in his direction, Her expression going from shock to suspicion. But he didn't react. He was too busy looking at what she wore. Bundled on the couch in a too-big jacket with Aero TV embroidered on the sleeve and a sweater that was just as big under it, she was holding herself around her knees. He had seen that jacket before. She was wearing one of the cameraman's clothes and he hated it, but he couldn't understand why. At least she was warm now. So why was it so irritating?

The cabin was warmer now but nowhere near as comfortable as his. And when he looked around he didn't see a cup or mug or plate. The stovetop too was bare but he did spot an empty wrapper on the table beside the couch.

'Is that all you've had to eat?' he asked her, trying very hard to keep his voice even.

'What's it to you?' she challenged.

'Answer the question, Katherine,' he said through gritted teeth.

'Yes, but I don't see how that's any of your business.'

Honestly, could she be more aggravating? He should leave. He had checked on her, she was alive, so now he could go and enjoy his hot food.

But if she had no food here, he couldn't just leave her.

'I've already said I don't want your death on my conscience,' Lukas replied. 'Get your things, I'm taking you to my cabin.'

'Why?' Katherine asked, making no attempt to move.

'Because it's warm and I have food.'

'Don't bother yourself. The storm is dying down, so the others will return soon.' She turned away from him to look at the fireplace, which had nothing but ash in it.

'We won't be seeing anyone for a few days. They don't know that we're here. They think we're out there somewhere,' he said, pointing at the door, 'because you ran off, which was an irresponsible thing to do. They won't risk any lives in this weather. Helicopters can't fly in this. There's no visibility and they will likely organise a search before they come back here and only when it is safe to do so. So, you will stay with me because you are useless at survival. Get your things and let's go.'

Katherine stared at him. The air grew thicker and thicker until it felt like he couldn't breathe it in, but he wasn't backing down. If she didn't listen, he would carry her out.

Do it, his body begged but he stood resolutely where he was.

'Fine.'

She disappeared from the room and he collected whatever food he could carry to his cabin to keep them alive. He waited an eternity that was truthfully only a few minutes, and Katherine returned rolling a small hardshell bag behind her.

'Let's go,' Lukas said, taking the bag from her and leading her through the snow into his cabin. 'Leave your coat and shoes by the door,' he instructed as they entered, 'and then sit in front of the fire.' It was so much warmer in here. With their coats hanging up, they would be warm and dry the next time they had to put them on.

'What smells so good?' Katherine asked, listening to him without complaint for once.

'Porridge and berries. Would you like some?'

'I would, but didn't you make it for yourself?' He watched her wring her hands, clearly uncomfortable to be in his space. A small, uncharitable part of him was glad of it.

'I did but I can make more.'

'Thank you,' she said, looking around as she made her way to the kitchen counter with three tall bar-stools on one side. His cabin was a lot larger than the one she and the crew shared. The touches more luxurious. There were perks to being who he was.

Lukas tried to ignore Katherine. Tried to ignore when she took hold of the spoon that had so nearly touched his lips, and ate his food. Tried to ignore her quiet moan and the way her eyes fluttered shut.

Tried and failed.

That sound, that expression was saved to his memory.

He forced himself to turn away and make another portion but all the while he could feel her eyes on him.

'You make that look so effortless,' she murmured, but he didn't turn to look. Instead, he kept his eyes firmly on the contents of the saucepan.

'What? Cooking?'

He heard no response, so he was forced to look at her, finding her eyes locked on to his hands. This was probably the longest they had ever interacted without sniping at each other. *I wonder how long it will last.*

'Can't you cook?'

Again, he got no response.

'I'll take that as a no, then.'

He stood where he was, the counter between them, and practically inhaled the bowl of food. Katherine had done the same.

'Thank you, that was really good.'

Lukas could see how hard it was for her to pay him the compliment.

'How do you know how to cook? I wouldn't have pegged you for the type.'

Lukas's heart constricted painfully. 'My father was a cook. He taught me.'

He saw her eyes light up with curiosity. It made her look breathtaking and darkened his mood further because this was exactly what he hated. People learning something small about him and then hungering for more information that they had no business to know.

'I thought your father was a mechanic.'

Lukas looked into his empty bowl. So much of the person he was was thanks to his father. His discipline, his skill. His preparedness. The reason he had extra provisions now was thanks to lessons his father had taught him. Know the risks and plan around them. 'He was both. He worked two jobs to support my racing career. Three, if you count how hard he worked to get me sponsors.' He chuffed. Anger curled in his stomach because the world already knew about his family. Neither he nor his father had had any privacy. 'Why ask about him when you already know? When you and everyone like you already went digging around in my past for a bit of juicy gossip?'

He picked up his bowl and tossed it into the sink with a loud clang. His pulse rushed in his ears as he remembered stories about his parents' divorce and his strained relationship with his mother being splashed around, forcing him to relive the agony of his family breaking apart. The fact that he was the reason they'd divorced in the first place. It was his fault, and he'd had to see it day after day for months.

He felt a hand grip his arm, making him turn around. Katherine's cheeks were red. Her lips thin.

'Don't you dare act like a victim when you're ruthless too.' Her voice was pitched low.

He stepped closer to her. That crackle was back. As though whatever this was between them would generate bolts that would tear the very cabin apart. 'What have I ever done that could even remotely be as unscrupulous as your actions?' He fought so hard not to raise his voice. Not to let her get under his skin but she'd burrowed there already. Katherine was the itch he could never get rid off.

'Are you joking right now?' she asked incredulously.

He had no idea what she was on about.

'You got me fired!' she yelled.

'You don't know what you're talking about.' There were a lot of media personalities Lukas didn't like but he had never used his power to get anyone fired. Especially not Katherine. He had, however, secretly tried to help her. Not that he would ever tell her that. Katherine probably wouldn't believe him if he did. And he certainly didn't want her to think that he *needed* her to think better of him.

'I don't know what I'm talking about?' She pushed him, hands on his chest. Her eyes glossy and bloodshot. 'You told my producer you didn't want to talk to me. Just me! It was a boys' club! They were just looking for a reason to get rid of me, and you handed them one. And why? Because I'm a woman? You're like all the other misogynists—just like your friend Roman—who want to keep the sport male-dominated, which is *so* incredibly hypocritical when your publicist is a woman. Or are you only happy to address the imbalance when it suits you?'

Lukas was shocked. First, Roman wasn't his friend. Lukas tolerated him at best. And second, he remembered those words, but he'd said them to Dominic, right after the very sight of Katherine had rendered him speechless. Only after he'd said the words had he realised Katherine's producer had heard him. He had even spoken to him, explained that it wasn't Katherine's fault. The producer had said it was fine.

Clearly it hadn't been fine.

But that didn't mean Lukas wasn't angry. Angry that Katherine hadn't come to him so they could clear the air. She hadn't known him and had assumed the worst from the very start. A person could only think so ill of another if they were already willing to believe that of them.

'Believe whatever you want,' he snapped, turning to leave.

'What I believe is true.'

Lukas laughed at that. A short burst of air clearly telling Katherine what he thought of that.

'I bet you're one of those people who underpays her compared to the male publicists too. Tell me, what were you paid in this last season after your bonuses?'

Lukas was tired of playing this game. This was public knowledge much to his dismay. 'Sixty-nine million euros.' The extent of his endorsement deals wasn't known so Katherine wouldn't learn about it now either.

'Sixty-nine, how appropriate for the man who will do anything.'

Lukas had had enough. She thought she knew so much about him, every single thing she knew was wrong. 'How much sex do you think I have?' he asked, doing nothing to temper his annoyance.

'Please,' Katherine scoffed, 'don't insult my intelligence. I've seen the number of women you appear with.'

Only because the media wouldn't give him an ounce of privacy and every time he had a dinner or arrived at an event a picture was taken. None of those women were ever in a relationship with him. 'Appear with. Not sleep with. Not date. My tastes in all things are very exacting.'

Katherine let out a taunting laugh. 'Okay, I'll bite. How many months has it been exactly?'

Knowing it would shut her up, Lukas leaned down. His lips brushed the shell of her ear. He felt the shiver that passed through her, the touch sparking as if they were statically charged. 'Three years.' He pulled away, smug at the shock on her face. 'What's wrong?' he asked venomously, 'Upset that it doesn't fit the narrative of me you're trying to peddle?'

Katherine was rendered mute. There were no comebacks. Satisfied, angry and tense, Lukas left her standing in the kitchen and walked away.

CHAPTER SIX

KATHERINE WATCHED LUKAS'S retreating back, breathing heavily. She'd never stooped so low as to attack a person the way she had Lukas right then but he made her crazy. As if she couldn't keep whatever she was feeling—anger, frustration, irritation—inside her when he was around. It all burst out of her in the most uncontrolled way and she hated that she could hardly temper what she said before she said it.

She had seen plenty of pictures of Lukas with women. They were almost never posed for. People talked. She wasn't the only one who had those ideas about him. That was no excuse though. As shocked as she was at his revelation, there was no denying he was telling the truth. No faking the offense he had taken, that flash of hurt in his eyes. Clearly something had happened there and she regretted her actions.

But she couldn't talk to him.

Not yet.

He had taken no responsibility for getting her fired. She couldn't forgive that. So here she was, upset at herself but still so angry at Lukas that she didn't know what to do with all this hate.

Her legs were finally able to move. They carried her to the door, but where would she go? A walk would help her cool off but a walk in a blizzard would get her killed. She could go back to her cabin and get some space but what then? She didn't really have much in the way of food or heat. And it was warm here. She felt infinitely better for having had something real to eat. Lukas didn't have to bring her here but he had. Even when he detested her as much as she did him.

Heaving a great big sigh, Katherine sat in front of the fireplace, staring at the hypnotic way the flames swayed and crackled.

As much as she hated to admit it, Lukas was right. While the storm wasn't blowing as intensely, it wasn't dying down sufficiently for help to arrive and she had no idea when it would stop. They were alone out here. They needed to rely on each other, so maybe the wisest thing to do would be to put their differences aside. She could be the bigger person. She had been when she didn't expose the reason she was fired from VelociTV.

Calmer, Katherine pushed off the floor and went looking for Lukas, which was harder than she had anticipated. She opened several doors in the cabin, finding a sauna, a gym, an entertainment room, a room with a large pool table in the middle. Finally, she tried a locked door and knocked gently on the wood.

'Lukas, can we talk?' she asked softly. 'Please.'

She heard shuffling and then the door swung inwards. Lukas stood there, one hand on the door-handle and the other on the frame. His knitted turtleneck sweater stretched across his chest, defining the incredible tone of his physique. The soft, camel colour warmed his grey eyes that so often reminded her of a winter storm, so at odds with his light brown hair.

How was this man single for three years? He was objectively rather beautiful.

She looked up into those intelligent eyes that were assessing her. He said nothing but if the roles were reversed she would probably do the same.

'I just want to talk,' Katherine said, waiting for a response.

Most likely a rejection. He pushed through the doorway and just before he could close the door, she spied a book lying face down on the king-size bed.

She really didn't think he was the reading type, but she hadn't thought he could cook, nor had she realised that he would be good at survival. He had gone looking for her equipped with a rope, had prevented hypothermia from setting in. There was a man behind the racer that she truly did not know.

He led her to the closest room. She took a seat on one of the buttery-soft tan leather couches and patted the cushion, hoping he would join her. See that she could be civil. To her relief he accepted, pouring himself onto the couch and draping his arm over the back-rest but he didn't look at her. He kept his eyes fixed to the black screen of the large television mounted on the wall.

Well, it looked like she would be doing all the talking.

'I'm sorry for what I said earlier, Lukas, it wasn't my finest moment.' All he did was blink but she could tell he was listening, so she ploughed on. 'I want to propose a truce.'

He looked at her then. Icy eyes piercing into hers. A shiver ran down her spine and she found herself leaning towards them just a little. She tried to pull away but couldn't.

'What do you think it was when I got you from that cabin, fed and warmed you?' She had never heard his voice so low. So robotic.

'I…' What could she say? That she didn't want to believe he could do anything kind or decent. 'I didn't see it for what it was,' she admitted. 'The attitude didn't help,' she added.

'Fine. So you want a truce. What does that mean?'

'It means that you're right, we're stuck here together and maybe we should work together to survive. I'll admit that I am lacking in some skills, but I can make up for them in other ways. All you need to do is teach me and I can help. It will be a lot easier if we coexist peacefully than if we're at each other's throats all the time.'

'Can *you* do that?' He turned towards her, folding one leg under the other as he focussed all his attention on her.

Can I...ugh, why is he so insufferable? It took a Herculean effort not to snap at him. 'I can try if you try too.'

He looked like he was thinking about it. It wasn't lost on Katherine that he could kick her out and live comfortably until help arrived, but anything could happen out here, and it wouldn't be smart to be apart when they could only rely on each other's help.

'I can agree to that. It's just until we're rescued, then we go back to our lives,' he said.

'Absolutely.' Katherine held out her hand. Lukas looked at it before he took it in his own much larger, warmer one, and shook it, scorching her skin. She did well to hide her gasp and pulled her hand away.

As she flexed her fingers, she caught a flash of something in Lukas's eyes that she didn't want to question.

Katherine was surprised but pleased by how well she and Lukas did over the days that followed. He did well to measure his tone when he spoke to her and cooked all their meals.

In turn, she tried not to remember that he'd gotten her fired, which helped a great deal in them being civil. It didn't help her blood pressure though. Being around Lukas was a constant reminder of what he had done. A constant reminder of the misogyny she faced. Of what her relationship with her father might become if she ever lost this career.

It made her burn, but they had a truce. A truce that ensured her survival, so as angry as she often found herself, as frustrated and bitter...she had to take a deep breath and force it all down. Still, her heart felt like it was constantly beating in her ears. Her stomach was constantly in knots. Even sleep was proving difficult.

The truce was temporary and soon they would escape each other.

Katherine was adding wood to the stove, feeding the fire, which was easy once Lukas had shown her how. And while she did that, he prepared their lunch.

'Thank you,' he said when she closed the door to the firebox.

'Can I help with lunch?' she asked, leaning over the counter.

'You want to help?' Lukas raised an eyebrow, incredulous. 'We have to be able to eat it afterwards.'

She wished he never knew of her weakness. She was preparing to throw a barb of her own when she noticed the corner of his lips kicked up in the most delicious way and realised he was teasing her.

'Don't be an ass or I'll eat all the yoghurt,' she retorted, forcing herself to calm down.

'Too late for that and you can help with the vegetables. Do you know what to do?'

'I've watched you enough.' She was watching him right now. The way he rubbed the marinade he had made with their limited ingredients over the chicken breasts. It was not normal to stare at his hands like this, so she yanked open the fridge. He was right, the yogurt had gone. In fact, a lot of the food had diminished. They were starting to run alarmingly low. Every meal was much smaller than Katherine knew he would really need. Obviously, he had to be mindful about how he rationed the groceries to feed them both. His supplies had been meant to be for him alone for no more than a couple days and the food he'd taken from the crew's cabin had been meant to feed them for two more meals.

'You know,' he said as she began chopping, 'that day in

the paddock, I was talking to Dominic. I hadn't realised that your producer overheard what I said at first.'

Katherine stopped breathing. Her knife pausing on the board. Her heart beat rapidly. They had avoided this subject since their argument.

'When I did, I told him discreetly that what he heard wasn't your fault. It had nothing to do with you. I told him that I couldn't explain further than that and he said he understood. I knew they fired you. I didn't know why.'

She handed her chopping board to him, careful to avoid his touch, careful to hide her shaking.

When he bent to place the dish in the oven, she asked, 'Why didn't you want to talk to me? We hadn't met before that point.'

Lukas closed the oven door, regret etched onto his face. 'It doesn't matter why. I'm sorry that it happened.'

There they were. The words she had wanted to hear for so long. She'd wanted to make him take responsibility for what he'd done to her and when he did she was never going to accept the apology. Was never going to forgive him. She hadn't once considered that he could somehow be innocent, or that his words were taken out of context. She had seen him speak into the ear of her producer.

'I didn't realise—that's not what he—' Katherine's mind was racing. 'Did you ever find out what he said to me? Did he tell you?'

'No,' Lukas said, stepping closer, 'because I don't grant interviews to VelociTV. I give them none of my time.'

'Why?' She had to know. Was it because of her? But that would be ridiculous wouldn't it because Lukas hated her and it had been three years. 'Why, Lukas?'

'It's not important. The point is that I didn't know.'

It mattered to her. It shouldn't but it did. Though, given

the fact that Lukas was turning away from her, she knew she wouldn't get an answer even if she needed it.

'Take a seat. I'll bring the food out when it's done.'

She was being dismissed. Why was he so opposed to talking about this? What was he hiding? Was she reading too much into it? She wanted to grab him by the arm and make him look into her eyes and spill his secrets. But she remembered the last time they'd touched, the handshake that still made her skin tingle when she thought about it, and she couldn't risk the move.

They ate in silence. Side by side. The atmosphere neither comfortable nor hostile for once. It felt like they were on the verge of something. Like words sitting on the tip of a tongue but refusing to fall. And when they were done and the place had been perfectly tidied—as she had learned Lukas needed—she sat in front of the fireplace fully expecting Lukas to disappear into one of the other rooms as he so often did. Except he didn't.

He joined her on the couch, wrapping a blanket around both their shoulders, huddling close as if he knew that having a smaller fire and the anxiety from the situation had chilled her. But having his body so close raised everything. Her awareness. Her heart rate. Her temperature. They weren't hating on each other now, so why was he still affecting her like this?

'Thank you for apologising earlier,' she said softly. She still wanted him to know what he had jeopardised without even knowing it. Or maybe it was that she was feeling rather alone with nothing but white beyond the windows and only Lukas for company. Maybe it was that she had gone longer than usual without talking to her father. Whatever the reason, she wanted to talk now. 'I was hurt but I was also terrified when I lost that job.'

'Why?'

'Because it was a dream I shared with my father and I was afraid I'd lost it before I even really had a chance to enjoy it.' A tremor passed through her at the memory and, mistaking that for cold, Lukas wrapped an arm around her, holding her to his body. But she didn't correct him. Didn't pull away. She wanted to stay exactly where she was.

What is happening?

'I come from a fairly large family. I have an older brother, a younger brother and a twin sister, and try as I might, I could never relate to them. They all got along so well but I was so different. Quiet. Studious. I preferred my books to company, while they were all so extroverted. The lives of the party. They had their little club and I was not part of it, which was fine because I had my own interests. I used to hang out in the library, they used to get into trouble. My sister, Paige, especially. And that has never changed. But through all of that, my dad and I had something to bond over. Something that only interested the two of us and that was Alpha One racing. During qualifying and the race, my dad was only mine for the entire broadcast. When it was over he had to go back to putting out the fires the others caused.' Katherine had seen how her siblings' behaviour would stress out her parents and she was determined that they would never have to worry about her. She still lived by that code as her parents were getting older. They had retirements to think about but how could they with three of their children still staying with them?

'Racing wasn't a realistic dream for you to have,' Lukas said. There was no judgement or mockery. It was a simple, unfortunate truth.

'No. Not just because there weren't any real avenues for female racers at the time but also, there would have been no way for them to support me financially. But journalism? That was something I could work towards and my father was always my biggest supporter. He celebrated every step with me.' And Katherine lived for that attention. It was the only time she felt seen.

'What about your mother?'

That was a lot more complicated to answer. While Katherine loved her mother, she was probably the reason Katherine was so set on never marrying. Never having children. Her mother's pressure still fuelled her drive in the opposite direction.

'My mother doesn't understand my need to succeed at all costs.' Katherine supposed the one person who could understand that was sitting next to her. 'She had a very promising career in marketing. She was climbing the corporate ladder and making a name for herself in the company but then she got married and had children. She left her corporate job for a lower paying one with limited growth that gave her time to spend with the family.'

Lukas's arm tightened fractionally. 'What's the "but"?'

'*But* she didn't spend much of it with me because I didn't need it as much as the others. She wants me to settle down like she did because, to her, that's the right way to do things. Pursue things when you're young and unattached but then make sacrifices for a family.' But to Katherine the sacrifices always seemed too big.

She had seen pictures of her mother from her corporate days. A sophisticated, polished woman. Stylish and elegant. She had seen her parents' wedding pictures where her mother had four bridesmaids. Her closest friends. Katherine hadn't met a single one of them in person and knew her mother had lost touch with them. The lack of time due to their chaotic family was to blame. Katherine knew it.

That bright sophisticated woman was gone, replaced by one run off her feet. Styled hair replaced by an untidy bun every day. The only people her mother spoke to daily were her husband and her children. Excluding Katherine, of course, because Katherine didn't need tending to. Her mother claimed happiness and yet, when they were younger, Katherine had seen the longing way she used to look at the handful of corporate mums who would drop their kids off in a hurry for school. On the weekends, when Paige used to flip through magazines, Katherine had noticed the way her mother—her own clothes covered in splatters from cooking or taking care of Nicholas—would gaze longingly at the fashion. The glamazons so reflective of how she once looked.

Her mother wasn't fulfilled but she had an unshakeable idea of what duty meant. Of what her role was. And for some reason she wanted Katherine to follow suit.

'And what do you want?' Lukas asked.

'I want to establish myself so firmly that no one thinks about Alpha One broadcasting without thinking about me. I want to follow this circus for the rest of my life. I want to grow bigger than I am. I want to—'

'You want to…' Lukas urged.

'I want to be successful. I want to take care of my parents when they're older. I know I'll have to, with Paige the way she is.'

Katherine looked up at Lukas and saw understanding on his face.

'They must be proud of you,' he said. 'Whether they show it or not.'

'I don't know,' Katherine admitted. 'Before coming here I was meant to have dinner with my family but they cancelled because Paige got into trouble.'

'Is it always like that?'

'Yes, but I understand. The others need my parents' support more than I do.'

Lukas shook his head. 'It shouldn't have to be that way, but I understand.'

'You do?'

The world knew about his parents' divorce, about his strained relationship with his mother, because tabloids had reported on it, but he was so private, more than that was purely a guess.

'My mother left because of me.'

Katherine's heart stuttered to a stop.

'My father spent a lot of time, energy and money on my racing. All those things could have been spent on the family and we could have had a more comfortable life.'

Katherine knew Lukas had come from humble beginnings. Everyone did. Just as everyone knew his father. A man who was at as many races as he could attend, which was nearly all of them until his death.

'Having to support a child through karting and everything else puts a huge financial burden on a family. My mother didn't sign up for that, so she divorced him and moved to Salzburg.'

Katherine put her arms around Lukas's middle, holding him tightly. If someone had told her days ago that she would be trying to offer him comfort she would have laughed in their face. But here they were and she realised something: They weren't so different.

'It was difficult but we were fine. My dad and I had each other until just over a year ago.' Lukas stopped talking. The anguish in his expression was hard to witness and even harder to feel. And she could feel it. As if her own heart was trying to tear itself to pieces.

Katherine remembered when Florian Jäger had died. It had been a short illness. Lukas had done absolutely no PR in the weeks leading up to his death. The whole paddock knew he was flying back and forth each night just to see his father while he could. Her stomach churned with guilt now because she remembered calling into question if Lukas would be able to remain competitive in the build-up to the race the next day.

If it was her father who died and that was what people had said afterwards, she would have likely set the world on fire. But she'd had to ask the question. It was on everyone's lips. Up and down the paddock. Online. At the network.

Katherine realised that at every turn she had assumed the worst about Lukas. She hadn't been good to him. But she couldn't apologise, because she'd only been doing her job.

'I'm not sure why I told you that.' It seemed like he said that more to himself than her.

'Because we're running low on wood and food and might succumb to the elements and die while in this over-the-top cabin,' she joked, hoping to bring some levity to the atmosphere that had grown solemn. And when she heard him chuckle, she felt an odd sort of relief.

'Are you comfortable?' he asked.

She adjusted against him. 'Mmm-hmm.' Then she glanced up and found him looking down at her. And she was caught. Frozen in place by a wintery gaze. One that reeled her in as if she were hypnotised. Her lips parted and so did his. Pink and soft. His breath hit her face. Cool and minty. He was so close now. Any movement might make their lips brush.

Just as they were about to touch, he pulled away. Blinking fast as if to clear away an enchantment. He pulled the blanket tighter around them, which forced her upright, breaking the connection of their bodies, and looked away.

What was that?

CHAPTER SEVEN

LUKAS'S HEART HAD thrummed in his chest. His skin had felt red-hot everywhere that Katherine had touched him. It was as if she'd ignited him and he'd burned up like flash paper.

And he was coming to see that she had brought out this reaction in him in every heated exchange. In every thought. Every touch. He'd needed to break the connection of their bodies and had done so, but he couldn't move away, because it was a thrill to be so close to her. Because she was cold and anxious. Because of all that she had told him.

So he stayed on the couch, under the blanket, with her. Sat with her in silence until they dozed off.

And when he finally opened his eyes to find the fire grown low, adding a log or two was not his first thought. Not when he looked beside him and found Katherine curled towards him in her sleep. With her head on his shoulder and her hands pressed under her cheek. Peaceful. Beautiful. Dangerous.

She was off-limits to him. He shouldn't want to brush her cheek or kiss her lips but he had wanted to earlier. He still wanted to.

He needed space. Air.

Laying Katherine down on the cushions as gently as possible, he extricated himself from the blanket and tucked her in tightly. Then he threw a couple logs on the fire and looked out the window. The wind had died down. The snow was no longer falling. The night sky lay beyond the filmiest of wispy clouds that were slowly blowing away.

He needed air and now he could get it.

He shoved his feet into his snow-boots and tugged on his jacket as he stepped out onto the porch. Nothing but thick, untouched snow lit up in a hint of silver from the crescent moon as far as the eye could see. The trees were like glittering pillars of white. Only the very edges of their needles poked through the pillowy snow that stood out in stark contrast to the black, shimmering night sky.

Lukas took a deep breath.

And then another.

And another.

Being away from Katherine cleared his head a little. He hadn't realised that it had happened but in the days they'd been together she had taken over his every thought. A pervasive presence. A woman he didn't want to be around and yet he so clearly did.

'How can you want to kiss her after all she's done?' he asked in the still night.

He would have loved to know the answer. Why did his body feel like it was breaking to get the smallest of touches? He hated her. *Hated* her.

It wasn't always that way.

No, it wasn't. The image of the first time he saw her lived in his head. The way she'd taken his breath away. There has always been something between them. Something electric. Something chemical. Something highly reactive to even the smallest stimulus. He couldn't deny that.

Lukas looked back at the closed door of the cabin. Part of him wanted to go back in there. Sit beside her pretending it was nothing, but inside he knew what it would be: an adrenaline junkie seeking out the thrill.

He turned away to lean against one of the large posts and

as he looked up, he saw the night sky shift. Light slowly dancing across the heavens. Muted and nearly white but the longer he stared at it the brighter it became. Brush strokes of pink and green dancing overhead between Lukas and the stars. It was breathtaking.

And he wanted Katherine to witness it with him.

He ran inside and knelt beside the couch.

'Katherine.' He fought and lost the urge to run the backs of his fingers down her cheek.

She mumbled sleepily making him smile. She was rather adorable like this.

'I think you'll want to see this.'

'What is it?' she slurred.

'The aurora.'

Her eyes flew open. 'What?'

He laughed at her reaction and fetched her snow-boots, slipping them onto her feet and then bundling her tighter in the blankets. 'Come on.'

He led her outside and held her back to his body, making sure her blanket didn't slip, keeping her warm. 'Look up.'

The lights were flaring beautifully now. Streaks of colour feathering to the heavens while jagged lines swirled and snaked against the black canvas of the sky.

'Wow,' Katherine breathed. 'Thank you for getting me. It's stunning.'

And then he looked at her. Saw the wonder in her blue eyes. The soft smile on her lips. She turned and caught him staring. Her smile growing full and contagious, stealing his breath.

'You're not looking at the sky.'

'I can't.' Pure honesty fell from his lips before he could think about what he was saying. But he couldn't take it back. Katherine was smart. She knew exactly what he meant. And he was sure his heart ceased functioning altogether when she turned in his arms. The smile dropping off her face as she searched his. Her eyes touching every inch of his skin before trapping his gaze. Something was sparking between them, and they were tinder catching alight. They couldn't fight it any longer. Not when they were moving closer, when their breaths mingled, when their lips touched and every explosive interaction, all that fire and electricity had somewhere to go.

Katherine gasped and Lukas wasn't sure if the sound he made was a moan, an anguished wail, a curse or prayer. Maybe it was all those things. His arms banded around her just as her hands peeked out of her blanket to fist the front of his jacket. And he kissed her. Slowly but desperately. Hungrily but savouring. Her taste consuming. Her tongue against his setting off a series of explosions in his body. Making him hard. Needy. Ravenous. And when she angled her head, he brought his hand up to the nape of her neck, holding her in place while he kissed her deeply. Losing control. Licking the roof of her mouth. His tongue dancing with hers. His teeth catching her bottom lip, and he ripped himself away.

He took two steps back and turned away from her. Adrenaline flooded his body. This was how he felt when he threw himself out of a plane, or went skiing off piste, or when he caught his car from spinning at three hundred kilometres an hour.

He was alive.

Katherine made him feel like this.

He shouldn't be surprised. Hate was a passionate emotion and there was unbridled passion here.

Do you really hate her?

No. He didn't. Not anymore.

He gripped his hair at the roots, then spun around and saw her watching him.

Every shackle broke loose.

Katherine saw the moment Lukas threw caution to the wind. He closed the distance between them. Everything about him screaming hunter. A silver-eyed wolf. But she wasn't prey. The moment he was within reach, she grabbed the front of his jacket and tugged him to her. She kissed him the same instant his hands cradled her face, breathing him in just as she heard him inhale this kiss. His lips were urgent but so were her hands and then he was spinning them around. Pushing her against the thick post. His body pressed against hers. Her stomach was in her throat. Chest heaving. Moisture pooling her core. Teeth and tongues clashing. Uncontrolled, just like they always were.

Whether they were arguing or kissing, there was never any controlling what they brought out in each other. And she wanted to touch him. Wanted him to call out her name and to make him beg, but there was no getting through his bloody jacket, and yet she felt his hands push through the gap in the blanket and slide under her top. His hands, surprisingly warm, left a path of tingles in their wake that had nothing to do with the temperature of their skin.

And then they were moving again but she stepped on the blanket and Lukas growled in frustration. Picking her up bridal-style, he took her back inside.

'The sky is beautiful right now, but I have no patience in me,' he said, teeth grazing her neck.

'I don't want you to be patient,' she confessed breathlessly. She just wanted him. He always heightened what she felt. It was no different when the sensations were physical. The moment he set her on her feet, she threw off the blanket, and his hands were pulling up on her top and pushing down on her leggings, desperate to get to her skin. But she understood because she was shoving him out of that jacket and tearing at his sweater. Lukas bent down, allowing her to yank it off his head.

Katherine had seen many impressive athletes in her life, but she was ill prepared for the perfection of Lukas's lean, cut body. Every muscle defined, hard and exquisite. And yet his skin was so soft, as if silk had been poured over a perfect frame to form him.

'Enjoying the view?'

She grinned. 'Yes.' She had always been brutally honest with him, there was no reason to hide her thoughts now.

That moment was all Lukas gave her before finally pulling her top off and laying her in front of the fire on the thick, fluffy rug. His fingers slid beneath the waistband of her leggings and underwear alike, pulling them both off in one. And then he was kissing her...there.

Everything was moving so fast but not fast enough. She wanted his lips on hers and his hardness inside her. There was heat in her veins and lightning in her belly. Lukas's tongue sent sparks of pure pleasure throughout her body but she wanted more. More. More.

Gripping his hair, she lifted his head off her. His eyes were half-lidded, drunk on the pleasure that was intoxicating her, and placing her hand under his chin, she urged him up her body but she didn't have to ask for what she wanted; he knew. He kissed her with a ferocity, holding himself up on his arms, allowing her hands to go to his pants and undo the belt, button and zip without looking. He shoved all the layers off him.

Finally, he was naked.

Gloriously so.

Impressively so.

God, this man should be on display in a museum.

'Glad you think so,' he said into her ear and she flushed red, realising she had spoken the words aloud. He sucked on a spot on her neck and she moaned out loud.

'Make that sound again,' he instructed. He begged.

His tongue teased the same spot, but this time his hands

travelled down her body, his fingers parting her sex, slipping in.

'Lukas,' she moaned louder.

'Mmm, that's even better,' he said, voice like gravel. He pulled his fingers away and brought them up between them, showing Katherine that they were drenched. And then he licked them clean. She couldn't take it anymore.

'Dammit, Lukas, give me what I want,' she demanded.

'And what's that?' he taunted.

'You inside me.' She couldn't breathe. She needed relief from the assault of pleasure on her senses.

'I don't have a condom, Katherine,' he admitted in a seductive voice.

'You can't leave me like this,' she begged. She was certain she would cry if he stopped now.

'I have no intention to. I'm happy to feast.' He licked his pink lips and she blushed to her roots.

'I'm on the pill and you haven't been with anyone in three years.' A fact she trusted because Lukas always spoke the truth. He was blunt and seemed like he didn't care how his words landed so there was no reason to doubt him now. Regardless of how much she hated him, his integrity was undeniable.

The thought made her realise something: She didn't hate him anymore.

'The pill wouldn't make a difference anyway,' he said against her skin. His fingers teasing her once again. 'Are you sure?'

'Yes,' she panted. 'I want you now.'

Lukas didn't need telling twice and thrust his hard, throbbing cock into her. She gasped loudly, arching her back. And then he raised her leg and set a pace that made her lightheaded. High. Her lungs were no longer adequately functioning and each of his growls and curses and pants raised goose bumps on her skin. Made her heart skip beats.

This was beyond anything she could have imagined. He kept pushing her higher, higher, higher. Like a firework rising above the clouds.

'Come for me, Katherine,' he commanded, and she exploded around him in pyrotechnic glory. Lukas, her pyromaniac, was close behind. He slid his large hand under her head, holding her forehead to his, cursing out her name as his body tensed, his muscles lower down undulating in waves until he could finally take a breath. Until he relaxed and let her leg down. Until he finally opened his eyes. They were molten silver.

'Lukas,' she breathed, scarcely able to believe what they'd done or how incredible it felt or how badly she wanted to do it again.

'I know,' he replied.

CHAPTER EIGHT

KATHERINE FOUND HERSELF in the entertainment room, an inviting warmly coloured space. She ran her fingertips along the edge of the polished pool table. Picked up a ball, testing the weight of it.

She had left a sleeping Lukas in front of the fire. In the aftermath of them having sex, she hadn't been able to rest. She couldn't stop thinking about how crazed they were for each other. How perfectly they fit. How he had been the best she had ever slept with. How frantic they had been.

And then she couldn't stop thinking about what he said.

The pill wouldn't make a difference anyway.

She didn't know what that meant but it made her think about her own choices. She didn't want love and children and sacrifice.

She fetched a wooden triangle with rounded corners hanging on the wall and brought it to the table. One by one she placed the coloured balls inside, but kept looking at the door as she did so.

'Get a grip, Katherine. The man is asleep.' But she wished he wasn't. She wished he was in this room with her and that was exactly why she needed a space to think. She stood back and looked down at the perfect J the solid balls had formed, then picked up the cue ball and took it to the top of the table.

'So this is where you are.'

She swivelled her head to find Lukas leaning against the

door-frame, hands crossed over his bare chest—well, she was wearing his sweater. His jeans sat low on his hips but the button was open. His golden-brown hair was mussed from sleep and sex.

'I thought you were asleep,' she said, turning around to lean against the table.

'I was, but then I needed something and the one I needed it from was missing.'

'Oh?'

Lukas pushed off the door-frame and stalked towards her. One hand went to her face, tilting it up to him, the other grabbed her hip.

'I need this,' he said before kissing her. Instantly, she was returning it. The passion from earlier that had lowered to a simmer was at boiling point again and she couldn't get enough of him. Couldn't pull him close enough, or touch his skin enough. He was utterly intoxicating. A drug made for her. A thought that made her panic and slow the kiss to a stop. She broke away from his lips but not out of his hold.

He smiled. 'I like the way my shirt looks on you.'

She liked the way it felt on her, yet she didn't welcome the feeling. She strived to keep her romantic partners at arm's length, but she was already breaking that rule with Lukas because they were stuck together and she couldn't help learning things about him. Connecting with him. Wanting him. Wanting to know him.

Like what he said earlier.

She needed to know, especially since they had been physical.

'Can I ask you a question?'

Lukas shrugged but there was caution in his eyes.

'What did you mean earlier when you said the pill didn't matter?'

That look of caution cleared away, but Lukas still took a

step back and shoved his hands into his pockets. She tracked the movement, knowing she should pay attention but his physique was distracting. She forced herself to look him in the eye as he explained.

'It wouldn't matter if you were on the pill, Katherine, because I've had a vasectomy.'

Well, that wasn't what she was expecting.

'You don't want children?' Katherine's heart was racing now. Nearly everyone in her circle criticised her choice but maybe Lukas was like her in yet another way. It made her hopeful but also wary because she really didn't need to see more ways that they were alike.

'No.' His answer was unequivocal, and it made Katherine want to cry because someone could understand her.

'I don't either,' she said through a lump in her throat.

He nodded, coming closer. 'I understand.'

'You don't need an explanation?' she whispered.

'No.' He brushed her hair behind her ear, a soft look on his face. 'You're an adult. You know best what you want and need. You don't have to explain yourself to anyone. Ever.'

Acceptance. It broke her apart and put her back together in a different way. A happier way. Now she wanted to explain to Lukas because he hadn't asked. He didn't feel entitled to tell her how to live her life, and she wanted to confide in him.

'My mother doesn't understand that. I don't want to disappoint her. She wants grandkids and is pressuring me for them, but I never want to be like her. I don't want to settle for a life that is only partially fulfilling. I don't want to give up friendships and I don't want to sacrifice my dream, my career I've worked so hard for, for a family and children that don't even appreciate or understand the sacrifice. And that's what a relationship is to me—a sacrifice. A threat to everything I've built. I don't want that. I don't even have pets. My plants are made from building blocks. I want a life where I'm free to go anywhere. Travel with Alpha One and then some more outside of it. I don't want to be tied down. But I also don't know how to make her anything but disappointed in me.'

Lukas shook his head as if he could make the words less true. Katherine wished he had that power. There was a softness in his grey eyes that offered her comfort but also reflected no small amount of hurt. He stood so close to her that they were all she could look at. He blocked out the room, standing between her legs as close as it was possible.

'My parents' divorce was entirely my fault,' he said. 'If it weren't for me and my racing, my mother would never have left. I know that. And I know she blames me. I try to financially support her to make up for it but I know it's not enough. And when the divorce and my relationship with her became news, I was confronted with that every time I switched on the TV or went online. It's why I can't let the media in. Because then people would see how selfish I am, that I sacrificed my father's happiness for my own gain. I'd rather stay private so no one else has to know that but me and my mother.'

Katherine brought her hand up to touch his cheek and her heart soared at his infinitesimal lean into her caress. She'd bared a part of her soul to Lukas and he didn't judge. He didn't offer unsolicited advice or tell her she was wrong. He'd shown her that he understood what a complicated relationship with a parent was like. That he saw her vulnerability and offered a piece of his own.

And now she understood why he hated the media so much. They didn't often look at him like a human. He was a celebrity. A public commodity for them to pry into and he was afraid that people would see him like he saw himself. They both had proud fathers and disapproving mothers, and she had to admit, she would hate for people to uncover that about her. It would hurt every time someone spoke about it.

Katherine realised how different the real Lukas was to the person the media portrayed him to be. She liked this man.

She kissed him softly on his lips. Her body tingled at the connection.

'Lukas,' she breathed and was met with a ferocious kiss. A kiss that made her mind go blank and her body light up like a Christmas tree.

'I have to confess something,' he said in between kisses. 'That day three years ago in the paddock, I thought you were the most beautiful woman I had ever seen. I walked away because I didn't want to talk to you. I didn't want to hear your voice or risk being charmed by you. I'd just had a relationship fail despite how much we loved each other, because I was so set on every part of it being in private. I couldn't be attracted to you when I was in a bad place. When you were the last person on earth I would ever consider being with.'

She rested her forehead against his. 'Because I'm a journalist.'

'The media has never been my friend, Katherine. I don't need the world prying into my life, analysing everything about me.'

They were so different. Wanted different things. Trusted different people. And as long as she was a journalist he would never trust her.

And she was never going to sacrifice her career for anyone. Least of all him.

'I don't know why you're so against the world getting to know you, Lukas. Everything I see makes me want to know you even more. Everything I uncover blows me away. I'm glad we got stuck here. I'm glad I'm getting to know you like this. You're extraordinary, why do you want to hide? You're not the one who needs to feel guilty or apologise, but your mother should. She owes you an apology.'

'That's not why I'm telling you this.' He cupped her face,

urging her to listen carefully. 'I can't be with you, Katherine. I value my privacy too much, that won't change. I gave up on a relationship because of the media, and after losing her, I won't enter into another relationship while I'm in the spotlight. Your career will always be in the way, but you're a drug and I'm addicted to you.'

He was right, on both counts. Their chemistry wouldn't be ignored. 'So we can have this time. Just until we're rescued and after that…'

'I'll go back to my life and you go back to yours,' he said.

So for now, she could just pretend.

Pretend as if everything was perfect so she could enjoy their chemistry. The pleasure. It would be a momentary distraction.

'I like the sound of that.'

The words barely left her mouth when Lukas lifted her and placed her on the pool table. A sudden rush of cool air greeted her most intimate skin and she watched him kneel in front of her. His eyes glinting wickedly as his mouth closed over her core. Feasting on her like a starving man.

She could definitely agree to their terms for this.

CHAPTER NINE

WATER RAINED OVER Lukas and Katherine. Steam billowing around them in the ultra-luxurious bathroom.

He held Katherine to him. His talented fingers playing a melody of moans as if she were his favourite instrument. Each string he plucked had her bowing and arching against him. It was the sweetest music. The very best dance.

Every morning since their talk had started like this. Every moment since he'd tasted her on that pool table, he had craved her more and more and to his great delight, the feeling had been mutual.

Unable to keep their hands off each other, the days had blurred together. Lukas hadn't even minded that, after the brief moment when the skies cleared enough to see the aurora, they were back to wind and snow.

Until that morning.

They had awoken to blue skies. It was so bright with the blanket of snow magnifying the sunlight. The clear sky looked vivid, as if someone had painted it. And good weather meant rescue.

Their time was up.

Lukas was determined to enjoy what little they had left. And he had been enjoying their time. Once he understood why Katherine hated him, it was only natural that he should apologise because he still wanted her to do the same. He had endangered her dream, and her articles had endangered his.

So, he understood and welcomed the fact that this attraction had no chance of a future, but God, did he want to revel in this passion some more.

'Turn around,' he instructed, high on the fact that she obeyed him so readily. He wrapped an arm around her waist, holding her to him, and kissed her fiercely while turning off the taps. Bodies dripping, he picked her up and stepped out of the shower, then heard the unmistakable roar of a helicopter overhead.

'I think help is here,' Katherine whispered. Her lips pink and full from his kisses.

'We should get dressed,' he replied but made no move to put her down.

He watched her stare into his eyes. So much passing between them. Electricity, regret, passion but the thwop thwop of the rotors only got louder and louder.

'Put me down, Lukas.'

Clutching her tighter at first, he forced his muscles to relax and then set her on her feet. He turned away from her, dried off as fast he could and dressed in the clothes close at hand.

He ran his fingers through his hair and turned to look at Katherine, unsure of what he should say. What he could say. Maybe it was best he said nothing.

He rushed to the lounge, just in time to see Dominic force his way through the door.

'Lukas.'

He had never heard his manager, his friend, sound so relieved or look older than he did right then.

He watched Dominic stride through the room and Lukas embraced him tightly.

'I told them you would be fine,' Dominic said, voice muffled. 'I made them start here.'

Lukas chuckled as he pulled away. 'You weren't worried at all.'

'Bastard,' Dominic grumbled.

'Thank you,' Lukas said with as much gratitude as he could muster.

'For knowing you so well or coming to get you?'

'Both.' Lukas smiled. He turned in time to see Katherine enter the room, her bag rolling along behind her. He noticed once again that she was in the cameraman's jacket. He wanted so badly to march over to her and rip the jacket off her. To wrap her in his own and claim her, but that would go against what they had. A momentary flirtation in private while they were snowbound. If he showed any interest in her now, rumours about them would get out and spread like wildfire. If a relationship he had been so committed to had ended because he was unwilling to budge on his privacy, he couldn't go against his principles for a tryst. So he clenched his hands into fists and stayed where he was.

Katherine noticed. He could tell by her slightly cocked head.

'Katherine!' Dominic exclaimed with surprise. His eyes growing wide when he noticed her. 'How did you… We thought you were…' He looked back and forth between Lukas and her. 'Did you two get trapped together?'

'Yes,' she replied, coming closer. Lukas could feel the distance between them closing as if she was hooked onto a spool within him and when she joined them a mere foot away, it felt like she was an entire chasm away. He wanted to touch her. To hold her. To tell everyone to leave them alone for a few more weeks but he bit his tongue instead.

'Lukas saved me, actually. I hurt my ankle and he found me and then I wasn't surviving very well on my own so he brought me here.'

He ignored the impressed look on Dominic's face. He didn't want to acknowledge the hate that no longer existed between them or explain what the past week had been like.

'Thank heavens for Lukas.' Dominic squeezed her in a one-armed hug. 'I'm very glad you're okay, Katherine.'

'Thank you, Dominic.'

'Your crew will be returning shortly to pick up their stuff,' Dominic said, 'But how would you like to leave with us now?'

'I would love to.'

The helicopter ride from the cabin to Rovaniemi was uncomfortable. Lukas said nothing the entire flight but every time he looked at her she could feel the heat in his gaze. Her body reacted to him but no relief would come now. He wouldn't kiss her or take her to bed. All those touches lived only in her memory now. Katherine knew she would compare anyone in her future to Lukas and they would always fail in comparison. But they were over. They were rescued and it didn't matter that her heart was imploding for whatever ridiculous reason, they had an agreement.

As soon as they landed, she and Lukas were bundled into separate vehicles. She didn't even get the chance to say thank you or goodbye.

'*Hei*,' she greeted the driver. As soon as she buckled herself in she switched on her phone, which still had battery life having spent the week powered down in her suitcase. A series of vibrations went through her phone. One of them being an email with a plane ticket out of Rovaniemi Airport straight to Heathrow.

'Perfect.'

She closed her emails, wishing she could be home already. In those walls she could safely let herself miss Lukas. She could replay the night by the fireplace and think about how different a man he actually was to the one she reported about.

Like in the feature article she'd written. The things she'd said wouldn't reflect the man Lukas really was, so it wouldn't be true. She couldn't let it run after all he'd told her.

Katherine dialled her editor, drumming her fingers on the door-handle as she waited for her to pick up.

'Katherine! It's such a relief to hear your voice! I was so worried—'

'I need you to pull the feature,' she said.

'What?'

'Jennifer, I know what I'm asking and that feature on Lukas Jäger can't run. I'm begging you.' Her palms grew sweaty. Katherine had never once asked to pull a story before. 'I'll write something else in its place. Please.'

'Why?'

'I don't think it's true anymore.' Katherine scrunched her eyes shut, assaulted with images of Lukas talking to her, taking care of her, pleasuring her, cooking. But she couldn't say any of that. She forced herself to sound more in control. Rational. 'It doesn't accurately reflect who Lukas is.'

'It's a great piece though, Kat. What's brought on this change of heart?'

'Being stuck in a snowstorm.' Jennifer wasn't going to respond to an emotional appeal. The story came first so there was only one thing she could say to make her editor change her mind and agree. 'I've just had the opportunity no one else will ever have. Full access to Lukas Jäger. I've got to know the man behind the persona and if we print the article I first gave you, we wouldn't be printing the truth.'

'I'll see what I can do…but this means I want a new article covering what you've learnt about him or we'll come up with something else to get us those clicks.'

'Thanks, Jen.'

'You owe me,' her editor said and then added, 'I really am happy you're okay. You had us all worried there.'

'I'm okay. See you soon.'

Katherine never had a reason to doubt Jennifer Harrison, but somehow, she didn't feel reassured. Maybe she had grown a little protective of Lukas, but all she could do was hope Jennifer kept her word.

To distract herself, Katherine opened her socials. Going a week without checking in was alien to her and she needed to know what was going on. As soon as she opened the first app, she was greeted by thousands of notifications all tagging her and Lukas.

'What the…' She looked at a few of them, closed the app, opened another but it was the same. Another app…the same result. Thousands of posts covering her and Lukas missing in Lapland. That she'd expected, because Lukas had been right. With the way she had run off, that was what the crew would have reported. What she hadn't expected was the explosion of speculation about her relationship with Lukas. There were always posts like that, but this was different. #Lukat was trending on several sites. Theories ranged from the believable—that they got caught in a snowstorm—to the absurd—they'd deliberately run off before the storm to have a secret affair and being missing gave them uninterrupted time alone.

Would Lukas see this? How would he react?

She was still scrolling, unsure of how she felt about being the subject of internet speculation, when her phone rang.

'Hi, Robert,' she answered.

'It's good to know that you survived. Did Jäger?'

'If you're asking if I murdered him, I did not.' But it was a miracle she was alive with the number of times he'd robbed her of breath. Stopped her heart. Had her writhing and panting and begging.

'I'm very proud of you. The reason I called is that there's going to be a meeting tomorrow, at 10 a.m. Make sure you're there.'

'Shouldn't I be getting recovery time?' Recovery from her and Lukas's explosive fling. They shared so much in common but all they could ever have was years of hate followed by a week so unforgettable her last thought in this world would be of him.

'Kat, you've done nothing in that tundra. That's enough vacation time for you,' he joked. 'Tomorrow.'

'I'll be there.'

She ended the call with unease in her belly. Robert hadn't said what the meeting was about or who would be there. All she could do was turn up and hope nothing horrible had happened while she was gone.

Katherine walked into the glass-panelled conference room at the Aero offices with nothing but her computer, which she placed on the table, and took her seat. The same seat she always sat at. Back to the window that overlooked London with its steel-grey skies, old and new buildings standing proud on the banks of the Thames. It was a lovely view. A distracting one, which was why she never gave herself any other option than paying complete attention to the meeting. It also allowed her to see what was happening on the floor. Who entered the room even when the blinds were drawn. They weren't used often, only when absolute privacy was required. The room let out little to no sound and today, the blinds *were* drawn. Not an oversight from a previous meeting. She knew how this place operated.

It made her anxious.

Katherine had replayed Robert's short call in her mind repeatedly but there was nothing to analyse. He had given her nothing to go on so she gave up. Instead, she'd lain on her bed, staring at the ceiling...missing Lukas.

Why didn't I say goodbye? Why didn't I take one last kiss?

She had eventually fallen asleep, curled around the pillow, wishing it was his body. Regret her only companion.

Now she tried to push away thoughts of Lukas but there was no getting rid of them. Even as she watched Robert enter with Jennifer and Scott Courteney, a network executive she hadn't ever met. Though she was the on-air talent, he operated at a much higher level than her. So what was he doing here?

Suddenly that knot of anxiety grew into an entire noose.

'Katherine!' Robert greeted, coming around the table to give her shoulder a squeeze. 'It really is good to see you. I wasn't joking when I said you had us all worried.'

'It's a good thing I wasn't alone,' she replied, wincing internally at the stab of pain that thinking about Lukas brought about.

A look crossed her producer's face that she couldn't decipher. None of this was making her feel better.

'Absolutely. Have you met Scott before?'

'No, can't say I've had the pleasure.' She held out her hand, which Scott shook firmly but there was a glint in his eye that didn't sit well with her.

'Shall we take our seats?' Scott gestured at the table as he placed himself at the head. Robert took the seat next to her, closest to Scott and Jennifer sat on her other side, sandwiching her in. She didn't like it.

'Is anyone else coming?' Katherine asked.

'Yes, they should be along shortly,' Robert said.

That wasn't much information.

'What's this meeting about?' She tried a different tack.

'I'm sure you have plenty of questions, Ms Ward, but I think they can wait just a little longer.' Scott's clasped hands were placed on the table. A man so used to power that he had no problem telling her to be quiet. Because that was exactly what that sentence meant.

'Why don't you tell us what happened in Finland?' Robert suggested. Was he here just to be a buffer? To smooth over anything Scott might say to her?

Katherine had already rehearsed the story she would tell everyone. She knew it would come up again and again. Everyone was interested in Lukas and now people were interested in her too, but she didn't want the world to know about their tender moments. How they'd confided in each other about their mothers or just how much their careers meant to them because their fathers believed in them so much.

She told them everything but did well to leave out the intimate parts of her and Lukas's snowbound week. The parts that made her ache.

She noticed a look pass between the three of them. She was reaching the end of her patience. Whatever was going on was obviously linked to her adventure in Lapland; she had no idea what, but she was going to demand some answers. Just then the door opened and in walked Dominic Wilson, Lukas's manager, Erin Walker, his publicist and right behind them, there he was. Lukas in jeans, boots and a leather jacket. His eyes landed on her the moment he walked into the room and it was like all the air had been sucked out and at the same time she took her first real breath since they had gone their separate ways.

Was that really only yesterday?

He didn't stop looking at her even when Robert and Scott shook his hand. He didn't stop looking at her when he sat opposite her. An entire conference table between them but she wanted to crawl over the top of it to sit on his lap and kiss him. To hell with their agreement and everyone who was watching.

And she could see the heat fill his silver eyes when he read her thoughts.

Finally, he tore his gaze from hers and she saw it settle on Scott. The heat replaced by something icy. 'It's obvious you all have been planning something, so I suggest we get to the point.'

Katherine smiled inwardly. Lukas wasn't bound by the same behavioural expectations she was. He couldn't be fired for not showing the reverence someone like Scott expected.

She wanted to mouth a thank you at him but instead sat quite still, waiting for all this secrecy to end.

'I think Robert should start,' Scott said and all eyes turned to the man sitting next to her.

He cleared his throat. 'Right. As we all know, there was some speculation about what happened to you both in Lapland. You were both on the news daily because there was no information about your well-being,' he said, glancing between her and Lukas. 'What we didn't expect was the level of speculation about the relationship between you two.'

Katherine got a sinking feeling in the pit of her stomach. Surely this wasn't heading where she thought it was.

'The public seemed largely to think that you two were an item or were going to be one and the level of interest that has generated can't be ignored.'

'Speak plainly,' Lukas ordered. His voice was growing lower. His brow furrowing.

Robert pulled some papers out of a folder in front of him that Katherine hadn't quite noticed before and handed them to everyone around the table. 'This is the increase in traffic to the Aero TV site since you two went viral.'

'We have seen similar impressions on Lukas's socials,' Erin added, and Lukas shot her a look that would have anyone shrinking. Katherine saw the apprehension on Erin's face but she pushed on. 'Here are some analytics on the Lukat hashtag.'

Katherine accepted the page from her but the words and infographics were blurring into one.

'This is why we've asked you two to be here today,' Jennifer said. She seemed as confident as always but, for the first time that day, Robert appeared nervous. 'This kind of attention is too great to ignore, so we think it would be best for you both to play into the rumours.'

This had gone exactly where Katherine feared.

'What?' Lukas growled.

There was no way Lukas was going to agree. She hadn't told anyone how they had connected, and she knew Lukas wouldn't have either. This was their secret. Something they had in private surrounded by a wall of snow. She didn't want to put themselves on display. Especially after they'd agreed on an end no matter how much her body and heart craved more.

Scott leaned forwards, placing his palm face down on the table, expecting everyone to give him their attention and everyone respectfully had, but Lukas looked at him with defiance.

He stared unwaveringly at the man and crossed his arms. Katherine couldn't imagine being more attracted to him than she was right now.

'No one is asking the world of either of you,' Scott said. 'You are both public figures. All that is expected is that you two pose as a couple for the next month and a half, which will bring us up roughly to the launch dates for next season's Alpha One cars. We will announce your break-up, and we'll have enough added interest to carry through testing and the season opener.'

'Entirely benefitting you,' Lukas sneered.

'It benefits everyone at this table.'

Lukas shook his head. His expression bored but Katherine knew better than that. He would be hating the very idea. His skin would be crawling. 'Absolutely not.'

'Lukas—' Robert started but Lukas cut him off.

'I will not have my private life splashed about the media like some performance,' Lukas spat. 'You are all entitled to my time on the track but away from it, none of you has any right to anything from me. This whole idea is ridiculous.'

Katherine tried not to take his vehemence personally but it still stung. Being together hadn't seemed ridiculous a day ago. But he was right. This idea didn't benefit her. She was only twenty-seven. She still had her whole career ahead of her. There was no guarantee that she would spend it all with Aero TV and if this ever got out, her career would be ruined. She'd done everything right from the moment she started school. Being the journalist she was didn't happen overnight. It had been a lifetime of working hard and now they wanted her to kiss and flirt with a man so they could increase their ratings. Make more money. But what about her integrity? Her reputation?

'What do you have to say?' Lukas asked her and all heads swivelled towards her. Encouragement on Jennifer's and Robert's faces, something hard on Scott's, curiosity on Dominic's and Erin's. But Lukas…he only expected an answer. Nothing more.

'I don't want to do it. It's too much of a risk to my career if it ever got out. It benefits everyone but me.'

'It benefits the network, Ms Ward,' Scott said.

'The higher ratings benefit you, Kat,' Robert said in a placating tone. 'Imagine how much further your name would go. Think about the clout you would have to negotiate your next contract.'

'Ms Ward.' Scott Courteney turned to face her. To intimidate her. 'You need to be a team player and do your part. We're all working to grow this network.'

'No.' Katherine refused to budge, and she could see pride in Lukas's eyes.

Scott's expression turned menacing. '*Kat*, do you want to work here?'

'What just a minute—' Lukas gritted out.

'You can't be serious,' Katherine spoke over him. She glanced at the man who just tried to stand up for her, who made butterflies take flight in her belly with just a look. Just a touch. And she saw pride had turned into glittering anger.

Jennifer swivelled her chair to face Katherine. 'We

could always find other ways to maximise interest, but they wouldn't be as mutually beneficial. Articles we could run.'

Jennifer's gaze bored into her own and a shiver passed down Katherine's spine. She would run the feature article despite being asked not to. Despite the fact that it wasn't true. But if everyone already thought Katherine and Lukas had been together in Lapland and an article came out that was written by her attacking him, the world would tune in for the drama. She would get a reputation for being unscrupulously ruthless and Lukas would lose any opportunities he had left. She couldn't do that to him. Do that to herself.

'The visibility will definitely be good for *both* of you,' Erin said, trying to diffuse the situation, but it didn't matter because Katherine was backed into a corner. Either she said yes or she lost her job, her reputation, Lukas's career. She'd worked too hard for all that she had achieved for it all to fall apart now. Scott would fire her and hire some other new face who was passionate about the sport. This was her dream career. And what if she said no and lost it all but Lukas's PR team still used the idea as a Hail Mary and forced him to go with it—because she knew how much his career meant to him? Would they find someone else to agree to this ridiculousness?

Some other woman who would get to be with him and touch him and listen to his voice and that accent she now found so endearing.

She hated the idea.

So here she was. She could agree or lose her job because of a situation with Lukas.

It's not his fault.

No, it wasn't but Katherine couldn't refuse. It would cost her her career and she would not let Lukas jeopardise her job again. Never again.

'Fine, I'll do it,' she said, defeat clear in her voice to all at the table.

* * *

Lukas wanted so badly to be angry at Katherine for agreeing. It had felt like they were on the same page in their opposition to this ludicrous proposition and it had felt good. Like maybe in this small way they could be a team. Be something more than the nothing they were forced to be by going back to their own lives now that they had left Finland. But he couldn't blame her. He knew what this job meant to her and this asshole threatening her career had Lukas seeing red.

Maybe it was good she had agreed because they wouldn't be able to blame her when he refused and brought this madness to a halt.

'But I won't be.'

'Lukas—' Dominic finally spoke up '—listen to them.'

He had never been more furious at his manager than right now.

'We are all aware of your current predicament in the sport, Lukas,' Scott said in a way that he clearly thought was charming, but really, all it did was make him come off as slimy. 'This is your last shot.'

'We're all working to leverage this attention for both of you,' Erin said. 'Despite the negative publicity that initially made them nervous—' she glanced briefly at Katherine '—teams would take you over someone in their academy or a pay-to-drive racer if they can get some sort of ROI with you. With all this attention, you would be bankable. You'd attract sponsors for the team. Your name would be worth even more money than it already is.'

Pay-to-drive. ROI. It was all so money dependent now. Where did talent lie? Lukas was confident he could take any car farther up the field than any of the teams still needing drivers could currently imagine being, but he was forced to consider how he could make them money away from the track too. As if championship winnings were no longer enough. It made white-hot heat fill his body. Blood pound in his ears.

'Lukas,' Dominic said. He knew the tone well. It was usually followed by something blunt he didn't want to hear. 'Do you want to have a drive next year? I'm doing all that I can. Erin and I both are. We wouldn't be sitting here if we didn't think this was your best option. There are two teams who haven't signed a second driver and at this point I'd say they are 75 to 80 percent more likely to sign two rookies. But we are trying our best to shift the needle here. Trying to get them to look at you as their saving grace, because we know you can be the difference between them earning sixty million or eighty million dollars.'

Those numbers meant that Lukas's options were firmly at the back of the grid, but at least he would be racing. If he could get the teams more sponsorships that meant more money and better car development, so maybe they would be able to fight even higher than that. But it would also mean that his privacy went out the window. That people could see who he was. That maybe they would see the boy who chose himself and imploded his parents' happiness for his own selfish reasons.

It occurred to him that if he took the team principal job he wouldn't have to deal with any of this nonsense. But he wouldn't be racing. All the sacrifice would have been for nothing. How could he have cost his father so much, only to see the dream die now? He owed his father.

He had to drive.

He pinched the bridge of his nose. How awful would agreeing be?

'Lukas?' He was giving Katherine his attention before he had even realised that it was her voice that called him. He wanted so badly to kick everyone out of this room and take her on the table. Show her how crazy he had been going since they got into that helicopter yesterday. This woman who was intelligent and beautiful. And who had just had her career threatened. If he said no, would he be jeopardising her career again? He knew how much it meant to her, because he knew how much his own meant to him. Their reasons were so similar.

Instead of hurting her he could help her.

And he could have a month with her. Extend the pleasure a little longer.

Yes.

His body cried out.

'I'll do it.' He was nauseous.

'Great,' Robert said but Lukas wasn't looking at him. Not at any of them, but Katherine. 'So now you will leave with Kat out the front of the building.'

'Yes, that will result in pictures on the internet for sure,' Erin agreed. 'It's best that we waste no time.'

'We have photographers stationed strategically as well to ensure there are a number of them,' Jennifer informed them.

'Enough.' Lukas brought his hand down on the glass table making everyone flinch. 'I've agreed to your plan but that's all you're getting out of me. None of you get to dictate anything further to me or to Katherine, am I clear?'

'Be reasonable,' Robert pleaded.

'All of you get out,' Lukas said to the others.

'Lukas…' He heard Scott's voice. The disapproval that he couldn't give a damn about.

He looked only at Katherine. 'I said get out. Leave us.'

He heard the shuffling. The footsteps. The snick of the door shutting. Once they were alone he got out of his chair and went to Katherine, taking her hand and making her stand before him.

The urge to touch her was too great, he couldn't stop himself from running his hand up her arm, over her shoulder, cupping her cheek. His thumb caressed her porcelain skin.

Are you okay? he wanted to ask. *Are you sure you want to do this because I don't*, he wanted to say, but he didn't. He couldn't. The future of their careers was hanging over their heads. What choice did either of them have if they wanted to hold on to their dreams?

Katherine seemed to understand what he wanted to say.

'It won't be forever,' she whispered.

'It won't.' But it felt like they were talking about so much more than this plan. They had another chance to be together. Weeks this time. Hours and hours to indulge the chemistry that was still so potent Lukas had to fight to stop himself kissing her here. But he would have to kiss her, and there would be pictures. His life that he had worked so tirelessly to keep private would be advertised for the world to see.

How could one person want something so badly and so utterly hate how they were getting it?

He was selling out his principles to keep his racing career alive. For a bit of time with Katherine. His father had always taught him to stand up for his beliefs, but he'd caved. What would he think of Lukas if he could see him now?

CHAPTER TEN

LUKAS SAT OPPOSITE Katherine in his private jet. She had said very little since they had left Aero. In fact, when he had said they would be travelling to Monaco to spend the time there, she had put up very little fight. Instead, she had seemed lost in thought.

That was fine. Once they got to his home, they would have the privacy they needed to talk. So for now, he gave her the space she needed.

Not that much space.

His jet had eight leather seats. Plus, he had a bedroom at the back of the plane hidden behind a polished wall. He could have sat anywhere else, but he didn't want to. He wanted to be around Katherine. Needed to be close to her. She didn't bring him peace. No. She made him feel like he was attached to a live wire. She focussed all his attention on her. Consumed him. And *that* was as close to peace as he got.

He led her by the hand to the waiting helicopter that would fly them to Monaco when they landed in Nice. Even while they buckled themselves in, he didn't let go. He didn't want to. It was only a seven-minute flight but with her hand in his and their shoulders brushing, Lukas was thrown into a dimension where every minute dragged for hours and yet somehow, he hadn't realised they had landed until the doors opened.

He needed to get home. Needed a moment with her in private to kiss her. To talk to her. To find a boundary he could work with, because right now he couldn't think clearly.

As soon as they stepped into his apartment Lukas could breathe again. Tension that had bunched his muscles from the moment they were rescued ebbed away. Here, he could be himself. There was no one watching, no one to judge him.

No one to support you. No one to be happy you've returned.

He was always greeted with silence.

'Lukas?'

Except today.

'I'll show you to your room. We can talk after,' he said, leading her through the entrance to his three-storey apartment. An apartment that was filled with so much light even though the sky was overcast and a drizzle fell as far as the eye could see.

'No,' Katherine refused, halting her steps and bringing her bag to a stop beside her. 'I want to talk first.'

'Fine. Come with me,' he said, placing his hand on the small of her back and leading her forward. 'Leave your bag. I'll take it up to your room.'

He took her into a lounge area with large overstuffed couches and a double height ceiling. A balcony to another floor wrapped around the square with tall narrow gold square poles placed in irregular intervals like a crown if a room could ever have one.

'We're just over two weeks into December and you have no Christmas decorations up.'

'I don't see the point of celebrating a holiday that does nothing but show me that I have no family to spend it with.' Lukas tried to keep his voice as emotionless as possible. He missed his father every day; he didn't need a holiday to make that worse. And his mother? Well, he understood her not wanting to see the reason her marriage failed.

'Have a seat.' When she obeyed, he sat on the coffee table in front of her. 'Do you want to go first?'

She didn't hesitate. 'Why did you bring me here? I'm still a journalist, Lukas. Nothing's changed.'

'You're right, nothing has changed and yet everything has.' Lukas leaned forward, clasping his hands between his knees to stop himself reaching for Katherine. They needed to establish rules before he allowed himself the pleasure. A pleasure he'd been robbed of since their rescue. One that he craved so badly he was currently leaving crescent-shaped indents on the back of his hands. 'I don't want to invite the media into my home and I'm *not* doing so. Understand that, Katherine. Whatever happens within these walls is not for a report. *But* it was best to come here. It's where I am comfortable. Where we can both be comfortable and have space should we need it. It's a place where we don't have to pretend, but when we step outside…'

'The cameras will go off,' Katherine finished for him. 'Monaco is small enough that it would take minutes to come back here should we need sanctuary.'

Lukas nodded, glad that she understood. 'There's enough space for you to work and you're free to use all the facilities in my home.'

'Thank you. But you still haven't addressed *us*.'

That's when Lukas noticed her hands. Fingers fidgeting with a ring. She needed to know where they stood just as much as he did.

He placed his large hand over hers. 'We're in this position because we had very few options and if it wasn't for that meeting we would have been over.'

'Does that mean you want us to remain that way? Over?' Katherine asked, her hands wrapping around his.

'We don't have a future. We're too different in the ways that matter.' Katherine slowly pulled her hands from his but he wouldn't let her. 'But I would be lying if I said that I want us to be a thing of the past. I'm giving you the choice, Katherine, because if it were up to me, you would be in my bed already. You would have barely made it into this apartment before I ravaged your lips and had your body against mine. Any second now you would have been screaming out my name but no one would have heard you. No one would have seen you and not because we were forced into a cabin in the middle of nowhere, but because we chose to take the privacy we're owed.'

'So you still want me.'

'I wanted you the very first time I saw you. That's never changed.' Lukas pulled Katherine off the couch to straddle his lap. She ran her fingers through his hair, tugging it back; he looked into the depths of her blue eyes made all the more vivid by her red lashes. 'Do you know how frustrating it is to be so attracted to the person you hate. Who you know hates you?'

'Do you still hate me?' she whispered so close to his lips that her breath tickled his skin.

'No.'

She smiled. 'I don't hate you either.'

And then he kissed her.

CHAPTER ELEVEN

KATHERINE AWOKE TO bright sunshine in a large, spectacularly appointed room with gold and marble accents. Monaco and the Mediterranean Sea lay beyond the windows, which had no treatments to distract from the view. She levered herself onto her elbows. Despite it being December, she saw plenty of people on the water in their yachts.

Never in her wildest dreams had she ever thought she would be in this position. Living in a driver's home, pretending to be in a relationship with him. *Pretending* was the important part. That's why after enjoying Lukas's passion in the lounge, she'd asked to be taken to her room.

This wasn't a real relationship. They were doing this because they were backed into a corner and neither of them wanted to risk their careers. Anything more than that was simply an opportunity to indulge in some pleasure, but pleasure was all it was. Katherine didn't want a relationship with anyone. She didn't want to move in with anyone. Love was dangerous. Love derailed dreams and then what would she be left with? A life of mediocrity and unfulfillment while trying to convince herself that she was just fine? No, thanks.

She wasn't her mother. Katherine wouldn't let that happen to her.

But thoughts of her mother made her realise that her parents would have been unprepared for the wave of news announcing her relationship with Lukas. Last time she'd spoken to them she was assuring them that she'd never been in any danger in Lapland. That there was no truth to the rumours, and she'd promised to visit the first chance she got.

Katherine groaned and flopped back on the pillows.

She reached for her phone and just as she expected there were numerous calls and messages from both her parents. Well, only one from her father—the only one that made her feel guilty.

Why didn't you tell us? You didn't have to hide it. Take care of yourself, Kittykat. Enjoy Monaco.

He loved the sunshine, would love it here.

Isn't it a pity that he'll never meet Lukas?

Yes. No. It wasn't a real relationship, so no, it wasn't a pity.

I have no family to spend it with.

Her father would never let Lukas feel so alone. He didn't let her feel alone.

For twenty weekends in a year, that was.

'No! Stop it, Katherine,' she ordered herself and got out of bed. Her phone lighting up as she did so.

It was a message from Robert.

Scott isn't happy that you two are hiding out in Monaco. I suggest getting out for some 'in public' time.

Scott Courteney being unhappy wasn't a good thing for her, so Katherine went down to the lower level—she had found out it contained the kitchen, two dining areas, a lounge and a home theatre, which was a lot of space to entertain for a man so alone—barefoot in her satin pyjamas. The aroma of freshly brewed coffee led her to the kitchen where Lukas was shirtless and sweaty in a pair of grey track pants hanging low on his hips, downing a bottle of water. Drop after drop of perspiration ran down his carved torso to the band of his pants where they were wicked by the fabric. Heat rushed to Katherine's face. A tightening in her core.

'Good morning.' There was a teasing lilt to his voice. Obviously he'd caught her staring. She did that a lot but honestly, how could she not when he looked like a fantasy given life?

'Would you like some coffee? I don't have any tea. I wasn't expecting guests.'

'Do you ever?' She walked up to him and curled her hands in the fabric of his pants, giving him the smallest of kisses, growing satisfied at his gasp. It was only fair to level the playing field.

'Not in recent years,' he admitted.

How lonely.

'I have a life, Katherine. I just don't like bringing the world into my sanctuary.'

'But you brought me here.'

'I did.' He said nothing else. Instead, he reached for a cup and poured her a coffee. It wasn't how she normally started her day, but she had always loved coffee. She developed the habit of drinking tea because that was what everyone else in her home preferred growing up and she didn't want to be demanding, so she had made do. Now starting her day with a cup of tea was habit.

'Robert messaged me, they want us to go out in public today.' She sipped the coffee, relishing the comforting warmth. It wasn't overly bitter, and she could taste notes of dark chocolate and caramel. It was delicious.

'I expected as much. It's a good thing I already had a plan, then, isn't it?'

'Oh? And what's that?'

'Get dressed and I'll show you.'

Lukas's plan was strutting down a street. Maybe that wasn't completely fair. They walked hand in hand down the most high-end street in Carré d'Or. Haute couture brands lined up everywhere she looked. Lukas had taken her shopping—a normally mundane outing yet with him it was anything but. Her heart hadn't found a steady rhythm since he'd held her hand. It was made even worse by the kiss he had given her outside a world-famous bag boutique that had rendered her light-headed. From one store to the next he had spoilt her. Something that wasn't spoken about in their agreement, but she had also never seen him in such a good mood and it made her wonder if he enjoyed taking care of people.

Hadn't he said he wanted to do so for his mother? But his mother didn't want to see him. Katherine moved closer to him, and he slipped his hand from hers, wrapping it around her shoulders.

Not real.

She had to keep reminding herself of that fact.

'You're quiet,' Lukas said, his dark sunglasses hooked on the front of his shirt.

'Aren't I always?'

The sound that came out of him was somewhere between a chuckle and a snort. It was the most undignified she had ever seen him and she had seen him use some colourful language on the team radio over the years. She couldn't help but laugh.

'Is that a no?'

'What is the saying you English use? When pigs fly?'

Katherine laughed harder then. He spoke so well that sometimes she forgot English wasn't his first language. She wiped a tear and saw a softness enter his eyes but he quickly looked away, so she did too.

'That jacket is stunning.' She tried to change the subject but it was clearly the wrong thing to say with Lukas being in such an odd mood, because he immediately led them inside.

'Try it on.'

'Lukas, it's really not necessary,' she tried to refuse.

Just then a very polished shop assistant came towards them. 'Can I help you?'

'No.'

'Yes.'

They said in unison.

'Yes,' Lukas insisted. 'She would like to try on that coat.' He pointed at the window.

'Of course, right this way.'

'You're being ridiculous,' Katherine whisper shouted.

'Am I, or are you?' Lukas challenged. 'How often do you get opportunities like this?'

Never, really. Katherine earned a very comfortable living and if everything went to plan it would only get better. That was why she was here, so that she didn't lose her career progress. So that she could eventually be rich and successful enough to take care of her parents. So that they could retire. And so that Paige, and to a lesser degree Christopher and Nicholas, would have a safety net. Buying a five-thousand euro coat wasn't on her radar. She had big-picture concerns.

'From the look on your face I'm going to say not often. So let me spoil you. You only have to put up with it for a month.'

Katherine hated the way that reminder made her mood plummet, but she forced herself to smile and said, 'Thank you.'

She went into the fitting room and tried the coat on. It was perfect. As if some magical tailor had made it to her exact measurements. She looked at the black fabric and white floral detail from every angle in the large cubicle fitted with the flattering light, and just as she slipped it off her shoulders and back on the hanger there was a knock on the door. She opened it a smidge and found Lukas on the other side holding a dress. Before she knew it, he was barging in and locking the door behind him.

'I want you to wear this.'

'What?'

'Try it on.'

'You realise you've walked into my fitting room, right?' The audacity of this man, barging his way in and making demands.

'Yes, I'm aware. I know I drive on a closed track, but I have a very good sense of direction.'

'You're impossible.'

He simply shrugged.

'Are you leaving?'

'Would you mind if I stayed?'

'No.' She really didn't. She loved the way he didn't hide his attraction to her, and how it made her feel. Was this appropriate in such an exclusive store? Katherine found that she didn't much care.

She took off her sweater and her jeans while looking at Lukas, whose grey eyes had darkened like a storm. Still, she watched him watching her as she slipped on the soft, heavy dress. The weight made sense since it was covered in sequins. The softness was surprising.

'Turn around.'

She obeyed and saw herself and Lukas reflected at her. Could see when he bent, trailing kisses up her spine as he pulled the zip all the way up.

'Beautiful.'

This dress was more than just beautiful. The long sleeves sat off her shoulders. From chest to toes she was covered in glittering sequins forming a silver and gold gradient. It fit every curve until her hips where it flared out just slightly in a sparkling column.

'Look at me.'

Her eyes found his in the mirror, watching him trail kisses over her shoulder, along her neck. His hands gliding down her covered arms to her waist and then he spun her around, pushing her against the mirror. Her chest heaving even though he hadn't done very much. But then his nose was running along her neck. His lips brushing after.

'You'll wear this tomorrow,' he said. Instructed.

'Why?'

'That's not what you should be saying.' He inched the dress up higher and higher, gathering the fabric of the skirt in his hands, allowing one of them to trail over the inside of her thigh until he reached her sex covered in satin and lace, and he hummed in approval.

'You should be saying, "Yes, Lukas."'

She could hear his smirk but couldn't look because his fingers were taking her apart and putting her back together.

'Lukas,' she breathed.

He chuckled, deep and low. 'That's half right.'

She couldn't think when a moan was building in her throat.

'Quiet,' he said, then he kissed her deeply, swallowing every sound she made as his fingers drove her to insanity. Her hips meeting the movement of his skilled hand, wanting, needing more.

'You're being so good for me right now,' he praised. His lips brushing hers as he said the words. The taunt of a kiss and it was all too much. His words and fingers and lips, and then his tongue was in her mouth silencing her as she climaxed in a fitting room in Monaco wearing the most expensive dress she ever had on.

'Yes, Lukas,' she agreed because, if this was a taste of what awaited, she would wear anything to have more of him.

CHAPTER TWELVE

LUKAS WAS PULLING out all the stops. An all-black Bugatti waited in the portico of his building, the headlights switched on. Gleaming the way it did against the late dusk sky, the car seemed like some kind of spectre. Dark and mysterious.

If Robert and Scott wanted her and Lukas to be seen, they would certainly get their wish.

Katherine had done as Lukas asked and worn the incredible dress he'd bought her. Her stomach felt like she was in a rollercoaster every time she thought about what had occurred in the fitting room. No matter what happened after this month, she would keep this dress forever—a reminder of the racer she had been so wrong about. The man who brought her to life. The passion that was only bestowed upon a lucky few maybe once in a lifetime.

'Ready?' Lukas asked beside her.

She nodded. 'Yes.'

He took her hand, led her to the car and helped her in before closing the door and getting in himself. Something about this night felt different. It had felt different since they'd left the fitting room but Katherine couldn't quite put her finger on what it was.

Was it Lukas? Was he being more attentive? Or was it her? Was it the way she felt about Lukas that was morphing into an affection she couldn't name?

She tried to pay little attention to what happened outside

the car as Lukas drove the short distance to the Monte Carlo casino, but she couldn't not notice the number of phones in hands that followed them as they drove by, and when they reached the valet and exited Lukas's car.

Katherine was always on the other side of the media and now, just as Lukas was watched and snapped and recorded every moment he wasn't in his home, so was she. She wasn't sure she liked it all that much. Yes, she was in the public eye, but it was never, ever like this.

She felt Lukas's arm around her shoulders and gave him a small smile. She really hadn't appreciated his patience before.

'You look beautiful,' he said.

'Thank you.'

'Ignorc them.'

Her steps slowed. 'What?'

'Keep walking and I said, "Ignore them."' His arm drew her tighter to him. More protectively. And when she looked up, there was a look in his eyes that took her breath away. 'The longer this goes on, the worse it's going to be. Cameras are going to follow you everywhere. The best thing you can do is ignore the attention.'

They reached the grand entrance to the casino where people the world over wished to visit but only a handful ever would. Lukas tilted Katherine's chin up and she gazed at his face. At the determined expression.

'And you can trust me to protect you.'

Katherine's throat went dry. Had he really noticed her discomfort with the attention she received? Attention was something she craved but never asked for. Now she was getting it in spades, so why was it bothering her?

'I—'

'Can protect yourself? I know you can, but this is something you're unprepared for. This kind of attention is invasive. It's not curious; it's entitled.'

'How did you…' Katherine wasn't sure what she was asking. *How did he know? What was he really saying?*

'There was attention that I craved and never received too, Katherine, but I knew this—' he tilted his head in the direction of flashing cameras '—wasn't it.'

Lukas understood her like no one else. If they stood out here any longer, the world would witness her getting emotional and she didn't want them to see her like that. Never mind that such a display would get the tabloids going crazy, because that was the unfortunate side effect of playing it up for Aero TV. The tabloids were having a field day.

'I think we should go inside.'

He smiled. 'That is probably a good idea.'

'So we're gambling tonight,' Katherine said in a light tone she forced when they climbed the stairs and walked through the historic doors.

'No.'

'Okay…then what are we doing at a casino?'

'Being seen and not heard.' His smile held a secret.

'You know what, I'm not even going to ask. Lead the way.'

Lukas noticed Katherine struggling with being in the public eye at this level. This wasn't anything like her job and he knew how violating it felt. Yes, she'd agreed to this, but it didn't mean she deserved to feel that way. He could help her. Was helping her. He was protecting her by bringing her into his home, taking her shopping where they would have constant reprieves whenever they went into the high-end stores, and bringing her here where the clientele was so exclusive. And that was why he took her into a restaurant.

'*Bonsoir,*' an elegant hostess greeted. '*Bienvenue.* Your table is waiting, Mr Jäger. Please follow me.'

Lukas placed his arm around Katherine's waist, holding her close as they followed the hostess through the stunning frescoed restaurant and into a cozy private corner near a window. The tables around them were empty. A reserved sign on each of them.

He held the chair out for Katherine and once she was seated, rounded the table to his own. The hostess handed them menus and left.

'Did you reserve all these tables?' Katherine asked. 'Is that how you made sure we wouldn't be heard?'

'I'm a selfish man, Katherine. I want your attention focussed solely on me.' A lie it was more convenient to tell, because the truth was that he wanted to spend all the time he could with her alone. He wanted her smiles and her candid honesty and her passion. He wanted them to be trapped in a bubble where he could lavish his attention on her and in return she would wholly want him. But wanting that much was a secret because she was only with him to save her career and enjoy some no-strings sex.

'I don't think that's true,' she said, leaning towards him. 'I don't think you're selfish. I think you were made to feel that way but really, you're generous and kind and protective.'

'Is that so?' He didn't want to say more than that and give away how he felt to have someone see him that way. He had never spoken to his father about his feelings regarding his parents' divorce or his mother's disapproval. He had never wanted his father to be forced to comfort him and lie to him. To tell him that his mother was wrong. It would have hurt his father to say that. It was better to be the son his father needed him to be.

'Yes.' She reached across the table and placed her hand on his. A burning, sparking touch he wanted pressed against his cheek, a comfort he wanted to soak up. 'And I truly don't understand how you've been single for so long or why.'

Because his choices had consequences, that was why. And he couldn't put another person through the way he lived his life.

A waiter approached the table and Lukas gestured to Katherine to order, all the while watching her. The way she smiled and laughed and bantered. The way her red hair glowed under the lights. The way the gleam from the candle on the table sparkled in her blue eyes. She was incredible. So full of life and determination. She was also the only person he had met who he could relate to.

'And for you, monsieur?'

'I'll have the same and a glass of your best Bordeaux for Ms Ward.'

'Of course.'

'You knew I liked red wine?' Katherine asked when the waiter left and Lukas was forced to show just how much attention he'd paid to her over the years.

'There was a discussion about wine between you, and some of the drivers when we were in France once. You mentioned a Bordeaux you tried—'

Her eyes grew wide. 'That I loved… Lukas, that was two years ago. You weren't even there.'

'I wasn't part of your conversation, but I was there. I watched and listened,' he confessed and then made another confession. 'And to answer your previous question, I've been single this long because of choices I made.'

Katherine's frown was a silent request for him to continue.

'I was in a relationship for two years. We lived together. I was certain I would marry her. I loved her and in my mind we were already committed to growing old together.'

'What!' The surprise on her face was almost comical. 'I had no idea.'

'No one did, and that was the problem. No one knew because I was determined to maintain our privacy. Protect us from the press and scrutiny. But keeping it hidden forced us to be so careful of what we did and where we went. Whether people would take pictures of us. We tried to be happy, but she grew tired of how viciously I protected our privacy.'

You're snuffing out the life in me, Lukas. I want to have fun. Not be sequestered in the shadows so no one ever sees us, or takes a picture of us. I won't wait for you to be ready to live. You need to figure this thing out with the media because they are never going away, but I am.

'She said she couldn't live like that. As if we were sneaking around doing something wrong.'

Katherine was quiet, listening and not interrupting. He could see her curiosity and a part of him wondered if he was being stupid, telling her something so private. She was still a journalist and only on this date because that career in the media had been threatened. But something in him wanted to keep talking to her, so he did.

'I thought we could just deal with the years I had to be in the spotlight and once I retired we could finally have the life we wanted and things would get better. But I was wrong. She was right to leave because I was being selfish again. *I* didn't want our relationship in the media, so I forced that on her without considering what she wanted. She said she just wanted to be able to live her life. It wasn't a great time,' he said, looking out the window at the sparkling lights of Monaco, certain that he saw a few flashes go off in the distance. 'Two weeks later we were at the season opener and I saw you,' he looked at Katherine then, remembering the way his steps had come to an abrupt halt when he'd seen her. She had taken his breath away. That attraction had never waned. Sitting here with her in that sparkling dress, it was stronger than ever. It had just magnified after getting a taste of her.

She laughed but it was sad. 'You saw me and were attracted to me and everything went to hell.'

'Yes,' he agreed. 'I decided after that it would be best for me to be alone until I retired.' He saw the waiter approaching and leaned back in his chair. Katherine followed his movements. They kept silent while their meal was placed in front of them then thanked the server and waited for them to leave. Only then did they resume their conversation.

'I don't understand something,' Katherine said. 'If driving hurts you so much at this point, why are you so adamant about continuing? I know what you said about your father, but how is this for you? You're the one who has to live with this career.'

'I don't have to. I have another option.' The words were out of his mouth before he could stop them, but now he wanted to tell Katherine. No one knew. Not even Dominic. 'I have an offer on the table from Vortex Racing.'

'Not to drive, obviously.' Because they already had a confirmed driver line-up.

'To be their team principal.'

'Wow,' Katherine breathed, sitting back in her chair. 'That's huge! But if you're still looking for a drive, that means you turned them down?'

'I haven't given them an answer,' Lukas admitted, picking up his fork, but all he did was push the food around his plate.

'This is a massive opportunity, Lukas.' Katherine sat up straighter, a small frown creasing her forehead as she placed her palms on the table. This was analytical Katherine. The side of her that absorbed information and made connections from it, and it was fascinating to watch.

'Okay, so they're new and unlikely to be very competitive in their first year. Their factory is small but they have attracted some big talent behind the scenes so I think they will have one of the better designed cars, which means there's potential even with them having a customer engine. With your name attached, more sponsors would invest and that could make a difference. Just your name attached…' She looked at Lukas and he stopped breathing, but it didn't stop him from listening to her. 'But with you leading the team, Lukas, I'd say two maybe three years at a push before that car's winning races.'

He placed his fork down on his plate. 'I don't know, Katherine. I don't know if I'm ready to leave the cockpit. If I'm ready to lead a team,' he admitted.

'You have already led a team as a driver. You have so much knowledge…such an understanding of the car and the craft that even from a technical aspect you could make a difference. Then there's the fact that you took Dudek's team from nowhere to a championship. You've done it with two different teams. If there's anyone who knows how to win a championship, it's you.'

'But it isn't driving.'

She leaned towards him, placing her elbows on the linen tablecloth and shaking her head. 'No, it isn't, but is driving what you're really passionate about?' she asked intensely.

Lukas couldn't answer that. He loved driving but he couldn't honestly say that he was as passionate about it now as he used to be. He was jaded.

'From where I'm sitting, driving is keeping you in this weird purgatory where your life is on hold. You're alone because of it. And you don't have to be alone, Lukas.'

'I could say the same thing about you.' He needed to move the conversation away from this topic because Katherine was starting to make more sense than he wanted to hear.

'That's different,' she said softly, picking up her utensils.

'Why? You are not your mother. You have achieved so much more than everyone else in your family has. Why are you letting your mother's choices warn you away from a possible future?' It was an invasive question, Lukas knew, but he wanted to understand everything about Katherine. He needed to.

'My achievements so far are precisely why I won't let myself fall in love. It's proof of what I can have without that distraction. Without the risk of having or wanting to give everything up for one person. I have responsibilities.'

'Tell me about them.'

She placed her knife down and picked at the duck on her plate with her fork. 'My parents are getting older and will soon have to retire, but that won't be possible if Paige keeps getting into trouble. One time it was shoplifting, another it was drugs. There's always something. She can't hold down a job. One time she decided on a whim to pawn a bunch of things and flew to Europe where she worked odd jobs to move around between countries until she ran out of money and my dad had to go and get her.'

'Did he miss something important?' Lukas guessed he must have. If Paige caused disaster after disaster, not every mistake would be remembered, but the ones that hurt in some way would.

'A celebration dinner when I got my very first media job. It was the first step in our plan and I knew he wanted to celebrate with me but he couldn't. I understood, but it still hurt.'

'You didn't have to be understanding. He could have made her wait. He could have sent her the money to get back and whatever happened after that would have been her choice as an adult,' Lukas argued, but Katherine's family history was starting to become so clear.

'I did have to. I'd vowed to be the one they never had to worry about. And that's why I have to be a success, Lukas. Because if I have the resources to take care of Paige, then my parents can enjoy their golden years. And then I'll have to care for them. Someone will have to pay for facilities they'll need later in life. Someone will have to cover for all the savings they lost on rescuing my siblings. And besides all of that, this sport is my life. It's my dream. I can't lose it. Not for anyone or anything.'

'I'm sorry, Katherine. I didn't realise just how much I jeopardised by speaking so carelessly back then. In your place I would have hated me too.'

'I'm sorry I didn't give you the chance to explain. Maybe we could have had this sooner.'

Lukas didn't care who was watching then, he leaned across the table and kissed Katherine bruisingly, wishing for the same. Wishing for more. Wishing that he had done a better job guarding his heart against her, because this affection for a woman he could never have hurt him more than hating her ever did.

CHAPTER THIRTEEN

KATHERINE WORKED QUICKLY and quietly to put the finishing touches on the Christmas decorations that now hung in the lounge.

After their dinner—and after that kiss that had felt so real her heart had started pounding in panic and exhilaration— they had returned home and Lukas had gone to his room and stayed there. When she'd come down for breakfast that morning, there had been no sign that he'd woken or worked out, which had been odd. But it had been an opportunity.

Katherine was now getting to experience what life was like for Lukas. Alpha One was his whole life, but there was so much that shouldn't have to come along with it, which he was navigating the best he could. The unwanted attention, the loneliness. And he was lonely.

A holiday that does nothing but show me that I have no family to spend it with.

Lukas was caring and supportive and generous and kind. He had been proving that to her over and over. Taking care of her in Lapland when he didn't have to.

At the meeting he'd deferred to her. Made her feel seen. Even her life choices—that her mother was critical of—had been simply accepted by Lukas because she'd made them. *He* wasn't critical, because he trusted her to make the right choices for herself.

And now that *she* was the one struggling with the media

attention, Lukas hadn't been smug. He didn't ask her how she liked it or say 'I told you so,' he'd opened up to her and helped her through it.

That man didn't deserve to be alone. Especially not at Christmas. Which had given her a brilliant idea. She had slipped from the uber-luxurious apartment and returned with all manner of decorations.

Green fir garlands now hung around the room. Woven through the gold poles with warm white fairy lights twinkling prettily between red and gold ornaments. The tree, which perfectly matched the garlands, was almost done. Katherine had only a few decorations left to hang. She quickly did so, then got rid of all the packaging before Lukas could see. There was one last thing to do, which she hoped he would do with her. Place the angel at the very top.

She'd just placed a plate on the coffee table when a gruff voice right behind her said, 'What's this?'

Katherine spun around, heart racing. 'I didn't hear you.'

Lukas placed his fingers on the pulse point on her neck, which did nothing to slow the beats down.

'You didn't answer my question,' he said softly.

Katherine was hit by a wave of doubt. Had she overstepped?

'I wanted to show you that you can celebrate the holidays,' she said. 'That you aren't alone.'

'Is that true?'

They stood exactly as they were. His hand on her neck. Her hands at her sides. Not moving a muscle. Not daring to breathe.

'Yes.'

For as long as he allowed her to be part of his world, he wouldn't be alone. So she stepped closer to him and wrapped her arms around his neck, not trying to kiss him or push for that passion that they so often lost themselves in, but just wanting to hold him. Give him the comfort he had been giving her.

His arms closed around her and he dropped his head onto

her shoulder. In that moment Katherine could have wept. She had never felt his heart so open to her. A sign that this wasn't just physical.

'Is that lebkuchen?' he asked before she could overthink what was happening.

'Yes.' They broke apart as he instantly reached for one. 'Abandoned for biscuits,' she tsked.

But Lukas had halted. Held the confectionary in his hand, making no move to eat it.

'Lukas, it's the off-season and it's nearly Christmas. I think you can allow yourself a few things that make you happy.'

He turned a burning gaze to her. She knew only part of that intensity was because of the lebkuchen and the nostalgia he would certainly be feeling.

Shaking himself out of whatever it was that had a hold on him, Lukas brought the biscuit up to her lips.

'After my mother left, at Christmas my father would make sure we never ran out of these,' he said. She bit into the soft, spicey glory, listening almost as if hypnotised. 'Most years there weren't any presents, but there was always a tin of these for me to open on Christmas Eve.'

He popped the other half into his mouth. She was mesmerised by his lips.

Katherine remembered Lukas saying his father had been a cook. 'Did he bake them?'

He nodded.

'How long has it been since you had any?'

'Nearly two years.'

Because his father had died the year before. They couldn't have spent last Christmas together. He had no one to spend it with anymore. A holiday filled with pain. Well, she was about to change that.

'I have one more thing to do on the tree. Will you help me with it?'

'Of course.'

She tugged him by the hand and gave him a box to open but he was inspecting a gold nut on the tree. There were many scattered among the branches.

'You thought of everything.'

'Never underestimate a determined woman, Mr Jäger.'

'I would never underestimate you.'

'Open that.' She tried to hide her flushed cheeks but it was no use. He caught her chin and placed a soft kiss on her lips. The first kiss since the restaurant.

He let her go and opened the box, revealing an exquisite iridescent shell angel with gold metalwork.

'Will you put it up top?' she asked.

'As you wish.'

While he worked to get it out of the box, she told him of a memory. 'When we were younger, the four of us would decorate the tree under my parents' supervision but there was always a fight for who got to place the tree topper.'

Lukas stopped what he was doing to listen to her.

'At first we had an angel. It was porcelain and so beautiful. We promised to be careful but when the others fought, it broke. From then on we had a plastic star. Whenever the fight broke out, I'd slink away to the corner, as far as possible from the fray.'

'What did you do for attention?' Lukas asked.

'What do you mean?' she asked, bundling up the fallen tissue paper, but he pulled it from her hands and brought her closer to him.

'It's clear to me to that you didn't get much attention and your siblings' behaviour would have attracted a lot of it. But you still wanted it, didn't you? Even though you sat there in the corner away from them, watching. So what did you do to earn it from your parents?'

Katherine stood there dumbstruck. A mouth full of cotton. She couldn't answer his question, which made her throat burn with emotions she didn't want to express.

'I think you chose this job to be seen, Katherine,' he said so simply, as if he wasn't about to strip away her armour, leaving her vulnerable.

'You and your father shared a love of Alpha One and maybe becoming a driver wasn't an option but given what you've told me, you could have chosen other routes. Engineering, perhaps. But you chose journalism. A job that would have you seen and heard by millions.' He caressed her cheek. 'Attention.'

She tried to look away but he wouldn't let her.

'You spent so long trying to be the good daughter who didn't need anything that you made yourself nearly invisible. You did what was asked of you when it was asked with no pushback ever, but you wanted to be noticed by your parents and the only time you were was when it came to racing and this career path. And you want to take care of them because you are good and kind but also so that they'll finally take notice of you. So now, here you are in the public eye demanding attention, standing your ground in your life because you have always been independent. But from your mother's point of view…she doesn't understand why you've changed. Why you suddenly won't listen to her advice and won't be invisible anymore.'

Katherine could feel her throat burning but she didn't want to cry. Not in front of anyone. Not even Lukas.

'You wanted to be so good, so easy to deal with that you hid yourself from them, but they should have worked harder to know you.' His warm hand cupped the back of hers, turning it over and in it, he placed the angel. 'I see you, Katherine.'

Then he picked her up and took her to the tree where she easily placed the tree topper.

Her heart was going to burst. She wanted to cling onto Lukas and never let go.

'We still have to make an appearance,' he started when he set her down.

In an instant she went from floating to falling. This was still a fake relationship. He had been given no way to refuse. She could never forget that.

'Tomorrow, I will take us out on my boat,' Lukas went on. 'We'll be seen quite easily but we'll be alone.' She shivered as he tucked a lock of red hair behind her ear. 'The paps can get their pictures, but we'll have complete privacy.'

'Tomorrow is your thirty-fourth birthday,' she said, feeling foolish for having bought him a gift.

'You knew that?'

'The world knows that, Lukas,' she deadpanned.

'I meant, you remembered.'

'Of course, I did.'

'Why? And don't tell me for your work.'

Well, there went that excuse. The truth was she didn't know. Most drivers celebrated their birthday during the season but not Lukas, so the date should have meant nothing to her. And yet she was always aware of it.

'I can't answer that.'

'Can't or won't?' he pushed.

'I don't know why.'

'I think you do but you don't want to think about the reason. It's okay, Katherine, I understand.'

He had it wrong. There was nothing to think about.

'I need to shower,' he said.

He didn't ask for her to join him, neither did she follow him when he left the room. She was left in the beautifully decorated lounge, alone, confused, heart racing for no explicable reason.

CHAPTER FOURTEEN

WHEN LUKAS HAD said 'boat' Katherine hadn't been sure what to expect. Yes, she had seen pictures of him on board— taken by paparazzi with their telephoto lenses—but the truth was that while she loved fast cars, she knew virtually nothing about boats. This one was bigger than her apartment, and far more luxurious too. But it wasn't anywhere near as fast as she had expected it to be. Lukas threw himself out of planes, raced cars, went skiing and mountain biking; she expected that to translate to the water.

'You seem surprised.' He looked amused.

'It's slower than I thought it would be,' she confessed, hugging her arms in her thick cable-knit sweater. Lukas stood at a large silver wheel, steering the boat easily, with Katherine at his side. They were going out just far enough to be alone, which was why they were up on the fly bridge and not inside at the main helm.

'I come out here to get away from everything. I don't need it to be fast, I need it to be calming.' Lukas stopped the boat, mooring them at a point out on the water from which Katherine could see all of Monaco. It was a completely different place during race weekends. Now it looked spectacularly beautiful, calm, peaceful. Though it would never again be peaceful for her.

Now every future trip would be full of memories of Lukas. His arms snaked around her waist.

Just an appearance, Katherine. This was his idea.

'Let's go down to the rear deck.'

His lips trailed up her neck causing a rush of excitement within her but her body reacting so readily to him also saddened her.

Are you wanting more from Lukas?

Before, she would have said 'no,' a flat out honest refusal. But she didn't know anymore.

He led her down to the rear of the boat furnished with plush couches around a fixed table.

'Have a seat, I'll be right back.'

From the couch she kept her eye on the principality, guessing from this distance where his apartment would be. Maybe she was growing too attached. Maybe she should leave. Lukas knew what her deal was. She couldn't change her mind on relationships, so he would understand if she made an excuse to go back to London.

After promising to stay for Christmas?

She didn't want to hurt him and pulled out a small gift box from her handbag.

'What's that?' Lukas asked, placing a plate of fruit on the table.

He sat close to her and her hand automatically went to his thigh as if she couldn't stand to not touch him. His hand closed around hers, keeping it there. Beneath the table where no one could see. No photographer would spy such a small, private show of affection. And it confused her more.

She placed the box in front of Lukas. 'Your birthday present.'

With his free hand, he pulled away at the ribbons and opened the box. She watched him pull out a crystal snowflake ornament.

'Seemed appropriate.'

He grinned. 'I'd say so.' With the ribbon the snowflake was attached to threaded around his middle finger, Lukas picked up the plate and stood. The sea breeze ruffled his light brown hair and plastered his sweater to his torso. 'Come with me.'

Lukas turned to walk through the glass doors, waiting for her just inside and shut them as soon as she was through.

'I thought we had to make a public appearance. What are we doing?'

'This is just for us, Katherine.' He took her hand and she paid no attention to the luxurious living area or the rooms they passed on the way to the main cabin, which was decorated in dark woods and soft lighting.

'Don't get stuck in your head,' Lukas said. 'This doesn't have to mean more than you want it to, but we've met our obligation, and I really don't want to share this part of you with anyone.' He sat Katherine on the edge of the bed, placing the plate down beside her and the snowflake next to it. 'Have I read your gift wrong? This is a reminder that we're temporary, is it not? Is no strings sex like we had in the cabin not what you want?'

Katherine had bought him that snowflake because no matter what happened between them, they would always have Lapland, the place where they connected with each other, memories of how good they could be together. But she could see how he would interpret it as a symbol of what they'd shared there, passion with an expiry date, and only that. A reminder that they were always meant to be temporary. She could have corrected his understanding, but what difference would it make? This wasn't forever.

'I want you, Lukas.' That was an irrefutable truth and the best deflection she could think of.

Lukas knelt before her, taking off her shoes one by one. 'Silly Katherine,' he said, moving to pop the button on her jeans, then pulling off her sweater. 'You can't want what you already have.'

But she didn't have him, not really.

I can pretend I do.

* * *

As soon as Lukas had said the words, he wanted to take them back because now Katherine would overthink them. She was falling for him, he saw it in the things she did, the words she said, in her eyes that hid so little, but she didn't *want* to. She was with him to save her career. If she was starting to feel more, she would likely quash those feelings because her success would always come first. He understood that. Respected it, even, because that was how he'd ended up in this situation too.

Except he couldn't lie to himself. What he felt for Katherine was far more than just passion or lust. The problem was they could never be more because she was still a journalist, and he didn't want a life lived in the media.

You've found a way around that right now.

A few weeks wasn't a lifetime.

A lifetime wasn't what Katherine wanted.

So now it was up to him to help them focus on something else. Get them out of their heads.

He lay Katherine on the bed and peeled off the rest of her clothes, dropping them to the floor and leaving her wearing nothing but the gold ring on her finger. Then he took off his own clothing, smirking as the look in her eyes changed from pensive to hungry.

He crawled over her, letting his skin brush hers, but he didn't kiss her in any bruising, intoxicating way. He kissed her lightly. Teasingly. Maddeningly. And when she tried to push up on her elbows to reach his lips, he grabbed her wrists and pinned them above her head.

'You don't get to rush this.' He wanted to take his time because when it came to Katherine, time was very much a finite resource. One day soon she would be gone and this connection that was more powerful than anything he'd shared with anyone else would be gone too.

'You're a damn tease, Lukas,' she complained.

'I am.' He reached over to the plate and plucked a piece of mango. 'But I'm a nice tease. I see that hungry look—' he leaned down to whisper in her ear '—and I'll feed it.' His cock twitched and at the same time, he brought the piece of fruit to her mouth and she obediently bit into it with a moan. Juice glossed her lips and ran down his fingers. He put the rest of the piece in his own mouth, savouring the sweetness. Katherine freed a hand and pulled his towards her, licking the tracks of juice up his skin to his fingers, which she took into her mouth, sucking them clean one digit at a time. It was his turn to moan out loud.

'And I'll happily take it all,' she husked.

Damn this woman. 'You're killing all the restraint I have.'

'Then let go.'

'I want to make this special for you,' Lukas confessed.

'Why?'

'Because I'm certain you've misunderstood my intentions for bringing you here today. You got so quiet after I told you what we'd be doing today—that we'd be making an appearance. I didn't say it to remind you of the state of things between us. I said it so you'd know that I respect your commitment to your career, that I wouldn't jeopardise it, which means showing up publicly. But I also wanted you to myself, Katherine.' He ran his nose up her neck, inhaling her scent. A scent that he both craved and didn't want in his bedroom because when she left and it lingered, it would be torment. 'And right now, we're perfectly alone. No one can see us. No one can hear us. You're mine and I'm yours.'

Katherine closed the gap between them, kissing him savagely and he wished that it wasn't just for right now. He wished things could be different. He wished he could call himself Katherine's without any quantifiers. But that wasn't reality. Reality was the ache in the base of his abdomen from how badly he craved her. It was his brain clouding over from the touch of her tongue to his. It was the pleasure encompassing his whole body as if he'd dived head first into a pool of pure ecstasy.

He needed her to know this pleasure too.

So he broke away from her lips, his stomach somersaulting from the half-blind way she looked at him—lust in her dilated pupils—and he kissed a path down her chest. He stopped to worship at her breasts, his body moving with hers as she writhed.

'Lukas,' she whimpered, 'more.'

He grazed her nipple, revelling in the way she cried out and continued kissing down her body until he was hovering above her sex. Her skin glistened with her arousal, making him curse under his breath. There was a look of anticipation in her eyes that matched the feeling burning through his body. He needed her. Wanted her. And he would have her now over and over so that she would chant his name until it was so embedded in her soul, she would never be free of him because he would never be free of her either.

His mouth closed over her smooth skin, his tongue delving through her folds as he sucked her clit into his mouth making her shout his name. He'd never known such satisfaction. He was thankful they were on the boat so no one would hear them but wished with equal measure that they were somewhere public so everyone would know it was his name on her lips. And maybe in her heart.

He feasted on Katherine, drinking from her as her breaths grew louder and her moans more insistent. Until she was pulling on her hair and on his. Until she was fisting the covers and bucking her hips. Locking her legs around his shoulders, he reached towards her with his hands so she could grab on to them. A tether as she threw her head back and screamed out her release.

Her hands grew slack and then she was running her fingers through her fiery red hair, eyes still scrunched shut and Lucas needed her in his arms through her journey back to earth. So he lay on his side beside her and pulled her to his chest, but it wasn't enough. He needed to be closer. He grabbed her thigh, hooking it over his naked hip, sliding his hard aching cock into her slick heat, groaning animalistically as he watched her face. His heart racing. Consumed by her taste, and her smell and her satin skin.

'Yes,' she said in a laboured breath with a content smile and flushed cheeks.

How was he ever going to say goodbye?

He had been protecting himself by keeping her in her own room, but tonight that would change. From this point on she would sleep in his bed and leave her presence all over his home. He would enjoy every bit of having Katherine tied to him while he could.

Until Lukas thrust into Katherine, making her sing a litany of moans and whimpers, he hadn't known a heart could soar and hurt at the same time. But Katherine's hands caressed his cheek, and he didn't care.

'More,' he begged. 'Touch me everywhere.'

Mark me for life.

'You're ruining me,' she said so close to his lips that they were breathing in each other's pants.

'You already have.' He tried to memorise her roving touch on his chest and back and hair. His hands travelled the length of her body, followed the perfect curve of her ass. Fingers digging into the soft flesh, and Katherine's movements, matching his, became more urgent. Any hope he had that he could take his time went out the window as he started thrusting harder, faster. Lost to sensation and lust and everything Katherine made him feel.

There was a coiling in his spine. Every nerve ending screaming for release.

'I—I'm so close,' Katherine stuttered through a frantic breath.

'Touch yourself.' He wanted her feeling as much pleasure as it was humanly possible to experience. He took her hand from his hair, brought it to his mouth, licking her middle finger and slid it between their bodies, making her gasp but he could feel her climax building in her body. In the way she gripped around him.

'Come for me, Katherine,' Lukas ordered. Demanded. Begged.

And then she was clutching onto him in a violent hold, her voice going hoarse as wave after wave of her climax washed over her pulling Lukas into the most intense release of his life.

'Fuck,' he growled, holding tightly on to her. He couldn't let go. He couldn't open his eyes. But he felt wetness fall from Katherine's face onto his arm and he knew exactly what she felt. This was different. This was so much more than any other time they had sex because this wasn't sex.

This time, out on the water, they made love.

They made love.

He loved her.

A woman he could never have. A woman fighting for her career in the media. The very same media he hated, but she was different. She had integrity, she was selfless and kind. And he trusted her.

He trusted her enough to be physical with her when he hadn't been with anyone for three years. He trusted her enough to confide in her about his mother…his career.

What would it be like to be with her?

Their whole relationship would be in the public eye. People would think he was accepting of the media because he was with one of them. But right now they were in his boat because he had found a way around the attention.

Could he do this all the time? Did he want to live his life this way for the woman he loved?

CHAPTER FIFTEEN

KATHERINE WATCHED LUKAS with a smile as he set a little Christmas tree on the table that sat between two armchairs in perfect view from his bed.

It was the first time she had set foot in here and it felt like they had moved beyond their agreement of just pleasure. Something had changed on the boat. Well, something had been changing before that but when she and Lukas had slept together earlier, it had been better than anything that had come before. There had been all the passion and fun she had come to expect but there had also been an intensity. A connection so strong between them she'd wanted to cling onto Lukas and never let go.

She didn't even know why she had cried but her heart had been about to burst.

Now she was in his bedroom. Proof that Lukas, that viciously private man, had lowered his walls for her.

'You know, you have a pretty large one of those two floors below you,' she said, gesturing at the small tree.

'But that tree won't have this.' He pulled out the snowflake she had given him and hung it on a branch. 'This is just for me.'

Lukas would never change. Hardly anyone came into his home and still he wanted to put barriers around what they shared. Hoard as much of the relationship for himself so no one else could peer in. Did he realise that that kind of behaviour made people more curious?

'Come here,' he called as he kicked off his shoes and settled on the large bed with one arm under his head, the other stretched out beckoning her.

She couldn't resist.

She joined him, marvelling at how tranquil, how content she was when his arm curled around her.

'I suppose that's a pretty good spot for it,' she said. 'In the morning, when the sun catches the crystal—'

'You'll be here to see it because you'll be in my bed.' He hovered over her and she ran her fingers over his soft lips.

'I thought you wanted some separation.' An assumption based on him having given her a room on a different floor. Her workspace was also away from his. So this was a big change. One that emphasized how real the feelings in this fake romance were becoming.

'I want you in my arms and in my home, Katherine. We might not be blessed with a lot of time, but we can make the most of what we've been given.'

But what if they had more time? She could wake up beside Lukas on some mornings, on others she would wake to the scent of coffee and him shirtless and sweaty. She could work in the office he provided her. Maybe they would travel to the tracks together. He'd race and she would report and then they would come back to each other every night. That didn't seem so bad. He'd had a vasectomy so there was no risk of a family that might force her to give up her dreams.

With Lukas, she was safe to pursue the life she wanted.

'I want that too,' she whispered, and he kissed her. It was volcanic. Their passion erupting around them. Sweeping them away and then a loud ping pierced the air.

Katherine groaned. 'I need to check that. It could be work.' It most likely was.

Lukas loosened his hold, and she pulled her phone out of her pocket and saw a new email from Jennifer. She opened the email and her stomach sank.

…I know you asked me not to run the article… Katherine read …but it will be out tomorrow.

Tomorrow!

No. No! This couldn't be happening!

'What's wrong?' Lukas asked.

'I'm not sure yet. I need to call Jennifer.' She tried to hide her trembling and gave Lukas a crushing kiss. This call would be make-or-break for them.

Katherine went down to the lounge, as far away from Lukas as she could get, and called her editor. Jennifer answered immediately.

'You said you'd pull the article.' Katherine didn't bother with pleasantries now. This was a disaster. Lukas could never see what she had written. Those words felt like a lifetime ago.

'I know I did, but there's so much buzz around you two right now, Kat. That article is a goldmine.'

Katherine pulled off the ring she wore on her free hand, anxiously toying with it while she tried to figure out a way to get Jennifer to change her mind.

'That's not the truth. Tell me why you're really publishing it,' she demanded.

'You want the truth? Fine. The truth is we asked the two of you to pose as a couple. Generate interest. What we got is a shopping expedition, Lukas trying to hide you away from the cameras and some shots of you standing on a boat.'

Every one of those moments was so much more than Jennifer made them sound. Right now, Katherine was in a room filled with Christmas decorations because that was how far they had come. 'That's enough to hint at a relationship, Jennifer.'

'Did we ask for hints? We wanted you to leave the meeting hand in hand. What does that tell you, Kat? I warned you in that meeting what would happen.'

'Warned me? Bringing up the article was more like blackmail, Jennifer. We established that the things I wrote aren't true. We have more information now that surely warrants a rewrite.' Maybe if she could speak to Lukas, she could pen something that he would be happy with being out in the world. A piece that didn't shatter this dream they had only just found.

'They aren't untrue, Kat. There's still a valid angle here,' Jennifer said, 'And having the article come from you is going to blow up traffic to the site, which is what I care about. But you know the others will be happy too, because people will tune in just to see what happens between you and Lukas in the aftermath.'

She was nauseous.

'Is there any way at all I can convince you not to run it. Anything?' She knew she sounded desperate now but she didn't care. The thoughtful man up in his room who had made her feel seen and protected deserved better.

She deserved better.

'No.'

'Damn it, Jennifer!'

Katherine hung up. She couldn't speak. She sank into the couch cushions and covered her face with her trembling hands. Lukas was going to hate her. All this contentment they'd found would be lost.

She had to find a way to get out ahead of it and the only way to do that was to talk to Lukas. After all, he knew what their dynamic was like. He knew she didn't hate him anymore. If she could get him to see reason, maybe it wouldn't be so bad.

She had to try. She couldn't lose him.

Lukas stood out on the balcony attached to his bedroom, leaning on the glass balustrade, watching the sun sink lower towards the sparkling horizon. Katherine had been gone awhile, but he understood how important her career was to her. Just how much her need to be successful stemmed from a need to be seen by her family. And while he was still struggling with the fact that her career required so much publicity, that it was in itself so invasive, he also wanted to be with her. For now, she was in his bed.

Even once she left and all the Christmas decorations were packed away, he would still leave that snowflake out. It was the only way he would never lose her, because he would never lose the memory.

One way or another he was determined that he would start the new season in the paddock. And Katherine would undoubtedly be there. How would it feel to see her? How would it feel when he got out of the car with adrenaline still pumping and emotions running high, then had to be interviewed by her?

You don't know that you'll be in a car.

He still had to face the fact that he was currently without a drive, but they were all working towards that goal.

You still haven't turned down the team principal offer.

He hadn't and he wasn't sure why, when he belonged behind the wheel. It was what he'd always wanted. What his father had wanted. Being a racer made him worth something. But Katherine had also made some valid points when he told her about Vortex's offer. Points that he had been thinking about.

'Lukas?'

He turned around to find Katherine standing in the middle of his bedroom, clutching her phone in both hands. There was something about the way she awkwardly shifted her weight from foot to foot. The way she looked off to the side as if she was avoiding his gaze.

He immediately went on high alert. Something was wrong.

'What's happened?' he asked. She opened and closed her

mouth but no sound escaped. 'Come here, Katherine.' He held his hand out to her and to his relief she walked towards him. When she was close enough, he put an arm around her waist, the other caressing her cheek as he placed a small kiss on her forehead.

'Whatever is wrong, we can fix it.' He would do nearly anything for her.

'Something has happened.' She swallowed hard. He could tell she was trying not to let her eyes well up. He never wanted to see her cry.

'Take your time.'

'Please hear me out before you say or do anything. Can you promise me? Please?'

'Of course.'

She nodded, pressed her lips together then said, 'Before we went to Lapland, before I even knew about Lapland actually, I had to write a feature on you for Aero's site.'

The words had irritation flooding through his system because anything involving media attention was never good for him. And if Katherine had written something before, they were trapped together, it was definitely going to be bad. But he couldn't respond as he usually did because it was his Katherine standing before him. Not the woman he'd hated, who'd hated him in return. So, fighting as hard as he could, he suppressed his irritation enough to respond calmly. 'And it's coming out now.'

He didn't like the idea, but if he had given it any thought he would have realised that she must have tons of work submitted that would only be published now. The truth was that he hadn't thought about it, because he was so lost in her. Another tendril of annoyance rose to the surface as he realised that fact, but he pushed it back too.

Stay calm. You don't know what she's going to say. It could be easily fixed.

'We've moved past the hate, Katherine, and if it's anything like what you've written before I've already seen it all.'

But she shook her head. 'No, you haven't,' she said gruffly. 'I called Jennifer after the helicopter ride and asked her to kill this article. She said she would.'

'But she hasn't.'

'No, she hasn't.'

'How bad is it?' Katherine wouldn't answer. 'Katherine, I asked you a question.' Still there was no response. And suddenly the sun lost all warmth. He was cold. Standing on a precipice. But it didn't have to be that way. Maybe if he could see what she'd said, they could figure out a way forward.

'Show it to me.'

Katherine stepped away from him, a pleading look in her eyes. 'Can we talk about this first? Do you really want to see it? We've come so far from the people we were.'

'We are still those people, we've just learned to understand each other. But I have to tell you that I don't like the fact that you don't want me to see it. When is it coming out?'

'Tomorrow,' she whispered.

'Great, then Dominic should know all about it.' Lukas turned to walk back into the bedroom, ready to call his manager.

'No. Wait!'

'One way or another, I will see it.'

'I know.' She covered her face. 'I just don't want you to yet.'

'There's no point in putting it off.'

Katherine tapped the screen of her phone a few times and then handed the device to him before taking several steps back until she was against the balustrade. As if she had to get a safe distance away from him.

'I feel sick,' she said more to herself than him but he could see it in her face, and it was this reaction that made him so adamant that he know what she had written. He looked down at the screen in his hand and began reading.

Lukas Jäger: One of the Greats or Overrated Has-Been?

A truth of Alpha One is that you're only as good as your last race. For Lukas Jäger, it has been a season to forget. Outside of showing brief glimpses of a talent he once possessed, it has otherwise been twenty-three races of mistakes, spins and slow practice times, which begs the question: Are we really surprised that he was replaced by Easton Rivers? The answer is no.

Lukas looked at Katherine, who had hugged herself, standing silently awaiting her judgement. She'd been there at those races. She knew the spins had been caused by a bad aerodynamics package. The practice times had been slow until they found a workable set-up for the race. Lukas had outqualified Will, his teammate, twenty races to three and finished all but one race ahead of him, and that one slip-up had been due to mechanical issues.

He went back to reading without saying a word.

But before we analyse his past season, perhaps we should look at his rise through the ranks thanks to experienced race manager, Dominic Wilson. Coming from a part of Austria not renowned for producing any racer of significance, Lukas received a lot of attention from the start...

Lukas could feel his pulse racing faster after each word.

...an argument could be made that, in his winning years, a lack of serious competition likely made him appear far more skilled a driver than he was. He did in fact have the most dominant car on the grid, which often meant he had no one to race, due to him starting from pole position.

With each excerpt that stood out to him, the calm he promised slipped away and was replaced with fury. This article covered his life in the worst way.

The question on people's lips right now is: Were Florian

Jäger's sacrifices worth it? A year or two ago, even in seasons that weren't Jäger's best, perhaps an argument could be made that they had been. But after this year, one could no longer answer that question with a definitive yes.

This was Katherine's magnum opus. Her masterpiece of all the pieces of utter hate she had written. She now knew exactly how badly Lukas needed to honour his father's memory, and perhaps she had seen it before. After all, they seemed to understand each other in the strangest way, so she'd known what a nerve writing this would strike.

Often described as cold by members of the paddock, Lukas has earned a reputation for being ruthless and selfish. He would be seen walking around with a notebook for the weekend. Data on the car, tyre performance and conditions collected from his observations, which he steadfastly refused to share with his teammates on the other side of the garage. Noted commentator Benjamin Stevens called the move immature and unfair. After all, it was the team that had to win the constructors' championship to remain competitive and to reward all the men and women working hard at the factory.

But no feature would be complete without a look at off-track antics as well. Jäger's publicist, Erin Walker, had her hands full after the scandal surrounding the strained relationship between him and his mother came to light—when it became clear that she had been all but exiled from their small Austrian hometown, where her son is hero-worshipped. In a sport like Alpha One where the media is your friend, Jäger opted to shun all attempts to get his side of the story, leading many to speculate about his culpability in her fate.

Lukas sat in the chair beside the small Christmas tree with the twinkling snowflake and read to the end.

...so we would have to say signing William Bell and Easton Rivers was a genius decision from Thomas Dudek, who has now secured a young, scandal-free, talented duo that will

take the team back to the top. As for Lukas Jäger, it was a good career while it lasted but perhaps bowing out of the sport now would be his wisest move. There's no denying his wealth of knowledge; perhaps a consultant role at a smaller team should be his next career choice.

Clack.

In the silent room the sound of Lukas placing the phone on the table beside him was as loud as a shout.

'Lukas, say something,' Katherine begged from the balcony.

He pressed his fingers to his forehead. 'What would you like me to say?' His voice was empty.

A sharp pain cut through his chest, his heart aching, his pulse thrumming. These words had eviscerated him. This article was going to undo all the work he, Dominic and Erin had done to win him a seat. The woman he loved would be the reason his career ended, and he could feel from the tone of the writing that that was exactly what she had wanted.

'Was this revenge for me accidentally getting you fired?'

'What? No? I'd like to think I'm more professional than that,' Katherine said defensively. 'I—I didn't know you like I do now. I told Jennifer we couldn't run it because it wasn't the truth anymore.'

Lukas laughed at that. Heat radiated from his eyes. His teeth ground together but he laughed. 'It was never the truth.'

He looked at her and she shrunk away from whatever she saw on his face, but then he witnessed her screw up her courage and approach him.

'Please, Lukas, please understand things were different when I wrote that.' She knelt at his feet and took his hands in hers. All he wanted to do was shove her away but he couldn't because even though he was furious and hurt, he always, *always* wanted more of her. It was infuriating. 'It was before you showed me who you are. Jennifer blackmailed me with this article in that meeting at Aero. If I didn't agree to fake a relationship with you, she was going to release the article. I couldn't let that happen. I told her I'd write something else. I thought you could have a say in it. I tried to fix this before it got out. I tried to make sure you weren't hurt.'

And then Lukas did push her away. He got to his feet, marching angrily away from her. Looking around wildly for some way to calm down but there was no use because Katherine was lying.

'That's bullshit and you know it,' he spat. 'You had several opportunities to come clean with this. In Lapland when you knew it would run, you had your phone and your laptop but stayed quiet. All the time here, even though you asked for the article to be killed you could have confessed and been open with me. You hid it and still you've made no apology.'

'Lukas, I'm—'

'Don't fucking say it now, Katherine. Just don't.' He gripped his hair tightly in his hands, the pain a welcome distraction. He felt stupid for ever trusting her. For falling so hard for her. 'The woman who wrote this would have no problem coming into my life under false pretences. I think this person—' he said, pointing at the phone '—would have cooked up a scheme with Robert and Courteney just to get those extra clicks.'

'That's not true.' She tried to cross the room to him but he wanted none of it.

'I should have seen it from the start. You only got close to me for a story.'

Katherine didn't stop the tears then. 'I would never do that!'

Lukas had enough. He went to Katherine and wiped the tears from her eyes. For all he knew, she was faking them. 'And to think that it was my good word that got you this job at Aero.' Her eyes widened, jaw slackened at his words, and he took pleasure in her shock. 'I told them it wouldn't hurt to have a beautiful woman who knows the sport on the presenter team. I said the drivers wouldn't mind talking to you.'

'You hated me.'

Lukas dropped his hand to his side. 'Leave.'

'You hated me!' Katherine cried, near hysterical.

'I didn't at first,' he said softly. A finality to his tone as he took a step back. 'Leave.'

'I don't want to,' Katherine said, her voice broken. 'Christmas is days away, I don't want to leave you.'

'Get out, Katherine.'

'Lukas, please. Maybe take some time to calm down and then we can talk.'

'I said get out!' he yelled. They stood there, staring at each other until she dropped her gaze and walked out of his bedroom.

He wanted no one in his home. Least of all this person who could be so utterly hateful towards him, even while he loved her. Never again. He was done with the media and done with love.

CHAPTER SIXTEEN

KATHERINE PULLED UP to a cream, three-bedroom semi-detached house in St Albans. A house she visited as frequently as was possible. A house that she'd grown up in, dreaming about a big career in London. She had no idea if her parents were home but as soon as she got off the plane from Nice—having spent the night at the airport waiting for the first flight out that morning—barely able to keep herself together, this was the only place she wanted to go.

She couldn't get Lukas's revelation out of her head. She blamed him all this time for almost destroying her career and maybe he did, but he was also the reason she was successful now. That she had a better role at Aero than at VelociTV. And she had used that opportunity only afforded to her because of Lukas to try to convince the world to hate him. To see the worst in him.

Her eyes misted up again, so she switched off her Mercedes and walked up to the door. Unable to hear any voices inside, she pulled out her spare key and let herself in.

'Mum? Dad?' she called, but there was no immediate answer. All the willpower she had to not fall apart ebbed away. The dam walls were fracturing and out spouted jets of anguish. She could feel her face crumble but she tried so hard to breathe through the pain of losing Lukas. A man she would have had to say goodbye to anyway but when he was kicking her out, she'd realised she didn't want to leave. She never wanted to say goodbye to him.

She turned to leave. 'This was a mistake.'

'Kittykat? I thought I heard your voice.'

Before she'd realised what she was doing, she spun around and launched herself at her father, who caught her in a tight hug. She never got so emotional that her parents had to comfort her. She could modulate her emotions on her own. Had done so since she was young.

No one else did.

No, her siblings didn't. They expected comfort.

She pulled away from her father, looking at the textured cream tiles that hadn't changed in twenty-seven years.

'This is unlike you,' her father said, his hand on her shoulder.

But was it? She did get upset. She'd been upset when her father had missed important days in her life because of Paige. She'd just made sure to mask it so that he wouldn't feel guilty.

...they should have worked harder to know you.

That thought of Lukas made it impossible to speak.

'Come, let's have some tea and we can chat in the living room. I have a fire going.'

'Can I have a coffee instead?' It wouldn't be like Lukas's, but she loved coffee and she missed him.

'Since when do you like coffee?' her dad asked as he reached into the back of the cupboard to pull out a jar of instant.

'I always have.' Katherine wasn't sure what made her say it. She was here to seek comfort, not to make her parents feel guilty.

He hummed as he switched on the kettle. 'I'm the only one here. Your mother is out with Paige, and your brothers are off somewhere.'

'That's fine.' She really only wanted her dad.

He finished making the drinks and handed a floral mug to Katherine. She took a sip of the milky coffee. It wasn't great but at least it was something she had asked for.

'Let's go talk.'

The lounge had remained unchanged. The walls were still a shade of peach she could almost taste. The comfortable, pillowy couches were in exactly the same places even if the upholstery had been replaced a few times over the years, always with exactly the same colour and fabric. In the corner stood a Christmas tree with a plastic angel on top. A new plastic angel.

'Who put the angel up?' Katherine asked, sitting in the chair farthest from the tree while her father sat next to it.

'Christopher won this round, though there were casualties.'

'I see that.'

'So tell me what's wrong, Kittykat. I imagine it has something to do with Lukas Jäger.'

It was a physical ache to hear his name.

'Do you want to explain what happened? One moment you were coming to dinner, the next you were missing and then you're in a relationship with a man I know you dislike. I've never had to worry about you, Kat, but these past few weeks have been worrying.'

Her father's words made her feel both angry and guilty. She never wanted them to worry about her and now she felt his disappointment in his words. Like she was being chastised.

'I know, Dad. I'm sorry. I found out about the Finland trip last minute and then Lukas and I got caught in the storm.' Katherine stopped. She didn't have to give her father the abridged version. He was her family. 'Actually, he saved me.'

'Saved you?'

And then Katherine told her father everything that had happened in Lapland, but she kept the passion a secret for herself. Even excluding that physical connection from the narrative, when Katherine looked back at their time, she realised how much they'd had together, how much more than lust. Even if they hadn't slept together, she would have left there wanting more of him. And then she confessed the truth about their relationship, how it had started. Saying it had all been fake felt like a lie.

Her father's eyes softened. He'd remained silent while she spoke, but now he moved across the room to sit beside Katherine, pulling her into a tight hug that made it hard to keep the tears at bay.

'It wasn't fake,' her father said softly, putting an arm around her shoulders and pulling out his phone from his pocket. Suddenly she was a young girl again watching racing with her father except this time she was the entertainment. He was showing her pictures of herself from news articles he had saved. And despite the devastation cracking her soul apart, a small piece of her shattered heart rejoiced because she was alone with her father getting a bit of the attention she had always craved.

'Look at this picture,' he said, swiping to one that was taken the day she and Lukas had gone shopping. 'Look at that smile on your face. Do you know when I last saw you smile like that?'

'No,' she breathed.

'Never,' he replied. 'And this one…' It was from the boat— Lukas holding a plate, her looking up at him. Was that only yesterday? 'Your mother hasn't ever looked at me like this and there hasn't been a day where the two of us have not been in love. Let me show you one more.' Her dad scrolled on his phone to a picture taken the night she and Lukas had gone to the casino. She was looking away but Lukas was looking at her. The emotion in his eyes took her breath away. 'That young man is not faking, and neither were you.'

'It didn't feel fake,' Katherine admitted, taking the phone from her father.

'What do you see? How does he look at you?' He squeezed her tighter.

'Like he'd fight the world for me. Like he'd hold back the oceans if I asked him to.' Except what they had wasn't meant to last. 'But he only agreed to this situation because he was forced to. He wants to drive. This PR stunt was his last shot at an offer.'

Her father took the phone from her and placed it on the scuffed coffee table then placed both arms around her. She wished she could have felt comfort like this growing up.

'How did he react in that meeting?'

'He asked for my opinion and then made sure I was okay.'

'I see, and after that?' her father pressed.

'He took me to his home that he allows very few into. He gave me privacy and comfort and support. He helped me when I was struggling...' with the media attention, with what her life was and why she chose this career. He never judged her. He kept her safe and treasured her and loved her.

And she loved him.

Katherine loved him so much it felt like a vital appendage had been lopped off. She loved him and she hadn't come clean to him about the article. Nor had she apologised.

'I never gave him the benefit of the doubt. After he cost me my job, I was convinced he was an awful person, but the truth was so very different.'

Was this revenge for me for accidentally getting you fired?

Maybe subconsciously, it all had been.

Katherine covered her mouth, muffling her voice. 'I was never impartial. If I had been I wouldn't have felt the need to pull that article in the first place.'

'Can you understand why he feels betrayed?' her father asked without judgement.

'It's my job,' she said but the words tasted wrong.

'I've always admired your commitment and your work

ethic, but I have also always worried that you put achievement above everything else in your life. Sweetheart, it's not your job that makes you important or worth listening to. You already are. Allow yourself to be happy outside of your career.'

That brought Lukas's words straight back to mind.

You are not your mother. You have achieved so much more than everyone else in your family has. Why are you letting your mother's choices warn you away from a possible future?

That night she had felt so close to Lukas. And that kiss afterwards would never fade from memory. It broke her and mended her. Made her want to cry and levitate. It was so raw, so desperate. And the next morning had been even better. When he placed that angel in her hand it felt like a missing piece of her soul clicked into place.

She looked at the tired Christmas tree in the corner with its supermarket ornaments and brand new plastic angel. A perfect reminder of the way she had been sidelined by her family.

'You say that yet you only had time for me when it came to racing or my career. Even then, when I finally broke into the industry you were gone to help Paige in another country.'

'Katherine—' Her father loosened his hold of her. Surprise on his face. But she spoke over him. She couldn't hold back the words this time.

'And how can I be happy and allow myself to love someone when Mum taught me that love means settling down and giving up my dreams? Dreams I worked bloody hard for. A career without which I wouldn't have even the little bit of attention you grant me now.' She got off the couch, tears she'd held back for years streaming down her face as she faced her father.

'Where is this coming from?' he asked. Hands on the couch, ready to stand, but Katherine ignored him. The dam had burst and nothing would stop the raging torrent.

'There's no winning, Dad. I either disappoint Mum, give

up the connection I have with you, or forego love and companionship. I can't have it all. I never could!'

His eyes widened. 'Katherine, you know... I...' He paused, shaking his head. 'That's not true.'

'I love Christmas, did you know that?'

Again, her father shook his head. 'You always seemed above it. You never got as involved as your siblings.'

'Think, Dad! Think back to what it was actually like. I never saw the point of fighting with my siblings who didn't really want me in their club anyway. This year I got to put an angel on an amazing tree, and it was one of the best moments of my life. Lukas made me feel seen in a way no one else in my life ever has.' Her skin replayed the memory of him lifting her up so she could reach the top of the tree.

Her father looked as if he'd been struck.

'I've always liked coffee, Dad. Every time we went out it was the first thing I ordered and yet you still didn't know that I liked it.'

She could see the shame in her father's expression, and it hurt her to see it, but she wanted more from her family. Hell, she wanted more from the world. From her job. She wanted respect and recognition.

'I need to apologise to Lukas,' she said softly. 'And then I need to go to the office.'

'Do what you need to, Kittykat,' her father said gruffly, 'and maybe after that you and I can talk. Maybe I have some making up to do as well.'

'Dad,' she croaked, and he went to her, engulfing her in a hug.

When he pulled away, Katherine could see his lashes were wet. 'I'm proud of you and I love you and I've failed you, but I promise that will all change. Go make your call. I'll be right here waiting.'

Katherine raced up the stairs to the bedroom she used to

share with Paige. She tried Lukas's number, praying he would answer, but it rang until she got his voicemail.

'Lukas, I know I messed up. I'm sorry. I'm sorry for the article, for how unfairly I treated you, for everything. Please, please can we talk?' She ended the call and sent a text. She held the phone in her hand, waiting. And waiting. And waiting. It had been delivered and seen but there was no response.

She had to find a way to get Lukas to talk to her. This man she loved didn't threaten her dream, he made her see a better one. And now she needed to fight for him.

CHAPTER SEVENTEEN

JENNIFER AND ROBERT were in the small meeting room when Katherine arrived at Aero TV. After a long talk with her father, she had called them requesting a meeting asap.

She was done being disrespected, had enough of her career being weaponised to control her. It ended now. Her heart pounded because she knew if this meeting went badly, it would be the end for her at the Alpha One official broadcaster. It would be a step backwards. The thought made her feel ill but enough was enough.

'What's this about, Kat?' Robert asked.

Katherine took her time pulling out a seat at the round table, ensuring she was visibly calm, then looked at him and Jennifer.

'We have some issues to discuss.' She placed her hands on the table. Fingers loosely knitted together.

'You're not still upset about the article, are you?' Jennifer asked. 'Do you want to see the traffic stats since it went live? It was great for you.'

'No, I don't.' Anger blazed through her. 'And it was great for you. Aero. Not me. Not Lukas.'

'What does Lukas Jäger matter? You were faking a relationship, badly I might add. Our needs are more important than any driver's.'

Katherine never wanted to work with Jennifer again. 'You

have no respect for people's lives, Jennifer. No respect for my work or reputation. For that reason, I am quitting the column.'

Jennifer threw herself back in her chair with a huff. 'Don't be so dramatic, Kat.'

She battled for calm with all her might because she wanted to rage at these people. 'Let's look at the facts, shall we? With no concern for our well-being after being stuck in a snowstorm, Aero forced Lukas and me to pose as a couple purely for publicity. Threatened our careers, threatened my reputation by blackmailing me with the article that we both knew contained false information, but still you used it to control me.'

'*Control* is a bit harsh, don't you think?' Robert said.

'What would you call it?' She cast her glare on him. 'Either I was fired if I didn't comply or the article was released which would call into question my ethics and integrity, my ability to be impartial and truthful. It would paint me as ruthless to the point of unscrupulousness. Who would hire me after that? That *is* control, Robert.' She wanted to throw herself out of her chair and pace the room, but she couldn't be emotional here. 'Tell me, if I was a male journalist would either of you have demanded this of me? Toyed with my career like this? I suspect the answer is no.'

Robert looked away while Jennifer refused to say anything.

'So here's how things are going to go. First, you're going to pull the article and issue a retraction—'

'Absolutely not!' Jennifer all but yelled.

'I'm not done.' Katherine stared her down. 'Second, the manipulation of me and my career stops now. You told me about the trip to Lapland at the last possible moment, Robert, when you would have known long enough to acquire service providers to carve a literal track in the snow. I'm not a pawn to be used, I am a journalist and deserve to be treated with the same respect you give my male colleagues. Third, in the place of the column, I will be added to the panel on *Track Talk* every Tuesday night. I know this sport, have great insights and bloody good access to information.'

'Kat—' Robert tried but Katherine was on a roll.

'A producer who treated me abominably once told me to go complain on a talk show, and you know what? He was right. If you don't comply, I will tell the world what happened. How you must have been planning to capitalize off our experience in Lapland before you'd even checked that I was okay, how you forced Lukas and me into a public relationship for clicks.' Katherine could see Robert turning paler with every word. 'How I asked you, Jennifer, to kill the article and why and how you blackmailed me with it. How Scott Courteney threatened my job. You think Alpha One will want to remain bound to Aero TV after that? They'll find another network. And I will never stop talking about this. Never stop talking about the institutionalised misogyny. I refuse to be treated how you have treated me.'

Robert swallowed thickly. 'I'm sure we can come to an understanding.'

Katherine stood firm. 'I want your agreement and nothing less or I will walk out of here and into another network because you know I'm great at my job. My fan base will come with me. We all know that would be a substantial audience. How many people do you think will believe my story?'

'Fine,' he acceded. 'We have an agreement.'

CHAPTER EIGHTEEN

A VIBRATION ERUPTED from the nightstand beside Lukas.

He didn't react at all.

He didn't blink. Didn't move a muscle to answer the insistent phone. He just lay there in his bed. Staring. Katherine had been right. The morning sunshine streaming through the glass caught the crystal snowflake. Light refracted across his bedroom in slow walking prismatic rainbows. It was beautiful. He hated it.

Still, he looked at the snowflake.

His phone stopped ringing.

Katherine had been calling constantly. Had been texting and leaving voicemails begging him to talk to her but he had nothing to say. How did he put into words the swirling betrayal. How did he express to her that he trusted her even though he shouldn't have. That he had fallen in love with her.

His phone started ringing again.

Lukas tossed off the covers and got out of bed, noticing when he did that the name on the phone wasn't Katherine's, but Dominic's.

He snatched the phone up and answered quickly as he went down to his kitchen.

'Took you long enough to answer,' Dominic complained.

'Sorry, Dom, I thought you were—'

'Katherine.'

'Yes,' Lukas said. Mechanically, he put on a pot of coffee and walked the length of the floor as he waited. Moving from room to room.

'You saw the article,' Dominic said in a resigned tone.

'Yesterday. Why are you only calling me now? Shouldn't you have warned me about this?' Lukas's hard tone surprised himself. He wasn't angry at Dominic; he was angry at Katherine. Or was he? Lukas would have walked away from Katherine after Lapland if Dominic and Erin hadn't conspired with Aero to force him into dating her.

You didn't want to walk away though, did you?

'I thought it would be best to give you two time to work it out. I knew Katherine wouldn't blindside you.'

'You knew that, did you? Like you knew what she had written?' Lukas stepped into the decorated lounge. A smiling angel looking down at him. Laughing at his foolishness. Yesterday he'd wanted signs of Katherine all over his home. Today it was hell. 'How badly has that article affected us?'

'Brock Racing has already informed me they will be going with another driver, but they won't make the announcement immediately. They don't want their statement to be overshadowed or seem reactionary. I haven't heard from the other team yet.'

'Funny how this was supposed to help all of us and yet only Aero has benefitted.'

Lukas sat heavily on the couch, phone to his ear, head hanging. Something hard pressed into his thigh. Reaching between the cushions he sat on, he pulled out a gold ring. Katherine's ring. The ring that glinted on her finger when he made love to her on the boat. When he had seen her that very first day.

'It's not over, Lukas.' But Lukas wasn't listening. 'Just give me some—'

He hung up on Dominic, tossing the phone aside as he inspected the piece of jewellery. His heart cracked wide open.

And when he looked around, his home had never seemed so full of life and yet so empty, the ghost of happiness haunting every room. Haunting him. He missed Katherine.

He got off the couch and threw the ring across the room with a shout. It hit the glass wall with a loud clang then clattered to the floor somewhere unseen.

'Fuck!' he yelled. In pain. In frustration. In anger at her and himself. He didn't want to miss her. She'd hurt him. Made him believe that he didn't have to be alone anymore. Made him believe that he had found someone who understood him. He'd been starting to think that she loved him and he'd been willing to be patient with her. To let her come to the realisation on her own. To let her decide if she wanted to take a chance on him, because now he realised that he'd been willing to do the same.

For a smart man he was very stupid.

He should never have let down his guard with a journalist.

He walked across the room and retrieved the ring, which had rolled under some furniture. It was a simple, antique fede ring. A ring for friendship. Well, the media certainly wasn't his friend. Katherine's article was proof of that.

But would she have written those things if she had known you?

There was no way to know.

He wasn't aware of any other driver who'd had a journalist force their way into their life like this, just to get more information. More clout. But he'd also never embraced the media like the other drivers had. A decision he could now see made him more enigmatic and fed people's desperate desire to know more, made photographers and journalists more hungry for a picture or a story.

As long as he was a driver, nothing would change. Maybe *he* would have to—maybe he needed to give a bit of himself to the public to satisfy them in order to have the privacy he craved. He didn't know if he could change that much.

Lukas dropped the ring into his pyjama pants pocket and walked out shirtless onto the high terrace. The cold took his breath away, but it was nice to have the physical discomfort. At least it lessened the urgency of his emotional upheaval.

He looked out at the streets of Monaco. In a few months he could be racing along them. The thought didn't fill him with happiness.

Is driving what you're really passionate about?

He loved racing but, no, driving wasn't making him happy anymore. He had more days filled with frustration and anxiety than exhilaration. He wanted to win championships. He was going to make no difference in a back-marker team. The only reason he wanted to stay on the grid was to make his family's sacrifices worth something. So that he wasn't just the selfish ass who robbed his parents of a good life together. But was that enough of a reason to keep racing? Was that a healthy reason?

He examined all the decisions he had made recently. This obsession with driving had made him ignore his principles. He'd agreed to pretend to date someone. He hadn't dated in three years and then only did so to deceive the world. Regardless of what Katherine had done to him or what he felt for her, he'd used her.

This wasn't the man he was.

He was honest. He had integrity. He couldn't let this quest for a drive change him.

But he didn't have to drive to remain in the sport.

You have so much knowledge...such an understanding of the car and the craft that even from a technical aspect you could make a difference.

Lukas leaned his elbows on the glass balustrade, the cold wind ruffling his hair. It hurt to think about Katherine, but a sense of peace settled on him as he thought about the team principal position that he hadn't yet turned down.

Katherine had been right about so much that night at dinner. And about one thing in that heinous article: He did have a wealth of knowledge. He could develop a team. He would have the power to make a difference. To influence decisions. To ensure that the right talent was in the seat without screwing over entire careers. He could make the team what he wanted it to be. He could take all that interest in his name, in him and make it work for the team. For him. There would be a lot of media attention as a team principal but nowhere near as bad as being the star of the team. It was a massive responsibility but without the lens of desperation of wanting to remain a racer, he realised that maybe leading a team was exactly where he should be.

He went back inside and retrieved his phone from the couch, then dialled a number he never thought he would actually use.

'It's Lukas Jägcr. I'm accepting your offer of team principal.'

CHAPTER NINETEEN

THE TRACK WAS a hive of activity. Thousands of fans streamed in a continuous line, wearing sunglasses and hats to protect them from the bright Australian mid-March sun. High-powered engines revved until they were practically screaming before being taken to a low growl. Quick short whines of wheel guns punctuated the air.

The first race weekend of the season.

It was only Thursday but that didn't mean that they were in for a quiet day. Drivers were being interviewed in fan zones, support races had practice and qualifying sessions, new drivers had to receive camera time, inserts were being filmed, and drivers and team principals had to hold press conferences.

Team principals like Lukas.

The man she had lost her heart to, the man she had hurt, who wouldn't take her calls or answer her messages. Katherine had tried for weeks before she'd been forced to give up. Every time she'd reached out and he'd rejected her, she'd felt a stab through her heart.

Give him time, Kittykat, her father had said. *Just don't give up.*

But she had to. She'd lost him.

She was on her way back to the Aero broadcast area when she saw Lukas talking to a group of journalists, most of them from European publications. Lukas talking to the media wasn't unusual. He's always had contractual obligations to fulfil. But Lukas in a grey-and-gold-collared team shirt talking to the media with a smile was.

Katherine watched him from afar. There was no scowl on his face. His body language was open, he was talking with his hands.

He was being friendly to the people he disliked.

Except for her.

Earlier in the paddock, she had seen that unmistakable golden-brown hair, those storm-grey eyes, that chiselled jaw. Lukas had walked towards her and her heart had skipped a beat. Butterflies had erupted in her belly. Her lips tingled with the need for his. His gaze had locked on hers for a moment. Just a moment when she tried to think of everything she wanted to say in those calls and texts. Everything she wanted to do to make her betrayal up to him.

'Lukas,' she had tried to say but it had come out strangled.

He had turned around and walked away.

Katherine was unable to get the image out of her head, even now as she joined her colleagues. When she was informed that they would be interviewing Lukas next, a thrill ran through her body. He would be close to her; he'd be forced to face her.

When he approached, she was ready, mic in hand, heart pounding in her chest.

Every step he took towards her felt like a piece of her was coming home. And when he joined them, she said, 'Hello, Lukas.'

But he didn't respond to her. Instead, he addressed everyone generally. 'This is a little bit different, isn't it?'

'Definitely,' James, the longest-serving presenter said. 'Not seeing you in a race suit is going to take some getting used to.'

'Well, I've swapped one suit for another,' Lukas joked.

He *joked*.

And when the camera light turned red, he continued being

charming and friendly. Was this the same man she had fallen in love with?

'What was the press conference like this morning, with Thomas Dudek also in attendance?' Katherine asked. Of course, the drama would appeal to fans but also, she was genuinely concerned about how that experience might have affected Lukas. He wouldn't even look at here, so asking was the only way she would know. It wouldn't be his words that told her anything—it would be his body. His eyes.

Lukas glanced at her so quickly before looking away, almost as if to look at her was poisonous. 'Thomas runs a team as do I now. He doesn't get a say in my team and neither do I have a say in his, but we do share a passion for the sport, and we will have to interact from time to time. Perhaps he made some questionable decisions when it came to me as a driver, but he did so for his team. And just because I'm not driving doesn't mean I can't take a team to a championship.'

That told her plenty. Of course, he was hurt having to see the man who had ended his career so heartlessly, but Lukas was trying his best to be diplomatic.

'We're different people,' Lukas continued, 'and will make different decisions.'

Meaning he would not be as unscrupulous as his previous boss.

'And do you think you can take a team as small as this to a championship?' James asked.

'Absolutely. We have to be realistic about our goals and the team is very new, but every team started somewhere, and we just have to be mindful to make the right decisions that will take us in the direction of those goals,' Lukas answered.

He answered every question without snark, without complaint and when James thanked him, Lukas handed back the mic, turned around and walked away without sparing Katherine a second glance. She could have been anyone. She could have been invisible and her already aching heart shattered like the most fragile glass.

Katherine handed the mic off to someone—she didn't really notice who it was—removed the transmitter and all the cables from her clothes, handing those off too, and walked away.

CHAPTER TWENTY

KATHERINE WAITED INSIDE a room filled with charcoal-grey tables and chairs. She was surrounded by three walls of black glass while the back wall was a glossy gold and the floors were light, tying the space together perfectly.

She had never been this anxious in a team motor home and had never been left alone. Journalists weren't usually unaccompanied, but the team had seen fit to let her stay.

So now she waited. She hoped and prayed that Lukas would see her. She had already been waiting awhile. Almost everyone she had initially seen here had left to perform their functions, but she wouldn't leave. Not until she spoke to Lukas.

After an age, he entered the hospitality area talking to a tall, broad, blond man with wire-framed glasses on his patrician nose. The logo of Command Technologies, a well-known tech company, on his shirt. Her instinct was to find out what he was doing here, but she ignored it. She wasn't here for work. She was drawing a line.

'Lukas.' She tried to keep her voice light, maintain perfect composure that wavered slightly when he looked at her. For a moment she thought she saw longing in his eyes, but it was gone faster than it appeared. 'Would it be possible to have a word?'

Lukas looked her over, processing her request before turning to the man and shaking his hand. 'Thank you for stopping by. We'll be in contact soon.'

'Definitely. Vortex Command Racing is going to be the start of great things for us, Jäger.'

Lukas smiled. It wasn't one of the heart-stopping smiles he had given her in Monaco, this one was practiced. Cordial and charming. No one would know the difference but her.

'I couldn't agree more, Matthew,' Lukas said and watched the man leave. The door had only just closed when he rounded on Katherine. 'We can talk in my office.' He led her through the back doorway to a set of stairs. 'I don't need you making a scene.'

'I would never do that.' It hurt to hear him think that way of her.

'Really?' They reached the top and he held a glass door open for her to step into. 'What would you call all those calls and messages, then?'

'Wanting to talk.'

He closed the door, sealing them inside a small, impeccably neat office. He had two visitor chairs on one side of his desk and a large comfortable-looking one on the other, but he didn't sit, nor did he invite Katherine to do so.

'You had plenty of opportunities to talk but when it mattered, you didn't.'

'Can you at least say my name?' It had been months since she'd heard him use it and all through the day he wouldn't acknowledge her. Now he was talking to her yet still wouldn't address her. It was tearing her up.

'Why?' he asked in a hard tone.

'Because I need to hear it.'

He shook his head and walked past her to stand at the glass wall looking out at the sunny paddock.

'Why are you here, Katherine?'

Every cell in her body came to life at the sound of her name on his tongue and she couldn't savour it. 'To ask for your forgiveness.'

'My forgiveness,' he scoffed.

'I asked them to scrap the article and they ran it anyway without telling me. You know this. I tried to fix it, Lukas. Yes, I should have told you about it, but I never meant to hurt your feelings.'

'Don't lie.' He turned towards her. Sadness, disappointment, hurt written all over his face. 'That's not true. Because the fact is you did write that article. You planned it, did research, thought of the words—the best words to get your point across—and then reread it before you submitted it.'

Katherine didn't know how to defend herself against that because he had a point. There was always a lot of consideration in her writing. 'You said you'd already seen all that I'd written, that we moved past the hate. Did you mean that?'

'You don't get to ask me that.' Despite his even tone, there was anger in his eyes. 'Are you proud of it?'

'No!' Katherine replied instantly. It was the least proud she had ever been of herself. No matter how disappointed Lukas was in her, it would never compare to how she felt about herself when she thought about how she had let her mistaken hate of him colour her judgement.

'When you first wrote it, Katherine,' he said slowly, 'when you typed it up and put it on an email that you sent to your editor, were you proud of it?'

Her insides squirmed. How she wished she could go back to that moment and do it all over again because she had been proud. Exceptionally so. 'Yes,' she confessed. 'But, Lukas, it isn't like that. I've changed!' She marched up to the man she loved and grabbed a fistful of his shirt, but his arms hung limply by his sides. He looked down at her, not pushing her away, but not touching her either. And even though it was the worst pain imaginable, she continued, 'I see you for who you are. I was wrong and I'm sorry, Lukas. I'm so sorry!'

He stepped back, forcing her to let go. 'You don't get it.

You did believe the things you wrote about me even if you no longer do. You were willing to believe the worst about me without ever talking to me or finding out the truth. You can only believe the worst about someone if you *want* to.'

'Lukas...'

'And you didn't just believe it,' he went on. 'You kept telling the world. You wanted everyone to think of me as you did. And even though you attacked me over and over again, I never said a bad thing about you, Of course, I vented to Dominic or my father because I am human after all. But not publicly, ever. Not once, Katherine.'

Her eyes welled with tears because he was right.

'I never once did the things you did.' He walked to the door and grabbed onto the handle about to pull it open but she stopped him.

Tears she couldn't control streamed down her cheeks. 'I'm not doing the column anymore.'

She could see that caught his attention. He let go of the door handle and turned towards her even though he remained at a distance.

'I'm done with opinion pieces.'

'What would you like me to say?' he asked plainly.

'I just wanted you to know.' Maybe then he could see that she was committed to being better.

'I never wanted you to give up your job, Katherine. I know what your success means to you. Means for your family. And I've been in the racing world a long time, I understand the need for you in it. The media is an important part of the sport, but it was never going to work between us. Don't give up your dream for me when we're never going to be together.'

'I just need you to forgive me,' Katherine pleaded.

'And then what? Hmm?' Lukas crossed his arms. 'How does it help? Where do we go from there?'

'Even if you can't be with me, maybe if you can forgive

me we can find a way to at least be friends. I confided in you, Lukas. I trust you. I can't lose you from my life.'

But all he did was shake his head. Katherine was breaking apart. Willing to settle for the crumbs of the affection he once had for her, but he wouldn't budge.

'I said I wanted you on the boat but I didn't want to think about why I wanted *you* so much, Lukas. I want all of you. I love you, but I'll settle for anything you're willing to give me.'

He pressed his back to the door, dropping his head back to rest against the glass, his neck exposed. He closed his eyes. Katherine wanted to scream for him to open them. Open them and look at her.

'Love doesn't hurt like you hurt me.' He ran his fingers through his hair as he said softly to himself, 'Maybe it does. What would I know about it?'

The woman he'd wanted to marry had left him because he was too zealous about protecting their privacy; his mother had left and kept punishing him for choices he hadn't made. Everyone Lukas loved had hurt him, including her. Katherine hated that fact. She wanted to wrap him in her arms and comfort him. Wanted to hear him say he forgave her and that he needed her. 'I know I hurt you, but I'm willing to make it up to you every single day, Lukas.'

Then he did look at her, and she thought she might combust. 'Why should I take you back?'

'Because you still love me. You loved me on the boat, and you love me now. If you didn't you wouldn't be hearing me out. You could have exposed our fake relationship—even though it wasn't fake to me—and ruined me, but you didn't. And I know I saw pride in your eyes when you saw me with the other presenters. It was so brief, but it was there.'

He pulled himself up to standing, shaking his head and pressing his thumb and finger to his eyes. Katherine saw his jaw twitch from gritting his teeth. His throat bobbed in a hard swallow and when he finally dropped his hand from his eyes and spoke, his voice was rough. Low and raw. Bleeding all the pain she could see in his stormy gaze.

'Of course I love you, Katherine. I can't turn my feelings off. I've never felt about anyone the way I felt about you, but I don't know how to trust you. It's just best if we have nothing to do with each other. It will be easier for both of us and save us the heartache.'

'Please, Lukas,' she cried.

'You can take a minute to compose yourself. Goodbye, Katherine,' he said softly. Solemnly.

She thought she had reached the bottom of the well when it came to this pain, but hope had kept her afloat. Now she was drowning. Couldn't breathe because every breath had shards in it, ripping her on the inside. Lukas, the only man she had ever truly loved, was gone.

CHAPTER TWENTY-ONE

KATHERINE NEEDED TO find a quiet place to breathe. To be alone. Somewhere she could hurt without being seen.

'Kat?'

She startled at the voice, thinking she had found solitude between the team trucks.

'Dominic.' He looked at her with sympathy, which made her feel worse. 'I'm not the best company right now.'

'Me neither, but I don't think the best is what either of us needs.'

It was only then that Katherine realised Dominic must be facing a very different dynamic with Lukas too. Lukas didn't need a manager anymore, and Dominic had been with him for almost twenty years.

'How are you holding up?'

'Could be better.' He shrugged. 'Don't get me wrong, I'm happy for Lukas. I didn't want him to end his career at the back of the field. But when your friend and client keeps something that big from you, it makes you question a few things. Like the wisdom of making him pretend to date a journalist.'

'You were trying to do your best for him.' Katherine leaned against the grey-and-gold truck. 'But you're right, maybe it was a mistake. How is he?' Dominic was the only means she had to get any news on how Lukas was *really* doing.

'Angry,' Dominic replied.

'At me?' It was nearly a whisper.

'You, himself, me. But here's the thing about Lukas, he can be quite fair even when he's upset. I mean, he didn't kick me out when I visited him on Christmas Day. Though he did put me to work.'

'What do you mean?'

Dominic chuckled sadly. 'He made me pack away Christmas decorations in the lounge. He didn't help at all. Didn't even look at them. He only joined me after I'd put everything into storage.'

He wouldn't even look at them. That's how much he hated Katherine now.

Lounge.

'Only the lounge? What about the tree in his bedroom?' Katherine's heart beat frantically waiting for the answer as if her life depended on it. Well, maybe not her life, but certainly her happiness.

'I don't know. I didn't go up there and he said nothing.'

Could he have kept that one reminder of her? The same man who walked away from her twice that day. Unlikely. It probably went into the trash. Her vision became blurry but she couldn't cry. Not at the track. Not in front of Dominic.

She swallowed hard, but her throat was closing. 'I need to…' She looked around. Eyes darting from one point to the next. Searching for an answer. 'I need to make this right.'

But how? Lukas didn't want to be with her. He didn't want to see her. By the sounds of it he was pushing Dominic away in his anger. Who was Lukas confiding in? She had gone straight to her father for comfort, but Lukas couldn't do the same.

Whether a future with him was lost or not, Katherine needed Lukas to be okay. She needed him to have someone he could lean on, so he wasn't so alone.

She was hit with a wave of inspiration and knew exactly what she had to do.

'I have to go!'

CHAPTER TWENTY-TWO

IT WAS THE morning of race day.

Lukas lay on his hotel room bed fully dressed. The image of a pleading Katherine in his head as it had been for two days.

Every atom in his body had begged him to take her in his arms. He'd wanted so badly to cave to her because he missed her. Every day without her was an ache in his chest that never faded. But the fact was that they couldn't be together. Offering her comfort wouldn't help them move on. And they both needed to.

The snowflake was still in his bedroom. He wanted to get rid of it but couldn't. So, it sat there taunting him every morning. He'd still looked for her at the track every day, albeit from a distance. When he'd failed to find her at all these past two days, he still couldn't help but worry about her absence.

'Why can't I stop loving you!' he said angrily to himself.

He had to concede that he was never going to stop thinking about her, but it was time to head to the track. He had work to do. But a knock on the door stopped him.

He opened it without checking to see who it was. They were a new team and he had made sure that their accommodation was kept a secret. If anyone needed him, it was likely someone from the hotel or team.

He was entirely unprepared for the person staring back at him.

'Mutter,' he said in shock.

'Hello, Lukas.'

He stood there, staring at the woman with sharply cut blond hair. She was a whole head shorter than him, with the same storm-grey eyes. Eyes that held apprehension.

His mother.

Curiosity warred with suspicion, but the former won out. He opened the door wider to allow her in. Door handle still in hand, as he watched his mother sit at the small, round, dark wood table.

Mechanically, as if his joints were in the process of seizing, he closed the door and approached Berta Jäger. Lukas was always certain about what he wanted to do. When racing was the wrong choice, he was still certain he wanted to do it. When he'd eventually let go of that obsession and considered the team principal move, he was certain of that choice. Even when he made Katherine leave his home, he was certain that was the end. But now, with his mother in his room and with no idea why she'd come, Lukas wasn't certain anymore. He didn't know if he should join her or keep standing or hover at the door. Should he demand to know why she was there or just be grateful that she was?

He didn't like being indecisive. He was used to making quick decisions, to reacting in two-tenths of a second. So he shrugged on the persona that made him so successful in his sport and approached the table.

'What are you doing here?' He kept his voice polite, but there was no missing the demand in his tone.

'I've come to see my son,' Berta said carefully.

He eased himself into the opposite chair, laying his arms on the padded armrests. 'You never have before. Why now?'

He could see his mother thinking of a response, but he didn't want that. He wanted anything she said to be completely unfiltered. After Katherine and the article and the fake relationship, he didn't have it in him to be patient with anything but the truth.

'I want the real reason.'

'A young woman came to see me this weekend and she brought me here, but she wanted to keep it a secret.'

Katherine.

'Who was it?' He held his breath almost praying for his mother to say her name.

'Katherine Ward.'

Lukas closed his eyes tightly. This was why he hadn't seen her for two days. She had flown to Salzburg. It was a long flight to get from Australia to Austria. She could have missed the whole race weekend. She *had* missed most of it. Why did she do this for him?

'She didn't want you to know but suspected maybe a talk would help us both.'

What did that mean? Had Katherine confronted her parents? Lukas found himself wishing he'd been with her if she had. Just like he wished she was with him now, which was ridiculous after she had hurt him.

'Is that what you want? To talk?' Lukas refused to allow himself any expectations. He knew what he was guilty of, he also knew how badly he'd wanted his mother in his life growing up and how much it had stung when she refused to see him as an adult.

'I don't really know, Lukas.' His mother wrung her fingers.

'Then why are you here? Why did you leave Salzburg? It's a long flight.'

She stopped fidgeting, folded her hands on the table and looked her son square in the eye. 'I guess I'm here because that young lady gave me a lot to think about.'

Lukas wanted to know every word that Katherine had said but couldn't ask. He was dying for any kind of information about the past few months and maybe he was regretting the fact that he didn't take her call. But he also didn't want to hurt himself by talking to her and making the chasm in his chest yawn wider.

'Go on.'

'She made me realise that I've hurt you. You see, Lukas, I had a great deal of resentment, and I put that on you instead of where it should have lain.'

'And where was that?'

'With your father,' she said without missing a beat.

'Don't. Don't blame him when he never did a thing wrong.' His father had sacrificed everything so that Lukas could have the kind of future he was enjoying.

'Then where do you feel the blame lies?' she asked, leaning forward just a little.

'With me,' Lukas said easily. He knew the truth and no one could tell him otherwise. 'It was my fault that he had to work two jobs. My fault that you were unhappy. My fault that you left. I know that. But I have been trying to make it up to you. To give you the life you wanted to have.'

His mother's eyes softened a fraction. 'I let you believe that, didn't I?' She shook her head sadly. 'Katherine told me I would need to take responsibility for what I had done to you and I see now that she's right.'

Lukas didn't know how to respond.

I'm not doing the column anymore.

He knew Katherine was trying to do the same—to take responsibility—but it didn't change things. He was a private person; he would make her miserable. And what about when she had to report on his team? Chances were they wouldn't have any big results for at least the first half of the season, how would he respond when she had to be critical?

'Your father could have said no when you wanted to race after that first time he took you to the track. Do you remember that day?'

Lukas shook his head. Those memories were blurry. He remembered getting into the kart and the feeling but not too much else.

'One of the families that he used to get your tyres from were getting rid of their kart, so your father offered to buy it from them. They gave it to him in exchange for him servicing their son's kart for the next year. His labour would be free, and he agreed. I wasn't happy. That was money we could have used, but your father took you to the track and you listened so carefully to the safety instructions and what to do. Then you got to drive. You went slowly at first because they told you to. They said the tyres would be cold and you did everything as instructed. We thought you would enjoy yourself and then we would go home but the next lap you went faster and the one after that, faster still. I remember it so clearly, Lukas, people started watching *you*. Not anyone else. It was like you were born to race. Afterwards someone told your father he should let you race, and you asked him if you could. You were so excited and he said yes. He didn't talk to me first. He made the decision.

'When we got home he spoke to me about what changes we would have to make to support your racing and I thought it was unnecessary. The chance of you getting into Alpha One was so small, what would we have for all that investment? And the days got tough after that, Lukas.'

'I know. I was there. I could see the toll my racing was taking,' Lukas said softly.

'I wanted a better life, and I resented your father for not allowing us to have that but I also didn't want to blame him, because I loved him still, so I blamed you. My son.' Lukas could see the shame in her drooped shoulders. In the fact she wouldn't look at him. 'But I watched you with pride, Lukas. I know it might not seem like it makes sense. I don't feel like I deserve to have you in my life now when you're successful.'

'That's why you don't want to see me. Why you're making it so hard for me to take care of you.' Lukas wondered then if Katherine would one day face the same barrier with her parents, because just like him, she wanted to take care of them. Make their lives easier.

She understood you.

She hurt me.

Others wrote hurtful and false things about you too. Why was Katherine's so much worse?

That was a good question. It made him really look at their past, how much attention he'd paid to her, the fact that he tried to make sure her producer knew that him not wanting to talk to her was *not* her fault. The fact that he mentioned to Aero that they should hire her. That he paid so much more attention to her articles than anyone else's. Her articles got under his skin because he had set her apart. He even called her 'Katherine' when no one else did.

'Yes,' his mother said, startling Lukas out of the reverie he had fallen into. He'd almost forgotten the question he'd asked her. 'I'm sorry, Lukas.' She reached across the table and placed her hand on his. The contact felt so alien, so unfamiliar, but he had craved it for so long. 'Can you ever forgive me?'

'Yes.' He didn't have to think about it because that was the path back to having family in his life. He had no siblings. He was certain it was his fault his mother had chosen never to start another family, because what if they were like him? His father was dead. All he had was his mother and he so desperately wanted her in his life. 'I forgive you, but do you forgive me?'

'There's nothing to forgive. It wasn't your fault. You're not selfish. You were just a child with a dream, and you made it come true. I should have supported you. I can't go back and undo the past but maybe if you let me, I could be at the track today?'

'I have always wanted that,' Lukas confessed. A small piece of the scattered puzzle his heart had broken into clicked back into place. The rest remained broken.

'These scars you carry should not have been yours to bear, *liebling*. Let the world look at you because they will find a strong, kind, determined man. Katherine saw you and she fell in love with you.'

'I don't know if Katherine and I can be together.' But, good Lord did he want that.

Not letting go of his hand, she brought her other hand up to cup his cheek and gave him a sad, watery smile. 'Everyone makes mistakes. I'm sure you made them too. You just forgave me after a lifetime of mistakes I made. Maybe you could do the same for her?' Her tone was gentle.

Maybe he could forgive Katherine. After all, he was excited about this new journey in the sport he so loved. It didn't matter to him now who was in his seat at his old team. He didn't care. If someone had asked him what his greatest goal was this weekend, he would say to have two cars finish the race and maybe score a point or two.

'I want to,' he confessed to his mother. 'But...'

'Lukas, do you love her?'

'With my soul.'

His mother got off her chair and went to stand beside him. He looked up at her, unable to remember when he last had a memory like it, and then her arms went around him, pressing him to her middle. A hug he had craved after she had left him and his father. So he held on to his mother, taking all the affection she was offering, wondering if it was too good to be true and would all be taken away in the blink of an eye.

'A love like this isn't easily found. She's brave, *liebling*. She told me things I didn't want to hear. She brought us together and didn't want the credit. She's as determined as you are. From what I can see, as selfless.'

His mother was right. Lukas would never have known Katherine had gone to Salzburg if his mother hadn't told him. Who did that? Who went out of their way to fix something so broken in someone's life.

Someone in love.

He let go of his mother almost in a daze.

'I'm going to go. I can see you have a lot to think about.'

Lukas gave his mother one last hug before walking her to the door. 'I'll see you later.'

It was unreal that he was able to say those words. He only could because of Katherine.

'Definitely.' His mother smiled and closed the door behind her, leaving him with thoughts only of Katherine. She did love him. She showed him as much at Christmas, with the snowflake, his mother and giving up the column.

She was so afraid of sacrificing her career like her mother did and yet she let her column go for him. She was willing to make changes to accommodate him. Showed him commitment. So why couldn't they be together? Why couldn't he trust her?

Love was such a risk to the life she wanted but she told him she loved him.

As if a light had switched on, Lukas could see how idiotic he was being. He needed to find her. They wouldn't be miserable together; they were miserable without each other.

He grabbed his keys and rushed out of the room, letting the door slam on their past mistakes. There was a future to fight for.

CHAPTER TWENTY-THREE

LUKAS STOOD IN front of a closed hotel room door. A quick text to Erin was all it had taken to find out where the Aero TV team was staying. And then he'd run. He'd run down to the street where he saw the back end of a tram disappearing into the distance. He could have taken his car but the only route he knew well was going from the hotel to the track. He never saw much of the city as a driver and was somehow seeing even less now. But from where he stood, he could see part of the building peeking through others…so he kept running until he made it here.

He knocked rapidly at the door and when it opened, a tired, puffy-eyed Katherine answered.

'Lukas,' she breathed. Eyes wide as if he was the last person she expected.

'Is that my…'

She pulled the hem of the shirt, looking down at the white cotton. 'I found it in my bag after we left Lapland. I wanted to—' She stopped herself. 'Do you want it back?' Her lip trembled.

But Lukas needed to hear what she refused to say. 'You wanted to…?'

Katherine clenched her jaw and straightened her spine, looking him in the eye. He loved that fire. 'I wanted to have your scent close to me because I missed you. I still miss you.'

'I miss you too, Katherine. Can we talk?' He was very

aware that she hadn't invited him into her room, seeing her
bloodshot eyes and red nose it wasn't hard to guess why.

Katherine didn't budge. He could see her warring emotions. She still wanted him but his refusal before had hurt.
Katherine wasn't the crying type. She had taught herself to be
controlled but he had brought tears to her eyes several times
and for that, he would never forgive himself.

'Please,' he added.

She stepped aside and in he walked. Her laptop was open
on the bed, her phone displaying a thread of texts beside it.
Scribbled notes on a writing pad lay on the table. The television was switched on but muted and on the bedside table a
small pile of crumpled tissues.

Katherine closed the door and joined him, keeping her
distance but he didn't want that. He reached for her hand
and tried to pull her closer, but Katherine would only move
so much.

'You said goodbye, Lukas.'

'I did but I shouldn't have. It was an idiotic thing to do
when I love you.'

Katherine didn't say anything. He'd admitted to loving
her before but had still pushed her away. This distance was
his fault.

'You were right, I do love you. I never stopped. You're my
first and last thought every day, Katherine. I wake up and
look at the snowflake. It's the last thing I see before I close
my eyes. I couldn't move it. I couldn't get rid of it. It hurts to
see it, because you're not there, but the thought of losing the
one thing that ties me to you hurts so much more.'

'Dominic said you made him take down the decorations.'
Her eyes welled up again. A tear danced on the edge of her
lashes but she was trying not to let it fall. She'd let herself
be vulnerable with him and now she was trying so hard not
to be. He'd let her keep her guard up if that was what she

needed but he would show her that it was okay to let go. That he would let his own barriers down so maybe she would too.

'I did. I was hurt. I couldn't enter that room and see the reminders of you. Of a moment when we were happy. But, Katherine, that isn't close to as happy as we could be. And I want to be happy with you.'

'But you said—'

'I hadn't coped well with seeing you. I still blamed you for everything, but I've had time to think and I want to try again.'

Katherine pulled her hand from his and moved to stand by the table. She tried to speak but nothing came out, so she swallowed hard and tried again. 'What's changed?'

Everything.

Lukas went to the window. He respected Katherine's need for space but that didn't stop him craving her closeness. His body constantly reaching for hers and maybe she felt the same, because even though she didn't directly look at him, her body still pivoted towards his.

'My mother came to see me this morning.' Katherine's eyes snapped to his. He needed her to see his earnestness. 'And I realised how much you love me and how much I can trust you. I confided a lot in you that you could have used but you didn't. Instead, you did the impossible and brought my mother back into my life. I don't know what you told her, but I can imagine how much you would have had to open up to a stranger to make her listen to you.' He went to Katherine then, whose tears refused to be controlled any longer, and he kissed the wetness away. 'That was a long way to go. You could have missed the first race of the season.'

'I would do it again for you, Lukas.'

'Katherine,' he breathed, his thumbs gently caressing her cheeks. 'I may not have liked or agreed with how you went about trying to get rid of the article, but you did try. I didn't make you feel like you could confide in me about your job.

I had a very black and white view on the media—they were the enemy and that drove a wedge between us. So I also have to bear some of the responsibility. It was wrong to put it all on you.'

'We both made mistakes,' Katherine said. Lukas didn't know if she had realised it, but she'd moved closer to him. He couldn't describe the elation that little movement brought him.

'We did. I'm trying to do better. I'm learning to give a little more of myself to the media and it has brought me some space in my private life. Though, without you, I don't need it.'

'Why?'

'Because without you, I'm not living, Katherine. I'm existing, and there is a very big difference in that.'

'I'm not living without you either.'

Lukas pulled her against his body. His fingertips tangling in her fiery red hair. His palm cupping her cheek. *This* right here was home. With his heart pounding frantically because that was just the effect her touch had on him. His spirit calm because she was close.

'Love is scary, I know that, and I know how difficult it would have been for you to admit you love me. But I promise you, we will be stronger for being together. I will support your career wherever you choose to go. Loving me will never mean you could lose your dream. Never.'

'I know that, Lukas. You made me see that my career didn't have to be my whole life. That with you I could have success *and* love. What you did for me… I'm sorry I used my position at Aero to hurt you.'

He had wanted that apology for so long and, while he appreciated it, Lukas found that he didn't really care anymore. There were more important things than being a driver or worrying about how the world saw him. He only cared what Katherine thought.

'That's behind us. And while I think you're incredible on

Track Talk, I think you should get your column back too. You're good. People need to hear from *you*.'

'I love you, Lukas.'

'I love you too, Katherine. Will you let me show you how much?' After months of being without her and having her body so close to his now, Lukas was suffocating, in need of the air that was her lips on his. He was cold, desperate for the heat of her skin on his.

'Yes.'

So he kissed her. He kissed her in apology and as a new beginning. He kissed her in a promise of love and show of devotion. He kissed her with his heart and soul. Her arms tightened around him and his tongue worshipped at her mouth. He never wanted to stop. He wanted this feeling every day until the end of time.

Katherine broke the kiss with a smile, but she didn't pull away. He could feel the puffs of her staccato breath on his lips and he wanted more.

'This doesn't mean you get special treatment. I still have a job to do,' she joked.

'I wouldn't dream of it, but if you could keep my personal life out of it, I would appreciate it. You see, my wife is going to be extremely well-known.'

Katherine laughed. 'Your wife, huh?'

'I'm hoping.' He kissed her briefly again. 'I'm never letting her go.'

'I like the sound of that,' Katherine replied.

* * * * *

MILLS & BOON®

Coming next month

SECRETLY PREGNANT PRINCESS
Lorraine Hall

Evelyne saw Gabriel's eyes widen. She tried to recover, but it was too late. He'd seen.

He pointed at her—at her stomach. 'What is that?' Gabriel demanded.

She had dreamed of this in her weaker moments. Telling him that he was to be a father. In her fantasies, she was calm, casual, disdainful almost. She did not give him the satisfaction of thinking that she needed him, wanted him, or was afraid of being alone.

She was determined to make fantasy a reality.

So, she beamed at him, made sure she sounded cheerful. 'In the States they call it a baby bump.' She ran her hands over the roundness, moved to give him a profile view. Refused to let the nerves fluttering through her show—she'd had ample practice at hiding those. 'Isn't that cute?'

He said nothing. Didn't move. She wasn't sure he breathed.

When he finally moved, it was with clear-cut precision. 'Explain yourself,' he said quietly, dangerously.

She chose to maintain her flippancy. 'Is it not self-explanatory, Gabriel? I am pregnant.'

Continue reading

SECRETLY PREGNANT PRINCESS
Lorraine Hall

Available next month
millsandboon.co.uk

COMING SOON!

We really hope you enjoyed reading this book.
If you're looking for more romance
be sure to head to the shops when
new books are available on

Thursday 15th January

MILLS & BOON

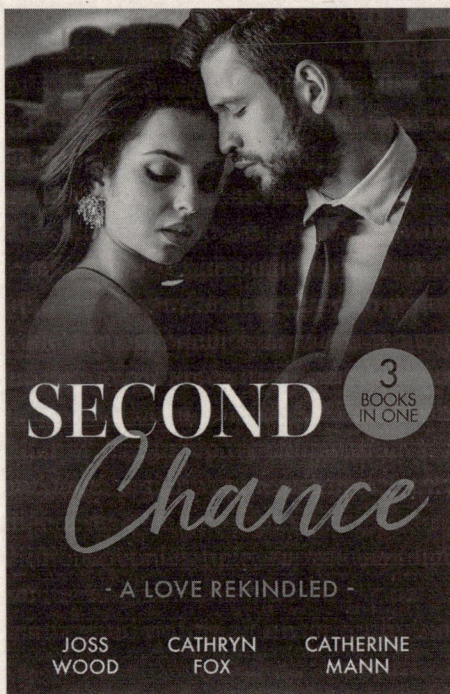